BJORN

BOOK THREE OF THE FRONTIERS

Jon R. Osborne

Seventh Seal Press
Virginia Beach, VA

Chris Kennedy/Seventh Seal Press
2052 Bierce Dr.
Virginia Beach, VA 23454
http://chriskennedypublishing.com/

Ordering Information:
Quantity sales. Special discounts are available on quantity purchases by corporations, associations, and others. For details, contact the "Special Sales Department" at the address above.

Cover Art by Ricky Ryan
Cover Design by Brenda Mihalko

Jon R. Osborne/Bjorn -- 1st ed.
ISBN 978-1950420551

Dedication

For Glenda Marcussen, my mother and a teacher who encouraged hundreds of young minds to read, including my own. Encourage a child to read, and they can change the world, or in the case of a writer, create their own.

Chapter One

Las Cruces, New Mexico

"Look out! There's a Tortantula on the left!"

Bjorn had already spotted the huge spider-like alien looming in the shell of a burned-out building. The ten-legged nightmare was the size of a car. More concerning was the small, furry rider mounted on the Tortantula's carapace. The alien was called a Flatar, and it wielded a powerful gun capable of punching through armor.

"I see it!" Bjorn snapped back as he slammed his CASPer to a halt. At nine feet tall and weighing almost a ton, the Combat Assault System, Personal screeched on the pavement, its armored feet sending up sparks. Bjorn fought the armor into back-pedaling in the nick of time. The three-dimensional Tri-V display in his canopy flashed as the Flatar fired at him. The hypersonic projectile missed Bjorn's suit by centimeters.

"I'm cutting south to catch them in a cross-fire," Roberto called. Bjorn's best friend was his wingman on both the football field and the battlefield.

"Mickey D and Blair, make sure those Besquith don't jump Berto," Bjorn instructed. Two of the werewolf-like Besquith had harried his group over the last fifteen minutes, trying to slink in close so they could pounce. The lupines were nearly as tall as a CASPer and twice as scary.

"Okay," Mickey D acknowledged. She probably hoped the Besquith would attack them—she preferred close up fights to stand-off exchanges of fire. Blair remained silent, as usual, but Bjorn could see his icon on the map follow behind Mickey D's.

Bjorn had bigger things to worry about. A laser mounted on the Tortantula burned a hole in the wall obscuring Bjorn from the spider and its rider. He couldn't use the CASPer's jump jets—he'd be the perfect target.

"Hang in there, Bjorn. I'm almost in position, then I'll light the spider up," Roberto said.

Bjorn's Tri-V display showed little in the way of cover. The Besquith had lured his squad here; a trap play he should have seen coming. Bjorn primed his rocket launcher and dropped the targeting reticle on the edge of the wall where the Tortantula would emerge.

"CRAP!" Blair broke his silence, panting into the microphone after his exclamation. Yellow symbols blinked above Blair's icon as his armored suit took damage.

"The big dummy stood out in the open, and the Besquith jumped him," Mickey D added, irritation in her voice. "I'll deal with the wolves and hopefully save the big lug."

The wall exploded as the spider crashed through it. A laser pulse illuminated the dust as the Tortantula skittered over the rubble. Bjorn adjusted his aim and unloaded both rockets in the launcher in rapid succession.

A smaller laser mounted on the spider's armor fired a staccato of pulses. The first warhead detonated halfway between Bjorn and the alien. The second rocket veered downward, below where the anti-missile laser could track. The rocket skipped off the pavement and detonated in the rubble below the Tortantula. The spider emitted a piercing screech as it arched through the air trailing smoke and ichor.

"There are two more Besquith!" Mickey D yelled, more anger than fear in her voice. "Dammit, Blair! Help out! At least fall on one or something!"

Bjorn glanced at the squad display. Red tell-tales blinked above Blair's icon and yellow indicators flashed as Mickey D's CASPer was damaged. "Berto, do you have eyes on the Flatar? I nuked the spider, but I didn't see the rider."

Roberto muttered a curse. "I thought it went with the Tortantula. It must still be—"

A sharp crack cut Roberto off and his icon went dark. A moment later Blair's icon winked out as well.

"Mickey D, look out! The Flatar is still on the field," Bjorn called. "It nailed Berto!"

"I've…got…my…hands full!" Mickey D snarled over the radio. More yellow indicators appeared over her icon, and one turned red.

"I'm coming!" Bjorn lowered his center of gravity and sprinted past the ruins of the wall. The metal feet of the CASPer reverberated against the pavement. As Bjorn broke cover, he engaged his jump jets, hoping the sudden boost would throw off the Flatar's aim.

Instead of punching through the operator's compartment, the hypersonic projectile grazed a leg of the armor, wrecking the servos controlling the limb. Bjorn's landing turned into a tumbling crash. He was thrown back and forth against the restraint webbing while the world spun in his Tri-V display. He wrestled the armor into a kneeling position as he slowed to a stop and raised his magnetic accelerator cannon. Several status indicators for his powered armor blinked yellow warnings, but he had enough power and ammo for at least one more shot.

A meter-tall chipmunk wearing an armored jumpsuit hopped onto a pile of rubble and lowered a huge pistol. Bjorn stared down the barrel as he triggered his MAC. The furry alien erupted in a spray of viscera as Bjorn's Tri-V display shattered into splinters.

* * *

"Simulation over!" the electronic voice intoned as the canopy swung open. Bjorn blinked against the bright light flooding the cockpit of his CASPer simulator as he unlatched the restraints. He could already hear Mickey D grousing from her opened cockpit.

"I took out three werewolves!" The tall blonde girl said as she extricated herself from the simulator. Alison McDaniels clambered to the arcade floor. "If Blair had done more than play wolf chow, we could have beat the scenario!"

"You guys asked me to play," David Blair protested. "It's not my fault Alison thinks she's a Besquith."

"Chill out," Bjorn said. He pulled off the haptic bands from his wrists and left them dangling from their cables. A real CASPer would require a haptic suit to pilot, but the simulator used footpads and armbands. "Alison is the only one here who wants to be a mercenary. For the rest of us, it's only a game."

Bjorn hauled his bulk out of the simulator cockpit. At sixteen, he already stood almost two meters tall and weighed 120 kilograms. It made the cockpit cramped, though not as tight a fit as Blair. David Blair was nearly as tall as Bjorn and packed an additional twenty kilograms. It helped in the offensive line on the football field, but it meant he struggled climbing out of the simulator.

"If these were real CASPers, we wouldn't need to grease the pod to get Blair out," Mickey D quipped. She grabbed one of the struggling lineman's arms. "Get the other side, before they charge us for extra time."

Bjorn stepped in and wrinkled his nose. He felt sorry for whoever used the simulator after Blair. The large boy left a liter of sweat behind. "On three—one…two…three!"

Berto laughed, holding up his phone. "You better hope Coach doesn't see this, or he'll put Blair on a diet."

"Dude, really?" Bjorn shook his head. "Don't put that on the Aethernet." The planet-wide network was modeled on the alien GalNet and had replaced the internet.

"Why not? It's funny," Berto protested. "I'll get a ton of clicks."

"Because I bet David doesn't think it's funny," Bjorn countered. Once Blair had his footing, Bjorn headed for the exit. As team captain, Bjorn watched out for his teammates. It was something the previous quarterback had taught Bjorn, despite the fact Bjorn had supplanted the senior.

"Fine," Berto relented. The running back was like a brother, but sometimes he got carried away, and Bjorn had to rein him in.

"Oh my god, you died!" Heather squealed. Bjorn's girlfriend leapt into his arms and planted a kiss on his lips. "You never get killed in sim runs!"

Bjorn set the blonde girl down. "I did this time. Goes to show why I shouldn't be a mercenary." Bjorn tempered his tone because of Mickey D. She wanted to join one of the military-for-profit companies and go out into the galaxy to fight aliens. Bjorn slipped his arm around Heather. "I'd rather stay here on Earth."

"Is your dad still ticked off?" Mickey D asked.

"That would be an understatement," Bjorn replied as their group made their way through the arcade.

Most of the teens in the arcade were engrossed in their games, but a few watched Bjorn and his friends with unmasked envy. Zagyg Arcade was the most expensive in Las Cruces, but kids from across the social spectrum flocked to the game complex. They all recognized the letter jackets from Mesilla Prep Academy.

"I can't believe he threatened to cut you off if you go to college instead of joining his mercenary company," Heather complained. Successful mercenaries lived like the rock stars of the previous century. While Bjorn didn't want to join the family business, he had no qualms about using his family's wealth to spoil his girlfriend.

"Even if he did, my grandfather still has me in the will. I'll receive ten percent interest in the company when I turn twenty-five, and another fifteen percent when he passes." While professional athletes didn't make as much as big-time mercenaries, they still made more money than Bjorn could see spending. "As long as I make it in football, or even baseball, I won't miss anything from the commander."

"Colleges are already scouting you," Heather remarked. "I bet there'll be a bunch of them in the bleachers for the championship game Friday."

"We better win, then." Bjorn chirped his car. Technically it was his mother's, but she let him use it. The fuel-cell-powered vehicle whirred to life. Since he wanted to drive manually, it meant only Heather could ride with him. Once he turned seventeen, he could upgrade his provisional license, but until then he was limited to one non-family member passenger under the age of 21. "Catch you guys tomorrow at school."

"You know it, *hermano.*" Roberto held out his right hand, which Bjorn clapped, then Bjorn held out his left for Berto to do the same. They slapped each other's hands hard enough to sting, but not enough to really hurt. It had been their "special handshake" for years.

"Are sure you don't want to let the car drive? We could ride in the back seat," Heather suggested.

It was tempting, but he needed to log enough operator hours to upgrade his license. "It only takes ten minutes to get to your house, and if we let the car drive us around for a while, your folks will be ticked at me for bringing you home late."

Heather mocked a pout. "We hardly have any time alone, and you're going away during winter break."

"It's a family tradition. We go to my grandparent's place in Alaska, have a few big meals, freeze our butts off, and wait for my dad and *Afi* to have an argument." Bjorn guided the car into light traffic. He knew the nanny-circuits were recording every move, so he made sure to follow the rules and resisted showing off. "We'll have more time after winter break, and there's always prom and spring break."

Ten minutes later, Bjorn brought the car to a halt in Heather's family's driveway. Heather's parents both had solid jobs, and the house showed it. It wasn't mercenary money, but it was enough to live in one of the affluent gated communities that had sprung up in Mesilla Valley on the south side of Las Cruces.

Their goodbyes stretched another ten minutes after Bjorn walked Heather to the front door. How long would it take for Heather's dad to find an excuse to come to the door? He was probably watching them on the security cameras. After a final good night kiss, Bjorn returned to the car.

A promising football career, top colleges courting him, and a gorgeous cheerleader girlfriend—Bjorn had plenty of reasons to smile on the ride home. His father could go off-world to fight aliens; Bjorn planned on staying on Earth.

*****

Chapter Two

Las Cruces, New Mexico

"What the—?" Bjorn fumbled his book bag and backpedaled toward the front foyer closet. There was a pistol hidden on the top shelf.

The dog-headed creature watched impassively. It stood as tall as a Human, with a bipedal stance similar to Humans. Drab tan coveralls concealed most of the creature. Once Bjorn threw open the closet door, it cocked its head to the side.

"Commander Tovesson, I believe I have startled your whelp." The creature's English was muddled but understandable, its hard consonants softened.

Bjorn's father stepped into view behind the alien. "Trip, settle down! Vurrg here is a Zuul contractor."

"What?" Bjorn froze with his arm halfway in the closet. He'd seen pictures of Zuul, but he had never met one in person. The only aliens he had seen up close were the lizard-like ElSha technicians who worked for the mercenary company and a purple bear-thing called an Oogar. The Oogar had given him nightmares all through fifth grade.

"Trip, are you hungry? I saved some dinner for you," his mother called from further in the home.

"Vurrg, this is my son, Bjorn Tovesson the Third, or Trip as we call him." Bjorn's father shook his head. "Trip, get your mitt away from the front door gun."

Bjorn's cheeks flushed in embarrassment as he regained his composure. He strode forward and tentatively held out his hand to the Zuul. "Nice to meet you Mr. Vurrg."

Vurrg took Bjorn's hand and shook it. "Your whelp must be nearly full-grown, Commander Tovesson. He is nearly as tall as you, but I can see from his incomplete facial pelt he has a hand of seasons to mature."

Bjorn blushed again. His father sported a thick, bushy beard, while Bjorn's wispy facial hair was limited to his chin.

Bjorn's father roared in laughter. "I'm sure he'll fill out. Come on, Vurrg, I'll show you the guest room."

"He's staying here?" Bjorn asked. Why had Dad brought an alien to stay in the house?

"I promised your mother I'd be home for dinner—which you were not, by the way. Vurrg is curious about Humans, so I thought I'd show him a taste of Earth outside of a startown or mercenary base." Bjorn's father chuckled. "Don't worry, son; he won't eat you in the middle of the night."

"Your mother fed me well," Vurrg added with a grimace full of fangs Bjorn hoped was a smile. "I look forward to seeing this game you play."

Bjorn tried to keep the alarm out of his voice. "What?"

"I told Vurrg how you were planning on chucking your heritage as a merc for playing a game," Bjorn's father replied. "He is fascinated by the notion of sports."

"I have seen many competitions on Tri-V, but never in person," the Zuul added. "I think being among the crowd will be an exciting experience."

Bjorn's father hardly ever attended a game. "You're bringing an alien to a high school football game—to *my* high school football game?"

"What's the problem, son?"

"I will wear a garment to be less conspicuous," Vurrg said. "Are you afraid the other whelps in your school will be scared as you were?"

"I wasn't scared; I was startled," Bjorn protested. "Usually when my dad talks about aliens, they're trying to kill him. Most of my classmates have never seen an alien in person; this isn't Houston."

"It'll be fine, Trip. I already cleared it with your principal. Come on, Vurrg."

Bjorn watched the pair disappear toward the guest rooms. Had anyone warned the housekeeper? Geneva could be in for a rude shock in the morning. Did Zuul shed?

"Trip, are you going to stand there or get something to eat?" his mother asked.

"Sorry, Mom." Bjorn followed her to the kitchen.

Automated cooking devices were interspersed among traditional appliances. While Geneva handled most of the cooking, his mother didn't want to feel dependent on servants and machines. Occasionally, his mom prepared meals herself because she enjoyed cooking.

"I was surprised by our house guest, also," Bjorn's mother remarked as she pulled a pan from the stove. "At first I thought he was a Besquith."

Bjorn's mouth watered at the smell of beef ribs and fried potatoes. He'd grabbed a sandwich after practice, but that was three hours ago. "Besquith are bigger and scarier. Why is he here?"

"Your father is working on a deal—it has to do with upgrades to the Casanovas," she explained. Bjorn's Berserkers were one of the few units who made use of the Combat Assault System, Vehicular. At some point, the CASVs were nicknamed Casanovas. "You know how your father is, always trying to find a way to make the Berserkers on a par with the Four Horsemen."

"Good luck with that," Bjorn remarked as he dug into the leftovers. The Four Horsemen were the premier mercenary companies on Earth. One hundred mercenary companies had left Earth on the first round of mission contracts known as the Alpha Contracts. Only four units had returned: The Four Horsemen. Since then, they had always been at the top of the merc company heap. "If he wants to catch up, he should invest in naval assets, so the Berserkers aren't so reliant on transportation sub-contractors."

"For someone who doesn't want to be a mercenary, you know a lot about the business," his mother remarked. She had encouraged Bjorn to seek a career outside of fighting aliens for pay.

Bjorn shrugged. "Hard not to growing up in this family," he said between bites. He shouldn't eat this late, but the food was too good to pass up. He'd do an extra 50 push-ups before bed. "Besides, when I go to college, I'm going to major in business and finance. I want to make my money last, including whatever I get from my shares in the company. They're only worth something if we don't waste money on gimmicks and make solid investments."

Bjorn's mother sighed. "Don't stay up too late, and don't leave your dishes out for Geneva."

"Good night, Mom."

"Good night, Trip."

Bjorn wolfed down the rest of his food and dutifully cleaned up after himself. When he was younger, he'd left messes for their housekeeper. As he got older, he appreciated how hard the woman worked and felt guilty for being a spoiled brat.

Once Bjorn reached his bedroom, he tapped on his slate. The computerized slab of glass lit up, notifications scrolling down its surface. A few swipes sidelined the generic social stream so he could focus on messages. There was one from Roberto asking a question about a play from practice. Two were from Heather, the last with a blinking icon indicating she was online for chatting.

He tapped the chat icon and propped the slate on the floor so he could chat and do push-ups at the same time.

"You'll never believe what I came home to," Bjorn said. He had to count his push-ups silently or the slate would type the count into the chat.

"What? Your dad said you could stay home for Christmas?" Heather followed the message with a smiley face.

"No, I wish." Despite the sanitizing of the winter holiday to remove various religious connotations, many still called it Christmas. "Dad brought home an alien from work—a Zuul."

"One of those wolf-things from the simulator?" An alarmed face emoji trailed behind the line of text.

"No, those are Besquith. Zuul are dog-like, but not as scary." It was easy to be brave now, without witnesses. "My dad is bringing the Zuul to the game Friday."

"Cool? Is this going to mess with the victory party?"

Mickey D's mother was out of town on a business trip, and she had pawned off her younger siblings on an aunt. The football team planned on celebrating their win or mourning their loss at her house. Having a Zuul house guest shouldn't affect Bjorn's plans—hopefully.

"I don't think so," Bjorn replied. "I might get tied up for a few minutes making nice. For some reason this Zuul is fascinated by Earth sports. I'll answer a couple of questions then make an excuse to split."

After another fifteen minutes of chatter, it was time to call it a night. No point in dragging tail at school tomorrow, not to mention making the last practice before the game harder.

* * *

Bjorn had almost forgotten about the Zuul until he spotted Vurrg sitting at the breakfast table across from Bjorn's father. Geneva bustled around the kitchen as usual, interspersing cooking with getting a start on her chores for the day. She ignored the alien other than to set a plate of bacon and sausage in front of him. Bjorn didn't know how much his parents paid Geneva, but he knew it was substantially more than most people paid domestic staff. As a result, Geneva had worked for the Tovessons for twelve years.

"I will get fat if I stay on Earth too long," Vurrg remarked. "I see your whelp has awakened. Good morning, Stumble!"

"It's Trip," Bjorn grumbled under his father's laughter. He poured himself a glass of orange juice—the real stuff, not the powdered imitation—and sat at the table next to his father. Without asking, Geneva plunked down a plate loaded with bacon, sausage, and eggs. A smattering of home fries and a single piece of French toast clung to the periphery of the plate. Bjorn had to watch his carbs, or he'd go from quarterback to linebacker.

"Trip isn't a morning person," the older Tovesson said. "He stays up too late playing kissy-face with his girlfriend over the Aethernet."

"Some of the idioms are lost on me," Vurrg admitted. "Does your wh—son have a mate, or is he merely sniffing at prospects? He should wait until he can grow a proper pelt before he sires his own pups." Bjorn fought not to choke on his eggs while his father guffawed.

"This is hardly proper talk for the breakfast table," Bjorn's mother protested as she approached the table. "However, he better not sire anything. Trip is too young to get serious."

"Good morning, Mrs. Lynn." Evidently the Zuul didn't have any customs regarding speaking with their mouths full of bacon.

Bjorn devoured the remainder of his breakfast despite his mother's disapproving remarks. He only half-listened to the conversation, which thankfully turned from Bjorn to Vurrg's experiences on Earth so far.

"I'll be home after practice," Bjorn said as he collected his dishes and left them in the sink.

"You're not going to get 'delayed' again, are you?" his mother asked.

"Nope. The coach wants us to go home after practice and get plenty of rest," Bjorn replied.

"At least the boy listens to someone," the commander muttered.

* * *

"I can't believe you have an alien staying at your house!" Heather eagerly reached for the door handle as soon as Bjorn stopped the car. Driving her home later would break the coach's injunction about not going out, but it was a short drive.

"It's not a big deal," Bjorn remarked. Hopefully his father wouldn't regale Heather with Bjorn's initial shock when he saw the Zuul.

A high-pitched whine filled the air as a matte gray VTOL emblazoned with the Bjorn's Berserkers logo swooped over the house. The flyer's turbine nacelles pivoted to hover mode and the vehicle sank out of sight behind the house.

"Must make for an easy commute to have your own air service," Heather remarked. "Think we could fly to Houston or Los Angeles sometime?"

Bjorn held the door open for Heather. "It may look fun, but those military flyers are not made for comfort." And minors couldn't hop on a commercial flight without leaving a data trail nosy parents could follow. "Besides, I don't think the commander would be cool with one of his pilots hanging out and waiting for us to go sightseeing or whatever."

"Hello." Bjorn's mother must have been waiting for them. "How are you, Heather?"

The departing VTOL shrieked overhead as Bjorn closed the door and took Heather's jacket.

"I'm great, Mrs. T. Thank you for letting me come to dinner. I've never met an alien before." Heather's bubbly enthusiasm would win his mother over.

"I'm happy to have you. Trip's father is bringing another co-worker, so we should have a full table." Bjorn's mother led them toward the dining room. His mother loved having guests for dinner. While she didn't flaunt their wealth, it was one of the rooms she took pride in. Antique chairs surrounded an imposingly large table, all crafted from real wood over a century ago. 3D printers had driven craftsman and artisans to the brink of extinction, so not a single printed item was in the dining room.

"Lynn, we're home!" Bjorn's father called, as though the screaming VTOL hadn't been enough notice. Vurrg's voice was muffled by distance and corners, as was Bjorn's father's reply. Heather grabbed Bjorn's arm in excitement.

"We're in the dining room, BJ," Bjorn's mom called back. Before Bjorn was born and became Bjorn Tovesson III, his father was Bjorn Tovesson Jr., an appellation he quickly switched to Bjorn II. Bjorn's mother was one of the few people who called his father BJ. A hearty guffaw betrayed that someone else was amused by the nickname.

"It's Commander Tovesson to you," Bjorn's father declared as he led Vurrg and a man in a charcoal gray Berserkers' uniform into the dining room. Bjorn recognized Captain Tom Davis. He commanded Grizzly Company, the second company in the Berserkers.

"Your boy's getting big," Captain Davis commented. "He may end up bigger than you, B-Boss."

"A shame he's going to waste it playing football," Bjorn's father said.

"BJ…" Bjorn's mother cautioned, drawing a stifled chuckle from Captain Davis.

"Vurrg, Captain Davis, this is my girlfriend Heather," Bjorn interrupted. "Captain Davis works with my father."

"I don't know, Boss, I can see why he'd want to play football," Davis remarked.

"Omigosh—you're a real alien! Oh no, is that the wrong thing to say?" Heather covered her mouth in alarm. "Are we supposed to call you non-terrestrial people?"

"You may call me Vurrg," the Zuul said, offering his hand.

"Wow, you have fingers almost the same as ours!" Heather declared before shaking the alien's hand.

"Were you expecting paws?" Vurrg asked with a toothy smile. Bjorn placed a reassuring hand on Heather's back. "It would be difficult to manage tools with such clumsy digits."

"I didn't know what to expect. You're the first Vurrg I've met."

"It is good she is pretty," Captain Davis muttered to Bjorn's father in Icelandic. The Nordic language was popular among the Berserkers. Bjorn's father stifled a chuckle.

Vurrg arched an eyebrow as he glanced at Bjorn's father. "My name is Vurrg, and my race is Zuul. I do not find the term alien offensive."

"Why don't we all sit so Geneva can serve dinner?" Bjorn's mother suggested. "She has been working on this brisket all day."

"It smells delicious," Vurrg remarked as he chose a chair.

"You speak English well, Mr. Vurrg. Was it difficult to learn?" Heather asked as she sat next to Bjorn.

"Compared to MinSha or Cochkala, English is a wind," Vurrg said. "You can learn a great deal about a people by learning their language. Although, I admit during important negotiations I turn on my translator."

"A breeze," Bjorn corrected. "English is a breeze, although non-English speakers might disagree."

Vurrg chuffed a laugh. "A breeze—thank you! How many languages do you speak, Trip?"

Bjorn ticked off on his fingers. "English, Spanish, Russian, Icelandic, and a smattering of Yup'ik."

"Impressive!" Vurrg smiled. "I would think with translators, Humans would be less inclined to learn other tongues. The Zuul only have one language, with a handful of archaic dialects used by scholars and hobby historians."

"When the Buma made first contact, Earth was still heavily balkanized," Heather remarked. "Half the world spoke about two dozen languages, and another 4,500 covered 99% of the remaining population."

Captain Davis arched an eyebrow while the table fell silent in surprise.

"We learned about it for a test," Heather added. Bjorn smiled and winked at Heather. She could play the vapid cheerleader, but she was smarter than people thought. At school, she was a solid B+. Since she didn't have any identity qualifiers, she was hoping family money and cheerleading would get her into a good college—hopefully the same one as Bjorn.

Geneva appeared with the first course to break the stunned quiet. Bjorn watched as Vurrg eyed the colorful salad placed in front of him.

"What is this?" the Zuul asked after Geneva returned to the kitchen.

"We call it salad," Bjorn's father replied. "It's a pile of leaves and vegetables. If you don't want it, pass it to the boy. My son eats enough for three."

Vurrg sniffed at the salad bowl in front of him, then turned to Bjorn. "I do not wish to offend the Geneva."

"I'll take care of it." Bjorn beckoned with his hand. Geneva wouldn't take offense if Vurrg passed on the salad, but Bjorn hated to see food go to waste. If he was going to pig out on anything, better it was something healthy rather than the fatty food bound to come later.

"It is good you have a strong appetite," Vurrg remarked, watching Bjorn dig into the second salad. "I assume your size gives you an advantage in sports?"

"It does for football," Bjorn replied between bites of salad. "I have to be careful though. If I get too big, I'll lose speed on the field. It's a balancing act—strength and mass versus quickness and agility."

"I hear you're as good a quarterback as you are a marksman," Captain Davis added. "I've seen your range scores, so those Albuquerque boys better watch out tomorrow."

"Range scores?" Heather asked.

"Marksmanship scores—in your boyfriend's case, pistol, though he's qualified on the rifle as well," Captain Davis explained.

Bjorn knew Heather's real question. She understood what a range score was; she was questioning *why* Bjorn still went to the range. "I practice with my grandfather's gun whenever Dad drags me to Bear Town."

Bjorn's father chuckled. "I remember when he first gave you that enormous hand cannon, you couldn't wait to take it to the range and try it out. Damn near knocked you on your butt."

"I got better," Bjorn protested. He knew the 12mm Heckler and Glock inside and out. Even after football and the decision not to become a mercenary, Bjorn kept in practice with the huge pistol.

"You did," Bjorn's father admitted. "That's why it's such a shame you—"

"BJ..." Bjorn's mother warned.

"Sounds as though you tread on thin ice," Captain Davis commented in Icelandic.

"He does," Bjorn's mother replied in Icelandic.

Geneva broke the awkward tension by arriving with the main course. Bjorn was anticipating the brisket as eagerly as Vurrg. The double helping of salad had taken the edge off his appetite, but Bjorn was salivating at the aroma of the smoked beef.

Heather watched Vurrg as he dug into his meal, visibly disappointed when the alien used his utensils the same as everyone else.

"Did you expect him to tear into it with his teeth?" Bjorn whispered. Heather gave a slight shrug. Vurrg glanced up from his meal long enough to give a toothy smile and lick his chops.

"Heather, do you have any plans after high school?" Leave it to his mother to fish for information.

"I definitely want to go to college," Heather replied. Luckily, she missed Captain Davis' eye roll. "My mother wants me to become a lawyer, the same as her." It was Heather's turn to roll her eyes. "My father is more flexible, as long as I land a decent career and not be—well, not be dependent on someone else."

Bjorn knew what Heather had almost said. Mr. Akins didn't want his daughter to be a "camp follower," a mercenary groupie who latched onto a mercenary boyfriend for the money.

"The hard part is finding a job not endangered by automation, but doesn't require technical skills," Heather added. "I suppose I could do tech, but it's boring. I'm thinking about public relations or advertising."

Bjorn didn't miss the scrutinizing gaze behind his mother's polite smile. He was glad Heather's family was well-off, which helped defuse the argument she was only interested in Bjorn for his family's wealth.

"Trip, please explain to me more how this football game works," Vurrg said.

* * * * *

Chapter Three

Las Cruces, New Mexico

Twenty-one yards and thirteen seconds stood between the Mesilla Prep Panthers and defeat. The Albuquerque Vocational Titans held a four-point lead, so only a touchdown would win the game. The Titan defense had dug in, resolved to keep the Panthers out of the end zone and preserve their lead.

"Mickey D—go to the left edge; Berto, fake the hand-off then run for the right edge. You know the rest." Both players nodded at Bjorn. "Blair, if I still have the ball after a five count, bulldog me an opening. Let's do this!"

The play clock ticked down as the team fell into formation. The defense shuffled in anticipation. The Titans knew he was going to pass, either deep to the end zone, or to the sideline seven or more yards away. At two seconds on the play clock, Bjorn called for the snap.

Roberto swept past him for the fake hand-off while Mickey D charged deep and left, two defenders shadowing her. Another defender picked up Berto, matching his lightning pace. The third receiver in the middle of the field had a single defender covering him. The Titan defensive linemen ground against the Panther offensive line in a pair of Human avalanches.

Both edges were covered. Bjorn locked eyes on the middle receiver, Felipe Gomez, and pumped. The defender responded in a flash, reaching to block the ball. There was only empty air.

Five! Blair roared as he slammed his bulk forward and to the right. Bjorn dashed through the gap, clutching the ball. Defenders fell back from the line to cut him off from the left sideline where he could stop the clock. Six seconds remained.

The defenders protecting the edge lost a precious second as Bjorn cut right. Gomez's coverage angled toward Roberto once he realized the pass hadn't gone to Gomez. The Titan switched back to intercept Bjorn. Three seconds—the clock no longer mattered. This was the last play of the game. The defenders on both edges collapsed back toward the middle while Berto and Mickey D went from receiving to blocking.

The defensive backs were faster than Bjorn. Time slowed to a crawl. Gomez's opponent would reach him first, followed by the Titan on Mickey D. Neither opposing player had anyone to hinder them. The other Titans were vying to get around receivers-turned-blockers. They might meet him at the one-yard line.

Bjorn vectored into Gomez's defender. The boy charged low; even though Bjorn was much larger, all the player had to do was trip Bjorn up and bring him down. The Titan dove for Bjorn's legs. Bjorn launched himself; if he stumbled, Bjorn had to make sure he didn't let the defender get a hand on him. The boy plowed into the turf, his arms grasping empty air as Bjorn sailed over him.

There were still five yards to go when a Titan charged in from the left. He leapt at Bjorn, and Bjorn had to resist the urge to stiff-arm him. At the last moment he threw himself into the would-be tackler. Bjorn had 30 kilos of mass on his side, and the Titan had expected him to flinch away from the tackle. The Titan bounced off Bjorn as if he'd tried to tackle a CASPer.

The end zone was almost within reach. The defender from the right found an extra surge of speed and threw himself at Bjorn. Ninety kilos of Titan landed on Bjorn's back. Two yards to the line. The defender from the left slammed into him, and Bjorn started to topple. One yard. He planted his foot and lunged forward. All three players tumbled to the turf…a yard past the goal line.

A roar erupted from the crowd. Bjorn extricated himself from the Titan players to regain his feet and hold the ball aloft. The scoreboard read 30 – 28. Mickey D and Berto tackled him, with the rest of the team piling on as they arrived in the end zone. Meanwhile, the defensive squad dumped the water cooler on the coach.

Bjorn's gaze swept to the cheerleaders, finding Heather. His girlfriend bounced in glee, waving her pom-poms. A canine howl pierced the crowd noise. Bjorn spotted Vurrg, raising his muzzle to the sky, next to Bjorn's father, who cheered along with the crowd.

His father was cheering.

* * *

The crowd milled about on the field, celebrating the Panther's victory. Bjorn hadn't missed whispers speculating about the next year. Bjorn was a junior, as were Mickey D and Berto. Next year, the Panthers would be an even greater force to be reckoned with on the gridiron.

"You took a heck of a gamble with your last second scramble," Coach remarked, clapping Bjorn on the shoulder. "Good job."

After the initial flush of victory, Bjorn noticed Berto's enthusiasm waned. As more people gathered to congratulate Bjorn, Berto drifted to the periphery of the crowd. Mickey D was talking animatedly to Blair. If she was less than thrilled at their victory, it didn't show. By the time the mob died down enough Bjorn could extricate himself, Berto had headed for the locker room.

Bjorn headed for the sideline. He hoped to meet with Heather first, but his father and Vurrg descended from the bleachers before he could get to her.

"This football is most exciting!" Vurrg exclaimed. He wore an extra-large hoodie, but many around him gawked at the alien's presence. "It reminds me of Zuul battlefield tactics!"

"That was a helluva play at the end, son," Bjorn's father remarked.

"The other guys left me with no other choice," Bjorn said. His father was actually praising his football prowess! Usually, the elder Tovesson groused at how Bjorn was wasting time with games that could be invested in mercenary training. The only reason he originally acquiesced to Bjorn playing football was the physical conditioning would be beneficial.

"The Zuul fight similarly to the way we play football?" Bjorn asked to cover his excitement at his father's approval.

"Yes! You have opposing lines. One side is defending an objective, while the other side seeks to punch through the defenses. A good Zuul defense finds the opposing command on the field and takes them out, similar to how they try to blitz the quarterback in your sport."

The analogy was fairly accurate, and it smelled suspiciously of a merc angle. "Did my father put you up to this?"

"I do not understand. He bought my ticket." The Zuul seemed guileless.

"Son, sometimes you have to take a compliment for what it is," Bjorn's father interjected. "You played a fine game. Take Vurrg's words at face value—I didn't coach him in some plot to sway you."

"I'm sorry, Vurrg." As much as it annoyed him, his father was right. Bjorn was so used to his father needling him about choosing football over mercenary work he looked for it everywhere. "Thank you. I'm glad you enjoyed the game."

"Bjorn!" Heather squealed. Bjorn turned in time to catch Heather as she threw her arms around his neck and kissed him. "You were amazing!"

"I hope Mickey D and Berto don't think I was hogging the glory." Bjorn set his girlfriend down, an arm still around her. "I expected one of them would get open."

"A good quarterback knows when he can't make a pass," a new voice interjected. "Hi, sorry to intrude. I'm Bill Weaver from the University of Georgia." He held up his phone, his business card displayed on the transparent plastic rectangle. "I know you're eager to celebrate, but in the next few days I'd love the chance to talk to you and your parents..." Mr. Weaver faltered once he noticed Vurrg. "Um, talk to you about our football program and scholastic opportunities sometime next week."

"We'll be out of town on a family holiday," Bjorn's father stated.

"Can we arrange something after winter break?" Bjorn asked, masking his annoyance at his father. "We'll be in Alaska visiting my grandparents."

"Absolutely. Can I transmit you my card?"

Bjorn's phone was in his locker. The coach didn't want the temptation for distraction anywhere near the game. Players the coach caught breaking the ban were sentenced to running laps—lots of laps. Bjorn's father would claim to have lost the contact card due to a glitch. "I don't have my phone—they don't hold up well on the field."

Heather unfolded her phone and held it forward. She beamed a bright smile at Mr. Weaver. "If you send it to me, I'll pass it on to Bjorn when he gets his phone."

"Splendid!" The Georgia scout flicked his finger on the surface of his device, and Heather's phone chirped in response. Heather showed the card to Bjorn before folding her phone and tucking it away.

Heather tugged at Bjorn's arm. "Come on. We have a pa—a celebration to get to, and you still need to hit the showers."

"I'll be in touch," Mr. Weaver said and shook Bjorn's hand. Heather must have sent the scout Bjorn's contact card during the phone exchange. "Again, congratulations on a great game!"

"Go on and have fun," Bjorn's father said. "Don't do anything stupid."

"I'll see you later." Bjorn allowed Heather to lead him in the direction of the athletic complex.

Vurrg whispered something to Bjorn's father.

"Probably," his father muttered, then called after Bjorn, "Be safe!"

* * * * *

Chapter Four

Alaskan Wilderness, Alaska

They had left the Snowcat two hours ago, but it felt like half the day to Bjorn. It didn't help that he was carrying twenty-five kilograms of gear on his back. Most of it was in case they got stuck out here in the middle of nowhere. The temperature had hovered a couple of degrees below freezing all day, so the snow wasn't light and fluffy. It fell in fat, wet flakes.

Bjorn regarded their trail from the Snowcat slowly filling with fresh snow. Other people might have admired the hushed landscape and the scenic mountains looming in the distance. They would be viewing it through a Tri-V, or a few steps from a warm, snug lodge. For Bjorn, it was a wet, cold pain in the butt. His boots were sodden and his feet chilled, despite two layers of wool socks. He glared at his father's back.

"Why are we out here freezing our toes off?" Bjorn complained. He knew the reason—his father thought some quality bonding time would help sway Bjorn from forsaking life as a mercenary. At least his grandfather had stayed out of the dispute—he didn't know how he'd handle it if both his elder namesakes ganged up on him.

Bjorn the Elder had retired recently, passing Bjorn's Berserkers on to Bjorn Junior. Since Bjorn III was an only child, his father assumed Bjorn would plan his life around eventually succeeding him as commander. Bjorn had been enrolled in the Mercenary Service Track in school by default. When Bjorn showed an interest in sports, his father considered it an opportunity for more physical conditioning and team building exercises. Once it became apparent Bjorn's prowess on the football field could open doors that would let him escape his mercenary destiny, his father changed his tune.

"You know, I could swing it so you could take your VOWS assessment this summer," the commander rumbled, breaking the hour-long silence. He stopped and turned to face Bjorn. "Given your fitness and grades, you'd do well. You could at least see what you score." Lingering under his father's words was the unspoken hope that if Bjorn aced the assessment it would change his mind about becoming a mercenary.

"The scout at the championship game isn't the only interest I've had," Bjorn stated, meeting his father's gaze. The older man stood a couple centimeters taller and packed an extra twenty kilos. Bjorn the Elder was the same—tall and meaty. Large men ran in the Tovesson family. "Most of the top ten football schools have been sniffing around. Any of them will offer a full ride scholarship, which pulls the teeth out of your 'not on my dime' crap."

"Ever since you became a quarterback, you've gotten cocky." His father brushed frost from his moustache with the back of his glove. "You should have stayed on defense. You were a quarterback's nightmare—you have a gift for picking apart the other side and seeing their weaknesses. It's a talent that would serve you well on the battlefield. Once you became one of those quarterbacks, you grew an ego."

"Like when *Afi* pinned the commander star on you? Now you think you know what's best for everyone?" Bjorn's voice rose, stoked by resentment. "You're ticked because I didn't drink the merc kool-aid!"

"What about after school? Four years of playing ball, a fancy degree, and then what?" Bjorn's father scoffed. "Even as good as you are, son, there's no guarantee you'll make the pros. What if you blow out your knee or something? There goes your free ride, and there goes your hypothetical pro career."

"Could something happen to me on the football field? Sure! At least I'm not going to get my head blown off on the football field!"

His father's expression flashed from icy scowl to wide-eyed surprise. "Look out!"

The brush behind Bjorn exploded in a spray of branches and snow. Bjorn spun and backpedaled as the Kodiak bear loomed over him and roared. Time slowed to a crawl as 500 kilograms of bear surged forward. His father was behind him—Bjorn needed to get out of the line of fire.

Bjorn's father cursed as his rifle went off. Red flecks joined the falling snow as the bear's ear was blown off. The bear snarled and shook its head, spraying saliva from its gaping jaws. Bjorn used the distraction to step back and raise his own hunting rifle. The hurried shot punched through the bear's neck, which enraged the bear further. The beast lunged forward and swiped with a huge clawed paw. The rifle was torn from Bjorn's grasp and spun off into the snow.

Bjorn caught a glimpse of his father trying to regain his footing in the snow—one leg had sunk into the snow up to his knee. Unable to free his leg, his father shouldered his rifle and fired. The *crack* of the shot was followed by a meaty *thunk*. The massive paw struck Bjorn again, and the bear's claws tore through his thick parka and snagged on his web gear. The blow spun Bjorn around and left burning gouges in his side.

His father's rifle cracked again as the beast eclipsed Bjorn's view. The Kodiak's stinking maw descended, the bear's breath hot and fetid. Teeth clamped over Bjorn's left sleeve, and his arm exploded in pain. A sickening crunch accompanied Bjorn's screams.

Bjorn's right hand found the huge Heckler and Glock pistol holstered at his hip. Bjorn didn't know if he lost the glove with his rifle or removed it before his hand grasped the handle of the pistol as he'd done a thousand times in practice. He jerked the gun free of the holster and flipped the safety off by reflex.

The 12mm pistol boomed again and again, the thunder of the gun drowning out his own screams and the roar of the bear. Freed from the bear's jaws, Bjorn sprawled in the cold, wet snow. Something warm sprayed him as the shadow of the bear collapsed.

"Son!" His father's voice seemed distant even though a silhouette blotted the gray sky. "Son, can you hear me?"

Bjorn's head lolled to the side. He could see the blurry brown hulk of the bear before the snowscape turned dark.

*****

Chapter Five

Anchorage, Alaska

"What happened?" Bjorn croaked. His mouth was dry. Pain circled like hungry dogs, kept at bay by drugs but eager to pounce on raw meat. Tell-tale beeps of medical monitors were the first noises Bjorn heard. He cracked his eyes open, squinting at the sterile brightness.

"Thank Frigg!" His mother's voice was close. "Sweetie, can you hear me?"

Bjorn nodded weakly. The shadow to his right must be her. "Where am I?" he rasped.

"Providence Medical in Anchorage," she replied.

A few disjointed memories returned—brown fur, white fangs, red blood. "There was a bear."

"Not anymore," Bjorn's father rumbled from the door, filling the frame. "You blew his fu—his face off."

"BJ." Mom was the only one who got away with calling Bjorn's father BJ.

His father rolled his eyes. "I caught myself. He's not ten. If a Kodiak bear couldn't kill him, an f-bomb from his old man won't. While I was on my butt in the snow, Trip pulled his sidearm and shoved it under the bear's chin while it was trying to eat him. Son, you put three rounds into the sonuvabitch's skull. I'm proud of you."

It only took getting mauled by a bear to hear his father say that.

"And I'm sorry, son. If I hadn't fallen, or if I'd spotted the bear sooner..."

"BJ, it was an accident. Trip knows that," Bjorn's mother chided. "You can't blame yourself. Besides, no one would expect Kodiaks to be so deep in the mainland."

Bjorn tried to flex his fingers. Everything ached. The fingers on his right hand budged, but not his left. He couldn't feel his left hand, or his left arm. There was no pain—there was no feeling at all. Fatigue swept over him as he tried again to move, or even feel, his left arm. "My arm?"

"Don't worry son," Bjorn's father said as darkness crept in. "You're getting the best care credits can buy."

* * *

Bjorn blinked, waiting for his blurry vision to clear. A flashing icon appeared next to the words *Diagnostic Complete. Boot Successful.* A moment later they were replaced by the words *System Ready*. The text floated in his field of vision. He turned his head, and the words moved with his gaze. After five seconds, the text faded.

"What the heck?" Bjorn muttered. *System query?* appeared before his eyes. He reached with his right hand and his fingers passed through the text.

"You are awake, yes?" The voice was nasal with a drawn out S. Bjorn followed it to the door of his room. A mountain lion wearing a lab coat stood in the doorway.

"I'm not so sure," Bjorn replied. The words faded away. The mountain lion glanced at a slate cradled in one of its hands. The digits were odd, but the creature definitely had hands instead of paws. Bjorn peered down—the mountain lion wore shoes. "What are you?"

Running query appeared in the air. A circle highlighted the lab coat-wearing feline. Race: H'rang—Identity: Doctor Shur'im. Bjorn closed his eyes and the glowing orange letters remained. He shook his head in an attempt to banish the words. After several seconds, they faded like the others.

"You are experiencing discomfort, yes?" the creature—the doctor asked. Bjorn opened his eyes and flinched back. The feline alien was half a meter away, staring with large, golden eyes. The doctor waited for an answer, unblinking.

"I have a headache, but I've had worse. It's a dull pain in the back of my head. What's a H'rang?"

H'rang—Galactic Union member race in good standing. Entry into GU 2,946 years ago (adjusted Earth calendar). Bipedal chordate mammalian analogs—superficial similarity to Earth feline physiognomies. Noteworthy for their aversion to conflict and hedonism.

"I am a H'rang. I am also one of your doctors, Doctor Shur'im, but I see your pinplants have already identified me." The doctor tapped at the slate in its hands.

"Why am I hallucinating words?" Bjorn asked. "Wait, you said pinplants—did someone pin me?" Bjorn had heard of pinplants. The brain implants allowed people to plug computers directly into their mind, and the more complex ones installed computers into the person's head.

"Yes. It appears the procedure was successful, yes?" The doctor grinned. "You are my first Human patient. The results are encouraging. In addition to installing your pinplant node, the interfaces, and the control matrix for your new arm, I was able to correct your asymmetrical coordination."

"What?" There was nothing wrong with his coordination.

Asymmetrical coordination—when a creature favors limbs on one side of its body when performing tasks.

"Stop it!" Bjorn shouted. The H'rang vaulted across the room, landing near the door and holding up its slate as though it were a shield.

"Son, what's going on?" Bjorn's father filled the doorway. Doctor Shur'im cringed from the older Tovesson's booming voice.

"BJ, move," Bjorn's mother ordered, and slipped through the door. "What's wrong, Trip?"

Bjorn pointed at the H'rang. "This…" H'rang. "Stop it! It put a fricking computer in my skull, and it's like someone glued a slate to my eyeball! Words keep appearing!"

"Calm down, Trip," his mother said. She tried to sound soothing instead of worried—it almost worked.

"What's wrong with him?" Bjorn's father demanded. "Did you mess up my boy's brain?"

Doctor Shur'im cowered, his ears flattened against his skull. "He isn't accustomed to the pinplants, no? He needs to learn how to use them." The doctor held up the slate. "The telemetry looks good, yes?"

"Why didn't you tell me I had asymmetrical…whatever? Why would you hide it from me?" Bjorn accused, pointing at his father. He realized both hands pointed. Both hands? Bjorn stared at his left arm. The hand and arm were a mix of metal and black polymer. "What happened to my arm?"

"It is not my fault, no?" the doctor declared. "The ElSha built your limb."

"ElSha?"

ElSha—Galactic Union member race in good standing. Entry into GU 30,147 years ago (adjusted Earth calendar). Bipedal chordate reptilian analogs—superficial similarity to 21st century advertising mascot. Noteworthy for their technical aptitude and adaptability to foreign technologies.

"That's what I'm talking about! I know what an ElSha is!" Bjorn waved his hand toward the words. The artificial left hand mirrored its organic counterpart. The explanation floated in front of his eyes for several seconds before fading.

Bjorn's mother placed a hand on his shoulder. "Sweetie, calm down a minute. BJ, stop terrorizing Doctor Shur'im! How can she help our son with you barking at her?"

"I…she…fine." Bjorn's father took a deep breath.

The H'rang edged along the wall toward Bjorn's bed. "Your son needs practice with the interface. You told him what to expect, yes?"

"No." Bjorn consciously rested his arms on the bed. Obviously, the encyclopedia entry regarding H'rang being averse to conflict was true. "I was mauled by a bear. I woke up here with no clue what was going on. Next time I woke up, I had this." He nodded to his left arm. "Also, words are mysteriously appearing as though I'm in some sort of virtual reality environment."

The H'rang bobbed her head. "I'll start from the beginning. Your arm could not be saved. It was amputated. You needed a prosthesis, yes? Yes. Advanced bionics require a pinplant interface, but the technology is new to your species. An ElSha, Frek, designed your arm, and I designed the interface to your brain."

"You were digging around in my skull?" Bjorn reached to side of his head, fighting to keep the artificial counterpart in place. Something hard protruded from the skin behind his ear. "You scooped out some of my brains and stuck in a computer?"

"It is a crude analogy, no? There was no excavation of brain matter. The process was performed with nanites. A tier-two implant was installed," Doctor Shur'im replied. "As I mentioned, I guided the nanites to correct your asymmetrical coordination. You should now have no degradation in performance regardless of which limb you use."

"What are you saying? I can write with my feet?"

The H'rang shook her head. "I only cured your bilateral disfunction. I suppose you could be wired to utilize your feet for tasks, but your digits—your toes—are not designed the same as your fingers. Do you wish to write with your toes?"

"No!"

"Trip, don't shout at the doctor," Bjorn's mother admonished. "Doctor, are members of your race ambidextrous?"

The doctor cocked her head. Was she reading ghost text? "Yes, we H'rang do not favor the appendages on one side of our body over the other. Your son's neural pathways indicated a predilection for utilizing his right hand and right eye. I have corrected the pathways so he will not be hindered utilizing the other limb and eye."

"You cured him of being right-handed," Bjorn's father interjected. He chuckled.

"I'm glad you think it's funny," Bjorn growled.

"Son, are you going to bi—complain because Doctor Shur'im made you ambidextrous while setting up your new arm?" Bjorn's father frowned. "I spent a lot of credits to get you the best care, and you whine because you got an upgrade in the process?"

Bjorn held aloft his artificial arm. "You call this an upgrade?"

Available upgrades—unknown. This cyber-equipment package is custom and does not have standardized features.

"Yes. It is superior to your flesh-and-blood limb. Once you become acclimated, the response rate will be seventy-five percent faster and the exerted force will be one hundred fifty percent of your original limb. It is faster and stronger. It is an upgrade, yes?" The doctor bobbed her head at the end of the question.

Bjorn pointed in the air, this time unable to stop his replacement limb from mimicking his gesture. "How do I stop the floating words?"

"You will need to practice with your pinplants so you do not accidently trigger queries," Doctor Shur'im replied. "It will be part of your recovery therapy, along with adapting to your prosthesis."

"How long am I going to be stuck here?" Bjorn asked. Winter break would end in two days. Heather must be worried sick.

The doctor counted off on her strange hands. The middle of her three digits was thicker than the phalanges on either side. "I estimate at least three to the third power Earth days. We must ensure there are no adverse reactions to the installed equipment. Also, your pain is abated with medicine and nanite treatment. You may not realize you are still healing from significant injuries."

"A month? I can't miss a month! School starts in a couple of days!"

"Trip, school is already back in session," his mother said. "It's been a week since your accident."

The time and date appeared in the corner of Bjorn's vision. He swatted at it as though the display was a fly. His fingers stung as his flesh-and-blood hand smacked into its artificial opposite. "Ow!"

"You will also require physical therapy, yes?" The doctor said. The feline turned to Bjorn's mother. "He need not remain here for the therapy. It is to acclimate him to the prosthesis, acquire muscle memory for the new limb, and adapt to the asymmetry correction."

"I'm going to fall behind in class," Bjorn complained. "Baseball tryouts are the first week of February."

"We can arrange for your schoolwork to be done over the Aethernet. Maybe we can organize a virtual presence in your classes?" his mother suggested.

"The video can stream directly to your pinplants. It will be as though you are in the class, yes?" Dr. Shur'im seemed relieved to talk to Bjorn's mother instead of his father.

"Son, you may not be able to play baseball this year," Bjorn's father said. "Before you get worked up, think about it. Wouldn't you be better off using the time for therapy and conditioning, to get into shape for next fall? The last thing you need is to get beaned by a line drive because something unexpected happened with your pinplants."

Odin's eye! His father made sense. If Bjorn wanted to be in prime shape for football in his senior year, he needed to figure out how to compensate for his prosthetic arm. Baseball was fun, and it helped keep him in shape for the second half of the year, but it was football getting him the scholarship and a career where an angry alien wouldn't try to laze his head off.

"Fine," Bjorn relented. He refused to say the commander was right. "I need to keep up with my studies and homework. It's not as though I have much else to do, seeing as I can't go—crap! What have you told Heather?"

"I called her parents and told them you had been in an accident, but you would be okay. I'm sure she's fine." Bjorn's mother pulled a slate from a nearby shelf.

"Fine? Mom, have you met Heather?" Bjorn asked as he accepted the slate and powered it up. His father stifled a chuckle. "There are 127 messages from her."

"Let's clear out so the boy can make kissy-face at his girlfriend," Bjorn's father remarked. "Be sure to wipe the screen off when you're done."

"I do not understand," Dr. Shur'im said as she followed Bjorn's parents.

Bjorn waited until the door closed before he pinged Heather. Her face appeared immediately on the screen.

"Bjorn, what happened?" she cried. Classmates behind her looked to see what was happening.

Device detected—Type 3 slate, archaic model. Pairing.

Bjorn flinched as the hospital room disappeared, replaced by a close-up of Heather's worried face. In the upper left corner, Bjorn's face appeared. The video stream was projected straight into his brain.

"Are you having a seizure?" Heather asked.

"No. I'm having an issue with the chat client on my slate, but I think I have it figured out," Bjorn replied. He used the smaller image of his face to aim his slate's camera. "What did your folks tell you?"

"Only you'd been in some sort of accident," Heather replied. "I tried to convince my parents to let me come to Alaska, but they were total tyrants about it. I've been so worried about you! Are you okay?"

"I'm not in any danger, but I'll be honest—I was hurt bad. A bear mauled me, and…and I lost my left arm."

"Omigawd! I don't care what my folks say—"

"Please don't," Bjorn interrupted. "I need to get a handle on this, and I don't want your parents to freak out. They'd call the authorities and turn it into a big deal." He didn't add they would try to blame it on Bjorn, even though they would. "I'm still pretty banged up. I'll be home in a month."

"Won't you miss…oh, I'm sorry." Heather blinked back tears.

"It's okay. I already figured out I'm going to have to skip baseball this year." Bjorn smiled into the camera. "On the bright side, I'll have more time for you."

"I wish I could be there."

"So do I." Fatigue seeped into his body as the last of the adrenaline from his initial shock and anger ebbed. "I'm getting tired. I'll ping you soon. Let the others know I'll be in touch."

Most of Heather's face disappeared as she leaned toward the camera and kissed her slate. "I miss you."

"I miss you too," Bjorn replied. "Don't worry, I'll be home before you know it."

*****

Chapter Six

Anchorage, Alaska

"What do you mean I can't play football?" Bjorn demanded. "I have half a year to get acclimated to this thing." Bjorn raised his artificial arm.

"They're not questioning your recuperation," Bjorn's father said. "Your…modifications disqualify you from playing football."

"What? I can't sit out my senior year. The colleges will think I haven't recovered; they'll think I can't play as well as before!"

Bjorn's father sighed. "You don't understand, son. They won't let you on the field—high school, college, or pro."

"No! That can't be right!" Bjorn slammed his left arm down. The side rail of his hospital bed crumpled under the blow with a metallic squeal.

"That's why. They're afraid you could hurt someone, or that your cybernetics would give you an advantage," his father said, gazing at the crushed aluminum railing. "I'm sorry. I know how much football means to you."

His father sounded sincere, which only infuriated Bjorn further. Ever since Bjorn discovered football could be a means to escape his destiny of becoming a mercenary, his father had been critical of the notion. Now that the dream was yanked from Bjorn's grasp, his father was supportive.

"Look on the bright side, son." His father's smile tugged at his beard. "After you finish physical therapy, you can still take your VOWS. You'll still be eligible for mercenary work once you get back on your feet and back up to snuff."

Bjorn clenched his cybernetic fist.

"I think the important thing is for Trip to focus on his recovery," Bjorn's mother interjected. She had always favored a path that didn't lead to her only child dying on an alien world. "He still has time to figure out what to do with the rest of his life."

"Of course," Bjorn's father muttered. He turned to gaze out the window. Snow swirled past a backdrop of gray clouds.

Bjorn glared at his father until the door opened. Bjorn recognized an ElSha without his pinplants responding to a query. The meter-and-a-half tall lizard resembled the advertising mascot from a century prior. Bjorn expected an English accent instead of the clicks and pops emerging from its mouth.

"Hello. I hope I am not interrupting." Bjorn's pinplants translated the lizard's speech as the creature's own translator pendant rendered the staccato noise into English, leading to an eerie echo. "My name is Frek. I wished to see how the hardware was performing."

Bjorn glared at the new arrival. "Great. I can wreck stuff, but I can't play football."

The reptile gave no indication of being intimidated. It blinked at Bjorn. "Odd. Your new limb should be compatible to all the physical requirements for recreational, vocational, and combat tasks. It will require some practice on your part. Your pinplants can assist by providing targeting data and performance feedback."

Bjorn held his cybernetic arm aloft. "The problem is whoever makes the rules thinks this thing will give me an unfair advantage."

"I imagine it would." The lizard blinked again. One eye strayed toward Bjorn's father. "Commander Tovesson instructed me to craft the best prosthetic limb money could buy, within the limits of your physiology and various weapon ordinances."

Bjorn shot his father an accusatory glance. "Can you dial it down so it's not any stronger or faster than my original arm?"

"I could, but why would you want me to do so?" The echo was getting annoying.

Pause integral translator function?

"Please, yes," Bjorn thought.

Integral translator paused.

"Because they won't let me play football with a CASPer arm attached to my shoulder," Bjorn replied.

Frek wrinkled his lipless mouth and did a good impersonation of appearing insulted. "Your limb is far more elegant and agile than a suit of battle armor."

"It wouldn't matter, son," his father interjected. "I already checked. Even if your prosthetic only replicated your original strength and reflexes, there's the question of having a player barreling across the field with twenty kilos of molybdenum steel and plastic. They're afraid another player could be seriously injured by a collision with a 'foreign object.' There are a bunch of liability issues, so they won't budge on it."

"Your father has spent a lot of time trying to find a way around this," his mother added. "We even hired an attorney to investigate the rules. I'm sorry, Trip."

"Would you like to crush something?" Frek asked, digging into a satchel. He pulled out a short length of pipe. "I wish to test the grip strength and record the sensory feedback. Judging by the increased blood flow to your face, you are experiencing anger or embarrassment, and the tones relayed by my translator indicate the former."

"Fine." Bjorn accepted the steel pipe with his flesh-and-blood right hand and squeezed it. Nothing. He passed it to his left hand and got a solid grip. Staring at his father, Bjorn clenched his fist. With a metallic groan, the pipe collapsed.

"Thor's hammer," Bjorn swore under his breath. Louder, he asked, "Can I punch out a CASPer? Flip a car?"

Frek whistled, which his translator rendered into laughter. "Your arm is a fine piece of engineering, but the rest of your body remains Human. You are still subject to the laws of physics. Please don't attempt something ridiculous and tear your arm off your flesh-and-blood body."

Bjorn accepted another length of pipe and crushed it. One of Frek's eyes went to his slate while the other remained on Bjorn. "Great, I can replace a trash compactor, but I can't play football. What am I supposed to do? And don't you dare say become a merc," Bjorn warned his father.

"Trip, take it one step at a time. Focus on your recuperation first."

"Your mother is right," his father added.

A robotic cart rolled into the room. *It must be dinner time.* The time and date appeared, but Bjorn didn't bother trying to dismiss it. If he ignored it, the display would fade after several seconds. A mechanical limb reached into a compartment and extricated a covered tray. The robotic arm deposited the meal on the table next to Bjorn's bed. Bjorn flexed his own mechanical limb as he watched the robot depart.

"Son, we'll go get some dinner and leave you to eat in peace," his father said. Bjorn's eyes snapped from the doorway where the robot had departed.

"Call us if you need anything," his mother added. "We won't be far."

Bjorn grunted and swung the table's surface holding his dinner over the bed. Frek was still regarding him. "What? Do you need me to crush more pipes?"

Frek shook his head. "I have the feeling I should get to work on future iterations of your arm."

"Future?" Bjorn popped the lid off the meal tray. A double serving of vat-meat hospital loaf and gravy with an extra-large serving of French fries. If he wasn't going to play football, maybe he should cut back on how much he ate? Loki take it, if he wasn't going to play football, what did it matter? "Isn't this thing finished? Or are you going to deck it out in some running lights?"

"Do you want running lights?" the reptilian alien asked.

"No, what I want is for people to not stare at me and feel sorry for me. I've seen the way people look at amputees. I've done it myself. You feel bad for them because they're missing a part of themselves. I don't want that."

"You want an arm that could pass for organic." Frek nodded. "A challenge—but I relish challenges. Based on the information Dr. Shur'im provided, you'll need at least one upgrade as you finish growing. I know you see this as a misfortune, but I will make sure you have the finest limb that can pass for organic."

Bjorn choked down a mouthful of vat-loaf, but there was still a lump in his throat. "Thank you."

"No need! I have many hatchlings, and your family will ensure they get good educations." Frek sniffed at the tray of food. "I think I will seek a meal myself."

"Frek? Are you going to help me learn how to use this thing?" Bjorn held up his arm.

"I'm an engineer, not a therapist. However, I'm sure your father will ensure you have a top-notch therapist. Now, if you'll excuse me, I will see if the commissary has stocked the grasshoppers as promised."

Suddenly, Bjorn was a bit less hungry.

* * *

Judging by the growing light, it was late morning. The sun didn't clear the horizon until after 10:00 in the morning this far north.

January 9, 9:42 am.

There had to be a way keep his pinplants from flashing the time and day every time he thought about it.

Do you wish to change the time-date settings? Select: always, passive request, active request.

Bjorn focused. "What is the current setting?" he thought.

Passive request.

"Change to active request." Hopefully that meant the time and date would only appear if he specifically asked the pinplants. What kind of lunatic would choose always?

Settings changed.

Crap. Instead of fighting these implants, he should have been customizing the settings as though he had a new slate. He glanced at his slate. Even though his friends were two time zones ahead of him, it would be hours before they got out of school. He still hadn't broken the news he was disqualified from football, not even to Heather.

Would she even want to be his girlfriend if he wasn't on the football team? He shook his head as though it would dismiss his doubts. She wasn't so shallow—she cared about him, not what sport he played.

"You shake your head so hard, you might rattle something loose."

Bjorn looked up. The hulking man in the door resembled his father, but the salt-and-pepper hair and beard resembled burnished steel. The fleece-lined buckskin jacket bore a Bjorn's Berserkers patch on the shoulder and Elder Futhark runes were embroidered down the sleeves.

"*Afi* Bjorn?" "Afi" was Icelandic for grandfather. Bjorn's eldest namesake approved of when he used the old tongue. "I thought you were snowed in?"

"We were until this morning. I think my pilot wet himself, though." Even though his grandfather was over 80, he was still vital and bright-eyed. "Your *Amma* said I shouldn't be so hard on him, but I remember when bush pilots flew these skies without fancy tech."

"*Amma*" would be Grandma Siqi. She was half Inuit and the source of the jet-black hair sported both by Bjorn and his father. If there was anyone more practical than Bjorn's mother, it was *Amma* Siqi.

"Is she here?" Bjorn asked.

His grandfather snorted. "Your *Amma* hates flying in winter weather, even when it's calm like today. I don't know what she's worried about; the snow is falling down instead of sideways." He approached Bjorn's bed and reached into a coat pocket. He drew out a string of bear claws arrayed around a hammer-shaped pendant and handed it to Bjorn.

"The Mjolnir pendant belonged to my father, Olaf. The bear claws are from the beastie who did a number on your arm," *Afi* said.

"What?" Bjorn assumed the animal's corpse had been left to the wolves.

"Once you were recovered and whisked here, they asked what to do about the bear you'd killed. We couldn't let it go to waste, especially considering the *blodth-price* you paid to bring it down. Much of the meat has been distributed, but I've saved the best parts," his grandfather said. "The pelt, the claws, the fangs, and the heart. I heard you killed the beast with the gun I gave you." His grandfather smiled. "A bear was mauling you and you remembered your training. You do the name Bjorn Tovesson proud."

"To be honest, I acted on instinct. I don't remember much," Bjorn admitted. What he did remember was mostly his screaming voice and pain. "I'm lucky you gave me the pistol. A smaller gun might not have dropped the bear."

His grandfather pulled up a chair. "I hear you can't play football. They're afraid you might hurt someone. I bet your father has already pitched the merc life."

Bjorn flexed his fingers one at a time. "He has. He knows I have few options since I'm disqualified from sports."

"Do you think he did it on purpose? Getting you the arm, I mean."

Why couldn't I have a thick beard to stroke in contemplation? Instead, Bjorn fidgeted. "I suppose not. I've read the rules forward and backward—a prosthetic foot or leg is allowed, but a hand or arm is not due to the chance for injury. Even if I had a dummy arm, with no cybernetics, they wouldn't let me on the field."

"There you have it," *Afi* said. "I won't tell you to quit being ticked at your father—you're a teenager after all. Consider this: your father did what he honestly believed was best for you."

"Sometimes I wish he'd let me die," Bjorn whispered, rubbing his thumb over the hammer pendant. "I don't know who I'll be. My friends, my future, everything was centered around football. What now?"

"I won't give you a glib answer or any of the feel-good bear-crap people spout." *Afi* rapped his knuckles on Bjorn's prosthesis. "This won't be easy. It may have fancy technology and cost a million credits, but it doesn't change the struggle you'll face. I've known several mercs who left part of themselves on the battlefield. No matter how tough they are, what comes after is never easy."

Bjorn met his grandfather's ice-blue eyes, another Tovesson hallmark. "My life is going to suck. Joy."

"Yes, it will suck. You'll be angry, you'll be depressed, and you'll want to give up," *Afi* said. "You won't, though. Many men would have soiled themselves and died out in the snow. You refused to let the bear take your life then. You won't let the bear take it in a month, or in a year. You won't let the bear win."

"But it took my dreams," Bjorn countered. "It took my future."

"Make a new future." His grandfather tugged on one of the dangling 10-centimeter-long claws. "You know the saying 'that which doesn't kill us makes us stronger?' Well, this brute made you stronger than ever. Use that strength."

Bjorn nodded mutely.

*****

Chapter Seven

Las Cruces, New Mexico

"Surprise!" a cacophony of voices shouted as the lights clicked on.

"Bjorn!" Heather squealed, bursting from the crowd gathered in the dining room. A Welcome Home banner stretched across the far wall.

Bjorn made sure to catch Heather with his right arm as she leapt to throw her arms around his neck and kiss him. Everyone else cheered, with Mickey D throwing in a whistle.

"I'm so glad you're home," Heather murmured into his ear, her voice full of promise, before Bjorn's friends descended on him.

Most of the crowd was from the football team and the pep squad, with their dates filling out the rest. One exception stood out—Vurrg. The Zuul remained at the rear of the crowd, observing the festivities with Geneva.

"*Hermano*, welcome back." Roberto held out his right, which Bjorn clapped and reflexively raised his left hand. As they'd done a hundred times, Roberto clapped the open hand. "Dang! It's like slapping a frying pan!" Berto shook his hand and realization spread across his face. "Hey man…"

"It's all good, *hermano*." Bjorn forced a smile. He'd remembered to pause his internal translator. He needed to figure out how to flag it not to translate Spanish unless he heard something he didn't understand. Right now, it was all or *nada.* "Later on, I'll do some party tricks and crush stuff."

Berto clasped him on the shoulder. "At least it wasn't your throwing arm."

"Right." Bjorn still hadn't told any of his friends, or even Heather, he'd been disqualified from football. He had waited to tell them in person, but now didn't seem to be the time.

"All right, let's cut the cake," Bjorn's father called, moving through the crowd of teenagers. "Geneva worked all day on it, so don't let it go to waste."

Bjorn followed in his father's wake, his right arm around Heather. It was the first time he'd felt normal since Alaska. Geneva cut up the cake and doled out slices on small plates. The crowd called for Bjorn to get the first piece.

A targeting reticle centered on the slice of cake, and the outline of the plate flashed in Bjorn's vision. Crushing cans was easy, but Bjorn struggled handling delicate items. The therapist in Anchorage told him it could take months.

Bjorn let go of Heather so he could use his organic hand to pick up the cake and place the plate in his upturned cybernetic palm. Everyone pretended not to watch him hold the plate in place until he could arrange his prosthetic digits to hold the plate steady without crushing it.

"Want me to feed you?" Heather asked with a giggle. "I promise not to leave you covered in icing."

"I can do it myself," Bjorn snapped. Heather stepped back; her expression hurt. The people closest to them turned, but at least he hadn't raised his voice. "Sorry, I still get frustrated with this thing. My therapist said I made a lousy patient."

"I'm sorry, I didn't mean..." Heather's voice faltered.

Bjorn summoned a smile. "It's fine, princess. I didn't mean to bark at you." He handed her a spork. "Why don't you help me with the first bite, then get some cake for yourself?"

Heather's smile returned, and she shoveled a large lump of cake mostly into Bjorn's mouth. The crowd noise resumed, some cheering as Bjorn wiped at the frosting.

Heather happily collected her own helping of cake. "I shouldn't eat this, but I'll make an exception for you."

"Welcome home," Vurrg said between bites of cake. The Zuul had waited until Heather was off huddled with her cheerleader friends. Watching the Zuul use the spork instead of devouring the cake directly off the plate seemed incongruous. "I shouldn't eat this cake, but it is delicious."

"Don't tell me you're worried about your weight," Bjorn remarked. Heather hadn't finished half her serving, handing it to Bjorn. When he practiced and worked out every day, Bjorn had no qualms about a few extra calories here and there. Now he had to watch it, or else he'd get as big as Blair.

"Zuul do not normally consume such complex carbohydrates." Vurrg scooped up the remaining sliver of cake. "It turns out we find them delicious, but we don't process them so well. I took a capsule to mitigate any ill effects so I could enjoy this treat."

"Your father spoke highly of your prowess and courage during your conflict," Vurrg added. "He said you acquitted yourself admirably."

"I screamed and reacted by reflex," Bjorn countered. "I didn't do anything special."

"I disagree." The Zuul lapped stray frosting from his plate. "Your *arn'harr*—first kill—was a formidable foe. You should be proud. To do so eye-to-eye is doubly impressive. It is why I asked to participate in your return-from-the-hunt celebration."

"This is more of a 'congratulations, you didn't die' party," Bjorn protested.

"Isn't that the essence of the hunt, or for you Humans, combat?" Vurrg asked. "Make the opponent die so you may live? After all, you are wearing the bear's claws instead of filling his belly."

"I guess," Bjorn muttered. He didn't want to agree with Vurrg, even if what the Zuul said made sense. His hand went to the bronze hammer dangling amid the string of claws.

"Hi, Mr. Vurrg," Heather said. She stood on her tiptoes and kissed Bjorn on the cheek.

"Hello." The Zuul sniffed the air. "I will let you cubs…celebrate. Good evening, Bjorn."

Tactile feedback indicated Heather had clasped his left hand. Bjorn was careful not to move the prosthesis.

"Do you think we could sneak off?" Heather whispered. The crowd had thinned, and after the initial wave of well-wishes and welcome backs, Bjorn had sidled out of the center of attention. His parents had vanished fifteen minutes earlier, having had their fill of teenage chatter and confident nothing would get trashed.

Bjorn checked the time with his pinplant. At least he had mastered something with the hardware crammed in his skull. "What about your curfew?"

Heather shrugged. "I haven't seen you in over a month. They'll cut me some slack over an hour or two, especially if I get weepy and lay on the guilt trip."

"Hey, *hermano*, I'm bouncing," Berto announced. He caught himself from extending his hand for their traditional exchange. "It's good to have you back. Um, Heather, do you need a ride?"

"No. My dad let me use the car as long as I leave it on autodrive. Hopefully it doesn't get flaky like when I took it to the Mesilla Galleria. The stupid car spent ten minutes circling the parking lot before it figured out how to get on the road."

"I'll see you in school, buddy," Bjorn said. "Thanks for coming out."

"For you, *amigo, por supuesto.* See you, Heather."

"It's a shame he doesn't have a girlfriend," Bjorn remarked. "I guess he's still smarting from Bianca dumping him for that senior girl."

"I know; he's such a sweet guy. Tricia from the pom-pom squad asked him out, but he blew her off," Heather said.

Roberto's departure may as well have been a signal for the other teens to make their exodus. Within fifteen minutes, only Bjorn, Heather, and Geneva remained.

"Geneva, do you want any help cleaning up?" Bjorn asked, despite Heather's tug on his arm.

Geneva snorted and tipped her head toward Bjorn's room. "I've got this."

Bjorn let Heather lead him away.

*****

Chapter Eight

Las Cruces, New Mexico

"Coach, there has to be some way around this," Bjorn pleaded. "It's not my throwing arm. We can wrap the damned thing in bubble wrap so no one gets hurt."

Coach shook his head and sighed. "I'm sorry, Bjorn, but there is no way a student with a prosthetic arm will be allowed to play. Not after what happened in Texas in 2091 and the lawsuits. I hate to lose you, but my hands are tied. On the bright side, I've spoken to the varsity committee, and they agree you can wear your letter jacket for your senior year."

"Great. I get to wear my jacket." Bjorn bit his lip and froze his face in a stoic mask. It wouldn't do to cry, especially in front of the coach. "Thanks, Coach."

Bjorn marched through the locker room and out of the athletic complex on autopilot. If anyone could have given him hope there was still a way for him to play, it was Coach. Bjorn had staved off depression under the pretense it wasn't final until he talked to Coach. Now it was final. His football career was over. If he'd been wearing the bear claw necklace, he would have torn it off and hurled it away, but the dress code forbade "outrageous adornments."

Bjorn sought somewhere isolated. He hadn't told his friends he was disqualified from playing. His nose began to run, and his throat closed up. Bjorn leaned his head against the lockers, breathing heavily. It wasn't fair! He was supposed to spend his last year of high school at the top. But instead of spending his senior year as a star quarterback, with colleges courting him, he was going to be no one. He'd be one of those washed-up has-beens whose glory days were behind them, and he wasn't even done with school!

Bjorn slammed his fist into a locker. The thin metal screeched as it cratered under the impact. He punched the next locker even harder, buckling the door. "It's not fair!" he bellowed, and sagged against the wall, sobbing. "It's not fair."

Fleeing footsteps echoed on the tile floor. Bjorn slumped to the ground and sniffled. A notification popped up in his field of view to remind him he had a physical therapy appointment in 30 minutes.

By the time Bjorn recovered his composure, one of the school resource officers was approaching, hand on his taser.

"Kid, you okay?" The SRO eyed the wrecked lockers and stayed out of arm's reach.

Bjorn wiped his nose with his sleeve. "Not really, but I guess it doesn't matter." Bjorn pushed himself to his feet.

The resource officer backpedaled and drew his taser. "Let's not do anything stupid."

Bjorn knitted his brows in confusion. His pinplants highlighted the taser and painted it as a threat. "Why are you drawing on me? I'm not hurting anyone."

"Put your hands up and don't move!" The resource officer aimed the taser at Bjorn. "I have a 10-15, first floor, south wing," the SRO added into his radio. "Requesting back-up."

"Are you kidding me?" Bjorn protested. He turned toward the other end of the hall. It was filled with students recording him on phones and slates.

"Freeze, or I will taze you!" the SRO yelled.

Bjorn spun back around and took a step toward the resource officer. "Up yours! My life has been ruined, and now—"

The officer's weapon popped as it launched the darts. Without thinking, Bjorn's left arm rose to shield him, and the taser darts embedded in his sleeve. The SRO jammed his thumb down on a button on the taser. The device snapped and cracked as it unloaded current through the wires. Bjorn's stump tingled where it interfaced with his prosthetic.

Bjorn twisted his cybernetic arm and yanked the gossamer wires from the weapon. "Knock it off!"

"Bjorn!" Heather's scream pierced the crowd noise. She broke through the throng behind the resource officer. "Don't shoot him!"

As the girl threw herself onto Bjorn, he caught her and twisted. The SRO unsnapped the restraint on his pistol. Bjorn hunched over Heather, holding her close and shielding her from the impending gunfire.

"Stand down!" Principal Martinez shouldered through the mob behind the SRO. "Officer Fields, put away your sidearm. I mean it! Mr. Tovesson, look at me."

Bjorn peered over his shoulder, still interposing his body between the SRO and Heather. Tears blurred his vision, and he sniffed again.

"Bjorn, take a deep breath," the principal urged, softening her tone. "For God's sake, Fields, holster your damned gun. You and Mitchell clear out these students. Lawson, go to the other end of the hall and help the teachers do the same."

Bjorn's pinplants painted Officer Lawson as he scooted past Bjorn as far away as the corridor would allow. Bjorn relaxed his hold on Heather, who trembled against his chest.

"You should go," Bjorn murmured. "I'm in trouble, but no one is going to get hurt. It'll be all right."

Heather shook her head against his shoulder. "I'm not leaving you."

"It'll be fine, princess. They've got to yell at me, and when my old man gets here, he's going to let me have it," Bjorn said, regaining his composure. It was the truth—his dad was going to blow a buffer panel, like a runaway fusion reactor overloading.

Principal Martinez took a tentative step closer. "He's right, Miss Akins. If your parents aren't picking you up, I'm sure you have practice."

Heather eyed the SROs chasing away onlookers, her eyes narrow. "How do I know they aren't waiting for me to get out of the way?"

"I won't put up a fuss," Bjorn said, as much for Martinez as Heather. With the adrenaline draining out of him, he wanted nothing more than to collapse in a chair. "The principal is right; you have tennis practice. Go on, I'll message you when the fireworks die down."

Heather bit her lip. "Fine, but I'll be waiting to hear you're okay." She rose on her tiptoes to give him a quick kiss, a breach of the school rules. Martinez said nothing. Heather paused at the corner and gave Bjorn a wan smile before she disappeared.

"Um, should I cuff him?" Officer Fields eyed Bjorn nervously.

"Is it going to be necessary, Mr. Tovesson?"

Bjorn shook his head, too tired to get angry again. "I said I won't resist. If you want to put the cuffs on me…whatever." Bjorn held out his hands.

"I think we can forgo the handcuffs," Principal Martinez said. "Let's go to my office and wait for your parents."

* * *

"What do you mean expelled? The boy is having a rough time. Odin's Eye, a bear ripped off his arm, and he lost any prayer of a football scholarship—my kid's life went in the crapper!" Bjorn's father shouted. He tossed a credit chit on the principal's desk. "That'll buy a couple hundred lockers!"

"Mr. Tovesson, it's not merely the property damage," Principal Martinez said, her hands folded on her desk. She didn't even glance at the plastic square with a red diamond chip embedded in it. At a thousand credits, it was worth 50,000 UN dollars, the common currency on Earth. "I'm sympathetic to your son's plight, but in the last half hour, videos of him squaring off against a School Resource Officer have spread through the Aethernet. Mesilla Prep has a certain image to maintain, and I've had several parents questioning that image in light of your son's actions. They're comparing us to public schools and threatening to withdraw their children."

"Loki's Get they will! The reason my kid is here, and the reason their kids are here, is this is the best school in town, and we're willing to pay the price." Bjorn's father jabbed his finger on the principal's desk. "How many families have you been able to draw in this year because of your football program? My boy is as responsible for that as your coaches."

"It isn't as simple as you think," the principle protested.

Bjorn's father slapped another credit chit on the desk. "Sure it is. We pay a fine, my boy does detention or mop halls, and we move on. Simple. If I'm not your richest customer, I bet I'm in the top ten."

"To be frank, with one child who has a single year left. The board of directors were explicit in their memo." Principal Martinez leaned forward and lowered her voice. "If it was up to me, we'd take the fine for damages, give your son a nominal punishment, and move on. He's been a good student, and you've been a good customer. However, it's out of my grasp."

His father snatched the credit chits off the desk and stood up, towering over the principal. She appeared nonplussed by two meters of mercenary. "Fine. We'll put him in another school."

Bjorn snapped out of his stupor. "Wait, does this mean I lose the entire year?"

"We paid for the year, dammit." Bjorn's father glared at Martinez.

"Given your son's scholastic performance, we can work out an online program to complete the remainder of the year," Martinez said. "However, he won't be allowed on school property or at school functions."

Bjorn's father frowned. "Good enough. Maybe it will give him time to get his act together."

* * *

Bjorn's father waited until they reached the matte gray personnel transport, a utility vehicle utilized by mercenary and military organizations. This one had the Bjorn's Berserkers logo emblazoned on the front doors. "What in the name of Odin were you thinking, son? Getting into a pissing match with a school cop? Did the bear crack your skull?"

Fresh anger spurred Bjorn from his lethargy. "Maybe it did. If you're going to screw up my life enough to make me a merc, might as well make me an idiot so I'll go along with it!"

"I'll take the blame for what happened in Alaska," his father countered as he wove the transport through Las Cruces traffic. He disliked handing control of the vehicle over to the autodrive. "I was too slow, and I lost my footing. It's on me, and there won't be a day I forget the sight of the Kodiak mauling you. I'll even grant you a temper tantrum with some property damage. Squaring off against a cop, not to mention in front of the rest of your school, is on you. Now we'll have to see if either of the other two private high schools can be bribed."

"Sorry to inconvenience you," Bjorn muttered.

"This isn't funny!" the commander retorted. "St. Bernard's is run by a bunch of pacifists leeching off vouchers. They could well turn up their noses at mercenary money. Latin Springs will give us grief because we're heathens. You could be stuck doing your senior year in a public school, which will hurt your chances of getting into college."

"Do you think I'll be able to get into college after this?" Bjorn remarked. He was a good student, but not stellar. His family's affluence would work against him in the admission process.

"I don't know. If you have good enough grades, maybe," his father replied. The bulk of college admissions were awarded based on a complex formula including academics, social inequity, and economic disadvantage. Those students had their tuition and expenses covered for four years by government programs. An exception were sports scholarships, which were agnostic regarding a potential student's background. All they cared about was athletic performance. "If you pull any more stunts like that, colleges won't even look at you."

Bjorn stopped paying attention as his father railed against the "liberal" education system. *I really screwed up,* Bjorn thought. How would Heather take the news that he was expelled? Would all his friends ghost him? Not only was he out of sports, he wasn't even in the same school any more. As an afterthought, he requested his pin-plants to query the Las Cruces Public Schools data. Aethernet data showed academic metrics, sports scores, and crime rates. The numbers were not encouraging.

* * *

"Are you okay, Trip?" At least his mother waited for Bjorn to gather his wits. "What happened?"

"Our son had a meltdown, destroyed school property, and disarmed a school resource officer," his father interjected. "He's lucky he didn't get shot."

His mother's tone turned cool. "I don't need an after-action report, BJ."

"I…I went to talk to Coach," Bjorn replied haltingly. "I guess I was hoping…hoping he would know some way I could still play."

"Son, we'd already been over—"

"I know!" Bjorn snapped, glaring at his father as he slammed his left hand on the table. The centerpiece jumped. He slowly lifted the hand, ashamed of the outburst. The cybernetic limb was a curse. He wanted to tear the hunk of metal and plastic off the stump. "I know. It didn't seem real, not until Coach told me there was no way I could play. After he shut me down, it felt as though everything was closing in on me. I was drowning.

"I lashed out and punched some lockers. When the SRO stumbled across me, he panicked," Bjorn continued, his voice subdued.

"What have we taught you about dealing with police?" his father said.

"I know, I know—cooperate and let the lawyers sort it out." Bjorn sighed, sagging in his chair. "I know I messed up. Now not only are my college plans ruined, I won't even finish school with my girlfriend or my friends. By next year, they won't even remember me."

"Your friends won't forget you," his mother promised. She didn't understand high school. Not only would Bjorn not be attending classes with his friends, he would be unplugged from their entire social ecosystem. Bjorn couldn't even go to any school-related activities.

"Have some dinner and get some rest." The commander pulled his hand down along his beard, a sign he was deep in thought. "Tomorrow you're going to base with me. Be done with breakfast and ready to roll at 0700."

"What? Why?" Bjorn couldn't muster much energy behind the protest. He envisioned a day of punishment details. How many latrines did the base have?

"You got your butt expelled, so I'm not going to leave you to goof off." His father grabbed a slate and tapped at the screen. "Once we have your class work, you will study in one of the offices at the base. You will do PT with the training cadre, and you will continue your Mercenary Service Track training."

"But—"

"I know, you don't want to be a merc, but MST is part of your school requirements and by Odin's Eye, you're going to do it right."

"BJ, are you sure he should be going to the base?" Bjorn's mother asked.

"Lynn, if we leave him unsupervised, he'll sulk around here getting fat." His father glanced at Bjorn. "All things considered, I think I'm going easy on him. It's not as though he'll be scrubbing latrines until he's eighteen—the thought did cross my mind. If I'm going to stay late at the base, I can send him home."

Bjorn's mother nodded. "The structure would be good for him."

"Great," Bjorn muttered. "I get to go to Bear Town."

*****

Chapter Nine

Bear Town, New Mexico

Bjorn and his father rode out of Las Cruces in silence. The LPT, or light personnel transport, had a radio—a misnomer for the audio streaming system—but neither Bjorn nor his father turned it on. Whoever picked an audio stream would have to endure the complaints of the other regarding their choice of programming. Instead, they rode in silence.

An autotruck roared past, cruising by at 150 kph in the lane dedicated to the huge autonomous trucks. The driverless semis hauled trailers of goods between depots, where a Human drover would guide the vehicle through the yard and to its dock. Maybe Bjorn could be a drover. The robotic trucks would be better company than he had now.

"Your *Afi* bought this land," Bjorn's father said as they exited US-70. The road south headed to a dilapidated military museum. They swung north, under the highway. "He always thought ahead."

"I know, Dad. Bjorn the First of Our Name bought the land from the cash-starved federal government, who realized most of their military assets were outdated and costly to maintain. He moved the Berserkers' operations from Houston because the presence of the merc industry drove up prices." Bjorn memorized the history as a child. "The tract including Bear Peak is lucky happenstance, or a sign from the gods, depending on *Afi*'s mood."

"At least you paid attention," his father muttered. They drove past a sign emblazoned with "Bear Town—1 km." If you were on this road, Bear Town was your only choice, barring turning around. His father had the sign installed because drivers were afraid they had gotten lost. "I wish Dad had picked a location a bit farther north. We're only eighty kilometers from the border."

South of the border lay the Federation of Mexican States. In truth, the various states were controlled by cartels. The Mexican government had collapsed a decade after First Contact, and to prevent anarchy, the cartels stepped in and assumed control of their respective regions. The UN General Assembly put their stamp on the arrangement to keep from having to bail the region out.

Bjorn's father halted the charcoal gray LPT at the gatehouse. The bored sentry snapped to attention once he spotted the name emblazoned above the Bjorn's Berserker logo.

"Good morning, Commander," the specialist said once the window was open. "I see you have a visitor today. Give me a moment to check it against the daily roster."

Even though Bjorn's father could command the sentry to admit them, he allowed the infantryman to go through the process. The sentry pulled a slate from his thigh holster and compared Bjorn to the image on the screen. "Your son? Very good, sir." The specialist gave his counterpart in the armored gatehouse a thumbs up and the metal gate rolled aside.

It was another kilometer before they passed signs of construction. Even at that early hour, crews were already at work. Bjorn guessed by the number of walls in the skeleton of the building it would be trooper housing. The Berserkers offered dormitory-style accommodations for single soldiers. Elsewhere on the base would be condominiums for mercenaries with families.

A huge structure loomed before them, uphill and backed up to the mountain. Its stone and wood façade was anachronistic compared to the utilitarian buildings they had passed. Large timber buttresses were carved into longship figureheads. The official plaque next to the door read Bjarnarsal, but everyone on base referred to the building as the Mead Hall. In addition to a huge mess area, the building housed the command and administrative offices of Bjorn's Berserkers.

"Much of the building is empty," Bjorn's father said as they turned away from the cavernous mess space. "Pops and I conceived this with room for the organization to grow. We've added a second company, and depending on how missions go, I'm hoping to add a third within two years, and maybe a fourth if I split off the recon elements into their own company."

Was this a sales pitch or idle talk? Better not to call the commander out on it—Bjorn had royally messed up, so he needed to pick his fights with his old man with caution. So far, his father hadn't said anything about cutting access to his accounts or threatened to turn off Bjorn's Aethernet access. A non-committal grunt seemed safest.

The elevator deposited them in the command lobby. A middle-aged man with dark hair turning silver glanced up from his large desk. Three different Tri-V displays hovered in front of him.

"Well hello there, young man," the man lisped, standing up. His shirt was the same dark gray BDUs, battle dress uniform, as Bjorn's father, but in place of a rank insignia there was a patch with a C followed by two dots which resembled a colon. It identified the man as a civilian contractor, the dots marked him as the rough equivalent of a technical sergeant. "The commander said you would be spending some time with us. My, you've grown. I think I last saw you two years ago; now you're as big as your father."

"Almost, Stefan," Bjorn's father remarked. Stefan had been the elder Bjorn's secretary for a decade. "Did you get everything together?"

Stefan gave the commander a wounded look. "Of course. Here's his badge, and I've downloaded the classwork that was already available from Mesilla Prep. The Cubs assemble for PT in thirty-seven minutes in the main quad."

Bjorn set a timer in his pinplants for 30 minutes. It only took two tries to get it right. It would leave him enough time to get to the quad for PT. A notification appeared in his pinview.

Berserker BTI HQ node is requesting handshake, the message read. Do you wish to accept?

"What's a Berserker BTI HQ node?" Bjorn asked aloud. "It's trying to ping my pinplants."

"The BTI is the Battlefield Tactical Intelligence," Bjorn's father replied. "Before you ask, no it's not an artificial intelligence. Think of it as a virtual assistant on steroids."

"The HQ node means it's the local iteration of the BTI," Stefan added. After Bjorn knit his brows in puzzlement, Stefan continued. "The BTI is a software swarm. There are multiple iterations, each in a node. For example, there is a node here in the headquarters, and there is also one in the mobile command center deployed in the field. When two nodes come in contact, they exchange data and updates."

"Isn't that how you get an AI?" Bjorn asked.

"You've watched too much garbage on the Aethernet," his father rumbled. "Think about it. How many copies do you think are floating around of the most popular virtual assistants? They're not going to change into some sort of hive-mind and take over the world."

"So it's safe to accept the handshake from the base node?"

"Absolutely safe," Stefan replied. "It sees your pinplants the same as a slate or phone. By the way, I'm a bit jealous. I've wanted pinplants since I first heard about them, but I'm afraid to let someone root around in my brain."

"It's easier if you're knocked out, and they don't ask you first," Bjorn muttered.

Bjorn's father either didn't hear Bjorn's remark, or chose to ignore it. "Stefan, you already memorize everything you read. Why would you want pinplants?"

"Accept," Bjorn instructed his pinplants. Several lines of text flashed by, ending with Connection established. "They're not as much fun as you'd expect," Bjorn said. "I've had them for over a month, and I'm still not accustomed to them."

"I could get twice as much done," Stefan stated. "Though I wouldn't use them with pinlinked weapons or as a CASPer interface."

Bjorn's father chuckled. "Stefan, when was the last time you were in a CASPer?"

"A long time ago, and the less said, the better." Stefan clucked his tongue. He led them along a hall lined with darkened doorways. "If I have to climb in a CASPer, the you-know-what has hit the fan."

"What did you say about pinlinked weapons?" Bjorn asked.

Pinlinked weapons—weapons with cybernetic sights that project a targeting reticle in the user's pinview.

"It's a newfangled accessory that lets you use your pinplants to aim," Bjorn's father replied. "Since we only have a couple of troopers with pinplants, it's not a big deal. Rumor has it the Golden Horde are huge fans and early adopters, but you can never tell. They tend to hold their cards close to their vest."

"Mark my words, Commander. Pinplants are the wave of the future. You heard what the Binnig rep said about pinplant control of CASPers." Stefan stopped in front of a doorway and reached inside. Lights illuminated a small office with a desk, chair, and desktop Tri-V display. "You can do your schoolwork here. The latrine is across the hall."

Bjorn's father scoffed. "The Binnig rep was trying to drum up pre-orders for the next model. Bjorn, drop your gear here, and head out to the quad. Come to my office at 1130, and we'll hit the mess for lunch. Got it?"

Bjorn nodded and set an additional alarm. He had 17 minutes until his first one expired but picking an argument over a handful of minutes felt pointless. He set his bag behind the desk. There was a whiff of fresh paint and new carpet in the office.

"I'll see you for lunch. Thanks, Stefan."

Better to be on his best behavior, despite how much this rankled him. He'd messed up, and now he had to take his lumps. He retraced the path to the main entrance to Bjarnarsal and stepped out into the chilly morning air. It was only five degrees Celsius—the desert got cold in the winter.

The main quad was 200 meters downhill. Only one building bordered the quad, belying its name. The BX, Base Exchange, sat opposite Bjarnarsal. It was little more than a glorified convenience store and only occupied half of the ground floor.

A knot of mercenary recruits mingled on the fused asphalt of the open square. Only a few gave any indication of noticing Bjorn as he approached, and they quickly dismissed him. Not knowing what else to do, Bjorn went through pre-practice stretches from football.

"All right, Berserkers, listen up!" A woman in work-out togs strode toward the quad. Her black hair was shorn short and a scar crossed her right eye. "We get the privilege of babysitting the commander's son for the next few months. So be on your best behavior, ladies and gentlemen."

Chuckles rippled through the crowd of 40. Bjorn scanned the troops—they were only a few years older than him, some fresh out of high school on early graduations. Only a handful were larger than Bjorn.

"Sarge, what if Baby Bear pukes? Do we have to carry his ass?" Bjorn couldn't identify the speaker.

The sergeant scowled. Bjorn tried to follow her glare, but the crowd obscured her target. "Stow that crap, Delmar. In answer to your question, we are not to give this young man any preferential treatment." Her gaze swept to Bjorn with the last statement. She didn't want him here any more than Bjorn wanted to be here.

Bjorn fought to keep his expression neutral under Sergeant's—what was her name? His pinplants highlighted her face.

BTI: Master Sergeant Karen Orr, senior training sergeant, Headquarters Company.

"Am I clear?" Sergeant Orr added.

"Crystal clear, Sergeant," Bjorn replied. His father had told the sergeant to be tough on Bjorn; the last thing he needed to do was make it personal by getting on her bad side.

"Fall in people," Sergeant Orr called. "We're starting off with a morning jog."

Not knowing where else to go, Bjorn moved to the rear of the formation. He regretted not keeping up on his sports regimen. He hadn't run much since the bear attack; he would need to pace himself.

"Don't puke, Baby Bear," one of the mercenaries muttered as Bjorn passed. A few stifled laughs were cut off by the sergeant's stare. Bjorn pretended not to notice.

Don't let them get under your skin. He had five months until the new school year, where he would join a Mercenary Service Track cadre at his new school. Given he was sentenced to attending a public school, the next few months might by easier than those that followed.

I'm an athlete, Bjorn reminded himself as the columns of mercenaries set off on a jog. Sure, these people would be better trained at operating a CASPer or firing a battle rifle, but Bjorn's focus for the past four years had been on physical conditioning and athletic prowess.

At the end of five kilometers, Bjorn's hubris was a stitch in his side and fighting not to gasp for air. The CASPer troopers had been through nanite hardening therapy. The process strengthened their connective tissues and made their bodies more resilient to the rigors of operating powered battle armor. The infantry troopers trained with kilograms of gear piled on their back. The only ones who seemed winded were the rumbler crews.

"Baby Bear is going to upchuck," someone whispered, followed by retching sounds.

"Sounds as though someone is ready for calisthenics," Sergeant Orr snapped. "Time for push-ups. Form up! Tovesson, on the left end, front row."

Bjorn hustled to where Sergeant Orr pointed and dropped prone. This would let him catch his breath, as his cybernetic arm could pick up some of the slack. He resisted the urge to show off; he could feel the sergeant's eyes boring into him.

Bjorn's respite was short lived as the cadre cycled through other exercises where his powered limb gave him no advantage. By the time they finished, every muscle was sore and sweat soaked his clothes.

"Last exercise before a leisurely stroll back to the quad." The sergeant guided the group to a quartet of climbing ropes hanging from tall metal frames. "You know the drill—get to the top, come back down without flaying the skin off your hands."

Bjorn only paid enough attention to keep his place in line. During their jog, the BTI had downloaded a base map to his pinplants. Now he scrolled back and forth across the map, picking out locations of interest.

"Tovesson! You awake?"

Bjorn's attention snapped to the physical world. "Yes, Sergeant!"

"Then climb the damned rope! These mercs want to get back to the quad."

Bjorn allowed himself a grin as he stepped to the rope, until he realized everyone was watching him. There were 40 troopers in the recruit cadre, making Bjorn the 41st. He was the only person staged to climb the rope.

Bjorn stared up the dangling rope. Even before he had a cybernetic arm, the rope climb didn't daunt him. His pinplants highlighted the rope. Bjorn bent his knees and jumped up, grabbing for the length of hemp. His hand registered as closed, but his haptic feedback didn't trigger. He missed! Gravity quickly threw him in the sand. Laughter rippled through the cadre as he brushed sand off the seat of his shorts.

"Why don't you try it again, Peter Pan?" The sergeant sounded amused. "Maybe this time take hold of the rope before you try to fly."

Bjorn's cheeks burned as he blushed. He turned his back to the crowd and seized the rope. No showing off this time. He hauled himself up hand-over-hand, pinning the rope between his feet each time he reached higher. In top condition despite his bulk, he used only his arms to climb the rope, but each heave with his flesh-and-blood arm reminded Bjorn he was three months out of practice.

Once he reached the top, he spared a glance down at the training cadre. Most of the troops ignored him, and the few paying attention watched with bored stares.

"Don't stay up there for the view, Tovesson!" the sergeant shouted. "Everyone is waiting on you." A few chuckles sounded among the crowd, and Bjorn descended with his back to everyone to hide his embarrassment. "All right, now back to the quad. Anyone who takes longer than fifteen minutes will get an extra watch duty."

"What about Baby Bear?" Delmar asked.

Sergeant Orr shrugged. "If he doesn't make it in time, it's up to Papa Bear. Maybe he'll send him to the motor pool to wash LPTs and rumblers."

The troopers set off at a jog. Bjorn fell in behind the throng and summoned the base map. It was two kilometers back to the quad. If he'd been fresh, it would be a piece of cake. After his first intense work-out since December, Bjorn resisted the urge to get overconfident. He started a timer in his pinview. He wasn't about to get stuck washing transports at the motor pool. With his luck, the six-wheeled armored rumblers would roll back from training maneuvers out in the countryside covered in mud and grime.

Bjorn became less sure as the path sloped uphill. Two kilometers over flat ground in fifteen minutes? He could power walk it, even soaked in sweat and with aching muscles. Stairs and ramps were highlighted on the translucent map in his pinview. They would also ascend 200 meters. With a grumble, Bjorn increased his pace. The cadre was no longer in formation, so he moved in among soldiers.

"Guess Baby Bear is in a hurry to get to his porridge," someone uttered. A few snickers mixed in with the measured breathing of the joggers. The stitch in Bjorn's side returned at 200 meters and one staircase out. The timer showed two minutes left.

"No stragglers?" Sergeant Orr called. "Maybe next time I'll make it twelve minutes to give you Cubs a challenge. Heck, Tovesson even beat some of you. All right, fall out until your afternoon training assignments."

The mercenary recruits scattered, ignoring Bjorn. What did he expect? They would be chums with the commander's kid? Bjorn trudged toward Bjarnarsal. He'd hoped it would at least mean they would take it easy on him. Good thing he didn't want to be a mercenary—a nickname like Baby Bear could haunt him. Bjorn had a bit over half an hour to shower and change before lunch with his old man. At least no one would call him Baby Bear while he was sitting with the commander.

* * *

"How was PT, Baby Bear?" his father asked, poking at his lunch. The lump on his plate was supposed to be some sort of meat and potato hash.

Bjorn prodded his own meal, labeled a tortilla-less burrito, it was a pile of rice, beans, vat-chicken, and salsa. He resisted the side of tortilla chips without his father even prodding him. He needed to eat as though he was still playing football.

"Don't call me that," Bjorn muttered over a mouthful. He swirled his protein shake. "Those guys are jerks."

"Could be worse," Bjorn's father countered. "It could be a lot worse. I won't tell you some of the names I got called when I joined Haynes Harriers right out of my VOWS. They knew who I was, but since my dad didn't own the Harriers, they had no reason to pull punches."

"You didn't start in the Berserkers?" This was news to Bjorn. He'd always assumed his father went straight into the family company.

"Nope. Your *Afi* told me I had to serve a year in another merc outfit before I joined the Berserkers. It ticked your *Amma* off, but Pops wanted me to see the business from a place where my name had no weight." He shoveled a heaping forkful of hash into his mouth.

"Were you going to tell me the same thing?" Bjorn asked. "Make me serve somewhere else before I could join the Berserkers."

His father shrugged. "I guess we'll never know since you decided you're too good to be a merc."

Bjorn glanced around, self-conscious and hoping none of the neighboring diners overheard his father. "I never said I was too good. I said I wanted to find a career that didn't get me eaten by an alien werewolf."

"Besquith," his father corrected between more hash.

"I know what a Besquith is," Bjorn protested. They had learned about alien races, especially the few races who served as the galaxy's mercenaries, early in the Mercenary Service Track. Bjorn could name them all with descriptions by fourth grade. "I don't want to get eaten by one."

"You'd be a lot more likely to die from weapons fire," his father stated matter-of-factly. "Besides, Tortantulas are scarier, especially with those furry little jerks who ride them. I hate Flatar—those chipmunks have guns that will punch straight through a CASPer."

"You're really selling the mercenary life," Bjorn said sarcastically. He peered around the cavernous mess hall. "You should get some guest restaurants in here."

His father furrowed his thick brows. "What are you going on about?"

"How many people work on base?" Bjorn asked.

"With support staff? About five hundred," his father replied. "Assuming we aren't deployed. We will be in two weeks. Why?"

"In our school cafeteria, we have guest restaurants. A different one serves each day out of a station. It gives us…it brings some variety to lunch." It was no longer his school, or his cafeteria. His friends would be having lunch without him right now. "If you go with mom-and-pop outfits instead of chains, you'd win points with the local community."

"If you think it's such a good idea, you draft a proposal while I'm gone. I want prices and logistics, including security."

Bjorn set down his fork. "It was just an idea. I wasn't volunteering for extra homework."

"Wasn't your plan to get a business degree with your football scholarship?" His father wiped stray shreds of potato hash from his moustache and beard with the back of his hand. "We'll be out on a three-month contract. It will give you plenty of time."

Bjorn stewed over the project for the rest of lunch. Now his father was giving him homework. He already had the schoolwork to get his credit for the year from Mesilla Prep, physical therapy three days a week, and joining the training cadre for PT. Now he was supposed to find time to research and write a business proposal? He jabbed the faux-burrito mound on his plate.

"Are you going to finish your lunch, or do we draw a chalk outline around it?" his father asked 15 minutes later. "Come on, I want to introduce you to your new therapist."

"I thought I was going to Arrowhead Medical for my physical therapy?" Bjorn protested. He wasn't a fan of the therapy sessions, but the facility was state-of-the-art, and the staff was extra considerate since the Tovesson's were paying customers as opposed to FedCare patients.

His father snorted. "You don't need affirming bull-crap and hugs. You need someone who knows what you're going through and isn't scared to give you a kick in the butt."

"Does Mom know about this?" Bjorn asked before polishing off the remains of his protein shake, choking down the sludge from the bottom.

"Whine to her if you want; it won't change anything." Bjorn's father stood. "Let's go."

It took fifteen minutes to reach the motor pool. Was this a ruse to stick him with washing company vehicles? He'd rather work on his school assignments.

"Where's Axe?" Bjorn's father asked the first person he spotted in the vehicle yard.

"Over in the main garage, Commander." The man's shoulder patch bore a technical private insignia. "Do you want me to get him?"

"No, carry on, Private. Keep up, son." Bjorn's father headed toward a large permacrete building with several open vehicle bays. Bjorn stepped aside nervously as a charcoal gray six-wheeled rumbler thundered past. His father didn't flinch despite the twenty-five-ton machine passing within half a meter.

As they reached the closest open bay, a bald man with a salt-and-pepper beard limped out to meet them. He wore technical sergeant insignia on his shoulder, and his name tape read Silver. Dark glasses concealed his eyes.

"Commander, what can I do for you?" the man called.

Bjorn's father gestured over his shoulder with his thumb. "Sergeant Axel Silver, this is my boy, Bjorn III. We call him Trip to keep it from getting too confusing."

"From what I heard you should call him Kodiak Killer," the sergeant replied. He limped forward and shook Bjorn's hand, peering over the sunglasses. His left eye was a mirrored orb. "Most folks call me Axe. Nice to meet you."

Bjorn's resistance faded. This was the first person in Bear Town who didn't treat him like a kid. The limp—Axe had a prosthetic leg. That was why Bjorn's father thought the sergeant could help—he understood how it felt to literally lose a part of yourself.

"I won't paint you a picture with puppies and rainbows," Axe said, pushing his glasses up. "You may never get used to the idea that part of you is machine. I've been a cyborg for five years, and I'm still not cool with the looks people give me, as though I'm some sort of freak."

"Some of my friends—I catch them looking at me as though they feel sorry for me." Bjorn flexed his cybernetic hand.

"Do you want to show me your hardware?" Axe asked, removing the dark glasses and stuffing them in a shirt pocket. "From what the commander said, your limb is state-of-the-art."

Bjorn rolled up the sleeve and held his left hand forward. "State-of-the-art means you get to be the beta tester," Bjorn remarked.

Axe whistled. "Is it fully articulated? It could pass for real if you didn't know it was artificial."

"Fully functional and then some. There's a fake skin sleeve covering it from the elbow down." Bjorn tapped the fingers to the thumb one at a time. "It's stronger than my meat-and-bone arm, but I'm still having trouble with finesse. Sometimes I miss what I'm grabbing, or I knock stuff over."

"Which leg is my prosthetic?" Axe pointed to his feet.

"The left one," Bjorn replied.

"Five years later, and you can tell by my limp," Axe remarked. "It took me four years to accept things will never be the same as before my injury. I lost my eye in the same battle."

"Why don't you get a more natural looking replacement?" Bjorn asked.

"I had a choice—trying to pass for everyone else or make the best of my situation. My eye is superior to the original. Maybe if I didn't have the leg, I would have opted for an organic appearance. People wouldn't stare. I decided the heck with them."

"What do you think, son? Axe has offered to give you an hour of time, three days a week," Bjorn's father interjected. "Or would you rather go to Arrowhead?"

Bjorn met the chrome gaze of the technical sergeant. "No. They don't understand me." He flexed his cybernetic hand. "They don't understand this."

*****

Chapter Ten

Las Cruces, New Mexico

"I still can't believe they expelled you," Heather said. "You didn't hurt anyone."

"I'm still hoping the board of directors will let me come back for my senior year." It was a fleeting hope. The board had already said they had no intention of letting a "violent reprobate" mar their school's image.

"The jerks—they won't even let you come to prom. Kim Houseman is bringing her boyfriend from Rio Grande High." Heather scowled into her low-fat latte. "It might as well be a juvenile prison."

"It's where I'll have to go if I can't come back to Mesilla Prep," Bjorn replied. He'd hardly touched his coffee. He wasn't a fan of it, but he bought one to justify occupying a table in the café.

"What? No! You'll get stabbed or shot!" Heather's protest abruptly ceased when her phone chirped. Bjorn recognized the ringtone—it was Heather's mother. Heather held her finger to her lips as she picked her phone and turned from Bjorn. "Hi, Mom! I know, I won't be out long. Hang on, Denise and Mya are saying hello." Denise and Mya were Heather's friends from the cheerleading squad. Bjorn could hear the girl's voices emit from the phone. "I'll be home in a little while. 'Bye."

Bjorn knit his brows in confusion. "What was that all about?"

Heather set the phone down. "My folks don't want me to see you. They're afraid you have post-mental-whatever. I told them you were fine, but the videos went viral—"

"Videos?"

Heather avoided looking him in the eye. "Yeah, a bunch of videos of your stand-off with Officer Fields are still floating around on the Aethernet. One broke six digits in views."

Just the thing to ruin any chance of going back to Mesilla Prep.

"So your mom thinks you're with Denise and Mya, not me." Prerecording a video of her friends and dropping it into the camera view of the coffee shop was creative.

"Yeah, so I can't stay out long." Heather reached across the table and took Bjorn's hand. "I wanted to make sure you were okay."

"I will be. I'm going to have to spend the days at my dad's work, which sucks because the mercs pick on me." Bjorn snorted. "I have to do PT—physical training—with the recruit platoon in the morning." He caught himself before he could mention the nickname the mercs had given him. Heather would find it cute, then the moniker would never go away.

Since Heather was holding his right hand, Bjorn had to use his cybernetic one to pick up his coffee. Computer code and physics formulas flashed across his pinview after he targeted the cup.

"Are you afraid you're going to spook your Colombiano Roast?" Heather remarked.

"I'm still getting the hang of this thing. I missed a rope on an obstacle today, and I don't want to douse us in coffee if I crush the cup." Hopefully his frustration didn't seep into his voice.

Heather edged as far back from the coffee as she could without releasing Bjorn's hand. "I'm sorry. I shouldn't have said anything; I forgot about your arm."

"Good. I don't want to be defined as the guy with the fake arm," Bjorn remarked. "I want to be a normal high school student—albeit with a rich family and hot girlfriend." His wink elicited a giggle, and the awkwardness passed.

Thirty minutes and half a cup of cold coffee later, Heather declared she had to go home. "At least my folks let me use the auto-car." She leaned forward and kissed Bjorn, her hand on the door. "It would be hard to convince them I was out with the girls if you dropped me off."

"What about Saturday night? Can you 'go out with the girls'? My mom is dragging my father to a charity gala. You could come over," Bjorn suggested.

"The basketball team is playing Deming High, and it's an away game." Heather frowned. "By the time I could get away, it'd almost be curfew."

"Oh, I guess I forgot about basketball."

"The season is almost over. Another four games, plus however far they get in post-season." Heather slipped from his grasp and slid into the car. "All I'll have to worry about is competitive cheer and tennis."

Bjorn watched the car whir away. He couldn't even lean in for a final kiss because of the internal camera. They would have more time in the summer, but it seemed so far away. He chirped his own car and headed home.

* * *

"Stupid basketball," Bjorn grumbled to the slate. "I bet Todd Purdy has been circling Heather like a shark. Now that I'm expelled, he'll smell blood in the water."

"*Hermano*, do you really think Heather would toss you over for some gangly, body-spray-wearing preppie?" Berto countered. "I mean, he was sniffing around while you were in the hospital, but Heather shot him down repeatedly. I wish I had a girlfriend who was as devoted."

"I know, I know." Bjorn paced in his room. The slate was propped on his desk and paired to a Tri-V display. Roberto's 3D avatar hovered above the desk, watching Bjorn. "I trust Heather. It's…Todd is such a smarmy creep."

"If it makes you feel any better, I'll be at the basketball game," Berto said. "I'll keep an eye on Heather and make sure Todd doesn't get her alone. I mean, she'll probably stick with the rest of the cheerleaders, but I'll keep a lookout in case he tries to separate her from her posse."

Bjorn paused. "Why are you going to basketball games? Especially away games—you said they were boring."

"Mickey D's brother Bobby is on the team, but if Blair goes with her alone, it might be a date." Roberto's avatar shrugged. "I tag along so they can't call it a date but stay out of the way in case it becomes one. Playing defense against Todd will give me something to do."

"Maybe Heather can introduce you to one of her friends," Bjorn suggested. He and Heather had schemed as much, but the trick was finding the right time amidst the whirlwind of high school drama. The friend had to be single, but she had to be far enough out of a relationship, and it couldn't remind her of her prior boyfriend. Bjorn had done physics homework with less variables.

"Maybe." Berto's avatar averted his gaze. Was he embarrassed? Roberto was terrible at reading signals—girls claimed they all but hit him over the head with a clue-by-four, yet he seemed oblivious to their intentions.

"I appreciate you having my back, *hermano*." Bjorn scratched Plan B off his mental list for Saturday. If he couldn't go out with his girlfriend, he'd hoped to have his friends over. At least Roberto would keep an eye on Heather.

"I have to watch out for the King and Queen of Mesilla Prep," Berto replied reflexively. "Oh, man, I'm sorry…I didn't mean…"

"It's cool. The King is in exile. After things cool off, I'm hoping my old man can wave enough credits under the directors' noses to convince them to let me come back for my senior year." Bjorn leaned conspiratorially toward the slate. "My dad is going out on contract in two weeks, so when he gets back, he'll be flush with credits. If nothing else, the shareholders may push the board to accept a donation."

"Do you think so?" Berto asked.

"Right now, it's all I've got. Well, besides you, Heather, and the rest of the gang. If I'm stuck in a public school, my chances of going to a decent college drop off a cliff," Bjorn said.

Berto's avatar scratched at his wispy goatee. "Can't your father buy you a slot? If you're not the richest family in New Mexico, I bet you're in the top ten."

"I'd rather not rely solely on my dad's blood money," Bjorn remarked. "If I have crappy grades from a public school, odds are I'll have to settle for a sub-par college, even with my father buying my way."

"*Amigo*, you should consider taking your shares in the firm and chilling," Roberto suggested. "It won't be raining red diamonds, but you wouldn't have to lift a finger for the rest of your life."

"I want to know what's going on with my money, regardless of how I get it," Bjorn countered. "I don't want to find out some manager has fleeced me of my assets, so I'm stuck living on the gigi." The GGI, government guaranteed income, only covered basic needs. Bjorn didn't want to be driving an electric chair through FedMart 30 years from now.

Berto's avatar nodded. "All right, man. Hopefully they let the King come home. I've gotta check out. There's still some homework I need to knock out."

"Luego, hermano," Bjorn said.

"Luego."

* * *

Bjorn froze in his tracks. An ElSha sat at the breakfast table, chomping down slices of bacon as though they were mealworms. His pinplants painted the lizard-like alien in his pinview, highlighting the markings on the creature's skin.

Target: elSha—identity: Frek—admin user access

"What are you doing here?" Bjorn asked.

One of the alien's eyes swiveled toward Bjorn. "Your Geneva is providing first-meal," the ElSha replied.

"I mean why are you here, in my house?" Bjorn hoped first-meal didn't include live larvae or rodents.

"Your arm submitted multiple bug reports," Frek replied. "I am here to troubleshoot them. It appears you are having some performance issues."

"If you mean I'm having trouble grabbing stuff, sure." Bjorn risked a glance at Frek's plate. There were bacon and eggs, but no larvae. "I don't have the timing down, and sometimes the hand overexerts the grip."

Frek gobbled another slice of bacon. "It sounds like some minor calibration issues and user...proficiency."

"Can you fix it?" Bjorn asked. He gathered his breakfast from the stove. He had 22 minutes before he had to meet his father out front.

"I can make the calibrations," the ElSha replied. "Fixing the spongy mass between your ears is on you, unless you want Dr. Shur'im to dig around in your gray matter."

"Pass." Bjorn shuddered. Maybe it was best he had been unconscious when they installed the hardware in the back of his skull. "I'm still sorting out the whole ambidextrous thing. By habit, I still use my right hand for almost everything."

"How much have you experimented with using your cybernetic limb for tasks normally performed by your handicap? No, by your dominant hand." The ElSha paused, a slice of bacon half lifted to its snout. "We would consider the inability to use both limbs equally a handicap. As I'm given to understand humanoid malfunction, 99% of your species has a dominant limb. I know Dr. Shur'im fixed this defect when she installed your pinplants, but you need to practice the use of the muscles."

Bjorn flexed his left arm. "Muscles? More like actuators."

Frek shook his head. "The driving force in your limb are bundles of artificial fibers emulating muscles. However, they are much more powerful and durable. As with your organic muscles, you need to become accustomed to the subconscious triggers through rote practice."

Bjorn sat down; his plate laden with food. He'd been worried about gaining weight, but he needed fuel for PT. He picked up his fork in his right hand and froze. Should he practice now? He had 19 minutes left. Nope. Eat now, practice later.

"Frek, when did you get here?" Bjorn's father asked. He grabbed a plate and shoveled heaping piles of eggs, hash browns, and bacon onto it. "Juice—orange," he told the refrigerator, which dutifully dispensed the requested beverage.

"One point two seven hours ago," Frek replied. "The air cab brought me here, and your Geneva was kind enough to offer me first-meal."

"She's a peach. Lucky you arrived when you did, otherwise there might not have been any food left. We can talk business while we ride to base," Bjorn's father said. He turned to Bjorn. "Have fun sneaking out with your girlfriend last night?"

"I told you where I was going and what I was doing!" Bjorn protested.

The commander snorted while he chewed a mouthful of eggs and hash browns. "I'm betting Heather's old man didn't know she was seeing you. He called me and told me to keep my delinquent son away from his precious little girl."

"What did you tell him?" It was bad enough that Heather's parents had banned her from dating Bjorn, but if his father fanned the flames, it would make getting together impossible. Heather's parents would watch her like hawks.

"I told him he needed to manage his family, and I would manage mine." Bjorn's father slurped orange juice to wash down the eggs and potatoes. "If you want to keep seeing her, it's your choice, not mine. If she chooses to keep seeing you despite your football career going down the drain and her folks forbidding her, it would move my estimation of her up a notch."

They finished breakfast in silence, save for chewing and gulps as all three hurried to finish. At least his father would not leave without Frek, and the ElSha's appetite for bacon rivaled Bjorn's. However, the bacon eventually ran out.

"Quite delicious." Frek swept his tongue across his lipless mouth. "I wonder if I flattened grub worms, soaked them in salt, and fried them, would they be as good as bacon?"

"I doubt it," Bjorn's father remarked, collecting his coffee thermos.

Bjorn didn't comment and pushed the image of flattened fried worms out of his mind while his breakfast roiled in his stomach.

*****

Chapter Eleven

Bear Town, New Mexico

"All right, Cubs, we're switching things around today," Sergeant Orr called. "Instead of our usual battery of calisthenics, we're going to work on hand-to-hand combat. You all remember it from your Mercenary Service Track training. Split into pairs."

Bjorn looked around. There were 40 recruits in the cadre, making him the odd man out. Maybe he'd be sidelined for this? It was one thing to let the commander's kid tag along for jogs and push-ups, but it would be another to compromise training so he could play along. Even if the morning run had taken less out of him than two weeks ago, Bjorn wouldn't mind the chance to cool his heels.

The sergeant's eyes fell on Bjorn. Was she going to use him as a demonstration dummy or send him off to run laps while the soldiers trained? Odin, please let it be laps. In response, his pinplants displayed the map and highlighted the running track.

"Eddings!" the sergeant barked. A short woman separated from the shifting pack of trainees.

Was this some sort of joke? Eddings was an armor gunner, not a CASPer trooper or infantry soldier. She didn't even reach Bjorn's armpit.

"Really, Sarge?" Eddings protested. "Baby Bear is a waste of my time. I bet he's afraid to hit a girl."

The BTI helpfully flashed Eddings's dossier into Bjorn's pinview. The gunner's scores and credentials scrolled past. A perfect score in VOWS hand-to-hand assessment, two accredited black belts, and commando training school. She was too small to handle a CASPer. *Lucky for the aliens,* Bjorn thought.

"No, Eddings, you're with me. I can't have you breaking someone's nose again." Orr scanned the crowd.

"It was Wick's fault for suggesting I needed a booster seat for my gunner position," Eddings spat back.

Sergeant Orr pointed at a recruit. "Clayton, you get Baby Bear. Try not to break him."

Clayton sauntered over. While shorter than Bjorn, he still possessed the beefy build typical of CASPer troopers. He was also saddled with extra guard duty because he finished behind Bjorn in the return run last week. Four people lost the sergeant's challenge to beat Bjorn back to the quad. Bjorn could have doubled the number, but antagonizing the recruits didn't seem prudent, especially since his dad left the day before for three months on a contract.

"What if I accidently yank off his fake arm?" Clayton asked, sizing up Bjorn. Yeah, he bore a grudge for the extra shift.

"Hope it's under warranty," the sergeant replied. "Pair off on the sand, people."

The first series of exercises Bjorn remembered from training at school. The second series was more advanced, and he hadn't covered it in MST yet. Clayton used the chance to slip a shot past Bjorn's guard and punch him in the gut.

"Don't cry on me, Baby Bear," Clayton taunted under his breath. "I owe you for the extra shift."

"Maybe you should have been faster," Bjorn hissed.

"It appears we have our first sparring volunteers," Orr announced. "Clear the sand. Clayton, Tovesson, you stay put."

Clayton grinned and paced on the sand. Bjorn assumed the ready position. Would it be wrong to wipe the smile off Clayton's face with a cybernetic left hook? They were supposed to pull their punches, but Clayton would have been through the nanite hardening therapy applied to CASPer troopers. His bones would be stronger and his connective tissues tougher.

"You know the drill," Orr stated. "No cheap shots, don't do any lasting damage. Go!"

"Come on, big boy; you know you want to take a pop at me." Clayton beckoned; his hands raised in a loose defensive stance. It was a trap of course. Bjorn circled, watching for the tell-tale of Clayton's attack.

"Are you two going to dance or fight?" Orr shouted.

Bjorn's eyes flicked toward the sergeant, and Clayton sprung forward. Bjorn brought his right hand up to defend his face, so Clayton landed a pair of body punches. Bjorn shoved the trooper away with his left arm, sending Clayton stumbling back.

By the time Bjorn closed the gap, Clayton found his footing. Bjorn jabbed with his right fist, but Clayton swept the blow aside. Bjorn dropped his left arm to cover his bruised ribs and Clayton's fist slammed into his jaw. Bjorn staggered as stars swam behind his eyes. He was used to getting hit on the football field, but that was under layers of protective gear.

Clayton stepped in, and Bjorn brought both arms up to defend. Clayton swept his heel behind Bjorn's knee, making him topple to the sand.

Clayton stalked back and forth and pumped his fist. "Yeah!"

"Congratulations, Clayton. You knocked a high school kid on his butt," Sergeant Orr said. "Tovesson, take a seat. Clayton, since you're showing the class how it's done, you stay in. Eddings!"

The smile fell from Clayton's face.

* * *

"Thanks for taking Clayton down a peg." Bjorn's ribs were still tender, and his jaw was sore.

Eddings snorted. She was one of the other recruits who earned extra guard shifts by falling behind Bjorn. Today she was keeping pace despite her shorter stride. "I didn't do it for you, Baby Bear. I hate jerks like Clayton. It doesn't mean I want to sign your yearbook."

Bjorn held his tongue for the rest of the jog back to the quad. After the cadre went through cooldown stretches and were given permission to disperse, Bjorn sought out Eddings.

"Where did you learn to fight?" he asked.

"My dad, my brothers, MST, a do-chang—lots of places," Eddings replied. "That's the secret. You have to learn from more than one place, otherwise you're limited. I had a friend in taekwondo who was pretty good, but when he got in a scrap with an experienced street-fighter, he got his butt kicked."

"Can you teach me?" Bjorn blurted out.

Eddings stopped and peered up at Bjorn. "Kid, I don't have time for some officer's puppy-eyed son to follow me around with a crush."

"What? No! I have a girlfriend," Bjorn protested. "This isn't some sort of lame attempt to…I want you to teach me how to fight. That's it."

Eddings sighed and started walking again. "You're too young for me, Baby Bear."

"I don't want to date you." Bjorn followed. Luckily, no one seemed interested in their conversation.

"Whatever. Have your old man teach you how to fight. It's how I first learned."

"The commander and I don't exactly see eye-to-eye." How his father would gloat if Bjorn asked him to teach him how to fight. "I could pay you!"

"What?" Eddings regarded Bjorn over her shoulder. A dangerous glint in her eye warned him he should pick his words carefully.

"You, or your family, paid your taekwondo sensei, right?"

"Sabumnim," Eddings corrected. "He also taught me some close-quarters kung fu because classic taekwondo is weak against a close-up opponent."

"I could pay you to tutor me," Bjorn said. "It's pretty obvious MST self-defense 101 isn't going to cut it."

"Word has it you don't even want to be a merc." Eddings stated.

"I don't, but next year I have to go to a public high school. With my luck, it will be the one I beat in the semi-finals this year," Bjorn replied. "Public high schools are tough enough, but you can imagine the welcome waiting for me."

"I'll think about it, Baby Bear." Eddings walked away.

* * *

Bjorn ate lunch by himself. While he and his father hadn't shared lunch every day, it was an hour no one was going to mess with him. Bjorn's concern that the troops, especially the training cadre, would hassle him now that his father was off-world appeared unfounded. The cavernous mess hall felt empty despite the hundred people scattered among tables.

The mess hall, or Mead Hall as the nameplate on the door declared, could accommodate ten times the number. Only two of the six food service stations were in use. Bjorn had taken notes for the project assigned by his father. Two of the darkened stations had no equipment behind the counters. The whole building had been constructed with future expansion in mind.

The extra space made it convenient for the troops to ignore Bjorn. It wasn't such a bad thing—Delmar and his buddies were on the far side of the hall and didn't spare Bjorn a second glance. Frek was having lunch with two other ElSha. One glance at their squirming meals was all it took to convince Bjorn not to join them.

Bjorn considered asking to join Axe and some of the motor pool mechanics. So far, the people who worked with Axe paid little attention to Bjorn when he arrived to work with Sergeant Axel Silver. They had too much work to do, and if Bjorn didn't get in their way, they could care less. It might change if Bjorn intruded on their lunch breaks. Even though Axe didn't treat him like a kid, the others had to view him as the boss' son. How could you relax if you were afraid the kid would go to his old man?

Bjorn picked at the mediocre vat-loaf. Even with the stigma and cost of natural meat, Bjorn was surprised it wasn't offered more frequently at the mess. It wasn't as though the mercs couldn't afford it, even if real meat cost five time the factory-grown equivalent. Maybe they preferred to splurge in town, either in Las Cruces or El Paso-Juarez to the south. Bjorn opened the project folder on his slate and made some notes.

Bjorn spotted Eddings with some of the other armor crew recruits, but he resisted trying to get her attention. He didn't want to scare her off from tutoring him by being a pesky kid, especially given her puppy-dog-eyes crack. If she said yes, where would he fit in training sessions? He hadn't thought about it when he asked her, but the idea was too good to pass up. His size and raw strength would only help so much.

Bjorn's slate chimed and his schedule manifested in his pinview. Three hours of schoolwork, then an hour working with Sergeant

Silver. Today, Frek would be joining Bjorn and Axe to follow up on some calibrations the ElSha made to Bjorn's arm.

* * *

"Stefan told me you played ball in school," Axe said after he slammed the engine compartment hatch on a rumbler. The tech sergeant slid down the sloped armor on the front of the vehicle. Bjorn noted he landed on his organic foot first.

"I did until the bear," Bjorn replied. He almost kept the bitterness out of his voice. Axe had no patience for people feeling sorry for themselves. "I was a quarterback with top college prospects. I also played baseball, but it was more to keep in shape during the off season and work on my throwing arm."

"Are you right-handed or a leftie?" Sergeant Silver asked.

Bjorn wiggled the fingers on his organic hand. "A righty, so there's one small favor."

"Actually, the doctor fixed that," Frek remarked from behind Bjorn.

Axe furrowed his brows, even though the one over his silver eye barely moved. "What do you mean she fixed it?"

"Something about asymmetrical…something," Bjorn replied.

Asymmetrical coordination, his pinplants displayed. *When an entity suffers coordinative deficiency on one side of a bilateral…*

Bjorn waved away the words. "Asymmetrical coordination. I don't think she realized it was natural for Humans to favor one limb over the other, so when they installed my pinplants, she also 'fixed' my right-handedness."

"They rooted around in your brain and made you ambidextrous?" Axe shuddered. "Here I thought them wiring my eye to my brain was bad."

"No one asked me beforehand," Bjorn remarked.

"Have you tested it out?" Axe asked. "Can you pitch with your new hand?"

"I haven't tried," Bjorn admitted. "All of the therapy exercises have been basic."

"Maybe your problem is you're treating your left hand as your off hand, but it isn't anymore," Axe suggested.

Bjorn looked to Frek, who shrugged, a very Human gesture.

Axe disappeared behind the rumbler. Bjorn could hear him rummaging through toolboxes. The tech sergeant emerged holding two baseballs and a softball. "We keep stuff around for the occasional pickup game when we're caught up. Come on, let's go out back."

A crude baseball diamond stretched across the sandy yard behind the largest motor pool garage. Crude, hand-made benches flanked the diamond parallel to the first and third baselines. A pitching practice net sat behind home plate, covered in dust and sand.

"It's getting warm enough to play, but we've been busy getting Bruin Company ready for departure," Axel remarked. "Why don't you go to the pitcher's mound and try to put these over home plate?"

"Sure. I'm out of practice, even with my right arm, so no guarantees." Bjorn accepted the balls and strode out to the middle of the diamond. While he'd enjoyed baseball, he was never devoted to it the way he was with football. Doing some football passing drills might bring out his melancholy side, but with baseball he could stay detached.

Bjorn set down the softball and one baseball and went through some warmup motions. It felt unnatural to mirror his expected movements, and his view of the plate was wrong. After several minutes of pantomiming a pitch, he wound up and let the ball fly. It skipped off the ground two meters in front of home plate, kicking up sand as it caromed off the ground and missed the practice net.

"Slow it down," Axel called from behind a piece of protective fencing. "Try lofting the softball over the plate. Don't worry about striking someone out—take your time and toss it."

It made sense. Bjorn picked up the softball. Despite the size, he could overhand pitch one across the plate. Again, he mimicked the motions of the throw a few times. He lobbed the ball overhand. The ball clanged off the frame holding the pitching net. Better than before, but not a strike.

American baseball strike zone. A glowing rectangle appeared over home plate. Where do you wish to target? A grid manifested within the rectangle.

Bjorn picked up the last baseball. "Dead center," he said aloud. A targeting reticle in the center of the strike zone replaced the grid. He took a deep breath and released it as he settled into his stance. He wound up the pitch, his eyes fixed on the glowing crosshairs. With a snarl, he whipped his arm forward. The ball's trajectory was traced in his pinview. It missed the target by ten centimeters. The frame of the practice net jerked off the ground and skittered back until it collided with the garage wall, two meters back.

How fast was the pitch?

Projectile velocity—53.6 meters per second.

Bjorn tried to do the math before his pinplants flashed 193 kilometers per hour. Bjorn stared at the space over home plate. His fastballs before had topped out at 145 kilometers per hour, and it was at some sacrifice for accuracy.

"Hey, Trip, you're out of ammo, right?" Axe called from behind the fencing.

Bjorn blinked, and the strike zone and the reticle disappeared. The ground at his feet was empty. "Yeah, it's safe. Thor be praised! The ball cracked 190 kph. No wonder they won't let me play!" Bjorn scowled. If he could pitch close to the 200-kilometer mark, how far could he pass? The length of the field, easily. Now it didn't matter.

"What was the difference for the third pitch?" Axe collected the balls off the ground. "It was night and day compared to the others."

"Some sort of targeting program kicked in," Bjorn replied, shaking off the malaise. "My pinplants projected the strike box and crosshairs."

"You still missed," Frek remarked, glancing up from a slate. "By ten centimeters. The software is struggling to compensate for organic variables."

"It was my third throw," Bjorn protested.

"Can this targeting be turned off?" Axe inquired, gazing at the practice net.

"I think so?" Surely it could be turned off. Frek nodded in agreement.

"We can work with this, Trip," Axe said, tossing one of the balls back to Bjorn. Bjorn snatched at the ball with his left hand, but it bounced off his digits. "You can use the targeting programs to build the muscle memory then turn them off to refine your natural accuracy."

"Why would I turn them off?" Bjorn asked.

"If you rely on the pinplants and its programs, it will make it harder to adapt when something unexpected happens," Axe said. "I had a buddy who went nuts on cyborg crap. I don't know what he was thinking. We were on an op and the enemy dropped an electromagnetic pulse grenade to blind our sensors. Luckily, I still had an organic eye. Gordon went blind and stumbled off the boat into the drink. He sank straight down and drowned."

"What happens if I get hit with an EMP with my pinplants?" Bjorn asked. What was even less comfortable than having computer hardware in his skull? Having fried hardware in his skull cooking his brain matter.

"Your pinplants have surge breakers, and the memory is quantum-optical, not magnetic," Frek remarked. "However, your arm could be vulnerable. I'll have to do some more research for your next iteration. Meanwhile, you can keep practicing to establish muscle memory."

* * * * *

Chapter Twelve

Las Cruces, New Mexico

"I should be the one taking pictures with you right now, not my best friend," Bjorn complained.

Heather pouted into her phone's camera. "I wish you were here. I can't believe they're being such jerks." Behind her, a flock of girls in colorful dresses swarmed and posed for each other amid peals of laughter. "With my mom playing chaperone, there's no way for me to get away, either."

Plan B had been for Heather to make an appearance at prom, then for Bjorn to pick her up. It was sunk by Heather's mother volunteering to help oversee the dance. Mrs. Akins had never showed an interest in school activities before, so she must have suspected either Bjorn would try to sneak in or Heather might slip out.

"Maybe in a couple of weeks you can wear your prom dress and we can go out on a fancy date?" Bjorn suggested. Since becoming a social pariah, he'd hardly spent any of his allowance. Food at the base was free, and by the time he got home he was tired. Only his weekends were free, but Heather had been busy.

"Speaking of fancy, check this out." Heather's camera swept across the crowd gathered in her front yard and settled on Blair and Mickey D. Blair was tugging nervously at his bow tie and collar.

"Why didn't anyone tell me Blair asked Alison to prom?" Bjorn lamented. He was out of touch with his friends. It felt wrong to call

Alison "Mickey D" when she was dressed up; Bjorn barely recognized her. How long until he didn't recognize his friends at all?

"She asked him." Heather giggled. "Berto described it as 'a hostage situation.' I don't think Blair had much choice."

The camera panned to Berto. He was shuffling his feet. When he realized the camera was pointed at him, Berto averted his eyes. Bjorn fought down a tinge of jealousy. Berto and Heather were going as friends. It smoked out the swarm of guys buzzing around Heather like bees, all asking her to prom since she didn't have a date.

Berto's tone had been laden with guilt when he broached the idea to Bjorn. Heather couched it as another scheme to hook Berto up with one of the girls on the cheerleading squad, but Bjorn had lost track of which one. Despite an irrational gnawing in his gut, Bjorn couldn't say no. A couple of the guys orbiting Heather were seniors. At least now he didn't have to worry all night about one of them trying to lure Heather away from her friends.

"Who are you talking to?" Bjorn recognized Mrs. Akin's voice. "It's time to go."

"I'll be right there!" Heather turned the phone to face herself. "I've got to go. I'll see you."

"Have fun," Bjorn replied. "I wish I was with you, princ—" The call disconnected.

Bjorn paced in his room for several minutes. It wasn't fair. His girlfriend was slipping away—they had barely spent any time together since his coming home party, let alone time alone.

"Mom, I'm going out! Can I take your car?" Bjorn called as he grabbed his key fob.

"You're not going to get into any trouble, are you?" His mother lingered near the foyer, as though she had expected Bjorn. "You can't set foot on the grounds."

"I know, Mom. I'm going for a drive. I won't be long."

"Trip, you're only going to make it worse," his mother said. "Don't pick at the scab; it will only take longer to heal. Why don't you watch a movie or something to take your mind off it? I could pop some popcorn, and you could order a pizza."

"Maybe…maybe I'll go to the arcade and blow some stuff up," Bjorn ventured. "Let off some steam and eat some junk food."

His mother smiled, but it didn't reach her eyes. "If you say so, Trip. Stay out of trouble. If nothing else, your driver's permit review is after your birthday next month. The incident at school didn't go on record, so if you stay out of trouble you can get your license upgraded."

"I'll stay out of trouble," Bjorn promised. She already knew he was lying about going to the arcade. Did she doubt this also?

"Okay. Be safe."

Bjorn chirped his fob as he stepped out of the house. The garage door opened, and the car rolled out. It obediently stopped and waited for him to climb in. He selected supervised manual drive mode. He might as well get credit for time behind the wheel. Halfway through asking the nav system for directions to the Misner Event Center, a map popped up in his pinview.

"Switch to first-person HUD," Bjorn said aloud. He still found vocalizing his instructions easier than thought-input. The map fell away into videogame display, with floating translucent arrows marking his upcoming turns.

"This is stupid," Bjorn muttered as he wove through suburban Mesilla. The event center was in a former private museum near the university. Balancing the urge to hurry versus the realization the car was recording every move was almost enough to distract Bjorn from the reason he'd set out. Almost.

A parking lot across the street provided the perfect location to watch and wait. Would they spot him, hanging out like some creepy stalker? Thank Odin the car was generic in appearance. His father had refused to get Bjorn the flashy car he wanted and hinted when the time came, Bjorn would inherit his mother's practical car. Bjorn had fumed at the time, but now he was thankful.

A parade of cars lined the street at the entrance to the Misner Center. After each car stopped, one or more couples emerged in their formal wear to stride down the red carpet stretching to the entrance. Most of the audience members had been hired to enhance the experience as though the students were strutting along the red carpet into some fancy Hollywood event.

Bjorn had been hyped at the idea when he was going to be a participant. Now, it was silly. A few dozen people were paid so a bunch of rich high school kids could feel like celebrities. Would he be sour on the idea if he was still walking the carpet with Heather on his arm?

Berto's car pulled to the front of the line. It was an older car, designed to emulate the vehicles of the previous century called muscle cars. Berto had bought it cheap and spent a year refurbishing it with his uncle. Bjorn had joked the car was Berto's real girlfriend.

He wondered what happened to the limo. Bjorn remembered the original plan was for a large shared limousine on the way to prom and smaller, more intimate rides for afterwards. Was this some sort of plot to leave Mickey D and Blair alone together?

Berto stepped out of his car and straightened his tux jacket. He slipped something to the valet—his keys and a gratuity. Berto circled the car and opened the passenger door. He extended his hand and helped Heather steady herself as she disembarked.

Bjorn sighed. She was beautiful, wearing a pink gown worthy of a Hollywood red carpet. He should be there, helping her rise from the low-slung car, holding his arm so she could take it, then leaning in so she could kiss him on the cheek.

Bjorn snapped out of his narrative. Heather had kissed Berto! It took a dozen pounding heartbeats before Bjorn composed himself. It was on the cheek—they were going as friends, plus they were hamming it up for the faux paparazzi. Bjorn couldn't see Berto's face. Was he self-conscious that it was his best friend's girlfriend on his arm?

Heather leaned into Berto and whispered something into his ear as they sauntered along the red carpet. Old-style flashes incandesced as they strode toward the doors. With modern technology, flashes were an affectation used for nostalgia. Heather waved at the ersatz paparazzi. How many people would believe she had dumped Bjorn for Berto?

Don't go there. Neither of them would betray Bjorn. He and Heather would get together in a couple of weeks and go out.

Inconsistent with data, appeared in Bjorn's pinview. He ignored the words to watch his girlfriend and his best friend disappear through the entrance. No calendar entry has been created for such an interaction.

Bjorn blinked and the text vanished. Sure, he hadn't made formal plans with Heather, but it was because they got interrupted. Tomorrow Bjorn would call her, and they'd make plans to go on a real date. Then he could put this self-doubt behind him.

The next vehicle to disembark passengers was a rental limo. Bjorn recognized the girls from his video chat with Heather. Nagging doubt clawed its way back to the surface. Why ride in separate cars? It defeated the goal of trying to match Berto with one of Heather's friends.

Bjorn was so engrossed in his thoughts he nearly missed it when Mickey D pulled up to the curb. Of course she drove. While Mickey D wore a traditional prom dress, she wasn't about to let Blair think he was in charge. Bjorn watched the couple walk the gauntlet of "paparazzi" and disappear inside. At least things worked out for someone.

What now? The time winked into his pinview then faded. It would be 3 hours until prom was over. He couldn't sit here and wait for the dance to end. It would be creepy, especially if he followed Berto and Heather. What if they spotted him? They would think Bjorn didn't trust them.

Bjorn drummed his fingers on the steering wheel, part nervous fidget and part exercise to coordinate his cybernetic fingers. He trusted them, right? It's not as though they snuck around behind his back. He was being an idiot and a jerk. He should go home.

He activated his slate and checked his social media feed. Nothing new from Heather or Berto since Bjorn had chatted with them. What was he expecting to find? He skimmed feeds from other former classmates. Nothing about the prom—they were too busy getting their pictures taken and having fun to fiddle with social media. Had he been sitting here an hour already?

The sun was down, so he'd be less likely to get spotted. Quit being stupid, he chided himself. What was wrong with him?

Diagnostic running. Pulse elevated. Blood pressure elevated. Levels of—

"That's not what I meant," Bjorn grumbled. He stared at the entrance, now abandoned save for a pair of bouncers dressed as doormen. He recalled the moment Heather had stepped out of the car and kissed Berto on the cheek.

As clear as day, he watched as Berto held out his arm, Heather took it with her gloved hand as she rose, and she leaned in and kissed Berto on the cheek. She whispered something in Berto's ear, then they proceeded up the red carpet. Bjorn blinked and the image froze in his pinview.

Playback engaged. Paused.

This was recorded in his pinplants?

Affirmative. Recording mode engaged at 19:47:03. Recording mode disengaged at 19:59:25. Video Length: 12 minutes 22 seconds.

Bjorn focused on his frozen pinview. A blue dot glowed next to the letters REC in the corner of the image. Why hadn't anyone told him he could record what he was seeing and hearing?

Pinplant functions are detailed in the user manual file. The user has not accessed the file.

How many hours did he have crammed in his brain?

Pinplant storage does not utilize host organic matter. It utilizes Galactic Union Standard Optronic Memory. This unit has 5.7 petabytes of memory, of which 2.1 petabytes are used by operational software. The user has 3.1 terabytes of saved audio-video stream.

Bjorn wished he had paid more attention in Galactic Union Technology 101. Since he had planned on remaining on Earth, he wasn't concerned about off-world tech. He had no clue what 3.1 terabytes entailed.

Your saved files represent 31.47 hours of streaming audio-video footage.

Bjorn sat back, his eyebrows arching in surprise. "I've accidently saved over thirty-one hours of footage in my br—in my pinplants?"

Your saved files represent 31.47 hours of streaming audio-video footage.

"What triggers the record mode?" Bjorn asked, grateful he was in a car so people wouldn't hear him talking to himself.

You do.

Bjorn drummed his fingers on the steering wheel. This time it was devoid of a pretense of practice; it was all frustration. "Be more specific. I need to know when I am triggering the record mode. If nothing else, I don't want to fill up my buffer, or whatever, with streams of me doing homework or eating lunch. I don't even know how much space is allowed."

The default partition is 5 terabytes. Do you wish to expand the default partition?

The default settings were there for a reason. What if he expanded his AV storage and wiped out his muscle memory of how to use a fork? "No."

Bjorn stared ahead, focused on the image frozen in his pinview. "How are stream files organized?"

Stream files are organized by time-date stamp in chronological order.

Bjorn thought back to his coming home party. He concentrated, and thought, *"Show files for February 16."*

A list of three files appeared. The first two were short. One would have been when they first arrived and the second was a few minutes later. Both were under two minutes in length. The third stretched for over an hour—from when Bjorn and Heather had gone up to his room alone. Given the events of tonight, did he even want to watch the footage?

The paused video of Roberto and Heather was replaced with an image of Heather following Bjorn up the stairs to his room. *"Play,"* Bjorn thought. Heather smiled and giggled, quickly covering her mouth to keep from being heard.

Bjorn watched the entire footage play out, remembering every expression on Heather's face, recalling every word, until the end.

"I love you," Heather whispered after a tender kiss.

"I love you too, princess," Bjorn's voice replied.

That had been less than two months ago. Bjorn scrolled through the date-time stamps until today, less than two hours ago. *"Play."*

He watched as Heather emerged from the car, lean in, and kiss Berto on the cheek. She pressed against Berto as they strode down the red carpet, arm in arm. Bjorn rewound the feed and played it again. After five more replays, he slumped back in his seat.

It would only be an hour until prom was over, and they would come out. He could follow Berto's car and see if this was just friends, or something more. A lump formed in his throat. But if they had betrayed him, then what?

Bjorn pushed the thought aside and powered up the car. "Destination: Home."

The car chirped its acceptance of the destination and pulled out of the parking space. Bjorn watched the front of the Misner Center disappear from his line of sight. The blue dot was illuminated in the corner of his pinview, along with the letters REC.

"Stop recording," he said aloud. The indicator winked out.

*****

Chapter Thirteen

Bear Town, New Mexico

"This isn't going to work if your head isn't in the game," Eddings remarked.

"Who cares, as long as we're getting paid?" Logan Wick was an armor driver who Eddings had recruited to be Bjorn's practice partner. Logan was almost as tall as Bjorn, and Bjorn suspected his presence was to ensure no one got suspicious.

"If I'm going to teach this kid how to fight, I'm going to do it right." Eddings pointed at a spot in the sand. "Get back in position and run through the drill again. Baby Bear, get your head out of the clouds. If this had been real, Wick would have punched your teeth in."

"Sorry. It's…I think my girlfriend is cheating on me with my best friend."

Wick laughed, doubling over.

"It's not funny," Bjorn protested. "They went to prom together, and for the past two weeks she's avoided getting together with me. Berto will hardly talk to me online, and he dodges me in person."

"You were cool with your girlfriend going to a formal with your buddy?" Wick exclaimed. "What did you think would happen?"

"They were going as friends," Bjorn protested. "Heather was supposed to set him up with one of her friends, but they went in his car instead of the limo with the group, and now I think there's something going on between them."

"I hate to break it to you, Tovesson, but you're right," Eddings stated. "So why don't you get good and ticked, then try to slug Wick?"

Wick stopped laughing. "Wait, what?"

"What's wrong, Wick? Think Baby Bear can tag you?" Eddings pointed at the sand square. "In the sand, now."

Bjorn sighed and trudged into the sparring square. He'd fought the urge to cancel the training session and stay home. He had watched the video-memory of Berto and Heather seventeen times this morning.

"Remember, this is supposed to be controlled contact," Eddings stated. Both Wick and Bjorn wore sparring pads, a luxury they weren't afforded in PT. "Wick, try to remember he's a kid."

Wick bounced in place opposite Bjorn. "Yeah, a 140-kilo kid with a bionic arm. All right, let's do this."

"Choon bi!" Eddings called. Ready appeared in Bjorn's pinview. He'd turned off translation for Korean, but now his pinplants were showing subtitles. *"Saejak!"* Begin.

Wick's fist jabbing for his face snapped Bjorn out of pinspace. He didn't so much dodge as fall away from the punch, kicking up sand as he fought to find his footing. Wick recovered from his missed punch before Bjorn regained his balance. Even with the padding, the punch to the ribs stung. He countered with an elbow strike to Wick's exposed flank. Even though the close quarters and awkward angle kept Bjorn from utilizing most of the cybernetic strength, not having to worry about injuring a meat-and-bone limb let him throw his considerable weight into the blow.

It was Wick's turn to stagger in the sand. "Sonuva—" The curse cut off as Bjorn stepped forward with a right counterpunch.

"Good! Keep pressing him!" Eddings shouted.

Wick ducked the next punch and hooked his arm over Bjorn's while he snaked his foot behind Bjorn's heel. Bjorn almost resisted the throw but couldn't get his other foot back in time. Wick let Bjorn topple, then sprung on top of him, slamming a fist down.

"Damn it!" Wick cursed as Bjorn intercepted the swing with his left arm. Bjorn twisted, throwing the other man off. Bjorn rolled away and rose to his feet.

"Kalyeo!" Eddings shouted. *Stop.* "You're out of bounds, Baby Bear."

"What did they make your arm out of, CASPer armor?" Wicks complained, shaking his arm.

Bjorn ignored the helpful composition index in his pinview. "CASPer armor would be too heavy. I think you hit my equivalent of a radius. It's a beta-titanium alloy, if I remember right."

"It felt like hitting a steel girder." Wick stood up, flexing his fingers. "I bet I'm going to have a bruise from your beta-titanium elbow."

"Thirty seconds and so many mistakes," Eddings interjected. "Out of curiosity Beta Bear, what is your dominant hand?"

"Before this," Bjorn wiggled the fingers on his left hand, "I was right-handed. The H'rang doctor who installed my pinplants thought asymmetrical coordination was a defect, so she fixed it while they were installing the hardware to support my arm."

"What does that even mean?" Wick asked.

"In theory, now I'm ambidextrous," Bjorn replied. "It's easier said than done. I don't have the muscle memory of doing stuff with my left hand. While I can write with my left, it resembles my writing exercises from 3rd grade. It's legible, and I even recognize it as my writing, but it's still crude and takes longer."

"All right, back to ready positions," Eddings instructed. "Let's see if Beta Bear can stay inbounds."

Bjorn wasn't sure he was a fan of the new nickname, but it was better than Baby Bear.

"Choon bi! Saejak!"

Wick wasted no time going on the offense. Two weeks of punching, blocking, and kicking drills helped Bjorn hold his ground until Wick went off script. Bjorn mistook a hook kick for a roundhouse kick. As he flinched away so Wick's heel wouldn't smack him in the face, Wick seized Bjorn's leading arm and threw him off balance. Bjorn twisted and fought to regain his footing before he stumbled across the boundary. He pinwheeled his arms and arrested his forward momentum. Then Wick planted his foot on Bjorn's butt and shoved him out of bounds.

"Kalyeo!" Stop, his pinplants reminded him, as if Eddings's tone wasn't enough. "Beta Bear, your footwork is awful. I thought you football guys had to be fast on your feet?"

"This is different," Bjorn protested. He'd gone for a whole day without remembering he'd been scrubbed from football. Nothing like a little salt for the wound.

"How?" Eddings demanded. "You have huge guys slamming into you and you need to stay on your feet. How is it different? Do football fields have artificial gravity?"

"Now you're being ridiculous," Bjorn complained. Everyone knew artificial gravity was something out of 20th century fiction.

"Am I? Tell me how a linebacker slamming into you is different than Wick trying to knock you on your butt."

"Well, he...I mean..." Bjorn stammered.

"Would it help if you held onto a ball?" Eddings continued. Wick snickered.

"Well, for one thing, the linebacker can't punch you," Bjorn retorted. "He can't kick you, and he can't trip you."

"Guess what, no one's going to call an Oogar for face-masking you." Eddings crossed her arms and nodded at the sparring square. "Back to positions."

The contest devolved into who could knock the other out of bounds. Wick won three of the five ensuing matches, though in the last bout Bjorn flattened him with a move he recalled from when he was a linebacker. He envisioned Wick as a quarterback with the ball and barreled into him as soon as Eddings shouted *"Saejak!"*

"Eddings, hold up a second," Bjorn called as the session broke up. Wick lurked further along the path back to the barracks.

Eddings stopped. "I swear, Beta Bear, if you ask me out, I will hurt you."

"What? No. Why would I—never mind. I wanted to say thank you. I know I've been distracted, and I appreciate you didn't give up on me as some mopey kid." Bjorn glanced along the sidewalk. "Besides, I'm not the one who wants to ask you out."

Eddings' eyes flicked toward Wick and she blushed. "Whatever. Practice your drills, and we'll have another session Wednesday. Don't let the stuff with the cheerleader get you down. You're kids, and you have plenty of time to figure this crap out. Almost nobody ends up with their high school sweetheart—they're like training wheels. It's fun at first, but sooner or later you need to move past them."

You haven't been watching the memory of your sweetheart with your best friend over and over. "Maybe. See you in PT."

"See you later, Beta Bear." Eddings turned to catch up with Wick, who was still waiting.

* * *

"You're putting in a late session," Stefan called from the office door. "Do you need me to arrange to have someone drive you home?"

"I had a training session with Eddings." Bjorn didn't glance up from his schoolwork. He thought getting kicked out of school would at least leave him with more free time. Between PT, therapy, training with Eddings, and schoolwork, it felt as though he had less time in the day. "I brought the autocar from home. If it's past curfew for permit drivers, I'll let it drive."

"You're not going to sit in here and obsess about *her*, are you?"

Bjorn stopped typing. "I'll do that while the car is driving me home. Right now, I'm trying to get this book report knocked out."

"If you say so, young man." Stefan cocked his head, as though remembering something. Bjorn doubted it, as Stefan never forgot anything. "Your father is going to a mercenary conference in Houston while you're on summer break. I know you don't want to become a merc, but if you have any interest in the business side it could be eye opening."

"I doubt my father would want me along, and my mother would be less than thrilled."

"You might be surprised," Stefan countered. "As for your mother, it's not as though you're going on a combat mission. This is a conference. You're more likely to get shot at that nerd convention in Indianapolis."

"I'll think about it. Thanks, Stefan."

"Any time. Be sure to turn out the lights when you leave." Stefan disappeared into the hall.

Bjorn watched three loops of the memory. He pinged Heather after the third time.

"Hey, Bjorn." He was surprised she picked up. "What's up?"

"I was thinking about you, and I hadn't heard from you in a couple of days."

"Aw, that's sweet." Heather smiled into the camera. "How are you holding up? You've been spending a lot of time at Bear Town."

"I do my schoolwork here, I do physical training here, and I do physical therapy here. It takes a lot of time," Bjorn said.

"I guess it's good you're keeping busy."

"I'd rather have the time to sit on the sidelines and pretend to do homework while I watched you at tennis practice." Bjorn hoped his smile seemed genuine. He resisted the urge to ask if Berto watched her practice.

"Any luck on you coming back for your senior year?" Heather asked.

Bjorn sighed. "No. The school's board of directors won't budge. I think my dad ticked them off. I'm stuck going to a public high school next year, unless I want to go to some posh private school somewhere out of town, which would defeat the purpose of finishing my senior year with my girlfriend and my friends."

Heather averted her eyes from the camera. Bjorn wanted to ask, *You're still my girlfriend, right?* "It would be a shame for you to have to go far away," Heather said.

"So, when can we get together?" Bjorn asked. He might as well, even if he expected another deflection.

"Friday night? At the coffee shop near Zagyg Arcade. I could be there by eight."

Bjorn blinked to mask his surprise. "Yeah, that would be great." He resisted the urge to suggest more. "I miss you."

Heather lowered her eyes before replying, "I miss you, too."

An indistinct male voice came from behind Heather. "I'm almost done," she replied over her shoulder before returning her gaze to the camera. "I've got to go. Take care."

The connection blinked out before Bjorn could reply. Who was there? Was it her dad? It would explain why she finished the conversation so abruptly and with a lack of affectionate nicknames.

Friday night was several days away, but now he had a concrete time. His father wouldn't be back yet—while he wouldn't forbid Bjorn from making the rendezvous, his father would heap on his "wisdom," and Bjorn was certain he didn't want to hear it. It would be all about how they were too young to be so serious—blah, blah, blah.

His parents hadn't met until his father was almost 30, so of course anyone younger was too young to be serious. Never mind that great-grandpa Olaf had met his wife when he was nineteen. Sure, most people waited until they were older to move out of the family home and get married. Most mercenaries wanted to make sure they had a good nest egg to provide for their family if a mission went south, and families on GGI found it easier to remain together and pool their stipends.

So much for his great plan. Get through college and propose to Heather after an NFL team drafted him. The family money made it improbable he'd end up on GGI, so what timetable did he hang the rest of his life on?

For now, he needed to finish this book report and go home. Then he'd need to resist the urge to watch either of the loops—Heather and Berto at prom, and the night of Bjorn's welcome home party. He hated to think how many times he had watched each recording.

107 and 37, respectively.

* * * * *

Chapter Fourteen

Las Cruces, New Mexico

"You're extra spiffy tonight," Bjorn's mother remarked. "Should I assume you're meeting Heather?"

"Of course I'm meeting Heather," Bjorn remarked. "Who else would I get dressed up to meet?"

"You've been spending a lot of time with Specialist Eddings." Bjorn suspected Stefan had leaked the info to Bjorn's mother.

"Mom, she's too old. She's at least twenty." Specialist Trish Eddings, Age: 20, appeared in his pinview. There was a BTI node installed in the home server, and it was close enough to Bear Town for the nodes to stay up to date on virtual gossip. Once Bjorn had let the base node connect with his pinplants, all of the nodes could do so.

BTI: The terms are file-sharing and database updating.

"If you say so. For the record, I agree, she is too old for you. Does this mean you've worked things out between you, Heather, and Berto?"

"I'm going out with Heather," Bjorn replied. "Berto has nothing to do with it."

"Of course. If you get back from your date early and want to talk, I'll be awake," his mother said. "I hope you have a good night. Drive safe."

"Good night. Don't wait up for me," Bjorn called as he headed for the door, especially since he hoped to sneak Heather back here after the coffee shop. They could leave Heather's car there, and Bjorn would return her to the family car at the end of the night. They could even leave her phone in the car in case her parents were suspicious.

* * *

"I've missed you, princess," Bjorn murmured.

Heather stiffened in his embrace. Had he hugged her too tightly with his prosthetic arm? "We should go inside," she said.

"Right, we don't want anyone to report you were with your reprobate boyfriend." Bjorn forced humor into his voice as he relaxed the hug. He held the door open and followed Heather into the coffee shop.

Heather gossiped about her friends in the cheerleading squad while they waited in line to place their order. Heather insisted on paying for her own beverage to leave a digital trail. It would be hard to argue she wasn't out for coffee when she had a receipt from a coffee shop.

Bjorn ordered his obligatory drink and followed Heather to a table. She picked one in the middle of the shop, instead of a table off in a corner as Bjorn had hoped.

Fifteen minutes of awkward small talk ensued, mostly about the people at school. Heather diverted any discussion about herself or her efforts to set up Berto with one of her friends.

"What about Mickey D and Blair?" Bjorn asked, picking a safe topic with threads leading to prom. "How were they at prom?"

Heather's smile lit up. "They were adorable—like two big puppies at play. They had no clue what they were doing or what to expect, and in the end Alison didn't care. I should send you some pictures."

"I saw some on social media, but I didn't see all of them," Bjorn replied. "I didn't see any pictures of you and Berto, either." He scooted his chair next to Heather's for a better view. He draped his arm over the back of her chair.

Heather's fingers faltered as she pecked at the surface of the phone. A folder of photos opened before she hastily swiped the album off screen.

"Weren't those the prom pictures?" Bjorn asked. They were only on the screen for a split second, but he could have sworn he recognized her prom dress.

"They're not the good ones I want to show you." She flipped through another folder before opening it. A patchwork of pictures spread across the screen. "Here are some nice ones of Blair and Alison. I thought Blair was going to faint during the first dance; I think he was holding his breath."

There were pictures of Mickey D and Blair, a few of Mickey D and Heather, and a half dozen of Heather and the rest of the cheerleaders. There was only one picture of Berto—of him and Blair trying to appear dignified in their tuxes.

"I wish I could have been there," Bjorn muttered as Heather continued scrolling through pictures.

"I know." She patted his hand but withdrew her hand when Bjorn turned his own to clasp it.

"That's a great photo of you," Bjorn remarked as a solo picture of Heather flicked onto the screen. "Gods, you're beautiful. Would you send it to me?"

"Um…okay." She tapped her screen a couple of times. *Why is she hesitant?* The picture was innocent, not at all provocative.

An icon appeared in his pinview when his slate reported receipt of the file.

Sharing protocols established. Do you wish to browse or download additional images or videos?

Despite the temptation to seek the pictures Heather had hastily skipped, Bjorn dismissed the prompt. He wasn't about to go digging around in her phone.

"I should get going," Heather remarked, picking up her phone.

"Already? You've barely been here an hour." Bjorn lowered his voice. "I was hoping we could go back to my house. My dad's off-world. We could leave your car here, and I can bring you back later."

Heather squirmed in her seat. "I really can't. I promised I wouldn't stay out late, and finals are coming up."

"I see." Bjorn didn't bother to mask his disappointment. "I want to take you out on a real date. I've hardly seen you, and we haven't…well, since the night of my coming home party."

"I know. I'm sorry, I really am."

Bjorn broke the ensuing awkward silence. "I'll walk you to your car."

In the past, Heather walked close enough for Bjorn to put his arm around her. It only took a few centimeters distance to make the gesture awkward, so he let his arm fall to his side after he held the door open for her.

"You know, we could have our own prom," Bjorn suggested as they crossed the lot. "You could wear your dress; I could rent a limo. How was the limo you guys rode in?"

Heather shrugged. "It was fine."

A stone formed in the pit of his stomach. Bjorn half-heartedly attempted to kiss her goodnight, but Heather turned so his lips brushed her cheek.

"Good night, Bjorn." Heather climbed into the car. Bjorn watched her drive away, before trudging to his own vehicle.

Bjorn sat behind the wheel for several minutes. She lied about the limousine. What else is she hiding?

Sharing protocols established. Do you wish to browse or download additional images or videos?

Surely Heather was out of range by now.

Target device is 367 meters away.

"Where?" Bjorn asked aloud. A map appeared in his pinview. A dot blinked nearby, around the block in Zagyg Arcade's parking lot. Why was she there?

Do you wish to browse or download additional images or videos?

What were those photos she swiped aside? He should have paid closer attention.

Do you wish to view recorded video from earlier?

Hacking into her phone would be an invasion of privacy. Watching something his own eyes saw would be a different matter. "Yes, start time index twenty minutes prior to receiving the image file, fast forward at times-four." Bjorn watched the footage advance rapidly. His pinplants must have started recording as soon as he moved to see her phone's screen. "Stop! Rewind at one-quarter normal speed. Stop. Advance at ten percent speed. Stop!"

An image of Heather's phone was frozen in his pinview. The picture on her screen was partially obscured by Heather's finger, but Bjorn could make out enough. It was a picture of Berto and Heather kissing at prom. Berto had snapped the photo and sent it to Heather.

Bjorn swapped the pinview to the map. "Pass location to vehicle navigation and engage autodrive," Bjorn ordered. He barely noticed the car whir into motion as he seethed behind the wheel. What should he do? What would he say?

Insufficient data.

The car parked itself in the arcade's lot. Bjorn clambered out and trudged toward the neon-lit entrance, almost getting run over as he crossed the parking lot. He ignored the epithets hurled at him by the driver. The usual crowd of high school and college students were standing in the entryway and the lounge beyond the foyer.

"Hey, Trip," the clerk at the entrance said. "Haven't seen you in a while. I think your pals are back past the CASPer simulators."

"Thanks, Ray," Bjorn muttered. He wove through the packed crowd. Colored lights and the glow of Tri-Vs illuminated the dim interior.

Blair spotted Bjorn first, and his eyes bugged out. Bjorn couldn't hear him stammer to Mickey D. Bjorn's attention was focused on Heather and Berto. Heather was leaning against Berto, who had one arm wrapped around her and was stroking her hair with his other hand.

Mickey D followed Blair's gaze and mouthed "oh shit" when she spotted Bjorn. While Blair gaped like a fish out of water, Mickey D intercepted Bjorn.

"Come on, big guy," Mickey D said, putting a hand on his chest. "You don't want to do this."

"You're right," Bjorn replied. "How long did you know? Is Berto the team captain, too? Is it why you've been avoiding me and didn't tell me? Blair is too chicken shit, but I figured you would have had the *cojones.*"

"I'm sorry, but it's not for me to tell," Mickey D replied. She fell back a step. "Please don't screw things up worse."

"It's okay," Berto called. Heather turned to see what the commotion was and gasped, her eyes going wide. Berto stepped away from Heather. "It was bound to happen sooner or later. Move aside, Alison."

Mickey D looked from Bjorn to Berto before reluctantly moving out of Bjorn's path. "I know they hurt you. Don't do something you'll regret."

Berto met Bjorn halfway. Some of the other patrons sensed the tension and shrank back from what appeared to be a brewing fight. Half of them pulled out their phones to record the proceedings.

Bjorn spied one of the public Tri-Vs used to share images to groups. He ordered his pinplants to pay the fee and transmit the isolated image. Berto's expression shifted from apprehension to confusion as Bjorn issued the instructions.

Heather's choked off cry caught Berto's attention. The picture of Heather's phone displaying the image of Berto and Heather kissing hovered in the projected display. Exclamations from the crowd rose above the background noise.

"I'm sorry, *hermano.* It's my fault, and I didn't mean for things to go down this way," Berto said. "Don't be pissed at her. If you want, beat the crap out of me. It's what I deserve."

"Don't you dare!" Heather surged forward to interpose herself between Berto and Bjorn. No matter how angry he was, he could never lift a finger against her, and she knew it.

"It's all right, Heather," Berto held Bjorn's gaze. "I hurt Bjorn; it's only fair he hurt me back. What do you say, big man? Do you want to take this outside?"

"No!" Heather cried.

"Is that what you want, Berto? Would it somehow absolve you if I beat the piss out of you?" Bjorn glared down at Berto. Blood pressure, blood oxygen, and heart rate metrics appeared in his pinview. "Berto, you were a brother to me. Heather, I was ready to spend the rest of my life with you. You've taken what little bit was left of my life and shredded it when I needed you both the most!"

Bjorn wiped his nose with his artificial arm. "How long have you been waiting to move in on my girlfriend? It's why you've always sidestepped any other girls, right? You were waiting…hoping for something to happen. Isn't that right, *hermano*?"

"I…I never meant…" Berto stammered.

"But you wanted it! You wanted her!" Bjorn shouted. "You must have been so happy when I was kicked out. How long did it take for you to console her?"

"Stop!" Heather yelled, getting in Bjorn's face. "If you want to blame someone, blame me! I was despondent when you were kicked out of school. Now you're going to be a merc, and you're going to get killed on some alien world."

"You know I don't want to be a mercenary!" Bjorn retorted.

"What other choice do you have?" Heather wiped tears from her eyes, smudging her mascara. "I loved you, but I don't want to see you die on some alien world to bring home a paycheck. I don't want a life of wondering if you'll come back. I don't want to be a CASPer widow."

Loved. Bjorn staggered back a step as though struck.

Video archived.

"I kind of wish you guys would slug it out and be done with it," Mickey D muttered.

Bjorn wanted to break something. A nearby arcade console was tempting. Servos in his hand whined as he clenched his fist. "I guess you've all washed your hands of me. I wish the bear had killed me—it would have been a mercy."

Bjorn turned on his heel and stalked away. The ring of spectators parted; a few patted him on the back as he passed through the throng. If only the bear *had* killed him. Once he reached the car, he slumped behind the wheel.

"Home," Bjorn uttered.

Command not understood. Please repeat.

"Go. Home," Bjorn said, angrily enunciating the words.

During the drive, Bjorn deleted all his social media contacts. His closest friends had betrayed him. He would attend a different school for his senior year. What did the previous years matter? Heather, Berto, and Mickey D all tried to contact him, but there was nothing else to say.

Bjorn shouldn't have been surprised when the lights were on when he arrived home. His mother waited at the table in the breakfast nook. A cup of steaming tea sat in front of her, with another across from her.

"You know I'm not a fan of tea, right?" Bjorn asked as he collapsed into the chair. The metal frame creaked under his bulk.

"Humor me, Trip. You might find it relaxing," his mother said.

Bjorn cradled the warm cup between his hands. "How did you know?"

"I didn't, not for sure, but I was a teenager once," his mother said. "Sometimes it's easier to see what's going on when you're a step back as opposed to in the middle of it. Besides, you're all young. Do you know how many high school sweethearts spend the rest of their lives together?"

"I know. You guys gave me the same speech when Heather and I got serious last year." Bjorn sniffed. "We're young, don't get caught up in thinking it's forever, blah blah blah. I guess you and Dad were right. I'm a dumb kid."

"You're not dumb. Every teenager thinks their first love will last," his mother replied. "Do you want something stronger than tea?"

Bjorn raised his eyebrows.

His mother laughed. "Do you think I don't know your father and grandfather have been slipping you schnapps and brennivín out in the garage? I don't condone it, but in this instance, I won't object to you having a drink to help you get to sleep."

"Thanks, but I'll pass." Bjorn's friends and classmates had snuck booze into parties, but he hadn't acquired a taste for it. The extra-hoppy beer they favored was bitter and smelled like dirty socks. "I'm going to go to bed."

"All right. Let me know if you need anything." Her smile was full of sympathy. Was she relieved he had passed on the drink? Her brother was an alcoholic, so maybe this was a test to see if he would turn out like Uncle Clayton.

Bjorn retreated to his room. He watched the video of Heather and Berto walking the red carpet to prom three times. He spent half an hour staring at the flashed image from her phone of them kissing. Another fifteen minutes was lost on the picture Heather had sent him. Thirteen loops of when she used loved instead of love in the arcade.

"Delete file," Bjorn rasped. Once the file interface hovered in his pinplant, he mentally highlighted additional files to erase. The kiss, gone. The promenade into prom, gone. Heather in her prom dress, gone.

The video file of their last time together, the night of his coming home party…The cursor hovered over the delete icon. "Archive file to slate," Bjorn instructed.

He rolled over and fell asleep, hoping to the Norns his dreams wouldn't be haunted by the evening's events.

*****

Chapter Fifteen

Bear Town, New Mexico

Bjorn knocked on the door frame of Sergeant Orr's office.

"What?" The sergeant glanced up from her slate. "Dammit, I forgot. Sorry, Tovesson, the training cadre troops joined their assigned units. There's no more group PT until the next batch of recruits roll in."

"How long will it be until the next cadre?" Bjorn asked.

Sergeant Orr shrugged. "When your old man hires another batch of recruits. There were only light losses on Tol'Vilk, so those will be filled by the reserve troopers. Unless he decides to add another company, it may be a while. Try not to get fat in the meanwhile."

"Thanks, Sergeant." Now what? School was done for the semester, so he didn't have classwork. It left him with a bunch of time to kill before he met with Eddings and Wick.

* * *

"Is Sergeant Silver around?" Bjorn didn't recognize the tech corporal, so it was best to stick to protocol rather than Axe's nickname.

"He's over in Garage Two," the corporal replied, jerking his thumb in the general direction.

"Thanks." Bjorn watched for traffic as he jogged across the motor pool lot, wary of a six-wheeled Casanova armored fighting vehicle rumbling across the fused pavement. The late May sun was already warming the air. Once summer proper arrived, the midday heat would border on unbearable.

Bjorn found Axe with two other technicians closing maintenance panels on a Mk 6 CASPer. The machine embodied its nickname: the Juggernaut.

"Hey kid, you're several hours early," Axe remarked as he wiped the grime from his hands. "Everything okay?"

"Yeah. The training cadre is finished, and school is out, so I didn't know what else to do. I figured I'd see if I could help out or maybe get in some therapy before lunch."

"You want to help, find us a haptic suit and a CASPer pilot," one of the technicians grumbled. "They think they're too good to help us out."

"Can't one of you drive the CASPer?" Bjorn asked.

"Not without a haptic suit," Axe replied. "Someone collected the spares we were using to move CASPers around in the maintenance bay. We need to get this mech back to its cradle, so we can get to work on the next one."

"Are these Block 3s?" Bjorn asked. When the CASPer simulator had arrived at the arcade, Bjorn had studied all the modern CASPer designs.

"Yeah, but what difference does it make?" one of the techs replied.

Bjorn brushed back the hair covering the pinlink for his pinplants. "If it's a Block 3, I can use my pinplants to interface with it. I can walk it over to the cradle and bring the next one back for you to work on."

The technicians turned to Axe. He asked, "Have you ever driven a CASPer?"

"My dad let me drive one last year, and I've had plenty of simulator time," Bjorn replied. "It's not as though I'll be fighting Besquith. It's walking one suit fifty meters and bring another back."

Axe stared at the suit. Its clamshell canopy was open. "Fine. I want to get the next one done before lunch."

"You need a step?" a technician asked.

"I should be good," Bjorn replied as he gauged the climb into the two-and-a-half-meter-tall war machine. He stepped onto the foot of the armor, set the toe of his boot on the kneecap of the suit, and grabbed the edges of the cockpit opening. He bounced a couple of times before he lunged forward and up. Bjorn caught the bar on the underside of the canopy with his cybernetic arm and latched on. He brought a foot up to the lower lip of the hatchway, hauled himself up, and pivoted. Turning 180 degrees so he could lower his legs into the suit was the hardest part.

Once his feet reached the pedals in the legs of the armor, clamps gripped his feet. He eased back against the pilot couch and fumbled for the first restraining harness strap.

CASPer Mk 6, Block 3.1 user manual.

Bjorn followed the instructions and secured the harness. He found the pinlink lead and plugged it into the port behind his ear. A Heads-Up Display manifested in his pinview.

Connection established. Pinlink control enabled.

"I'm pinned in," Bjorn stated. "I'm going through the power-up sequences."

"Have him skip—" one of the technicians remarked before Axe cut him off.

"Let the kid do it the right way," Axe said. "Unless you want to explain to the commander how his son got hurt because you wanted a rookie pilot to cut corners?" The technician shook his head. "I didn't think so."

Bjorn scrolled through the checklist, ticking off one item at a time. "All systems are green," he reported. "I'm closing the canopy."

"Roger, closing the canopy," Axe responded. The armored clamshell swung down and sealed the suit. "Releasing maintenance clamps. You are free to maneuver."

Readouts flooded his pinview. Bjorn swatted the graphics aside until they all lined up along one edge of his field of view. He shoved his arms into the upper arms of the CASPer and gripped the controls below the suit's elbow. Bjorn checked his display one more time before taking a tentative step forward.

The armor lurched out of the maintenance cradle, each armored foot clanging on the concrete. Bjorn straightened his posture, and the CASPer responded. Another step rang out on the concrete, then another.

"I think I'm getting the hang of this," Bjorn said into the channel Axe had set up. Each stride was ponderous, but the suit's larger stature meant it covered more ground. A map appeared in his pinview with directions to the parking cradle.

"Don't get cocky," Axe countered. "Keep it nice and steady."

Bjorn glanced at the HUD projected in his pinview. There were twice as many elements as the simulator game he played with…well, he used to play. Only a fraction of them mattered for the brief walk. Balance indicators flashed yellow when he stumbled stepping from the garage to the motor pool lot. Four centimeters, and he almost tripped.

"You good, kid?" Axe called.

Bjorn nodded, then chided himself because Axe couldn't see the gesture. "I'm fine."

The CASPer lurched into motion again, pausing halfway across the motor pool to let a LPT roll across his path. By the time he reached the CASPer Armory, his gait had increased to a slow walk. The lip of the armory floor behind the open door flashed yellow in his pinview.

"Take it to Cradle Seventeen—the first empty one on the left," Axe instructed.

Bjorn's projected path adjusted. He strode between two rows of battle armor facing each other until he reached the empty spot. He turned the CASPer away from the cradle and cautiously backed between the waiting clamps.

"All right, raise your upper arms thirty degrees while keeping the forearms parallel to the torso." Axe moved to gauge the alignment of the clamps. "Hold the monkey pose and move a little to your left. Good, ease back until you make contact."

Even though he was careful, the CASPer jarred to a halt against the storage cradle. Bjorn winced and waited for Axe to admonish him.

"Bjorn, confirm the clamps are green," Axe said.

Clamp alignment within parameters. Green for engaging storage clamps.

"Confirmed." Bjorn felt a slight bump as the cradle arms extended and grasped the CASPer.

"Good job. Shut it down. I've got the guys prepping your next ride."

The shutdown checklist manifested in his pinview, and Bjorn methodically went through the items. The second to last item was to pop the canopy. The clamshell rose and let in the fresh air. "The simulators are more forgiving than the real thing."

"You want us to put the next one in training mode?"

Training mode automates several functions at the cost of pilot autonomy.

"No. My dad must have had the one he let me tromp around in training mode," Bjorn said as the machine went dark with shutdown. He disconnected his pinlink and clambered out of the cockpit.

Axe pointed at a lever. "Pull on the manual canopy release until the hatch closes. The next one is two aisles over."

The return trip proceeded quicker. Bjorn navigated the CASPer with more confidence, increasing the gait to a steady walk. He was still wary of other traffic in the motor pool yard, but nothing else rolled through. At the halfway point, external microphones picked up the shriek of a low flying VTOL. His HUD painted the aircraft as it zoomed overhead, the IFF—Identification, Friend or Foe—coloring the vehicle as a friendly.

BTI: Commander Tovesson has returned.

Bjorn was afraid the program would rescind his control of the CASPer, but he resumed his progress unimpeded. He was in the process of extracting himself from the cockpit when his father stormed into the maintenance garage.

"Why the hell did a CASPer paint my ride? What—" Commander Tovesson froze when he saw Bjorn half out of the battle armor.

"What in the name of Loki were you playing at, boy? Were you trying to give my pilot a heart attack?"

"The suit did it automatically," Bjorn retorted. "I didn't know who it was until the IFF flagged it as friendly, let alone that you were onboard."

"Commander, it's not your son's fault," Axe interjected. "BB107 has a faulty sensor relay—it's stuck in active mode. We made sure to unload its ammo and safe its weapons as a precaution. Even if it flagged you as a hostile, it couldn't fire on you."

"Which brings me to my next question, Sergeant Silver." The commander pointed an accusatory finger at Bjorn. "Why was my son tooling around in a CASPer? Are you running some sort of kiddie ride?"

Bjorn hopped to the concrete floor, seething. "It's not his fault. With school out and the training cadre done, I had some free time. I pestered the sergeant and his team into letting me help."

"Help?" His father's expression was incredulous. "How is letting you joyride a CASPer helping?"

"He did help, commander," Axe said. "Someone yanked our haptic suit, and Bjorn offered to lend a hand since his pinlink would let him drive the CASPers we were working on without a haptic suit. We didn't even need to put the mech in training mode. It saved us time we would have spent trying to find a damn suit."

"You think CASPer funk is bad, you should smell a shared haptic suit," one of the techs muttered to Bjorn.

"It was good practice for me and these pinplants you had them shove into my skull," Bjorn added.

His father regarded Bjorn, his moustache twitching as he pursed his lips in thought. "Obviously we need to find some more stuff to keep you busy for the summer. Come on. It's almost lunch time. Carry on, Sergeant Silver."

"Yes, Commander."

Bjorn followed his father back into the afternoon sun. Approaching midday, the temperature was over 30 Celsius. An LPT waited on the shimmering lot. Bjorn had expected to walk 800 meters uphill to Bjarnarsal for lunch.

"So why were you itching to pilot a CASPer?" Bjorn's father asked as he wound the LPT on the looping road to the HQ building.

Bjorn shrugged. "They were working on one, and I didn't have anything scheduled until 1500. Axe—Sergeant Silver—can't work with me on physical therapy until his work is done, so it seemed the best idea."

"If you say so." A smirk twitched his father's beard. "If school is over, what's at 1500?"

"Private Eddings is coaching me on hand-to-hand," Bjorn replied.

The LPT whirred to a stop in a reserved parking space. "She's the short hellcat in one of the CASV squads, right? What does Heather think?"

"Heather and I broke up." Bjorn threw the door open, climbed out, and stomped into the building.

"What happened, son?" The smirk disappeared.

"After I got kicked out of school, she and Berto started spending time together. They went to prom, and well…yeah." Damned dust from the parking lot. "We broke up a couple weeks ago once it finally got through my thick skull."

"Did you kick Berto's ass?"

Bjorn shook his head. "I wanted to…I wanted to punch his face in, but I couldn't. Even though he betrayed me, I couldn't bring myself to knock his lights out."

"There's no shame in that, son, but truth be told, I wouldn't have blamed you if you slugged him. Taking another man's girl is low, especially when he's deployed."

"I'm not a merc. I wasn't off-world." Bjorn surveyed the food stations prepared for lunch. He headed for the guest restaurant, Qomida. A bowl piled high with rice, beans, and chicken would fit the bill.

"You might as well have been," his father protested. "It's dirty to move in when a soldier can't be around. What's this place?"

"Remember when you told me to research my idea of bringing in guest restaurants? They're here on a month-long trial to see if it works for both parties."

"I didn't authorize bringing someone in," his father protested. "I wanted you to get me some numbers."

Bjorn collected a tray and waited to place his order. The line was long, but the food was better than the other mess hall stations. "Stefan authorized it. It turns out he has a lot of latitude over civilian contractors, especially when you're not around."

His father grumbled something about operation security as he grabbed a tray. "Are they serving real grilled chicken?" he asked once they came within sight of the food options.

"They bring it in from south of Juarez. It turns out the cartel has a solution for vegan activists trying to drive farmers who raise animals out of business," Bjorn remarked. "The Mexican poultry farms produce fresh meat at a quarter the cost of lab-grown, and it tastes better."

"If you and Heather split, what's going on between you and Eddings?" his father asked after ordering.

Bjorn rolled his eyes. "I already told Mom, there's nothing going on. I think Eddings is seeing Wick, and she's…it's not like that. Trish is a badass, and my first week of hanging with the training cadre reminded me I wasn't. I'm paying her to tutor me."

"Probably the smartest thing I've seen you spend credits on," his father remarked as they sat. "Don't let it go to your head. Even if you're able to kick some ass, someone better than you will come along. It's why I run the Berserkers as a mixed outfit. You don't want to become dependent on a single weapon."

Bjorn dug into his lunch. "Makes sense. Is that why you've invested so heavily in the Combat Assault System, Vehicular when everyone else wrote it off in favor of CASPers?"

"Some armored outfits field the lighter fighting vehicles," his father countered. "CASPers get the glory, but even badasses need a ride. While proper tanks can carry more armament, they are sitting ducks compared to Casanovas."

Bjorn nodded. "Why haven't we invested in naval assets? Wouldn't it be cheaper if we had our own transports to get our dropships to the operational theater instead of hiring out?"

His father glanced up from his taco salad, oblivious to the flecks of salsa and lettuce in his beard. "Before I answer your question, I'm glad you've picked up an interest in company operations."

"I hear a but coming," Bjorn muttered.

"You obviously haven't researched the upfront cost of acquiring space assets and the infrastructure needed to support them. We had our own mercenary cruiser until six years ago." A mercenary cruiser, despite the name, was a glorified transport with enough shields and weapons to deliver ships to the target world—in theory.

"What happened?" Bjorn asked.

"Some XenSha shot it full of holes during a contract. We won the ground fight but paid an exorbitant fee to the XenSha to give us a lift back to civilized space." His father speared a tomato slice. "We lost the cruiser and three dropships, two with all hands. I sold the wreck for scrap; it was too expensive to fix."

"Why didn't you have some ships to protect it?" If the cruiser was intact and most of the dropships made it to the ground, the XenSha advantage couldn't have been overwhelming.

"We're not the gods-damned Winged Hussars!" his father snapped.

"They're not the only merc units who have space naval assets," Bjorn said. "There are even outfits specializing in combat transport operations. We should buy one them. It's what one of the Horsemen did instead of building their transport fleet from scratch."

"We're not at their level…yet." His father poked at the remains of his salad. "How'd you like to meet some of them?"

"Some of who?"

"The Four Horsemen," his father replied. "There's a conference in Houston. Most of it will be bullshit, but you could meet some of the big dogs in the business."

"Why would they give a fig about who I am if I'm not going to be a mercenary?" Bjorn countered.

"It doesn't matter what they think. Do you want to go or not?"

Bjorn scraped some stray rice from his bowl to stall. "Sure. It's not as cool as going off-world, but I could use a change of scenery."

"Good, because I would hate to think I had that fight with your mother for nothing," his father said.

*****

Chapter Sixteen

Houston, Texas

"This is why we were airborne at 0700?" Bjorn grumbled. The flight to Houston had only taken an hour via dropship, and with the other travel logistics they were at the Berserkers' Houston office by 0900.

"Getting here early let us beat the traffic," his father retorted. "Sorry if I cut into your busy schedule."

Bjorn snorted and returned to tapping his slate. Even though it was faster to use his pinplants, Bjorn still used his fingers out of habit. He pretended not to peek over the screen at the pretty receptionist manning the desk in the lobby. *She must get bored here.* In two hours, Bjorn had seen two people come by the office besides his father and himself. "Why do we rent a half-empty office suite in a half-empty building?"

"Because we got in on the ground floor when they built this tower. It meant our rent is locked in as we're an investor," his father replied. "Most mercenary outfits maintain a presence here in Houston, including the ones based in other nation-states. Even the Golden Horde has offices here."

"I thought they owned the starport in Tashkent," Bjorn said.

His father shrugged. "They pretty much built the damned starport in Uzbekistan. My guess is Colonel Enkh wants to keep her fingers on the pulse of the merc industry, and Houston is the heart of it. Now get your butt out of the chair; we're going to meet Vurrg for lunch."

"I thought he was at Karma," Bjorn remarked, stowing his slate.

"He came back for the convention. There will be representatives from several alien companies here. Binnig may manufacture CASPers here on Earth, but the best gear otherwise is alien made."

"I wonder how much time he had to waste?" Bjorn followed his father out of the office. Downstairs, they exited the air-conditioned office tower into the furnace of afternoon Houston in the summer. With the temperature in the low 30s, it was almost as hot as Bear Town.

"I don't know what you're complaining about. You've spent the past two hours ogling Sasha."

"I didn't ogle her," Bjorn protested. "I glanced at her a couple of times, sure. It's not as though I stared at her."

The older Tovesson chuckled. "Sure. How much footage have you stashed in your pinplants?"

Twelve minutes of video in 7 files.

"Whatever." He spotted a knot of four mercenaries walking toward an unmarked storefront in what looked like a vacant strip mall. "What's that place?"

"The Lyon's Den. It's a merc hangout."

"Why don't we go there for lunch?" Bjorn asked.

"One—you're not a merc. Two—it's not a tourist attraction. Three—I don't even know if they have food. I drank there a couple of times, but the only thing on the menu was tall tales and war stories. We're meeting Vurrg at the Hunnu Mongolian Barbeque."

"Is it an all you can eat place?" He shouldn't pig out, but if a Mongolian barbeque didn't cry out for indulging, Bjorn didn't know what did.

His father shook his head. "In a startown full of big, hungry, mercs? Don't be ridiculous. It's by the bowl, but feel free to go nuts. Who knows how long it will be until we grab dinner? I wouldn't want you to waste away."

"Whatever." Bjorn rolled his eyes. "There sure are a lot of aliens here. I thought they considered Earth a backwater."

"To them, we're a bunch of rubes. Even better, we're a bunch of rubes rolling in mercenary credits. Business has been picking up, and Humans have been getting a reputation," Bjorn's father said. "A lot of it isn't flattering. We don't fit into niches, and they find it hard to pigeon-hole us. Bakulu excel at naval combat, XenSha are button-pushers, Oogar are shock-troopers, but we want to do everything and are damned good at it. It gets on the aliens' nerves."

"What are those goat-looking aliens following us?" Bjorn asked. He'd spotted the four trailing them five blocks earlier and through two changes of direction. The hunched over bipeds almost came up to his shoulder, at least as far as he could judge from a couple of glimpses.

Khabar—carnivorous bipeds who superficially resemble Earth goats. Home world: Khabrix. They are members of the Galactic Union. They were denied certification as a mercenary race due to chronic breach of contract.

"Don't stare at them," his father warned. "You'll piss the Gruffs off. I don't want a brawl in the starport, or worse, find them waiting in an alley for us on the return trip."

"Are they tough?" Bjorn fought the urge to glance over his shoulder again. According to the map in his pinview, they were only two blocks from Hunnu.

"Not as tough as Zuul, but tougher than your average Human," his father replied. His hand casually drifted toward his holstered pistol. "They're not stone-cold killers. If they jumped us, they would try to put me out of commission and kidnap you."

"Why?"

"Unless you're an assassin or a bounty hunter taking death marks, there's no money in murder." The restaurant loomed ahead, a large structure with huge horse figureheads flanking the entrance. A pair of bear-like Jivool lumbered in.

"Our bank accounts would say different," Bjorn remarked.

"With mercenaries, both sides know what they're getting into," his father said. "If someone hires you to protect something, it means they've ticked off someone else enough for them to pay mercenaries to hit the objective. It's a transaction, a bloody one, but it's business."

"At last you are here!" Vurrg exalted as they entered the dim, cool foyer. "The scent of meat has me drooling. I feared you would never arrive."

Cooked meat, spices, and seared vegetables combined into a delicious aroma. Bjorn's mouth watered. The hostess, an Asian girl clad in a semblance of Mongolian garb, wasn't fazed by Vurrg's presence when she asked how many were in their party.

"It will be about fifteen minutes," she remarked as she handed Bjorn's father a translucent glass square with the restaurant's logo on it. The device would light up when their table was ready.

As they moved away from the hostess station to join the waiting crowd, Bjorn caught a whiff of an earthy odor reminiscent of mulch and fertilizer. At first Bjorn thought it was the waiting Jivool, then two of the Khabar brushed past him. Their odor up close was strong enough for him to wrinkle his nose.

"Welcome travelers," the hostess intoned. "Are you familiar with Earth cuisine?"

One of the goat-like aliens spoke, his translator pendant rendering his gravelly bleats into English. "Yes. Your flesh is delicious."

The hostess blanched.

"Meat. Your meat is delicious," the other Khabar corrected. "We prefer our meat fresh, less cooked."

"Fresh," the first Khabar agreed, eyeing the hostess.

The girl regained her composure. "Table for two?"

"Yes. Two of us."

The hostess held out one of the squares. "This will flash when your table is ready. It should be about fifteen Earth minutes." She was accustomed to dealing with aliens—the use of Earth minutes reduced the chance of a translator error.

The Khabar clutched the device in a hand composed of two thick fingers and a thumb anchored to the creature's wrist as opposed to the side of the hand as with Humans. Thick nails with sharp points covered the two large phalanges.

"Are those the same goats who followed us?" Bjorn asked his father in Icelandic. The aliens' translators were probably programmed for Russian and Spanish, but Bjorn was hoping they didn't have the more obscure languages in their translation matrix. Vurrg cocked his head in confusion, reinforcing Bjorn's guess.

"Yes. There are few of them on Earth." His father's Icelandic was rustier than Bjorn's. "The other two are waiting out…waiting outside."

Bjorn spent the next twelve minutes avoiding directly looking at the Khabar. He stole enough glances his pinplants assembled a composite image of each alien.

"How many of these people are in Enkh's employ?" Bjorn's father asked after the hostess escorted them to their table.

Vurrg chuffed a laugh. "Hard to say. The Golden Horde is renowned for their intelligence network, but embedding operatives in a Mongolian Barbeque seems…how is it you say, on the nose?"

"Why would the Golden Horde have spies in a Houston restaurant?" Bjorn asked.

"Information is valuable," his father replied. "It's why the Galactic Union has a guild dedicated to it."

Vurrg nodded. "You can tell something is worthwhile if there is a guild. There is the Mercenary Guild, the Science Guild, the Cartography—"

"We learned about the guilds in school," Bjorn interrupted before Vurrg repeated the entire litany of guilds. The Galactic Union had little in way of actual government, and the bulk of it was wrapped up in the guilds.

"Quit watching for the Gruffs," his father remarked. The arrival of a server, also clad in Mongolian garb, cut off Bjorn's retort.

"Why are they following us?" Bjorn asked after the server departed with their drink orders.

"Don't worry about it right now," his father countered, leading the way to the huge horseshoe shaped flattop grill. Patrons chose ingredients from a buffet, placed them in a bowl, and handed the bowl to the cooks manning the grill.

Bjorn's stomach growled as he accepted the bowl back from a cook, piled high with steaming meat, veggies, and rice. One of the Khabar watched him from across the horseshoe. Bjorn pretended not to notice and returned to the table.

"These goat-dudes are creeping me out," Bjorn muttered.

"Ignore the Gruffs," his father replied. "Take your time and eat as much as you want. Maybe they'll get bored and move on."

Bjorn made three more trips to the grill. During the last, one of the Khabar stood next to him. The creature had a bowl piled high with pork and little else. The creature made a snuffling noise. Did it sniff him? A chill ran down Bjorn's spine.

"Your flesh is strange." The Gruff's pupils were dumbbell shaped. Was it remarking on Bjorn's selection—a mix of beef, chicken, and duck on top of a bed of rice and mushrooms—or on his inedible cybernetic arm? "Meat. Your meat is strange."

The cook tapped his spatula on the grill for Bjorn's attention. "It's a mix," Bjorn said as he handed the bowl over the sneeze guard. "What's in your bowl?"

"Flesh, like yours." The Khabar ran its tongue over the serrated bony ridges that served as teeth. "Delicious."

"Maybe I should have tried some mutton or goat," Bjorn replied.

The Khabar waggled its tongue and made a choking sound. "Ha ha ha," sounded from its translator. "Well spoken, kid."

The cook set Bjorn's bowl on the counter and took the Khabar's. Bjorn returned to the table, fighting the temptation to peer over his shoulder.

"What was that all about?" His father pushed aside an empty bowl.

"The Gruff was trying to get my goat." Bjorn set his bowl down and glanced back at the grill. "Why are they so fascinated with us? Are they planning on robbing us? Is this how they case a target?"

"Khabar tend to resent Humans," Vurrg remarked after licking the last of the bits of food from his bowl. "The Khabar sought to become recognized as a mercenary race. They have the temperament for war, but they thought they were above the rules. They were denied after repeatedly breaking the Union Rules of Engagement. They broke one of the cardinal directives of legal mercenary combat—no planetary bombardment from above sixteen kilometers. The third time they did it, the Mercenary Guild authorized a punitive strike against Khabrix, their home world.

"The XenSha and Bakulu who executed the assault were..." Vurrg paused, then chuffed when he recalled the English word, "enthusiastic. They were enthusiastic in their retributive strike. The Khabar had wronged both races."

"So they're ticked at Humans because we got in the Merc Guild, but they didn't?" Bjorn asked.

"A generalization, but not inaccurate," Vurrg replied, sniffing toward the grill. "Their global economy was devastated, and three-quarters of their population perished. Now they rely on work from those too cheap to hire mercenaries, or patrons who mercenaries will not or cannot work for—mostly criminals—without getting on the guild's sensors." Vurrg stood. "One more bowl won't hurt."

"So are these guys going to jump us?" Bjorn asked, no longer enthusiastic for his bowl of barbeque. "Maybe they saw the logo on your jacket."

"Quit being a worry-wort, son." The commander flagged down the server and requested another beer. "You have until I finish the next beer to decide if you're going to poke at your third helping or eat it. Since I'm paying for it, I suggest the latter."

Bjorn speared a chunk of grilled meat. "I don't know how you can be so calm knowing they'll try to mug us."

His father shrugged. "My bet is they'll try to kidnap you. A smart merc doesn't carry a bunch of hard currency around, so the best way to get money out of me is a ransom. The two in here will confront us in a block or two—"

"And the other two will try to grab me while you're distracted," Bjorn finished. "It's not comforting. Why don't the Peacemakers do something?"

"Involving the Peacemakers in anything short of a high-profile crime is expensive," his father replied. "There isn't even a Human Peacemaker yet. The few Human candidates who have applied have washed out."

"Great." Bjorn dug into his bowl without gusto but finished it by the time his father had drained the beer. Vurrg finished his last serving before Bjorn, licking his chops. As they left, the Khabar quickly stood and followed.

"When we walk a block away, take out your stone," his father said in Icelandic as they emerged in the warm Houston evening.

"You are rusty," Bjorn remarked before switching to Icelandic. "I understand. Will they attack then?"

His father shook his head. "No. It will give them time to walk ahead."

Bjorn slipped back into English. "We're making it easier?"

"Trust me." His father winked.

At the next intersection, Bjorn stopped to unholster his slate. "Why do you need this?"

"Do you want ice cream?" his father asked.

"No. I'm stuffed," Bjorn replied. "When you said 'eat as much as you want,' I took you at your word."

"It's fine. You can put your slate away." His father flicked his eyes along the road. The two Khabar from the restaurant hurried past. In a whisper, he added, "Bruin Actual to Jackson, what do you see?"

When his father resumed walking, Bjorn fell into step with him. He queried his pinplants for tactical radio, but the result was negative. The pinplants could connect to a personal area network, but not the more powerful comm channels.

Bjorn composed the query in his mind. "Closest PAN, excluding devices carried on my person?"

After a moment the reply appeared in his pinview. BB-BruinA-09G301.

"Can you access the network?" A PAN connected devices used by a person, such as a slate and an earpiece, or, in this case, his father's comm unit and his earpiece.

Working.

"Heads up!" his father hissed.

"—on your six!" The voice may as well have originated next to Bjorn.

The two Khabar stepped from an alley, pistols ready. Bjorn spun to face the pair of Gruffs behind him. One Khabar swung a black baton while another moved to grab Bjorn.

Blitzing the quarterback. Bjorn twisted out of the grasp of the lunging Khabar, and the baton connected with his raised cybernetic arm. The weapon emitted a threatening sizzle, and the stump of Bjorn's amputated arm tingled where it connected with his prosthesis.

The goat-man blinked in surprise. Bjorn slammed his right fist into the Khabar's cheek, staggering it. Two gunshots echoed in the street, causing pedestrians to scramble for cover. The Khabar who had grabbed for Bjorn bleated and crumpled.

The Gruff with the baton shook its head and swiped at him again. The weapon clipped Bjorn's elbow before bouncing into his ribs. For a split second his entire body felt as though it was plugged into a light socket.

Neural overload countered.

The Gruff gave a tongue-waggling laugh until he realized Bjorn was still standing. This time Bjorn drove his cybernetic fist into the alien's skull, where the Human temple would be. Something crunched under Bjorn's artificial knuckles, and the Khabar's eyes rolled back as it collapsed to the street.

A dark-skinned man in gray Bjorn's Berserkers BDUs with sergeant's stripes followed the falling alien with his sidearm.

"We good, Commander?" the sergeant asked.

"Yeah, the last one got the heck out of Dodge," Bjorn's father replied as he holstered his sidearm. "I don't think this one will be a problem anymore."

The sergeant strode forward, keeping his pistol trained on the Khabar Bjorn had punched out. "Your boy clocked one. Do you want me to finish the job?"

"No." His father lowered his voice. "Too many witnesses. If he wakes up before the scavengers get to him, I guess Tyr was looking the other way. Thanks for watching our backs."

"Can't let the guy who writes our paychecks get whacked by some billy goats," Jackson replied. "Your son took the other one like a champ. I thought for sure the kid would take a nap after the second hit by a stun baton."

"Really? Two hits?" His father kicked the club away from the unconscious Khabar.

"I caught one on my left arm," Bjorn replied. Servos whined as he flexed his cybernetic fist.

"Good job. Let's not stand around lolly-gagging." Bjorn's father beckoned. "Trip, Sergeant Tyson Jackson is our recruitment sergeant. He works out of the Houston office."

"Nice to meet you, Trip." The sergeant smiled. "I can't wait to see your VOWS scores."

"I'm not going to be a mercenary," Bjorn protested.

Jackson glanced back at the Khabar lying in the street. "What a shame."

*****

Chapter Seventeen

Houston, Texas

"Quit looking over your shoulder, son," Bjorn's father muttered.

"Where are the cops?" They had left the Khabar lying in the street. While a simple mugging wouldn't merit a police investigation, a broad daylight robbery of a wealthy person should prompt law enforcement's interest. "Aren't they going to be ticked we left the scene?"

"This is the startown, which means it's under Galactic Union law, or more appropriately the lack thereof. A Peacemaker isn't going to be interested in a pissant robbery unless I want to fork over enough credits to make it worth their while. There's probably not even one on-planet at the moment, anyway, unless there's a reason for one to be here."

Bjorn learned about Peacemakers in his Mercenary Service Track curriculum. They were marshals with broad authority and deadly reputations. While each world in the Galactic Union were required to provide personnel to the Peacemaker Guild, only an elite few beings became badge-carrying Peacemakers. So far, no Humans had qualified, though many worked as bounty hunters for the Peacemaker Guild.

"Most of the aliens who work on your world are employed in the startowns," Vurrg remarked. "Being an armed guard is not as lucrative as a mercenary, but it is far easier."

"The local thugs and hoods learned the hard way that shoplifting from a MinSha shopkeeper could literally get their hand bit off," Bjorn's father said. "It's why they don't let locals wander in without cause. It's to keep Darwinism from running its natural course."

The autocab turned a corner and their destination was visible ahead. The First Horsemen Historical Museum was hosting the mercenary conference. The Cartwright Historical Preservation Society had turned an old airport into a museum since the facility was inadequate for use in the new starport, but still lay within startown. A few of the hangars had been kept as multifunction spaces.

The cab slowed for the checkpoint manned by Cartwright's Cavaliers' personnel. Odds were they were cadre—troops in training frequently drew the crap assignments. Bjorn's father lowered the window as one of the guards approached.

"Sorry, but the museum is closed for a private event," the guard remarked, his eyes flicking across the passengers. He couldn't have been much older than Bjorn. They should have brought Sergeant Jackson—he was in a Berserkers' uniform. Bjorn's father could have passed for an aging biker on the hunt for a bar.

"We're here for the merc confab," Bjorn's father said. "I'm Commander Tovesson of Bjorn's Berserkers."

"I'll need to see your credentials," the guard stated, his voice edged with doubt. Bjorn's father waved his UACC, Universal Account Access Card, over the guard's slate. The young man's eyes widened when the display showed Commander Tovesson's picture and information. "Excuse me, Commander Tovesson. The conference is in Hangar Four and the exposition hall is in Hangar Five. Your autocab will be updated to drop you off at the welcome entrance."

Bjorn's father grunted. "Thank you, Private." After the cab rolled through the gate, he chuckled and added, "I guess I don't look reputable."

"To be fair, it is a vague standard for mercenaries," Vurrg said. "I've learned you Humans are not cohesive in your approach to uniform doctrine."

"Small units think the big outfits are pretentious for having uniforms. The big boys think the little guys are unprofessional slackers because they dress as though they raided a soldier's laundry bag and put on the first clothes they could find." Bjorn's father gestured to himself. He had stripped off his jacket from earlier and wore a T-shirt with the company logo. "I'm not above letting people underestimate me, especially if it makes me more comfortable."

The autocab whirred to a halt in front of a huge metal building. A variety of vehicles, ranging from chrome and black motorcycles to beat up rumblers cluttered the parking lot. A tank sat alone in one corner—no one appeared eager to park next to the 50-ton behemoth. A banner stretched above an awning read Welcome Mercenaries.

"I must go check on my associates," Vurrg announced as he climbed out of the cab. "I need to make sure they haven't bankrupted our company or promised miracles."

"We'll catch up with you later," Bjorn's father said, heading for the doors under the awning. A short line was queued in front of the entrance.

"Can you pull rank and cut line?" Bjorn whispered.

"Why? We're no more important than any of these guys. It's a quick way to be labeled a jerk and told no at the same time."

Bjorn activated the search field in his pinplants. "Query: Bjorn's Berserkers ranking in Earth mercenary companies."

The reply only took a moment to manifest in his pinview. Bjorn's Berserkers—17th in deployable troops, 29th in deployable CASPers, 27th in annual earnings in the last reporting year, 19th in years active.'

"Crap—we're not even top ten," Bjorn muttered.

If his father heard him, he gave no indication. After fifteen minutes in the sweltering heat, they finally reached the air-conditioned entrance. Another fifteen minutes brought them to the registration booths where they received their badges and slate updates for the conference schedule.

Bjorn checked the schedule through his pinplants. Boring, boring, and boring. Half the seminars were thinly veiled pitches by sponsor companies, and they didn't even seem relevant to the Berserkers.

"What now?" Bjorn asked.

"We'll go through the exhibit hall," his father replied. "There's a networking session in a couple of hours I want to attend."

"Joy—sounds like a blast," Bjorn grumbled.

His father snorted. "It won't kill you to make nice with some of these people. If nothing else, when I'm dead you might be selling the company to one of them."

"Don't tempt the Norns," Bjorn said as he followed his father between rows of temporary meeting rooms. Even with sound dampening dividers, the murmur of dozens of voices filled the cavernous building, competing with the hum of industrial air-conditioning units.

His father snorted. "I tempt them every time I climb in a CASPer. I have to hope it's not my time to take the trip to Valhalla."

Signs directed them to turn 90 degrees and led them to another set of doors. They stepped back into the furnace of Houston heat. A fenced and covered pathway connected the hangar to the adjacent building.

"I hate to think how much it costs to air condition these buildings," Bjorn's father muttered as the cool air gusted through the open door. "Even with this blazing sun, those solar cells won't cut it."

The huge exhibit hall dominated the cavernous hangar. Rows upon rows of exhibitor booths lined the floor, competing for attention. The Binnig display dominated one end of the hall, illuminated by flashy holograms. A crowd surrounded the Binnig pavilion.

"Come on." Bjorn's father turned the opposite direction. "Binnig is all hot and heavy about the new Mk 8s they're developing."

"Don't you want to know about the new CASPer?" Bjorn asked. A female Sirra'Kan in a skimpy parody of a merc uniform winked at him as they passed her booth. Bjorn's cheeks reddened, and he barely avoided colliding with an attendee gaping at the humanoid alien.

Image saved.

His father stopped two booths away. The centerpiece of the booth was a suit of powered armor. The red and gold paint job reminded Bjorn of a sports car. A CASPer would dwarf the armor. Bjorn gauged the height of the suit, taking the pedestal into account. The outline of the armor flashed in his pinview.

Height: 182 centimeters.

Two Jeha lurked at the rear of the booth, regarding Bjorn and his father. A hologram of a Human woman manifested next to the display. "I see you are interested in our latest innovation, the APEX suit. The Armored Powered Exoskeleton provides battlefield protection and physiological augmentation without the clumsiness of the more primitive CASPer."

Bjorn's father nodded at the armor. "What's this, some sort of model?"

The hologram gestured toward the suit. "This is an actual working prototype APEX suit."

"You're kidding." The commander squinted at the armor. "My sixteen-year-old son is bigger than your suit. Most CASPer operators wouldn't be able to squeeze into it."

"The APEX can accommodate an operator up to 170 centimeters in height," the hologram stated. "This allows APEX-clad troopers to ride inside the passenger compartments of most vehicles."

"I don't see any weapon mounts," Bjorn remarked. A modern CASPer would have a mount on each arm, plus larger mounts on the shoulders.

"Due to space, weight, and power constraints, the APEX does not equip onboard weapons. However, conventional arms can be easily modified for use by an APEX operator." The hologram smiled and posed next to the display armor.

"Loki-cursed deathtraps—that's what those suits are." Bjorn's father turned away. "Come on."

After several paces, Bjorn asked, "Do you think anyone would buy those APEX suits?"

"Nope. Ever since Binnig's patent on CASPers expired, plenty of companies, both Human and alien, have been trying to get a slice of the pie," Bjorn's father replied. "Mercs are a superstitious and conservative lot. I'll ride a bucket-of-bolts dropship that got me through half a dozen landings rather than trade up for a shiny but untested craft. Mercenaries know Binnig works—dabbling in something else tempts fate."

"What about the Casanovas?" Bjorn countered. "Hardly any mercenary firms use them."

"Sometimes you have to go with your gut." Bjorn's father slowed at a booth featuring CASPer accessories. "I get a good deal on the CASVs, and they're flexible. Here we go. These guys are smart; instead of trying to reinvent the CASPer, they specialize in aftermarket modifications and support equipment. If you're dead set on getting a business degree, there's a lot of credits to be made selling to mercenaries."

"Good afternoon, gentlemen." A man the same age as Bjorn's father broke away from a discussion. He pushed up a pair of glasses—a rare sight as FedCare covered basic eye treatments. Were the spectacles for show? "I'm Ramon Tejedor. What can Griffith Technology do for you?"

Bjorn's father unholstered his slate. "I'm interested in the Gen3 Obsidian Mirror Laser Shields." A three-dimensional image of the collapsible ablative laser shield hovered over the slate along with scrolling text.

Mr. Tejedor smiled broadly, but Bjorn quickly lost interest in the conversation when it devolved into haggling and delivery dates. Bjorn wandered among the displays; the booth was the size of a store at over 100 square meters stretched along the hangar wall. The salespeople paid him little attention. He stole a glance along the aisle in the direction of the Sirra'Kan. Even though there was a feline aspect to the alien's features, her form resembled a Human female. What was she selling? Whatever it was, two mercenaries in dark camo BDUs and maroon berets were interested.

Bjorn angled for a better view and bumped into a large metal container. The box stood two and a half meters tall and was nearly two meters on a side. One entire side was a hatch. The sign in front of the container read CASPer Coffin.

"What's got your interest, Trip?" Bjorn was grateful his father hadn't spotted him moments earlier trying to check out the Sirra'Kan booth model.

"It's our CASPer Coffin," Mr. Tejedor said, following Bjorn's father.

"Could you have picked a worse name?" Bjorn's father asked.

Mr. Tejedor shrugged. "Maybe. I told them it was awful, but someone higher than me is a big fan of alliteration. I lobbied to call it the CASPer Vault."

Bjorn's father regarded the container skeptically. "I'll bite. What's the big deal?"

"These are CASPer transport containers. They are designed to be handled by heavy loaders." The salesman pointed to the lift brackets. "The cradles inside include connections for power and diagnostics. They have Galactic Union standard data ports and heavy power ports, as well as attachment points for standard cargo brackets and cargo straps."

"It would be a pain to get the CASPer into it," Bjorn's father remarked.

Bjorn peeked down the aisle. The Sirra'Kan was waving at some passing attendees with her tail.

"Not at all. It has a standard maintenance cradle. Let me pop this open." Mr. Tejedor tugged on the handle. "Damn it, they keep pulling out the leverage bar. It's design to be opened by a CASPer or with a bar through the handle. An industrial spanner or a prybar will work as well."

"Maybe I can open it," Bjorn suggested, flexing his left arm.

Mr. Tejedor chuckled. "You're a good-sized fellow, but you can't muscle it open by the handle."

"How much you want to bet?" Bjorn's father's beard couldn't conceal his broad grin.

Mr. Tejedor pushed up his glasses. "If your son can open the CASPer Coffin without any help, I'll include what's inside if you buy a platoon's worth."

"My outfit runs twenty-five CASPers in a platoon," Bjorn's father replied. "What's the list price?"

"We sell them for two thousand credits each," Mr. Tejedor replied. "If your son can't open it without using any sort of tool, you'll buy a platoon's worth at list price."

"Sounds like I'm on the hook for fifty thousand credits either way." Bjorn's father nodded. "All right, it's a bet. Trip, if you get this thing open, I'll take you back to the Te'Warri booth to get your picture taken with the cat-girl you're pretending not to check out."

"For the record, I wasn't staring." Bjorn stepped to the CASPer Coffin. A social media picture with a hot alien might tweak the nose of a person or two. He pushed the petty thought aside and focused on the task at hand. Bjorn grabbed the handle of the CASPer Coffin with his left hand and braced his elbow against the metal container. The servos in his cybernetic arm whirred as Bjorn laboriously pulled out the handle. A loud metallic clank reverberated through the container and the hatch swung open to reveal a CASPer.

"Son of a—I hope I don't lose my job." Mr. Tejedor's eyes went from the CASPer to Bjorn. "What are you feeding your kid?"

"Red meat," Bjorn's father replied. "Is that a real CASPer or some sort of mock-up?"

"It's real, but stripped-down," Mr. Tejedor replied. "It doesn't have any of the higher order electronics. Those were fried under its previous owner. Still, it set us back fifty thousand credits. My boss is going to kill me."

"Maybe he'll take heart in that you sold a quarter million credits worth of laser shields," Bjorn's father remarked. "If they perform as advertised, I'll be buying more."

"I hope so," Mr. Tejedor said. "Don't forget about our Coolflex haptic suits. They keep your troopers cool, so they aren't distracted by the heat and dehydrated from sweating."

"We'll see how the six work out. I'm a bit concerned you top out at a 3x." Bjorn's father thumped his chest. "Don't fall for the Mk 8 bullshit. Us big boys need to be able to squeeze into our suits."

"We could investigate accommodating larger sizes should the need and business arise," Mr. Tejedor stated. "I can't imagine a Mk 8 would work for your son, especially if he's not done growing."

"The way he eats? Not a chance." Bjorn's father chuckled. "Come on, Trip. I bet I can convince your cat-girl to give you a picture to make a certain someone jealous."

*****

Chapter Eighteen

Tovesson Family Lodge, Alaska

"It's not out there."

Bjorn turned away from the bay window overlooking the wooded mountain slope. "What's not out there?"

"The bear," his grandfather said. "You've been here a week, but you haven't step foot out of the yard."

Bjorn's hand drifted to the bear claw necklace. "Our closest neighbor is a three-hour hike. The closest village is an hour and a half driving on a track carved through the forest. There's not much reason to go traipsing through the woods."

"It never stopped you before."

"You think I'm afraid, *Afi*?" Bjorn released the claws.

His grandfather shrugged. "It would stand to sense. I know I would be."

Bjorn snorted. "You've fought more battles than I've played football games. You've fought Besquith and Oogar—I doubt a grizzly would scare you."

"Buttoned up in a CASPer, no." The corners of *Afi*'s white beard rose. "If I ran into one with only meat and bone, then I would wet myself."

Bjorn shook his head. "I doubt it."

"The bear took a lot from you," the old man said. "If you're not afraid, you must be furious. Football, college, your girlfriend, your friends—all gone because of a *helvítis bjorn.* It's ironic your life was wrecked by our namesake."

"I hadn't thought about it. I was too busy watching my world crumble to think about semantics and linguistics," Bjorn replied dryly. His grandfather was in his eighties, and Bjorn immediately felt guilty.

"Follow me." Despite his age, Bjorn I was no doddering old man. His grandfather led him through the huge house, past the kitchen where Bjorn's mother and grandmother were pretending not to be preparing a birthday feast for Bjorn's 17th birthday.

Bjorn had originally protested the idea of coming to Alaska on his birthday, but he had no friends to celebrate with back home. If nothing else, being in Las Cruces for his birthday would rub salt in the wound.

Bjorn froze in the doorway to his grandfather's den. A huge bearskin rug sprawled on the floor. Bjorn still had nightmares followed by sweats from the attack. "Is that…?"

Afi turned and followed Bjorn's gaze. "No. It's not the bear you killed. I have the hide if you want it someday, but I wouldn't spring it on you. This rug has been here for years. You saw it the last time you were here."

Bjorn hadn't paid it much mind before. It was an odd decoration as opposed to the avatar of ruining his life. He edged around the pelt. Other hunting trophies decorated the room, but at least there were no Besquith heads on the walls or stuffed Flatars in the corner.

"I thought if I gave this to you now, it might avoid a confrontation with your mother. Since Junior is out on a contract, I can't count on his support." *Afi* placed a large case on his antique wooden desk.

At first glance, Bjorn took it for a guitar case, but the shape was wrong. *Afi* flipped the clasps and opened the case. A double-headed battle-axe rested on the velvet lining.

"I had this axe made fifty years ago. The blade is a hardened molybdenum-titanium alloy, and the handle has a carbon-fiber core." Bjorn's grandfather lifted the weapon and held it out to Bjorn.

"These runes spell our name, right?" Runes decorated the blade near the haft. While Bjorn could speak Icelandic, he had never studied the ancient runic alphabet. The B and R were recognizable. Bjorn accepted the weapon—his grandfather hadn't struggled despite its impressive weight. Bjorn turned the axe over and examined the blade. Several faint scratches marred the surface, despite the metal's toughness. CASPer blades were made of the same alloy.

"I killed my first Besquith with this axe," *Afi* boasted, a smile lifting his silver beard. "A couple of werewolves jumped us when we were..."

Bjorn let his grandfather spin the tale. He'd heard it a dozen times and knew when to nod and appear impressed. Bjorn experimentally hefted the weapon in his cybernetic arm. Numbers scrolled across his pinview—mass, dimensions, striking edge, center of balance.

Weapon profile compiling.

Bjorn carefully "typed" a query in his pinview, so as not to interrupt *Afi*'s story. He was getting to the point where one of the Besquith killed his best friend in the platoon.

Does this mean I can wield the axe now?

You will still need to learn how to use the weapon. Systems are optimized to assist but cannot replace training.

"...and I drove the axe into the werewolf's open maw. I made his smile even bigger!" His grandfather laughed, and Bjorn chuckled along. "Some are going to tell you a double-bladed axe is an inefficient weapon, and you'll get more chopping power with a single-edged axe. Tell it to the Besquith running up behind me! When I yanked the axe free, it smacked him right in the snout. The blade buried fifteen centimeters into his sinuses. A single-edged axe would have thumped him, but he would have still been standing and as mad as an Oogar."

"I'll take good care of it, *Afi*."

"I know you don't want to be a mercenary, but you should learn how to fight with the axe." *Afi* pointed at Bjorn's left arm. "It may help you master your gift from Tyr."

Tyr was the Norse god who allowed the dread wolf Fenris to bite off his hand so the beast could be fettered. Bjorn knew the story well but hadn't drawn a parallel to his own situation. "*Afi*, Tyr willingly sacrificed his hand. I was mauled by a bear."

His grandfather gave a dismissive snort. "Maybe the gods have a different plan for you. Did you ever think about that?"

Bjorn raised his cybernetic hand. "If this is their way of giving me a hint, then the gods are jerks."

"If you've read the *Edda*—the old stories and poems—you know you are right. The gods, and the Norns, move in mysterious ways and can be assholes. Of course, you might have gotten unlucky and merely stumbled across a ticked off bear, but I prefer my version."

Bjorn carefully replaced the axe in the case. Since his grandfather had retired, he'd become more vested in the Ásatrú religion and the old Norse legends. "Good thing I'm not flying commercial."

Afi poked Bjorn in the chest. "Remember what I said. Learn how to wield your Nafnøx and let it make you stronger."

"Nafnøx—Name-Axe?" Bjorn had to rely on his own memory rather than the pinplants.

"Calling it *Björnøx* would have been a bit on the nose," his grandfather replied. He clicked shut the lid of the case. "Your *Amma* has been glaring down the hall for a couple of minutes. They must be waiting to surprise you with your birthday cake. Later, we'll come back here, and I'll pour you some brennivín. A glass will make my stories easier to swallow. Now come along."

* * *

"Your grandfather didn't give you another gun, did he?" Bjorn's mother asked.

Bjorn shook his head and immediately regretted it as his brennivín-inflamed brain bounced around inside his skull. He vowed to never drink the unsweetened Icelandic schnapps again. "No. He gave me a trophy from his merc days. It's not a gun, or a laser, or anything that can shoot."

"Okay. I'm not a fan of that huge pistol he gave you a couple years ago, and the last thing you need is another gun."

The huge pistol had saved his life, but Bjorn didn't feel up to arguing the point. A VTOL flyer idled on the landing pad behind *Afi*'s garage. What would be worse—the high-pitched shriek of the VTOL in flight or the ballistic sub-orbital that would convey them from Anchorage to Houston? Bjorn's skull throbbed at the prospect. He didn't want to pile on an argument with his mother. Instead he wordlessly lugged their baggage to the waiting craft.

"Remember what I said," *Afi* chided, bright-eyed despite the three glasses of brennivín last night. "Nafnøx will make you stronger if you let it."

"I'll remember," Bjorn promised. If nothing else, the heavy weapon would provide a good work-out.

Bjorn's grandfather turned to Bjorn's mother. "Lynn, it's always a pleasure."

"Be sure to keep our boys in line," Bjorn's grandmother added.

* * *

The sub-orbital was worse. The screaming turbines of the VTOL made his head pound, despite the noise-dampening earphones. The thunderous ascent on the sub-orbital hammered at his skull, and during the few minutes of micro-gravity at the apogee of the flight, Bjorn fought to keep down what little he'd eaten for breakfast. His mother watched worriedly as he clutched a bag in case he lost the battle with his stomach.

"Trip, are you okay?"

Bjorn nodded and replied through clenched teeth. "I guess…something I ate…is disagreeing with me." The nausea was almost enough to distract him from his aching head. Never again would he drink brennivín. He must have made the promise twenty times during the trip.

By the time they boarded a Bjorn's Berserkers' VTOL for the flight from the Houston starport to Las Cruces, Bjorn wavered between numbness and sullen misery. The pilot wasn't gentle—either she was a rookie, or she knew her passenger's state and gleefully added to his suffering. Bjorn's stomach lurched every time the VTOL weaved and bobbed. Was the pilot practicing combat maneuvers?

They reached home, and Bjorn finished unloading the last of the luggage moments before the VTOL shrieked into the sky to return to Bear Town. Once the craft disappeared into the distance, Bjorn's headache subsided to a dull throb. He wanted to go into his room, close the blinds, and lie down.

"Still feeling the aftereffects of your grandfather's war stories?" Bjorn's mother asked as he set the last of her bags on the floor. He still had to drag his luggage upstairs to his room.

"Something like that," Bjorn replied, grabbing a duffle and the case containing the axe.

"Remember it the next time your grandfather, or anyone else, offers you something to drink." Of course she knew. "I'm not going to ground you—it was with family. Don't think it gives you carte blanche to drink."

"The last thing I want now is anything to do with alcohol."

"Good," his mother said. "Drink plenty of water and get some rest. You only have two days before school starts."

"Right." As if Bjorn wasn't miserable enough, he'd been sentenced to Rio Grande High. New school, no friends, and classmates who would hate him—maybe he should have stayed in Alaska.

*****

Chapter Nineteen

Las Cruces, New Mexico

"What a dump," Bjorn muttered. The school had been built twenty years after First Contact, but before the boom of mercenary money pouring into government coffers. When it was originally built, the 3-story school had been utilitarian. Eighty years later, the best adjective Bjorn could think of was grungy. Mesilla Prep had been scoured stone and gleaming metal. Rio Grande High School was dingy concrete and rust-stained steel.

The autocar whirred away, and Bjorn hiked down the block toward the school. He could smell the school's namesake less than 200 yards away, the trickle of the Rio Grande obscured by a levee. Hopefully no one had seen him climb out of the family autocar—it would mark him as coming from a well-off family and put a target on his back.

Bjorn joined the queue to pass through the metal detectors. He patted the card in his vest pocket for the fifth time. Mesilla Prep had security, but it was both high-tech and less obtrusive. The security at the entrance to RGHS would have appeared at home in a century-old picture from airports.

Bjorn set his bag on the conveyor and stepped through the metal detector. Lights flashed and a klaxon sounded. The students froze, their eyes zeroing in on Bjorn. Three guards gathered in front of Bjorn. One, the youngest, dipped his hand to his holstered taser.

"Freeze!" Another guard shouted. One of her hands rested on the butt of a stun baton.

Bjorn drew a calming breath. "I have a prosthetic arm. I am holding my medical card in my right hand. Can I show you my card?"

"Don't move!" The young guard unsnapped the strap holding his taser in its holster. "If you move, I'll taze you!"

Bjorn bit back a retort. He wasn't eager to be tazed again, and even though Bjorn was certain he could thrash the pasty-skinned man close to half his mass, he didn't want to get kicked out of another school.

"If I can't show you my medical card, someone is going to have to come and take it," Bjorn stated. Deep, slow breaths. No one seemed eager to get in his reach. "Maybe I could set it on the—"

The young guard ripped his taser out of the holster. "We said don't move!"

Bjorn muttered a few choice oaths in Icelandic.

"What's going on?" Another security guard muscled his way through the throng. This one was older, with a weather-beaten face the color of tanned leather.

"Sergeant Arroyo, this student set off the detectors," the female guard replied. "The field strength indicated a significant mass."

"Sergeant, I have a prosthetic arm. I'm holding my medical card, but everyone seems afraid to come close enough to check it." Bjorn waved the card slightly, hoping it didn't provoke Pale-Boy to taze him.

Arroyo stepped toe-to-toe with Bjorn, holding his gaze. The sergeant asked, "Are you trying to be funny, *muchacho*?"

"No sir. We seem to be at a stand-off, and I'd rather get to class than get tazed."

Arroyo took the card and scanned it. "Give me a wand. Mathers, put away your *maldita* taser before I zap you with it."

The woman handed Arroyo a device that resembled a curling iron. Arroyo waved it along Bjorn's cybernetic limb. The device squealed until Arroyo swept it to Bjorn's other arm. After the device was silent during passes over Bjorn's legs and torso, Arroyo handed the wand back.

"You're new here?" Arroyo asked.

Bjorn nodded. "Yes, sir. I'm supposed to report to the administrative office before first period."

Arroyo returned the card. "How'd you lose the arm?"

"A bear."

"No shit?"

"Nope. A bear mauled me in Alaska," Bjorn replied.

"He only got your arm?" Arroyo asked.

"Yes, sir. I blew his brains out before he could chew up the rest of me."

Arroyo laughed, deepening the wrinkles in his face. "*Muy bueno.* The office is to the right. Let's get these lines moving folks! *Vamanos!*"

* * *

"Mr. Tovesson, as I've already discussed with your parents, we don't need any more troublemakers." Principal Figueroa stared out the small barred window overlooking the front of the school. "You may be used to certain…indulgences your family's wealth and status provides, but I assure you they gain you no favors here."

If his family had so much pull, he wouldn't even be here. The principal wouldn't appreciate Bjorn's candor. "I want to keep my head down and finish out my senior year."

"I like your attitude," the principal said. "If you hold on to it, we won't have any problems. Good luck, Mr. Tovesson."

* * *

Bjorn's luck lasted until lunch. The morning classes had been uneventful. The teachers assigned seating based on names or student ID numbers, so there was no drama of the "you're in my seat variety." Once Bjorn stepped into the cafeteria, he might as well have been in the Wild West. There was no rhyme or reason to how cliques were distributed among the tables.

Once he emerged from the lunch line—his tray laden with vat-meat and wilted vegetables—Bjorn scanned the room. He spied an empty table and bee-lined for it. The less he had to interact with people, the better.

Bjorn was halfway through his lunch when a handful of seniors and juniors gathered around him. One of them reminded Bjorn of the pale security guard with the taser.

"You're at our table."

"There's plenty of space," Bjorn said. "Have a seat."

"I said this is our table." The alpha of the bunch loomed over Bjorn.

"Well, I'm new here, and there's nothing marking this table. There's no reason you can't sit and eat your lunch, unless you need to prove how little your manhood is by picking on the new guy."

Chuckles mingled with the muttering. Alpha puffed his chest, such as it was. "Do you know who I am?"

"I don't care," Bjorn replied. "I want to eat my lunch and get on with the day."

"I'm Mitch Brackin."

"Nice to meet you. I'm Bjorn." How much lunch could he wolf down before one of them tried to dump what's left over his head? His pinplants highlighted each member of the gang and initiated queries of social media and other Aethernet sources. "So, are we done with posturing, or is this part where one of you tries to grab my milk and pour it over my head? It may have been funny in the old-time videos, but it's pretty played out."

"You think you're a tough guy?" Mitch demanded. A couple of his cronies chuckled.

Bjorn gulped the remainder of his milk. "In fact, I do. Unlike you, I don't need to prove it. Your buddies already know how tough you are and, frankly, I don't think it's worth whatever they hand out as punishment around here for fighting."

"Aw, he's afraid of getting in trouble," Mitch mocked. Cue the laugh track from his squad. "All right, New Guy. I'll be waiting for you off school property. We'll see how tough you are. Come on, let's go chase the Pony Boys off their table."

"*Hombre*, you must have some *cojones* on you."

Bjorn glanced up from the last scraps of his meal. Two Hispanic teenagers stood at his table holding lunch trays. "Last time I checked."

"I'm Tomas Garcia, and this is my cousin Grace. Can we sit with you?"

"It's a free country," Bjorn replied. Grace caught his eye. She was cute. He pushed the thought aside. The first day of school, and he already had an after-class fight with the local bully. The last thing he needed was to add drama. "I'm Bjorn."

"You're new here," Grace said as she sat across from Bjorn. "I would remember someone as big as you."

Could his pinplants suppress a blush?

No.

"This is my first day. I transferred from Mesilla Prep."

Several seconds of silence hung over the table before Grace broke it. "A bad boy?"

Tomas coughed. "If it's cool to ask—what did you do to get booted to public?"

"Nothing badass. I had a…bit of a meltdown, punched a locker, and yelled at a security guard when he tazed me."

"*Hombre*, we call that Tuesday. They kicked you out? I knew the private schools were uptight, but that is *loco*." Tomas dug into his vat-meat.

"The guard tazed you and you yelled at him?" Grace was ignoring her meal.

Bjorn shrugged. Was there something wrong with the air conditioning in the cafeteria? It felt warm, especially when he caught Grace studying him. "It's not as impressive as it sounds, and unfortunately for me, it was a viral video. The school didn't want the public relations black eye of letting me go unpunished, so here I am."

"What's this? Fresh meat on the first day?" A new arrival plunked her tray on the table. "Grace, did you pick up a stray over summer and not tell us?"

"No, we met him five minutes ago," Grace replied. "I haven't picked him up…yet. Bjorn this is Aisha, and the quiet blonde is her girlfriend Amy."

"Smooth girl, you took me off the board right away," Aisha remarked. "Lucky for her, I'm taken. When I fancy boys, I prefer them big and brawny, and you fit the bill. Tell me you're on the football team."

A lump formed in the pit of Bjorn's stomach. "I can't play sports. I'm not allowed."

"Why is there a new person at our table?" a dark-skinned boy demanded, pointing at Bjorn. He was every bit as tall as Bjorn, but slender as a rail. "You know I don't deal well with change. It's bad enough half our clique graduated. Why didn't anyone warn me there was—crap! Why are you sitting with the enemy?"

"What are you talking about, Larcell?" Tomas asked.

"Why are you sitting with Bjorn Tovesson, the quarterback for the Mesilla Prep Panthers?" Larcell pointed a long finger at Bjorn. "He knocked us out of sectionals last year."

"I had help," Bjorn protested. "It wasn't as though I played by myself."

"Bull! You tore our defense apart like wrapping paper on Christmas." Larcell set his tray down. "It was the worst beating since the Alpha Contracts!"

"I remember that game," Grace said. She gazed at Bjorn through her lashes. "That was you? You were amazing."

The air conditioning was definitely on the fritz.

"My *prima* is a big fan of football, or should I say football players," Tomas remarked. "I think you made her boyfriend cry."

"My *ex*-boyfriend."

"They broke up after prom," Aisha added. "The jerk had his side girl at the dance. Can you believe it? I'm surprised she still has the hots for football players."

Grace gave Bjorn a smile before pursing her lips around the straw in her milk.

"Too bad I don't play football anymore," Bjorn said, tearing his eyes away.

"Are you crazy?" Heads at adjoining tables turned at Larcell's cry. "How can you not play football?"

"The prosthesis," Amy interjected, her voice low. "His prosthetic arm disqualifies him."

"What?" Tomas looked from Amy to Bjorn.

"She's right," Bjorn said. She must have been at the entrance this morning. "I have a prosthetic arm. It's why I can't play sports anymore."

"So that's how you whipped our butts," Larcell accused. "A bionic throwing arm!"

"No, I lost my arm after the football season," Bjorn retorted. "I was all flesh-and-blood when I kicked your butt."

"How did you lose your arm?" Aisha asked.

"A Kodiak bear shredded it," Bjorn replied, fighting to keep his voice even. "Everything below my left shoulder is hardware now."

"How did you survive?" Tomas asked.

"I blew the bear's brains out."

* * *

"So you don't take the bus?" Grace and Tomas fell into step with Bjorn as he headed south. He'd given the autocar instructions to pick him up three blocks south of school.

"Not if I can help it," Bjorn replied. "Even if I walked the whole way home, it would be quicker than taking the school bus."

"We live in the housing block a half mile south of here," Tomas said. Bjorn was familiar with the complex. His family was among the well-to-do who had protested the housing projects would drive down property values in the area.

"I live a bit further." Would they judge him when the autocar pulled up? Maybe it wouldn't be there and he could gracefully part ways. At least it wasn't Tuesday or Thursday, when someone from the Berserkers was supposed to pick him up and take him to Bear Town. "I could walk the whole way home if necessary."

"I guessed right." Mitch and a half dozen cronies ambled out of an alley into Bjorn's path. "I thought you might come this way. This isn't your lucky day, New Guy."

Bjorn shrugged off his backpack. He could see the family autocar idling half a block beyond Mitch and his cronies. "You know, I hoped my first day at a new school wouldn't be so cliché as to face off with the school bully."

"You mean getting your butt kicked by the Big Man On Campus," Mitch countered, cracking his knuckles and flexing.

"If you're dead set, let's do this." Bjorn gauged his opponent. Mitch was ten centimeters shorter and 40 kilograms lighter. However, Bjorn bet Mitch had street fighting experience beyond the MST self-defense courses.

Bjorn assumed the standard defensive stance taught in Mercenary Service Track self-defense courses. A feral grin spread across Mitch's face.

"You brought this on yourself, New Guy." Mitch feinted into the first step of an MST self-defense drill but changed up his attack at the last minute.

The spin kick caught Bjorn off guard. Even though Mitch's heel only clipped his head, Bjorn staggered back a step seeing stars. Mitch pressed his advantage, throwing a reverse punch-snap kick combo. Great, in addition to street fighting, his opponent was into martial arts. The punch caught Bjorn in the ribs as he swept aside Mitch's foot.

Bjorn stepped into his opponent, smothering the next kick. Mitch jabbed an elbow strike into the sore spot left by his punch. Bjorn had squandered the advantage of his reach. He could hear Eddings chiding him for being so sloppy.

"Not so tough now, are you New—"

Bjorn planted his left hand on Mitch's chest, braced his feet as though he was on the football line, and shoved. Mitch's arms pin-wheeled as he fought to keep his balance. To his credit, Mitch stayed upright, but before he could recover, Bjorn plowed into him with a linebacker charge. This time Mitch hit the pavement.

Mitch rolled to his feet as Bjorn closed the gap. The same trick wouldn't work twice, and kicking was an invitation for Bjorn to end up on his ass. Mitch ducked a right jab and spun out of Bjorn's reach.

"All right, big guy, you've got some moves." Mitch bounced on the balls of his feet, his arms in a loose guard position. He feinted to gauge Bjorn's reaction. "Tell you what—ditch these fence-hoppers, and you can hang with us."

Bjorn recognized the decades-old pejorative. "Screw you." Bjorn dropped his fighting stance. "I'm not hanging with a bunch of bullies."

"Can't say I didn't give you a chance," Mitch said. He lunged forward in a knife hand-kick combo.

Bjorn snagged Mitch's wrist while his fingertips were ten centimeters from Bjorn's Adam's apple. Bjorn twisted so the follow up kick caught him on the hip instead of the crotch. Bjorn locked the grip on his cybernetic hand clutching Mitch's wrist. Mitch tried to wrench his hand free, to no avail.

Bjorn slammed his right fist into Mitch's gut and again below his solar plexus. Even though it was his organic fist, the strikes landed like hammer-blows. One more punch crashed into Mitch's jaw, and Bjorn released his opponent. Mitch staggered backward and collapsed onto the sidewalk.

Bjorn retrieved his backpack. "When he can see straight, tell him to stay away from me," Bjorn commanded. Hopefully that would be the end of it.

"*Hombre*, I think you're in for a world of hurt," Tomas muttered. They sidled past Mitch's cronies, who tended to their fallen alpha.

Bjorn shrugged. "I kicked his butt, but it's not as though I supplanted him in his gang. I'll be happy if they leave me alone."

Bjorn slowed as they approached the waiting autocar. "This is my ride."

Tomas whistled. "What does your family do? This is last year's luxury utility vehicle."

"Typical—judging someone based on his ride," Grace scoffed.

His mother was using her car, so he'd used his father's LUV. "My family is in the mercenary business," Bjorn replied.

"Dios Mio!" Tomas slapped his hands together. "Why didn't I make the connection? You're part of the Berserker family!"

"The family name is Tovesson, but yeah, you're right. My family owns Bjorn's Berserkers, named after my grandfather."

Grace held out her phone. "For the record, I was already going to give you my number before I found out you were from a merc family."

*****

Chapter Twenty

Bear Town, New Mexico

Axe arched an eyebrow as Bjorn approached. "What happened to you? I thought Eddings and Wick were out on contract?"

"Oh, you know, the typical first day at a new school; run afoul of the local bully and get in a fight." Bjorn set the heavy case down.

"Don't tell me you got kicked out on the first day," Axe lamented. "Your dad will be angrier than a shaved Oogar."

"No. It was off school property, and before you ask, no, I didn't pop him with my left hook."

Axe shook his head. "You couldn't keep your head down and stay out of trouble?"

"Trouble found me!" Bjorn protested. His slate chimed with an incoming message. Grace's avatar popped up in his pinview, followed by a selfie.

"You okay? You're a little flush. Did the school find out about your brawl?" Axe asked.

Bjorn shook his head and shoved the images out of his pinview. "It's a message from someone I met today."

Image saved.

"Would someone happen to be a girl?" A broad grin spread across Axe's face. "Good for you, kid. It's about time you quit moping over the cheerleader."

"It's nothing…I just met her…"

"Fine. I'll change the subject." Axe pointed to the case. "What do you have there?"

Bjorn squatted and popped open the case to reveal Nafnøx. "You talked about fighting with archaic weapons. I'm hoping you can help me learn to use this." He lifted the axe out and stood.

"Wow. That is a serious hunk of metal," Axe remarked.

"Hey, Sergeant Silver, we got the last CASPer back in its cradle. Are we good to—" The technician froze when he saw the axe. "Whoa, that's awesome. Is it some sort of CASPer weapon?"

"It's too small for a CASPer," Bjorn replied.

"I guess you're right," the technician admitted, studying the axe. "If you blew it up 100 percent in all dimensions, it would be big enough."

"It would be eight times heavier," Axe remarked.

"It wouldn't be a problem for a CASPer," the technician countered. "In fact, you'd need the extra mass to transfer enough kinetic energy to the target to make it worthwhile. Anyway, we finished with BB059. Can we knock off for the day?"

"Go ahead." Axe eyed Nafnøx. "Why do you want to wield such an impractical weapon?"

Bjorn hefted the axe. "First: Bjorn the First gave it to me; it's a family heirloom. Two: I thought it might be good exercise and training for my bionic arm. Third: how many people wield axes?"

"Fine. Let's go to the practice yard."

Bjorn followed Axel Silver around the main garage. The yard next to the crude softball diamond was littered with relics from Bjorn's physical therapy. A pitching net, a football target, and a handful of bats leaned against the building.

Axe paused in the shade cast by the garage. "I don't suppose your granddad taught you anything?"

"Only not to drink Icelandic schnapps," Bjorn replied.

"Not germane to what we are doing," Axe said. "I'm good with swords and the quarterstaff. I didn't mess with axes or polearms much. Your heirloom isn't even historical—there's no evidence for double-bladed axes in antiquity."

"I don't care about history. Can you teach me to fight with this weapon?" Bjorn asked.

"Sure. It's not as practical as a CASPer blade, not to mention the hand cannon you call a sidearm," Axe replied. "I think it's unwieldly and inefficient, but I'll concede it'll give your cybernetic arm a work-out. It will take a lot of effort to control."

"Let's get started." Bjorn set his pinplants to record. He squelched incoming messages from his slate. The last thing he needed was another picture of Grace appearing while he was swinging a six-kilogram axe around.

An hour later, sweat soaked Bjorn's work-out clothes.

"I bet you thought your arm would take up most of the slack." Axe grinned. "Swinging around a heavy weapon takes your whole body. Your artificial arm gives you more control—normally you sacrifice accuracy for power because your wrist and elbow can only do so much."

"Sometimes I felt as though I had to fight it," Bjorn remarked, wiping his brow.

"A heavy weapon has more inertia, so it takes more energy to redirect or stop it." He pulled a fencing rapier out of a time-worn golf bag. "A lighter blade is easier for parrying and recovering from misses. Once you swing your beast, you're committed. Even as strong as you are, it will never be good for defending."

"It's not as though you could parry a battle-axe with a rapier," Bjorn countered. "Even if you could hold the sword against the blow, your blade would snap."

"I would get out of the way of your swing and stab you before you could bring the axe around to defend yourself."

"Oh, good, you're still going at it." The technician had returned with an ElSha following him.

"We were finishing up, Wathen," Axe said.

Wathen jerked a thumb toward the ElSha. "Egg and I were talking about B-Three's axe and the application as a CASPer weapon."

The ElSha nodded. The insignia on the small reptilian alien's equipment harness marked him as a technical contractor and his nametape read Egk. "While I contend such a weapon would be inefficient compared to a CASPer blade, it makes for a challenging thought exercise."

Axe shook his head. "Good thing you're wasting your off-duty time with this nonsense."

"Could we examine the weapon?" Egg asked.

"Sure." Bjorn held the axe out.

The ElSha rotated one of its eyes toward Wathen. "Collect Tri-V images so we can create a virtual reconstruction. What is the metal?"

"My grandfather said it was a titanium-molybdenum alloy, the same as CASPer blades," Bjorn replied. He opened his hands and balanced Nafnøx across his palms. "The handle has an artificial core of titanium and carbon-fiber."

"Is it true you won a CASPer?" Wathen asked while he passed a ruggedized Tri-V camera over the axe.

"I guess. My father bet a vendor I could open one of those CASPer vaults without a pry bar. It's a stripped-down demonstrator model. I don't even know what happened to it. It's not as though I'm ever going to use it."

BTI: CASPer BBXX3—designated user—Bjorn Tovesson III—Location: Houston Logistics Depot.

"Please rotate the weapon 90 degrees," the ElSha asked. "The symmetry will make it easier to model."

"How much does it weigh?" Wathen slowly moved the camera over the axe head.

5,893 grams.

Bjorn repeated his pinplant's estimate. "Do you want to put it on a scale?"

"This data should suffice," Egg said. "We can extrapolate the mass of the axe head by its volume and composition."

"Think we can make it for a CASPer?" Wathen put away the camera.

"Of course we can make it," Egg replied. "The question is whether it will be functional. The haft will be a challenge."

"Remember you two—no working on this 'experiment' while on duty," Axe chided.

"Of course not, Sergeant Silver," the ElSha said.

"Waste of time," Axe remarked. "Kid, you should get a move on if you want to clean up and hit the mess hall before it goes to self-serve."

Bjorn returned Nafnøx to its case and checked the time. With school dominating so much of his day, it meant he was having to cut back and shuffle his usual routine around. Plus, he still had homework after he got home. At least he still had his office and access to the shower in Bjarnarsal.

* * *

"Trip, did you have a good first day?" his mother called before he shrugged off his backpack.

"It was fine, Mom," Bjorn replied. He'd eaten at Bear Town, but he wouldn't mind a few leftovers to nibble on while he did his homework. Homework on the first day! Sure, it was only two chapters spread across two subjects, but the principle galled him.

His mother rounded the corner as he surfaced from the refrigerator with leftovers from two meals. "Someone had a rough day in after-school PT," his mother remarked. "Does Private Eddings use a step-stool?"

"She normally has me spar with her boyfriend," Bjorn replied. His mother had noticed the bruise from Mitch's first kick. He needed to distract her. "I made some friends at school. I met a girl."

His mother whirled from the coffeemaker. "Oh?"

"Her name is Grace." He couldn't exactly tell his mother Grace was hot. "She's really cool, and she follows sports."

"Good. I was hoping you'd meet someone." The "to take your mind off Heather" remained unspoken. "How did you meet?"

"Lunch. I sat with her, her cousin, and some of their friends," Bjorn replied. "One of them recognized me from the Panthers."

"Will it be a problem?"

Bjorn shook his head. "No. None of them are on the football team."

"Did you have any trouble?" his mother asked. Had she heard about the scuffle with Mitch?

"I set off the metal detectors, and security freaked out until their sergeant arrived and checked my medical card," Bjorn replied as he doled leftovers onto a plate. "The principal gave me the 'stay out of trouble' lecture."

"So when am I going to meet Grace?"

"I only met her today," Bjorn said. He returned what remained of the leftovers to the fridge. "Let's see where this goes. We might turn out to have nothing in common."

Another message silently pinged his slate and passed to his pin-plants. Grace's avatar appeared, followed by another selfie captioned good night.

Image saved.

"We'll see where it goes," Bjorn repeated as he hurried from the kitchen.

* * * * *

Chapter Twenty-One

Las Cruces, New Mexico

"Form up! For those of you who are new here, I am MST Sergeant Kimble. My comrades call me Snake. You will address me as Sergeant Kimble! Is that clear, you little pukes?" The Mercenary Service Track trainer stalked along the line of high school seniors. A tattoo of a snake wound its way around the sergeant's bicep.

They were in preparations to take their Voluntary Off-world Assessment exams. The battery of tests would generate scores used by potential mercenary employers to gauge their prospects. They wouldn't be a big deal since Bjorn had no intention of becoming a mercenary. However, if he couldn't play sports, the competitive voice in his mind urged him to get as good a score as possible.

"Am I boring you, newbie?" Sergeant Kimble shouted in Bjorn's face.

"No, Sergeant!" Bjorn responded. *What was the sergeant saying?*

"Your slack-jawed drooling says otherwise, newbie. What did I just say?" Sergeant Kimble demanded.

"The days alternate on a weekly basis, Sergeant." Thank Odin for his pinplants. "This week is Tuesday and Thursday, next week is Monday, Wednesday, and Friday."

Sergeant Kimble stepped back, still glaring. "You look familiar. What's your name?"

Bjorn suppressed a gulp. "Bjorn Tovesson the Third."

"You're from Mesilla Prep, aren't you? You're the quarterback who had a meltdown and got kicked out of private school. Well, welcome to the real world, princess. I don't care if you're the son of a merc commander, and I don't care if you're a varsity all-star. Here, you're another maggot. Got it?"

"Yes, Sergeant."

"You know you fractured two of my little cousin's ribs? He played at Deming High School. I bet you're used to being the big man." The sergeant scrutinized him until a smothered chuckle sounded from down the line. The sergeant's head whipped around. "Does someone think I'm being funny?" Kimble stalked past the teenagers, glowering at them one by one. "Holy crap, what happened to you, Brackin? You fall under a truck?"

"No, Sergeant."

Great, Brackin was in the advanced MST class, along with several of his cronies. Bjorn hadn't spotted anyone he met yesterday, so they were in the much larger intermediary class.

"All right, let's see how fat and lazy you pukes got over the summer. Give me a two-mile run, forty push-ups, then five pull-ups. Once you finish all three, park your butt in the bleachers." Training assistants moved to the area designated for push-ups and the pull-up bars. "If you toss your lunch or call it quits, go to the bench."

Bjorn had rejected throttling back his work-out regimen after the training cadre ended. He still ran and exercised, but he didn't push himself without Sergeant Orr's scrutiny. The hand-to-hand training and workouts with Sergeant Silver helped but didn't cover all of it. At the beginning of summer, the routine Kimble demanded would have been easy.

The two-mile run immediately showed who had sluffed off over the summer. Bjorn wasn't at the lead of the pack, but he didn't want to wind himself and rely on his cybernetic arm. Mitch bumped Bjorn as he ran by. Bjorn ignored him—hopefully he'd only be a jerk where Mitch knew Bjorn couldn't retaliate.

Bjorn finished the run shy of the 14-minute mark. Out of the 40 in his class, seven finished ahead of him, including Mitch. Only one person threw up and another was lamed by a Charlie horse. Bjorn suspected a third didn't make the 15 minute "passing" time, but he didn't stick around to watch.

"Reduce armature power by 50%," Bjorn commanded through his pinplants. A graphic in his pinview displayed the decreased power to the artificial muscles and servos in his prosthetic. He dropped into the proper position and counted off his push-ups. A training assistant recorded the students' progress on a slate linked to a camera.

The push-ups would have been a cakewalk if he wasn't a bit winded from the run, even with the decreased power. He still completed them in under 2 minutes and moved on to the pull-up bars.

"Hey, Sergeant! Tovesson has a fake arm; he's cheating!" Bjorn didn't recognize the voice, but when he spotted the speaker it was one of Mitch's crew.

"Tovesson! Is this right? Are you using a cybernetic arm to cheat?" Sergeant Kimble stomped to face Bjorn. The snake tattoo reared up and bared its fangs—a morphogenic tattoo.

"I've dialed down my prosthetic, Sergeant," Bjorn replied. "I don't need to cheat on PT drills."

"Why should I believe you?" the sergeant demanded.

Bjorn reached and grabbed the pull-up bar with his right arm. He turned so his shoulders were perpendicular to the bar and laboriously hauled his body into the air. Once his right shoulder brushed the bottom of the bar, Bjorn eased himself back to the ground.

"Restore armature power to default levels." The graphic in his pinview displayed 100% power and faded. Bjorn waggled the fingers in his left hand; the servos were barely audible. "My right hand is flesh and blood, my left is metal and plastic."

Kimble's eyes flicked to the bar before returning to Bjorn. "Go sit in the bleachers, Tovesson."

"Yes, Sergeant." Good thing Axe had included strengthening Bjorn's right arm as part of his therapy exercises to keep Bjorn from becoming over-reliant on the cybernetic limb. He hated one-arm pull-ups, but Bjorn had to admit Axe was right when he asked what would happen if something went wrong with Bjorn's prosthesis.

"I bet you think you're hot stuff," Mitch muttered from behind Bjorn. "It's how you beat me yesterday. You used your fake arm."

Bjorn kept his voice low. Even though the training assistants were engaged supervising the other students, Bjorn didn't want to draw their attention or Sergeant Kimble's ire. "If I had beat you with my cybernetic limb, you wouldn't already be back in school. Leave me alone, and I'll do the same."

Mitch snorted, and it was the end of the conversation. If only it would be the end of the nascent feud.

***

Bjorn claimed an empty table and wondered who would arrive first—Mitch and his gang, or Grace and the others. Bjorn propped his slate so the camera could watch behind him and feed the video to his pinplants. Bjorn spotted Mitch and his crew—they held a hurried conference and chose a table on the other side of the cafeteria.

"Hey." Grace claimed the seat across from Bjorn. "Are you doing homework during lunch?"

Bjorn stowed his slate. "Not quite."

"Going through your messages?" She flashed a mischievous grin, reminding him of yesterday's pictures.

Tomas asked, "How are you doing?"

"Did you thrash that loud-mouthed bully Mitch Brackin after school?" Aisha sat next to Bjorn. Amy gave Bjorn a sidelong glance before she sat on the other side of Aisha. "I heard you punched the stuffing out of him."

"I wish I would have recorded it," Grace added. She patted Bjorn's hand. "Brackin needed to be taken down a peg."

Larcell joined in. "Why didn't you tell us there was going to be a rumble? We could have been there. Strictly as moral support—I'm no good in a fight."

"It's not a big deal," Bjorn protested. "It's not nearly as impressive as it sounds. I almost got my clock cleaned by Brackin. I didn't know he was some sort of kung fu black belt."

"When he kicked you upside the head, I thought it was going to be lights out," Tomas admitted between bites of his lunch. "I don't know who was more surprised—you, or him because you were still standing."

"Bjorn kicked his ass." Grace glared at her cousin. "Mitch was the one sprawled on the ground."

Tomas held up his hands in mock surrender. "I'm merely stating the facts."

"He's right," Bjorn interjected. "As much as it galls me to admit, I got cocky. I assumed between my size and my hand-to-hand training he wouldn't be a serious contender. I hope since he got rocked, he'll find someone else to hassle."

"You really are new here," Larcell commented.

* * *

Today the autocar was only half a block from school, barely out of the traffic pattern.

"You brought your ride closer. It's a good call,"

Tomas remarked.

"You guys want a lift?" Bjorn offered as he circled to the driver side door. "If nothing else, if Mitch and his minions are lurking somewhere ahead, they wouldn't be able to hassle you guys in lieu of me."

"Even if it wasn't blazing hot, there's no way I'd say no," Grace replied.

Tomas grabbed the front door. "No way am I riding in the back, *prima.* You're so short, we could put you in the trunk."

Grace stuck out her tongue and uttered something in Spanish Bjorn couldn't make out before relenting and climbing in the back seat.

"Don't take this the wrong way, but I expected the interior to be tricked out," Tomas remarked before reciting his address for the car. "What's the point of a prime ride if you're interior isn't posh?"

"Ask my dad. It's a family car, and he isn't big on frills." Bjorn considered driving on manual, but he would have to pay attention to traffic rather than watch for Mitch and his gang or peak in the rear-view mirror at Grace.

Grace met his eyes in the reflection. "What's the deal with the gnarly necklace?"

Bjorn's hand went to the hammer dangling amid the bear claws. "The claws are from the bear that mauled me. The pendant honors Thor; he gives me strength."

"The big guy with the hammer from the movies?" Tomas asked.

Bjorn shook his head. "I'm not talking about *Mjolnir vs. MinSha.* I'm referring to the Norse God of Thunder."

"For real?" Tomas stifled a laugh. Grace reached over the seat and whacked her cousin on the shoulder. "You're serious. Those are characters from videos and games."

"Dude, don't bag on my faith, and I won't diss your religion," Bjorn said. First Contact threw traditional religions into upheaval when mankind learned they weren't alone in the universe. Atheism flourished, but there was also a resurgence of less formal religions.

Grace interrupted Tomas' rejoinder. "If the bear maimed you, why do you carry around parts of it? Is it some sort of Viking trophy?"

"In part, but it's also to remind me I'm stronger than the bear or the wound he gave me." Bjorn rattled the claws. "He cost me a lot, but I'm alive. He's a rug."

Grace leaned forward. "Really? Do you keep it in your bedroom?"

Sweat broke out on Bjorn's brow. Was there something wrong with the car's air-conditioning?

Tomas sighed and rolled his eyes, then thumped the seat. "Hey, there's Mitch's crew."

There was no sign of Brackin himself, but four of his buddies were milling about in the alley from yesterday. None of the group gave any notice as the autocar rolled past.

"Good thing I had the car pick me up close to school." Bjorn's pinplants highlighted each the teens and captured facial images.

Facial recognition—running.

The car veered east, toward the tower blocks past Mesilla. The federally funded housing towers were only a few blocks from Bjorn's gated community, but until today he'd paid them no mind. As the autocar turned into the tower complex, a multitude of eyes followed it. There were hardly any vehicles in the complex, and the ones Bjorn saw were mostly antiquated.

"Maybe we should have gotten out at the entrance," Tomas muttered.

"It's no big deal," Grace countered. "They'll think it's someone dropping off their *domesticos*."

Tomas huffed and mumbled, "I'm going to be an architect, not some *gringo's* gardener." His eyes flicked to Bjorn. "No offense, man."

"None taken." The car whirred to a halt.

Tomas climbed out and waited while Grace lingered. "So."

"So?" Bjorn echoed. Words evaporated from his vocabulary.

"So when are you going to ask me out?" Grace gave him a mischievous grin.

His schedule appeared in his pinview with his commitments highlighted. "Saturday?"

"You're going to ask me out Saturday?"

Heart rate elevated—aerobic pace achieved.

"No. Ummm…" Bjorn stammered.

Grace mock pouted. "You're not going to ask me out?"

"Yes. I mean…do you want to go out Saturday?" Bjorn asked. Why was it so hard to get the words out?

Grace smiled. "I thought you'd never ask. We can work out the details later. Tomas is getting impatient."

Bjorn watched as Grace followed Tomas into the tower lobby until she disappeared behind an unmanned security station. "Home," Bjorn instructed the car. Should he catch Tomas somewhere and make sure he was okay with Bjorn dating Grace? What would he do if Tomas said no? It wasn't Tomas' business, but Bjorn didn't want to seem disrespectful.

A shout caught Bjorn's attention. A convertible with the top down idled next to Bjorn's car at the traffic light. The occupants were all Hispanic men a few years older than Bjorn and Coahuila Rap blared from the car's speakers. Were they gang-bangers? Had they seen Bjorn and Grace and were rallying to scare off Bjorn? The passenger in the front gestured for Bjorn to lower his window.

"What's up?" Bjorn asked as the window descended.

"Nice ride."

"Thanks?" The light turned green and the convertible turned in the opposite direction.

* * * * *

Chapter Twenty-Two

Bear Town, New Mexico

"What's up, Trip?" Private Burr gave Bjorn's pass a cursory glance.

"Normal kids have sports or drama after school. I come and hang out with a bunch of mercs," Bjorn replied. "You're stuck with the PM gate duty again?"

"Yeah. I overslept and missed a muster for infantry PT," the guard replied. His partner hunkered inside the guard shack and ignored the conversation, engrossed in his phone. "Word has it your old—the commander is on base."

"Hopefully he's been too busy to worry about what I've been doing while he was gone."

Private Burr chuckled and hit the button. "Good luck with that."

Once Bjorn parked the car, he checked his messages. He'd taught his pinplants to hold all but emergency messages while he was driving. A quartet of messages from Grace with pictures of her proposed outfits for their date tomorrow populated his pinview. It was good he wasn't driving.

"Surprise me," Bjorn replied to Grace's query as which one he preferred.

There was a message from Eddings. "Not even 48 hours after I get home? Meet me at the motor pool."

After his run-in with Mitch, Bjorn was eager to resume his hand-to-hand tutelage under Eddings. So eager he hadn't thought to check and see if she was okay after the mission. Eddings had a successful contract under her belt, so Bjorn's tutoring payments would be chump change. Maybe she was going to tell him she didn't need to waste her time with a kid for a handful of credits.

Three rumblers roared past Bjorn as he hiked to the motor pool. Further out in the desert, he could see the six-wheeled vehicles rolling out of dropships. The fourth rumbler, a battle-scarred Casanova, skidded to a halt next to Bjorn.

"Hey, kid, Eddings says to get in!" a woman shouted from the crew hatch. Bjorn clambered into the armored vehicle, and it lurched into motion.

"Get up here, Baby Bear!" Eddings shouted over the whine of electric motors and the crunch of armored wheels over gravel.

Bjorn crawled forward until he could see Eddings in the driver seat. She jerked a thumb toward the vacant commander seat. "Park your butt," Eddings ordered. The Tri-V in front of her displayed the road, though the lower left quadrant flickered.

Bjorn sat and reflexively strapped himself in. "Sorry, I should have waited a couple of days instead of pestering you as soon as you got back."

"What happened to your face?" Eddings asked. She slowed the rumbler as they approached the motor pool yard. A line of rumblers waited ahead of them.

"What's going on?" Bjorn asked.

"The techs are doing triage on the rumblers to figure out which one gets fixed in what order." Eddings pulled back on a handle and the deep *thrum* from the rear of the vehicle diminished. "You didn't answer my question."

"I got into a fight with a jerk from my new school."

Eddings laughed. "Hasn't it only been a week? Please tell me you gave better than you got."

"He caught me off guard at first, but he ended up on his ass," Bjorn said. "I've got the footage on my pinplants, and I can cast it to a slate."

"In other words, you got cocky," Eddings chided. "What did I warn you?"

"Not to assume because I'm bigger and have some merc training I'll automatically be able to kick someone's ass," Bjorn replied. "He's some sort of ninjutsu martial artist."

"Ninjutsu my ass." Eddings threw another lever forward and released her harness. She climbed out of her seat and pulled out her tactical slate. "Dump the video to my slate. I'll watch it while you keep our place in line."

"Wait, what? I can't drive a Casanova."

"You're a commander's kid and you've never driven a rumbler?" Eddings hunched in the cramped space. "Hurry before the line moves."

Bjorn fumbled with his harness then squeezed past Eddings. This was why most rumbler crew members were smaller. He wedged himself into the driver position. The vehicles in front of him were rolling away.

"The red handle will release the parking brake. Use the joystick on the right to drive. The pedal on the floor is the brake." Eddings leaned over his shoulder. "Pretend it's a video game."

Bjorn released the brake, and the rumbler lurched forward. He stomped on the brake when the rumbler ahead of him ground to a halt.

"Keep your foot on the brake and strap in." Eddings pushed away from the back of his seat and clicked her restraints into place. "Watch the rumbler in front of you and take it easy on the brake. Let me know when we're at the front of the line."

Bjorn instructed his pinplants to send the video to Edding's slate. A small window in his pinview mirrored the video but keeping pace with the other vehicles in the line dominated Bjorn's attention. His dad would blow a gasket if he found out Bjorn had crashed a rumbler.

"Yo, Eddings. My teeth are rattling back here," the sysop called from the rear of the vehicle. "You sure it's a good idea to let Baby Bear drive?"

"It'll be fine, Carmen. If he burns up the brakes, we'll chalk it to combat wear." Eddings studied the video, pausing and rewinding it to rewatch portions of the fight. "It's some sort of Hip-Hop-Kido mixed with a middle belt of kickboxing."

"Hip-Hop-What?"

"It's a modern blend of shorin kempo, taekwondo, and aerobics. It's as much for fitness freaks as martial artists." Eddings snorted. "You fell for this kick?"

Bjorn bit back an excuse and focused on bringing the 25-ton rumbler to a gentle stop as the line of vehicles shifted. "Yeah. It nearly took my head off."

"Maybe I should have varied your sparring partners," Eddings murmured, replaying the scene. "Logan doesn't do this jackrabbit crap. Someone does a jump kick on you, knock them on their butt. Okay, good, you got a clue and used your bulk against him. It's how you should handle these bouncy bastards."

"You told me to play to my strengths. I'm big and strong."

"Why aren't you punching his lights out with that sledgehammer you call an arm?" Eddings froze the footage on an image of Bjorn pounding Mitch with his right fist. "One slug could knock half his teeth out."

"No one is going to say boo about a couple of high school punks duking it out. If I cave his head in with my cybernetic fist, it might be enough to draw some police attention, especially if some of the local law enforcement have a beef with mercenaries because we're 'above the law.'" Bjorn's father had often warned him not to cross the police. Between those who thought mercenaries weren't contributing enough to society, and those who were failed mercs themselves, there was too high a risk of running into a cop with a chip on his shoulder for mercenaries.

Eddings made a non-committal noise. "Was this fight over a girl?"

"It had nothing to do with Grace."

"Grace? Did you finally get over the cheerleader?" Eddings laughed. "Maybe people will quit asking if I'm robbing the cradle with the commander's kid."

"I'm not much younger than you," Bjorn protested. "To answer your question, yes, I'm over Heather. I'm going out with Grace Saturday night."

"Good for you."

How was he going to fit in hand-to-hand training on top of his sessions with Axe and homework? Bjorn juggled his schedule in his pinplants while waiting for the procession of rumblers to move.

"I'm instructing advanced hand-to-hand classes a couple nights a week. Are you interested?"

Of course he was interested. Did she think he was qualified for an advanced class? He'd carve time out of his schedule—sleep was for the weak. "Sure. How much?"

"Ten credits a session."

Bjorn nearly stomped on the brakes. Ten credits equaled five hundred dollars! He muttered a Norse oath that translated to "do you take me for a dwarf?" "I don't have that kind of money."

"I forget you're not on the payroll." Eddings drummed her fingers on the commander console. "Tell you what—since you were my first student, I'll give you a discount. Two credits a session, but you can't tell anyone about it. I don't want people to think I'm going soft."

"What about my dad? He may ask why I'm converting $200 a week to credits and spending it."

"Fine, you can tell the commander. I don't know what the big deal is; it's not as if you can get into any trouble at the startown for four credits."

He could swing the fee from his allowance, but it would mean he would hardly have anything to save for a car or to put in his college fund. Maybe he'd hit his father up for the tuition. It would mean Bjorn spending more time at Bear Town.

The rumbler in front pulled away, exposing the motor pool yard. "We're at the front of the line."

"Carmen, send our diagnostic report," Eddings called. "See the guy with the green batons? Follow his directions. If his batons turn red, stop immediately."

"Aren't you going to take over?" Bjorn asked.

"Why? You haven't hit anything yet."

The man waved his batons to the right. Bjorn released the brake and eased the rumbler into a turn. Closer to the garage, another signal person waited. She crossed her batons as Bjorn approached.

"Bring it to a stop—they're still arguing over which bay to put us in," Eddings said. Once the rumbler ground to a halt, the woman lowered her batons. After a minute, she raised them and gestured right, along the row of vehicle bays. Several rumblers waited on the pavement, their crews dismounting.

Another person with batons beckoned them along the building. At the third bay from the end, he gestured into the bay with his left baton and twirled the other.

"He's telling us to back into Bay Three," Eddings advised.

Bjorn's growing confidence at the controls waned. "Back in?"

"Yes. Slow down, and as you reach Bay Four, turn the stick hard until our butt is pointed at the building."

Bjorn jerked the joystick, eliciting a curse from the back of the vehicle.

"There's a button by your pinky. Hit it to toggle your cameras to the rear." Eddings unbuckled her restraints so she could lean over Bjorn's shoulder. "See the green line projected on the image? It's your path of travel. Ease the stick backwards and aim for the bay where green-sticks is standing. He'll signal you to adjust your direction."

BTI: Do you wish to enable a pinlink interface to CASV17?

"No, I think it might confuse me more," Bjorn replied aloud.

"What?" Eddings sounded puzzled. "How is he going to confuse you?"

"I wasn't talking to you. The base's tactical intelligence asked if I wanted to plug my pinplants into the rumbler," Bjorn replied. He nudged the joystick as he guided the vehicle at a glacial pace. The signal person beckoned impatiently. "Maybe if I had started off driving while plugged in it would help, but now I think it would mess with me, and I don't want to drive through the motor pool wall."

"You're doing fine. Don't let him rush you," Eddings said. "I didn't even know you could jack into rumblers. I thought pinheads could only plug into CASPers…no offense."

"None taken."

BTI: CASV rumblers are equipped with pinlink interfaces for all four positions.

Bjorn mentally typed a response. "Are you eavesdropping on my pinplants?"

BTI: I am interfaced with CASV17 and using the onboard wireless node as a relay.

"A little more to the left," Eddings cautioned.

Bjorn mentally swiped the exchange with the BTI from his pinview so he could concentrate. In the Tri-V, the frame of the door into the garage flashed green. The signal man stepped to the side. As the vehicle backed into the bay, the distance to the rear wall appeared in the Tri-V.

"Stop at three meters from the wall," Eddings advised. "Our nose will barely be inside, but it gives them space in case they need to drop the aft ramp."

Bjorn watched the number scroll down—4—3.8—3.6—3.4—3.3—3.2—3.1—3.0.

"Throw the red handle forward to set the parking brake. Pull the handle next to the joystick back until it clicks to set the drive system in stand-by. Congratulations, you parked a rumbler without putting it through a wall or running anyone over." Eddings patted him on the shoulder.

"Thank Entropy!" Carmen called from the rear. "All the bumping and jerking has me ready to piss myself!" The metallic clank of a hatch opening reverberated through the vehicle.

"Hit the yellow button above the power lever to put the rumbler in stand-by mode. Good, now the red button to power down." Eddings headed back. Bjorn popped his safety harness and followed.

"Eddings! Why are you driving like my grandmother and holding up my motor pool?" Sergeant Silver demanded.

"I was breaking in a new driver, Sergeant," Eddings replied.

"Hey, Axe, sorry if I created a traffic jam," Bjorn said as he squeezed out the hatch. "I needed to confer with Eddings about almost getting my head kicked off."

Axe's remaining organic eye bugged out as he sputtered an expletive. "Kid, are you telling me you were driving a half-million-credit armored fighting vehicle through my motor pool yard?"

"Yes?"

Axe rubbed the bridge of his nose. "Good thing you didn't hit anything. What's next? You want to try a VTOL flyer?"

"Can—"

"No! I was being sarcastic. Now get out of here before someone figures out you've been joyriding in a Casanova and tells the commander." Axe pointed at Eddings. "You stay and go over the diagnostic report with Melinka."

Bjorn slipped out the back door of the building to reduce the odds of anyone associating him with the rumbler that had creeped across the lot. He decided he could practice some pitches; he'd gotten as good with his left arm as his right, and his left-handed fastball clocked 179 kilometers per hour. It would appear as though he'd come for one of his physical therapy sessions.

Incoming call.

"Son, are you on base?"

Why ask the question if he knew the answer? Did he know Bjorn had been driving a rumbler? "Yeah, Dad. I'm by the motor pool."

"Sergeant Silver has his hands full, and you don't need to be in his hair," his father said. Bjorn released a breath he hadn't realized he'd been holding. "Meet me at the mess hall for dinner."

* * * * *

Chapter Twenty-Three

Bear Town, New Mexico

"Your mother says you've met a girl."

Bjorn had barely sat across from his father before the interrogation began.

"She also says you've been fighting," his father added. "Trying to squeeze everything into your first week?"

"It was one fight, and I didn't start it. It wasn't even on school property," Bjorn protested. "One of the local bully-boys decided to make an example of the new guy."

"It looks as though he got some licks in," his father remarked without glancing up from his meal. Mom must not have been distracted enough by the news about Grace. "I've already been over this with Axe and Eddings. I got overconfident, and I paid the price. While we're on the subject—could I get a raise in my allowance?"

Bjorn's father studied him while chewing a mouthful of salad. "Were you fighting over this girl? Need some merc money to impress her?"

"Grace had nothing to do with the fight, and the money isn't for dates." Bjorn had saved a bit of money since he and Heather broke up. Another expense to factor in. "Eddings is teaching an advanced hand-to-hand class. Obviously, I need the training."

"Son, she's charging mercs for this class. I signed off on it, but troops have more money than they know what to do with. While her rates are reasonable for mercenaries, they're a bit pricey for regular folk."

"What, a civilian can't get his butt kicked?" Bjorn countered. "This time I managed to win without resorting to my 'left hook' and putting him in the hospital. It would have been easy to slug him with my cybernetic fist and finish the fight. Sergeant Silver has helped me acclimate to my artificial arm, but if I don't want to rely on it as a crutch, I'll have to get better at using the rest of me."

The commander pointed his fork at Bjorn. "How long have you been working on this speech?"

"I only found out about the class in the last hour," Bjorn replied. It was a good speech, but would it work?

"I'll meet you halfway," his father said. "I'll pay your tuition for Eddings' class, but I'll pay it directly to her."

"Awesome. Thanks!" Not only would Bjorn not have to pinch pennies, Eddings would get the full tuition.

"So when do we meet Grace?"

Bjorn sighed. "You're as bad as Mom. I'm taking Grace out Saturday night."

"First dates are hard enough. My first with your mother was a disaster—it's a wonder I got a second date, let alone married her." Bjorn's father chuckled. "If you think you're going to keep dating her, we'll arrange something. You can bring her over for dinner, or maybe we could invite her family for a cookout."

How big was Grace's family? How would his father react when he found out they weren't rich like Heather's family? "I haven't met most of her family yet. Maybe something low-key would be better first."

His father grunted. "How long has this food vendor been in the mess hall? Another part of your experiment?"

"They went into the rotation two weeks ago," Bjorn replied. His idea of guest restaurants was a hit with personnel. Stefan warned the per person expense was 10 percent higher than relying on their own cafeteria services for all meals. They had floated the idea of having diners pay the vendors directly, but included chow was considered a perk of an outfit with a large base such as the Berserkers.

"I suppose you're going to want the car for Saturday night?"

What, were they going to walk? "Mom's been letting me use the car."

"Your mother has her own car," Bjorn's father replied.

"Can I borrow the car?" Bjorn asked. His father being back hadn't entered the equation for Saturday. "If you need it, maybe I could borrow a LPT?"

Bjorn's father chuckled. "What's next? Want to borrow a rumbler?"

Bjorn stifled a cough as a chunk of baked potato threatened to go down the wrong pipe.

"It's fine. You can use the car," his father continued. "If I need to go somewhere, I'll call an autocab or have someone pick me up. Besides, if you're in the car I know you won't get into any serious mischief."

His parents could keep tabs on the autocar through the GPS and onboard cameras. "Thanks. I wasn't planning any mischief—first date and all."

"Maybe I should keep a LPT at the house for when you need to borrow my LUV," the commander commented.

"You know, if I had my own car, I wouldn't need to borrow yours." Bjorn tried to sound casual. His own car would also afford him some privacy.

"Nice try. First you hit me up for a raise, now you want a car?" His father chuckled. "Let's see how your grades are this semester, then we'll talk about a car."

"It's not as though I'm asking for an aircar."

"Good, because my answer would be easy," his father said. "A car, I'll think about it. A flyer, no way. I don't even use the things. The Parvo family died because their aircar had a duct-fan failure."

Bjorn didn't want an aircar. He shared his father's concerns regarding the alien-manufactured vehicles with a VTOL's worth of machinery crammed into a car-sized chassis. However, his request for a regular car would seem reasonable compared to one of the advanced flying cars.

"Maybe I should buy myself a new car and give you the family car?" Bjorn's father pushed back the empty dinner tray. "I could get myself a sporty number since I wouldn't have to haul your butt everywhere."

Was he teasing? *Don't take the bait.* "You could. I could knock out the back row of seats for more room. There'd be enough space in the back for hauling stuff, going camping, or…other things."

His father chuckled. "Well played. Either way, let's see what your mid-term grades are before you plan out your rolling hotel room."

"Did Mom tell you about the present *Afi* gave me for my birthday?" Bjorn asked.

"The axe? I told the old man ten years ago it was an impractical weapon," Bjorn's father replied. "Give me a sword or CASPer blade."

"I've asked Sergeant Silver to teach me how to use it," Bjorn said. "I know it's primitive and unwieldly, but with my arm I think I can handle it."

"When do you think you'll walk around with a double-bladed battle-axe strapped to your back?" Bjorn's father asked.

"You never know. Some of the techs are working on a CASPer-scale battle-axe."

His father sighed. "I know big, heavy weapons feel powerful, but they're also cumbersome. When you're fighting Besquith or Tortantulas, you need a responsive weapon. The aliens may be big, but they're also fast."

"So am I." Bjorn resisted the urge to snatch away his father's tumbler of tea to demonstrate how fast he was.

"You're a civilian, remember? You won't fight aliens."

"Wouldn't it be a useful recruiting and advertising image?" Bjorn suggested. "I don't plan on fighting, but I am trying to understand the business. We want to draw more customers and troops. Projecting a badass image benefits both goals."

His father was trying to think of a counterargument; Bjorn could see the wheels turning. "I think it's ridiculous, but you're going to do it anyways. I'll admit, an axe-wielding CASPer would go with our Viking motif, but I don't think it will amount to more than branding."

Bjorn suppressed a grin. He'd learned early never to gloat over his victories with the commander.

"I suppose next you'll want simulator time."

"We have simulators?" Bjorn assumed all CASPer training was practical.

"We do, but they're not videogames," his father replied. "I'm not going to waste my technicians' time so you can goof around."

"I didn't even ask," Bjorn retorted.

"Good."

*****

Chapter Twenty-Four

Las Cruces, New Mexico

"First time I've seen you cleaned up all fancy since…" his father's voice trailed off—*since before the bear attack*. "In a while. Is that a new shirt?"

"Yeah, I outgrew my old ones," Bjorn replied. His mother had let him go shopping with the family account when Bjorn discovered how snug some of his shirts had gotten.

"Too much time chowing down in the mess hall," his father remarked. "No wonder our mess expense has gone up."

"First of all, I only eat there four times a week," Bjorn protested. "Second, I got those shirts at the beginning of last year."

"Whatever you say, Chunky." His father chuckled.

Bjorn's mother *tsked*. "Stop it, BJ, or you're going to give him an eating disorder."

Normally, weight gain would have been a concern over the summer, but Bjorn had worked out more this summer than he had when he played football.

"Trip's not some fragile flower. Do I need to give you any speeches, son?"

Bjorn shook his head. "Don't do anything stupid. It's a first date, so the second topic won't be an issue, but to make you feel better—I know, and I have some. Be home by midnight. Don't ding the car. Did I miss anything?"

"Nice try. Be home by 2300," his father replied.

"Come on, I'm a senior."

His father scowled. "So your senior buddies get to stay out all night?"

"BJ, maybe we could compromise?" his mother interjected. "He is seventeen, and next year he may be off at college."

"My cadre soldiers have a curfew," Bjorn's father countered.

"Not on Friday or Saturday." Bjorn fought to bridle his tone. Getting too confrontational would only make his father dig his heels in.

"Fine. Be back by 2330." The commander's tone was final.

He would take what he could get. "Awesome. Don't wait up," Bjorn said.

"Good luck—but not too much luck," his mother called.

Bjorn's father's laugh was audible as Bjorn reached the front door. "Did you tell our son to get lucky?"

"Shut up, BJ."

* * *

There were more people out and about in the complex than Bjorn expected. Between the heat of the day and the lure of 500 channels worth of Tri-V programming, most people should have been ensconced in front of their Tri-V sets. At least it's what the commentators on certain channels favored by the affluent claimed.

Kids played in the street—an unnerving obstacle course. People walked their dogs. A group of men clustered around a petrol-burning car with its hood up. It certainly wasn't a hive of the indolent masses eating their government dole in front of Tri-V sets.

Bjorn parked and messaged Grace he had arrived. Would her mother demand to meet him?

"Mama wants to meet you. Tower B, Apartment 1214." Bjorn winced.

He composed a respectful and earnest speech waiting for the elevator and during the ride to the twelfth floor. As soon as he knocked on the door, the words evaporated from his mind.

Grace beamed at him as soon as she opened the door. "Don't worry, Mama doesn't bite."

Grace led Bjorn to the living room of the apartment where four children clustered in front of the Tri-V set. They ignored Bjorn in favor of a cartoon depicting the exploits of a fictional mercenary outfit. A teenaged girl younger than Grace worked on a slate. She glanced at Bjorn and remarked in Spanish, "Cousin, he's a big slab of beef."

"Corina, you're too young to speak like that," a middle-aged woman called from the kitchen, also in Spanish.

"I've been called worse," Bjorn said. Hopefully he didn't botch the verb tense in Spanish. Corina flushed.

The woman emerged from the kitchen, wiping her hands on her apron. "So, you are the new *gringo* my *menina* is all excited over. Corina is right—you are big."

"Mama!" Grace hid behind her hands in embarrassment.

"Do you play football?" Grace's mother asked. "If you don't, you should."

"I played until last year," Bjorn replied. "I, um, had an injury, so I can't play anymore."

The woman grunted.

"I'm Bjorn, by the way. It's a pleasure to meet you."

"Bjorn." The woman eyed him. "Your name rings a bell. Why?"

"Mama, you promised no inquisition on the first date," Grace protested.

"*Bien.* Have her home at a reasonable hour. If my husband was here, he would show you his machete collection." She headed back toward the kitchen.

"How many machetes does he have?" Bjorn had never heard of anyone who collected machetes.

"Only the one," Grace replied. "He enjoys menacing boys I date."

"Where should we go?" Bjorn asked once they were in the car.

Grace shrugged. "What's your favorite restaurant?"

"Herman's," Bjorn replied without missing a beat. He'd taken Heather there several times, but he hadn't been back since they broke up. "All of their food is great, but I especially love their chickenaki—it's a spicy teriyaki on boneless grilled chicken. I haven't had it in a while."

"Sounds like we're going to Herman's for dinner."

* * *

A glance at Grace quickly dispelled any concern about ghosts dampening the mood. Bjorn wasn't here to dwell on old memories. The waiter held his breath when he asked for their drink orders until they both ordered soda. They both laughed about it once the server was out of earshot.

"We're sitting in the family section. Did he expect us to order beer or tequila?" Grace asked once she caught her breath.

"I think he's new," Bjorn replied. "Maybe kids have been trying to order, which is silly since our Yacks include our birth dates."

"So if you don't want to be a mercenary, what do you want to do after school?" Grace asked once they exhausted the basic small talk regarding their respective families.

"I guess I'll go to college and learn to handle the business side of the operation," Bjorn replied. "Since I'm the only child, I stand to inherit the company when my father retires or gets killed. A lot of mercenary outfits go under due to mismanagement. They don't lose a battle; they simply go broke."

"So where are you going to study? Some up-scale east coast school?"

Bjorn shook his head. "Not without a football scholarship. I've applied for scholarships at a couple of universities here in New Mexico. Hopefully being local will offset some disadvantages in the application process."

Grace furrowed her brows in puzzlement. "Why do you need a scholarship?"

"Mercenary families don't qualify for FedEd—the Federal Education Grant. Since my father won't pay for me to go to college, I have to figure it out on my own."

"That's crazy."

Bjorn shrugged. "The commander is bitter because I don't want to be a mercenary and eventually take command. My grandfather, Bjorn the Elder, founded the Berserkers. There has been a Bjorn Tovesson in command for over forty years, and I stand to break the streak."

"Your family is loaded. He should buy you an admission to whatever school you want." Most universities had a handful of "bid admissions" that allowed wealthy families to guarantee their child a spot while bringing in funding for the school. Grace paused as their meals arrived. "If my papa had the money, he would do the same for me."

"What do you want to do?" Bjorn had dominated the conversation with his drama, and he knew very little about Grace.

"I'm thinking political science with an intent to go to law school."

"You want to be a lawyer?" They hadn't been in school long enough for Bjorn to get an idea of Grace's grades, and it seemed rude to ask a date about their grade-point average.

"Surprised?" A bemused smile lit up her face. "Most people think I should be a cosmetician or go into the service industry."

"It's a lot of school to become a lawyer," Bjorn remarked. There was also a lot of money to be made, especially in corporate law. "You must enjoy studying or arguing."

"Maybe a little of both," she replied with a wink. "Anyway, I've applied to the University of New Mexico. UNM is the only law school in the state, and I'm hoping the in-state bonus points will help. Between my family being working poor, my grades, and my extra-curriculars, I think I have a solid shot."

"Extra-curriculars?" Bjorn was so busy after school that he hadn't even checked into what the new school offered.

"I'm on debate team—surprise—and show choir. If I get elected again, I'll be on the student council, which doesn't do much but pad my application." Grace plucked a french fry off Bjorn's plate. "How about you? You used to play football and baseball before the accident. What now?"

"I spend a lot of time at Bear Town. It's east of here, north of Highway 70 after you get through the mountains. There's a sergeant who's an amputee, and he's helping me adjust to this." Bjorn wiggled the fingers of his cybernetic hand. "I still go there to work with him, and I'm taking an advanced hand-to-hand class. I got to drive a 25-ton combat rumbler the other day—but don't tell my dad."

"For someone who doesn't want to be a mercenary, you sure hang out with them a lot," Grace teased.

"After Mitch almost took my head off, I figured I needed more training," Bjorn replied. "Even if he backs off, someone else with a chip on their shoulder will pop up. Since I'm already there for work outs, I usually eat there and study in my office."

"You have an office?" Grace claimed another fry and chewed on the end of it. "Can I see it?"

"Now?" Bjorn hadn't considered using his office for anything but studying, but now Grace was giving him ideas.

"After we eat."

It was tempting. Getting her past the gate wouldn't be hard if she ducked down. The guards only gave him a cursory glance when he arrived. Bjarnarsal would be a different issue. "We're not dressed for it. We'd stick out like sore thumbs."

"You don't like how I'm dressed?" Grace gave him a mock pout.

First date, Bjorn reminded himself. "I do, but everyone would know something's up. Maybe another time, when we can dress like off-duty mercs and not high school kids out on a date."

"Fine. So what will we do for the rest of the night?" Grace rested her chin on her hand as she watched Bjorn.

"We could go to the cineplex or the arcade. There's Club Jove—all the music and dancing without the booze or creepy old dudes."

"You don't strike me as the club type," Grace remarked. She was right. Bjorn had taken Heather to the teen club a couple of times, and she had spent most of the time hanging out with her friends. "A movie is intriguing, but we won't be able to talk." She winked.

Bjorn's collar felt tight. *Was it warm in here?* "The arcade has a putt-putt course and a bowling alley. We could—" He missed a beat as he spotted two of Heather's friends from the cheerleading squad watching him and whispering.

Grace leaned forward. "What is it?"

"Nothing. Two of my ex-girlfriend's squad are talking about us," Bjorn replied. "It caught me off guard. Want to get out of here?"

"Not until we take a first date selfie." Grace circled the table to sit in Bjorn's lap and pulled out her phone. "Say 'ex.'" She kissed him on the cheek as the camera clicked. "Now we can get out of here. I'll send you a copy so you can put it on your social media."

Bjorn squared away the check, and Grace put some extra sway in her step as she led him past Heather's friends. The girls whispered behind their hands as Bjorn and Grace passed. He didn't know if Heather even paid attention to his social media, but Bjorn suspected word of this picture would get back to her. Why should she care? Why did it matter to him?

* * *

"Cutting it close," his father remarked as Bjorn closed the door.

"I have a whole three minutes," Bjorn countered as he followed his father's voice to the kitchen. The commander sat at the breakfast table, nursing a cup of coffee.

"I bet you had to put the car in manual to make it." His father grinned over the steaming cup. "So how did it go? Given how close you are to curfew, either really good, or so bad you needed the time to sulk. Given the grin you're trying to hide, I'd say good."

"Yeah. It went well, especially for a first date." Bjorn fished a soda out of the fridge and sat across from his father. "We went to Herman's for dinner, played putt-putt, and drove around a little bit."

The older Tovesson chuckled. "You mean you parked on Monte Vista or on the access roads around the antenna farm above St. Augustine Pass. Don't worry, I didn't peek on the cameras."

If he did, he'd known Bjorn had covered the cabin camera. Not that things had gotten too hot and heavy—it was a first date after all, although Grace was more forward than Heather had ever been.

"Just don't let things get too serious too quickly." His father slurped his coffee; the habit drove Bjorn's mother nuts. "I know you got tired of hearing me say it when you were with Heather, but you're both young and have plenty of time. I didn't marry your mother until I was almost thirty."

He had to bring up Heather. Bjorn's good mood waned. Not long ago, Bjorn assumed he and Heather would get married someday. He shouldn't get the same notion about Grace. Loki curse it; his father was right.

"Don't worry, I'm not making wedding plans," Bjorn remarked. "My whole six-year agenda went out the window on the hunting trip."

His father masked the flicker of remorse across his face by raising the coffee cup. Yeah, it was an unfair barb; it wasn't his father's fault there happened to be a Kodiak bear lurking in the vicinity.

Incoming message: Grace Garcia

"Can't wait until our next date. See you at school."

The attached video showed further why Bjorn should look forward to their next date. He might need to review it a few times when he wasn't sitting across from his father.

"Do you need to take a call?" his father asked.

Bjorn shook his head and pushed the video aside into a corner of his pinview. "No, it's only a message, not a live call. How could you tell?"

"When you're focused on your pinplants your eyes glaze over, and your pupils contract." His father gazed into his coffee mug. "For the record, I'm glad you found someone. I was afraid you were going to get a crush on Eddings."

Bjorn scoffed. "She's badass and pretty awesome, but no. I couldn't see dating her."

"Not even after she let you drive the rumbler? Oh yeah, I know all about it."

Crap! Maybe he really did have eyes everywhere on base. "Did Eddings get in trouble?"

"I thought about it, but in the end, I decided against calling her out and dressing her down. It can be good to let the troops believe they can get away with a little transgression here and there. They think they're clever, it improves morale, and it doesn't reveal how much I see so I can deal with real troublemakers."

Good thing he hadn't tried to smuggle Grace onto base, let alone into his office in Bjarnarsal. Bjorn chugged the rest of his soda. "I'm going to bed. See you in the morning."

"Good night, son."

Once Bjorn reached his room, he restored the message window in his pinview.

"Play video."

*****

Chapter Twenty-Five

Las Cruces, New Mexico

"All right, maggots. This is the confidence course. I don't know why—I have no confidence many of you will finish!" Sergeant Kimble bellowed.

Bjorn resisted grinning. The only obstacles of concern were ones requiring a tight squeeze, where his large frame would slow him. Given CASPer drivers were larger than average, he didn't expect an MST course to overly penalize him for being big.

"This is a timed course. In the spirit of mercenary service, your success doesn't only depend on your performance, but those of your brothers-in-arms. You may hate their guts, but you must have their backs!"

Oh no. No good could come of this, especially since Kimble had it in for him.

"You will be paired up. Your scores will be based on the slowest time of the pair." Kimble's grin widened as some of the MST students moaned and grumbled. "Quit bitching! Be glad I didn't invite the remedial squad to join us! There are a couple of butterballs who would be boat anchors. When I call your names, form a column behind the starting marks. *No trading partners!*"

Bjorn scanned the cohort. Who would Kimble saddle him with? Henszey? She had the lowest scores overall and barely made the advance class. Lozano? He couldn't outrun a zombie but could do push-ups until the sun went down.

"Tovesson and Brackin—get in line!"

Of course, the one person in the school with the biggest chip on his shoulder against Bjorn. Their scuffle was over a week ago, but Mitch glared at Bjorn every chance he got. Mitch and his cronies had steered clear, but Bjorn could tell he was itching for a rematch.

"Great," Mitch muttered as they lined up. "I get to haul your lard ass down the course."

Lard ass? He might not be as trim as during football season, but he'd fought against packing on pounds. "Try to keep up, Brackin. It won't all be about having twinkle-toes."

The column moved forward as the trainer at the starting line flagged each pair and gave them the signal.

"I should let your ass fail the course," Brackin whispered.

Bjorn snorted. "I don't want to be a merc. I could sit at the starting line and it wouldn't matter."

Brackin's eye twitched. He wanted to be a mercenary. He had bought into the fame and fortune spiel. The scores from MST were only a small portion of the VOWS assessment, but if you wanted a prime placement in a training cadre, you needed every point you could get.

"You sandbag and I swear—"

The trainer cut off Mitch. "Pair Seven—go!"

Kimble was a double jerk. Not only had he paired Bjorn with Mitch, but Sergeant Kimble had placed them behind slower pairs. They would lose time if they overtook the previous pair at an obstacle.

Mitch sprinted the 100-meter dash, but Bjorn paced himself. Burning too much energy up front could be disastrous later on.

"Come on, Lard Butt!" Mitch yelled. He traversed the dash in under 11 seconds, while it took Bjorn a full 12 seconds.

Two rows of staggered tires awaited them. Bjorn was well familiar with this obstacle from his football days. The staccato step remained in his muscle memory and he caught up to Mitch.

"Come on, Twinkle-Toes!" Bjorn yelled as he dashed to the next section. Two rows of hand-over-hand bars stretched above a mud pit. He snagged the first rung and swung out over the mud. Even without his cybernetic arm, his upper body strength would have offset the disadvantage of his mass. When Bjorn landed on dry land, Mitch was only a quarter of the way across the bars.

Bjorn loped to the climbing wall. The pair ahead crossed over the top of the wall as Bjorn reached the base. A standard rope climb—a piece of cake. Bjorn hauled himself to the top by the time Mitch reached the bottom of the wall.

"Grab the rope!" Bjorn shouted as he seized it at the top of the wall and brace himself. Mitch clung to the rope and Bjorn hauled him up the wall and over the top. Without a word, Mitch clambered onto the net stretched from the top of the wall to the ground.

By the time they reached a pair of logs over another mud pit, Mitch had pulled ahead. The balance logs increased the gap by another second, which lasted until they reached another wall. This one was shorter, about three meters tall, but had no rope. Another pair was eyeing the top.

"I'll boost you to the top," Bjorn told Mitch.

"Great, but how do we get your beefy carcass up? You're too big for me to haul up."

Bjorn repressed a sigh. "All you have to do is keep me from falling. When I jump up, grab hold, and I'll pull myself up."

"I don't—"

"The clock is running," Bjorn interrupted and laced his fingers together to boost Mitch.

"Fine. I hope you don't dislocate my shoulders." Mitch placed his hands on Bjorn's shoulders and stepped into Bjorn's hands.

Bjorn heaved Mitch up, nearly launching him clean over the top of the wall. Seconds ticked by while Mitch lay on the top of the wall and stretched his arms down. Bjorn backed off a couple of paces, then charged ahead and bound up, reaching with his flesh-and-blood hand. Mitch snagged it and held on with both hands, grimacing as Bjorn hauled himself high enough to reach the top of the wall with his cybernetic hand.

"I ought to knock your butt in the dirt," Mitch mumbled before Bjorn could gain the top of the wall.

"Go ahead," Bjorn retorted. "I already told you I don't care."

"Then how come you're trying so hard?" Mitch asked as Bjorn clambered over the top of the wall.

Bjorn glanced at the angled rope anchored to the ground. Sneaky bastards—it would be much quicker to drop to the ground and run, rather than climb down the line and try to avoid rope burns on the palms of your hands.

"I guess I have a competitive nature," Bjorn replied as he lowered himself from the top of the wall and dropped the last bit. He didn't wait for Mitch as he trotted toward the last obstacle—logs stretched over a water pool. Unlike the previous logs, these weren't secured—they rotated freely. Several students were wading through chest-deep water.

"Crap," Mitch uttered. "Might as well jump in and swim."

"It's another teamwork obstacle," Bjorn countered. "I'll hang onto the end of the log while you cross. Then you grab the other end, and I'll come across."

"Damn, Tovesson. You're not as dumb as I thought." Mitch positioned one foot on the log and waited for Bjorn to seize it.

"Go on," Bjorn said. The rough surface helped his fingers gain purchase. Mitch quickly tip-toed across. Some of the people in the water swore when they saw the solution.

"All right, go for it," Mitch called as he held the other end. Bjorn stepped onto the log and briskly covered over half the length before Mitch lifted his hands and declared, "Oops, splinter!"

Bjorn unceremoniously spilled into the water. "You jackass!" he shouted at Mitch's receding back. The thick mud at the bottom of the pool clung to his boots, so he hauled himself along the log the last few meters.

Dripping, Bjorn trudged toward the finish line. His water-logged boots squelched with each step. Mitch doubled over in laughter as Bjorn crossed the finish line. Sergeant Kimble watched with a bemused grin and glanced at his assistant's slate.

"Your little stunt cost you boys twenty-seven seconds," the MST sergeant remarked.

Mitch caught his breath. "Totally worth it to see the expression on Chunky's face when he realized he was going in the drink."

"Oh, you think it's funny?" Bjorn stepped forward and cocked his left fist. Mitch flinched and scrambled back several paces and assumed a defensive stance. Sergeant Kimble put a hand on his assistant's shoulder and shook his head at another trainer.

"That's right, I've already shown I can kick your butt." Bjorn glanced at the sergeant. "Not worth the trouble to do it again." Bjorn turned his back on Mitch and slogged toward the locker room.

* * *

"I heard about MST this morning," Tomas remarked as Bjorn sat at the lunch table.

Grace leaned forward. "What happened?"

"I'm surprised you ain't heard." Larcell covered his mouth to keep from spraying crumbs. "Our boy threatened to knock Mitch Brackin's head off his shoulders. Then he turned his back on Mitch, and RGH's favorite bully was too chicken to do anything."

Wow, it had spiraled fast in a couple of hours. Maybe it would have been better if someone had caught the confrontation on video.

"Are you *loco*?" Grace asked.

"First of all, someone is exaggerating a lot," Bjorn protested. "Mitch intentionally dumped me in the water obstacle even though we were partners, and I had helped him. All I did was raise my fist and point out I didn't need to kick his tail again. Everything went down in front of Sergeant Kimble and a couple of assistant trainers."

The assistant trainer had been holding her slate, and the camera could have picked everything up. An image appeared in his pinview from when he glanced at Kimble. His pinplants overlaid the near-field communication IDs of every device in his field of view. The assistant held a generic, Earth-made ruggedized slate—cheaper by a factor of 10 than an alien-manufactured equivalent, and with only one percent of the processing power.

Accessing school network through public node. Searching…networked device found. Handshaking…do you wish to run decryption from on-memory resources?

Bjorn wasn't a hacker, so he hadn't downloaded any toolware to his pinplants or slate beyond what the ElSha, Frek, had given him. "Estimated time?"

"It's only a quarter past noon?" Larcell replied. "Is he having some sort of seizure?"

Thirteen seconds. Executing. Copying cached video files from timestamp. Compiling.

"He better not be messaging his ex-girlfriend," Aisha commented, earning a glare from Grace.

"He's using his pinplants," Amy muttered. "Must be neat."

"Give me a second, guys," Bjorn said. He pulled out his slate and set it flat on the table. "Okay, here's what really went down."

Bjorn played the video from the assistant's slate. The camera showed Mitch kneeling at the end of the log. He raised his hands, laughed, and sprinted for the finish line. After 20 seconds, Bjorn hauled himself from the water and jogged to the finish. The camera followed him, but also caught Mitch and his words. The rest of the scene played out, ending with Bjorn walking toward the school building while a couple of other MST students teased Mitch.

"That's bad," Tomas said once the screen went dark.

"What do you mean? It clearly shows the gossip is way overplayed. Mitch dunked me intentionally," Bjorn retorted.

"He means Mitch lost face," Aisha said. "Back it up a few seconds. See those guys hassling Mitch? It means he's been knocked down a peg or two."

"Good." Bjorn picked up his faux-burger. Let other people shame Mitch and save Bjorn the trouble of taking the wind out of his sails.

"It means he's going to need to do something to restore his 'honor' with his cronies," Tomas countered. "It means you have a target on your back."

"I don't want something to happen to my future boyfriend," Grace said.

"Future boyfriend?" Bjorn raised an eyebrow.

Grace winked. "Depends on how the second date goes."

"Way to go, big—" Larcell aborted his remark when it drew an irritated glance from Tomas.

"I guess I better plan something special for Saturday, assuming I live that long." Bjorn scooped up the slate. "At least now I have a reason to stay alive."

*****

Chapter Twenty-Six

Bear Town, New Mexico

"I heard you soldiers had a problem," Axe called as he led Bjorn into a large metal building labeled Training 3. A metal framework suspending twelve CASPers dominated the center of the chamber. A pair of technicians surrounded by Tri-V displays manned a pair of computer consoles.

"Hey, Sergeant Silver," one of the technicians said. She gestured toward the CASPers. "I don't know why you were called here. The problem isn't technical. One of the squads is short a man."

"I know. I brought them a spare." Axe jerked a thumb toward Bjorn. "He's pinned, so we don't even need a haptic suit. Stuff him in a tin can and spool the simulation up."

"Wait, what?" Bjorn peered at the simulator rig. One of the CASPers rested on the floor with a mounting step in front of it. "You want me to go in a CASPer sim-run with troops?"

The other technician stifled a laugh. "This should be good. Should we avatar him as a second lieutenant?" He couldn't contain his laughter any longer.

"Go on, kid. You've driven a real one. This will be a step up from your arcade games. Hey, Bennett. I bet you fifty credits the kid makes it to the end."

Bennett stopped laughing. "Serious? You know we won't dial things back because he's Ba—he's the commander's son. I'm good for fifty."

"I wouldn't expect you to cut him any slack," Axe said. "Tully, you want in on this action?"

The technician shook her head. "Too rich for my blood, Sergeant. The big man pays us well, but not so much I'm going to throw away a month's pay."

"If you make it, Bjorn, I'll cut you in for half," Axe remarked.

Great, nothing like being put on the spot. "Fine. I hope tech sergeants are paid well." Bjorn threaded his way between machinery to enter the circle between the CASPers. His pinplants flagged them as Mk 6, and if they had pinlinks, they were Block 3s. Bjorn mounted the steps and wriggled his way into the CASPer. Once he was securely in the armor, Bjorn grabbed the clamshell armored canopy and pulled it down, sealing him in the suit.

He found the interface cable and clicked it to his pinplant port. The simulation flashed through the normal checklist and start-up sequence. With a lurch, winches and servos hauled his suit into the air until it clicked into place in the rig. His pinview showed an emulation of the CASPer's Tri-V heads-up display.

"Grizzly Bravo Two Five, checking in," Bjorn called as he was linked into the unit network.

"At last," Sergeant Kolaček called. "I was afraid I'd piss my haptic suit before they found someone to replace Goff. Who are you, new guy?"

The countdown to the start of the simulation flashed large, with only twelve seconds to go.

"Guy Nýr," Bjorn replied. They didn't have time for the drama associated with his real name, and no one would catch the joke behind the Icelandic *nýr* for new.

"All right, Neer, you're with Rutger. The mission is to seize a dropship from the enemy without blowing it to kingdom come. Neer, my board shows you in a generic load out, so support your partner and don't do anything stupid."

BTI: Creating alias—Guy Neer. Establishing access—CASPer operator.

"Roger, Sergeant." Bjorn blew up the map as he fell in behind his teammates. It appeared straightforward—fight their way up the middle to the landing pad and secure the objective. Two locations stood out where opposition forces would have a significant advantage. Bjorn flagged the zones with his pinplants and sent the marked-up map to the sergeant.

Several seconds passed as the squad followed Grizzly Bravo One along the boulevard. When Bravo One was 50 meters from the first point Bjorn had marked, Sergeant Kolaček instructed them to vector off to the left. Bjorn couldn't tell whether the sergeant in Bravo One protested, as they began taking fire from Zuul forces.

"Good eyes, Neer." The sergeant led them down the side street, past the battle. As Bravo Two approached the next zone Bjorn had highlighted, the lead CASPer relayed an image of a Zuul crew-served laser emplacement.

"Do we take it out?" Rutger asked. His CASPer had a heavy weapons package, and he sounded eager to use it.

"No. Let Bravo One draw their fire. Keep moving," the sergeant replied. "Rutger and Neer, you're on point until we reach the wall."

The *snap-pop* of laser fire announced Bravo One had engaged the emplacement. The tactical display showed additional Zuul swarming out as Bravo One troopers plinked at the emplacement, at least until one of them lobbed a K-bomb over the sandbag barricade protecting the weapon crew. Zuul scattered, one way or the other.

Bjorn and Rutger crept the last twenty meters to the wall surrounding the landing pad. It would be easy to use their jump jets to hop over the wall.

"This is a skeet shoot," Bjorn remarked. "We jump over the perimeter, and they blast us from the sky. Do we have anyone with K-bombs or demolition charges?"

"Flowers, get up there and do your thing, but save some boom-boom in case we need it later," Sergeant Kolaček said.

Jim Flowers chuckled over the comms. "I'll try not to get carried away, Sarge." The CASPer lumbering toward Bjorn and Rutger carried additional K-bombs in place of an external magnetic accelerator cannon. Half the explosives were flagged in Bjorn's pinview as shaped demolition charges.

A clang resounded through Bjorn's CASPer. "Quit daydreaming, Neer!" Rutger snapped. "Watch the other side in case the Zuul try to flank us."

"Right." Bjorn shuffled his CASPer out of the way to let Flowers work.

"You boys get ready to bounce when I set this off," the demolitions expert stated. He hummed tunelessly as he smacked blinking charges on the wall. "You might want to step back and dampen your audio pick-ups."

As soon as the explosives breached the wall, weapon's fire poured into the gap. Laser trails incandesced in the settling dust but found no targets. Six CASPers bounced over the walls on either side of the breach, several meters away from the fusillade into the opening.

Bjorn spotted a Zuul crew-served weapon emplacement as he crested the wall. As soon as his targeting reticle zeroed in on the heavy laser, he triggered his magnetic accelerator cannon. The hypersonic projectile carved a path of destruction through the equipment supporting the laser. A cloud of coolant made the crew scatter.

Three squads of Zuul, not the advertised two. Bjorn scanned ahead as he stepped forward to clear the landing zone for his squad mates. They hadn't lost anyone yet, but Bravo One was down two CASPers already.

It still left the Besquith. It was unlikely the "intel" confused the third squad of Zuul for Besquith. The dropship was visible behind a row of buildings ahead. Sergeant Kolaček urged the squad forward.

"We're almost there," the sergeant called.

Besquith erupted from the building ahead of him.

Bjorn already had his arm-mounted laser raised when the werewolves charged. His first shot was sloppy and grazed the shoulder of the snarling Besquith. Enraged, she lunged for Bjorn.

"Dammit, now I wish had the axe," Bjorn growled as he fended off a snarling werewolf.

BTI: Weapon loaded into simulation.

Bjorn reached to where a CASPer carbine should be and found the haft of an enormous axe. He pulled the weapon free of the mount. "Time to put the dog out."

His first swing was clumsy, and he smacked the werewolf with the flat of the blade instead of the edge. The force of the blow was still enough to knock the alien back a pace. It retreated another step to avoid Bjorn's backswing. A supersonic tungsten slug from one of Bjorn's teammates punched through the Besquith's combat armor.

"Dammit, Neer! You're too far forward," the sergeant called. "Mendiz, Rutger, move up to support the rookie. Holman and Flowers, form on me. We need to pressure those Zuul eager to join this fracas."

Bjorn shifted his grip. The haptic feedback meant he could feel the shape of the handle in the CASPer's hand. The next Besquith who lunged at Bjorn pulled up short when blocked by the axe. Bjorn and the Besquith circled each other until the werewolf grew bored and lunged forward. Bjorn chopped off one of her hands.

Bjorn was slammed around in his armor as tell-tales lit up and an external camera showed a Besquith clinging to his back. Claws screeched across the armor, and one of his shoulder servos flashed yellow. Bjorn goosed his jump jets and leaned backward. He flew a few meters in the air before thrust cut out and his suit plummeted. The werewolf was squashed between the falling CASPer and the tarmac.

Bjorn shook stars from his head as he rolled off his foe and put a laser round into her to make sure she stayed down. No point in taking chances. Another Besquith dropped into a kneeling position with a laser carbine. Bjorn's laser shield snapped out, and the beam dissipated against the shield. Bjorn counter-fired with his own laser. The Besquith dove aside, right into Rutger's beam.

"Are you done clowning around, Rookie?" Mendiz asked as she took position on Bjorn's left, her carbine ready.

"Where the hell did you get an axe?" Rutger demanded, covering the right.

"Can the chatter!" Sergeant Kolaček barked. "The Zuul are falling back between the hangar and the mechanic's shack toward the objective. Mendiz, pair with Flowers."

"I'm too sober for that," Mendiz quipped.

"Screw you," Flowers responded.

"Knock it off. Our two fire teams will push toward the objective. Rutger take Neer and support Bravo One. They're down to three."

"Roger, Sergeant," Rutger said.

Bjorn watched the blips of identified enemies funnel away from them and disperse beyond the buildings. "Sergeant, it's a draw play. I bet there are more Zuul and Besquith waiting for you past those buildings."

A direct channel pinged on Bjorn's comms. "Have you run this sim before? Be straight with me."

"No, Sergeant. You can check—I've never run this sim, but it's an obvious trap," Bjorn replied. It was obvious—Bjorn could see the Xs and Os of a football play in his mind, except the linebackers were 200-kilogram werewolves.

"Very astute, Neer," the sergeant said over the squad channel. "Rutger and Neer, your orders stand. The rest of us will swing wide and try to avoid falling for the dogs' trick. Move out!"

He was going to miss taking the objective. It rankled Bjorn until he reminded himself this wasn't a videogame, it was a training exercise for the troops. There were no points. He lumbered along behind Rutger as they approached the forces guarding the gate from behind. The Zuul exchanged fire with the remaining CASPers of Bravo One, both sides hunkered down behind cover.

"Let's do this!" Bjorn charged forward. "Valhalla awaits!"

"Dammit, Neer!" Rutger lumbered after him and fired his shoulder-mounted rocket at the farthest of the two clusters of Zuul.

As the Zuul spun in reaction to the explosion, Bjorn fired his laser at the closest enemy, then hit his jump jets. The Zuul reacted quicker than he expected, a couple snapping shots off as a ton of machinery, armor, and soldier arched into their midst. One shot ablated on his shield, but the other caught him in the knee joint. The knee indicator flashed red and Bjorn felt a sting in his own knee. As he slammed into the Zuul, one fell under his blade and lost a leg.

Bjorn's suit crumpled into a kneeling position as the knee servos failed. Only his axe embedded in the pavement kept him from falling over. He lasered another Zuul as they scrambled out of his reach. Fire from Bravo One and Rutger cut half their number down. Bjorn sought another target when he noticed the metal balls the size of a baseball, each with a blinking blue light. Zuul grenades.

The CASPer rattled as his display flashed white before going dark.

Simulation ended.

Bjorn had to wait eleven minutes for the simulation to wrap up. One of the prices you paid for dying in a simulation was boredom. At least he could take advantage of the time to knock out some reading homework.

The CASPer jerked as the simulator rig lowered him to the ground. A metallic thud punctuated the end of the descent. Indicator lights blinked on inside the cockpit before the clamshell canopy swung upward. Bjorn blinked against the light streaming in as he detached his pinlink.

"Not bad," Sergeant Kolaček remarked. "We took the objective with less than 50% casualties. Taking the objective at all is considered a win in this scenario."

"Our survival rate would have been better if your rookie hadn't gone on rampage at the end," the sergeant from Bravo One said.

Bjorn didn't recognize her. She counted off the CASPers around the circle until she found Bjorn. "This isn't some game…Sonuvabitch."

"The charge at the end was bone-headed, but he spotted two of the three big traps in the scenario." Kolaček followed her gaze. "What?"

"Don't you recognize him?"

"Damn, it's Baby Bear," one of the troops blurted.

"Is this some sort of test or joke?" Sergeant Kolaček demanded, turning toward the techs and Sergeant Silver.

"The call came out that you guys needed an additional driver," Axe said. He pointed at Bjorn. "The kid has driven CASPers for me in the maintenance yard, so I figured he was better than going in a man short."

Kolaček turned to Bjorn. "How many hours have you logged in the sims, kid?"

"None," Bjorn replied. "I've played the dumbed down civilian versions, and I've driven CASPers in the motor pool. My pinlinks did some of the heavy lifting."

The other sergeant approached. Her name strip read Glass. "You're wired? I wouldn't trust alien tech inside my skull. You must be nuts."

Axe sucked in his breath, but Bjorn cut him off. "I didn't have much choice. The hardware in my head runs the machinery replacing the arm I lost."

Sergeant Glass blinked. "Shit. I didn't know." Her eyes went to Axe. "Still, I don't think it's funny that you snuck the commander's kid into our sim-run."

"What would you have said if I asked, Barb?" Axel crossed his arms. "You would have said no and cooled your heels. Frankly, the kid did better than I expected. I figured he'd draw fire and let your soldiers stay in the run longer. I didn't expect him to call out trigger points in the sim or download a weapon."

"Where did you get the axe?" Rutger whispered. The CASPer operator was nearly as big as Bjorn, but with close cropped platinum blonde hair. "It was pretty bad ass."

"I guess the base's tactical assistant program had it on file," Bjorn replied quietly. "It was a surprise to me."

The sergeants dismissed their squads. A few gave Bjorn a glance before filing out of the simulator chamber. Rutger gave him a thumbs up.

"Kid, did you hack the simulator?" Sergeant Silver asked as they emerged from the building. Even though the sun was low, a hot breeze gusted across the complex. "Your axe is not standard gear. The file manifested while the program was under way."

"I wished I had my axe and Bettie loaded it into the simulator environment," Bjorn said.

"Bettie?"

"The BTI. I'm guessing it pulled the data from the working files Egg and Wathen are using," Bjorn replied. He hadn't heard from the pair, so he had no clue where they were on fabricating a CASPer-scale version of his battle-axe.

"You shouldn't give virtual assistants names," Axe cautioned. "Remember the panic around Circe, the virtual assistant everyone was afraid had gone full AI?"

"It was before my time, but if I remember right, the whole thing was a false alarm," Bjorn countered. "A true AI requires more powerful hardware than we can supply on Earth. Bettie isn't about to go AI and start the next galactic war."

BTI: Alias accepted—Bettie.

*****

Chapter Twenty-Seven

Las Cruces, New Mexico

"Come on, you don't know her favorite flower?" Bjorn asked. A social media search had turned up nothing.

"She's my cousin. How the heck would I know what kind of flower Grace likes?" Tomas protested. "What's your cousin's favorite flower? Pick any cousin."

"I have no close cousins," Bjorn countered. "My dad is an only child, same as me. The only cousins I know of branch off a couple of generations back, and I've met them maybe twice, three times. Grace might as well be your sister."

"*Verdad.* I still don't know what her favorite flower is," Tomas said as they paused for the traffic light. Grace had remained behind at school for debate team practice. "I can tell you she hates roses. Her last boyfriend gave her a bouquet of roses and she tossed them in the trash."

Good information. Bjorn mentally crossed roses off his list—they had been the first choice for romantic flowers.

"Any idea why—" Bjorn was interrupted as a van screeched to a halt beside him and Tomas. The side door was flung open as the vehicle disgorged figures in plastic masks. Two of them grabbed Tomas while the other four encircled Bjorn.

"You're too chicken to show your faces?" Bjorn challenged. In response, all four assailants produced riot batons, a popular purchase from militia surplus stores. Bjorn debated triggering a 911 call when the first attacker lunged forward. If there was a bored police officer nearby, he might respond.

Bjorn blocked with his cybernetic arm and hammered his right fist into the masked figure's ribs hard enough to send him stumbling back to the van. Pain blossomed as a blow landed across his back. Bjorn whipped his left fist in an arch. Another attacker flinched back out of reach, but the guy who had struck Bjorn was too slow. A meaty *thwack* accompanied a spray of teeth and plastic mask shards.

Another baton glanced off his head, causing stars to swim in his pinview. Bjorn stumbled as he spun to face his assailant, who danced away as his partner struck Bjorn from behind over his kidney. Bjorn resisted the urge to face the newest assault—they were trying to keep him disoriented so they could pound away at him. Bjorn rushed the attacker in front of him.

The man swung again, but Bjorn snagged the baton with his artificial hand and ripped it away. Bjorn drove his shoulder into his opponent, sending him sprawling onto the pavement. Bjorn whirled in time to partially deflect a swing aimed at his skull. It grazed his head, drawing more stars and pain.

The attacker who'd been knocked toward the van lunged in, forcing Bjorn to deal with him instead of the assailant in front of him. Bjorn's right side faced the new attack, so he employed Edding's teachings. Bjorn snagged the assailant's wrist and bodily threw him into the sidewalk. Two down for the count.

One of the remaining goons landed another blow on Bjorn's ribs. Something cracked, and Bjorn doubted it was the baton. Each breath hurt. It was two on one, but the pair kept themselves on opposite sides of Bjorn. Were they from the MST class, or merely experienced street fighters?

The assailant in the devil mask lunged in a feint. His goat-masked partner stepped in and swept his baton low. Bjorn was too slow, and the tip of the weapon clipped his knee. Fury mixed with pain.

Bjorn snatched the weapon before goat-mask could recover and drove his cybernetic fist into the side of his attacker's head. The mask slewed sideways as the goon crumpled to the pavement.

Bjorn hunched forward so the expected strike landed on his shoulder rather than his skull. Bjorn jammed his left elbow back, but devil-mask retreated. One on one now.

Concussion detected—seek medical treatment.

Bjorn circled his last opponent, who held his baton ready. Devil watched Bjorn's unsteady steps, biding his time. Bjorn's knee throbbed. For the first time, Bjorn was glad he wasn't playing football. Devil made a couple of fake swings to gauge Bjorn's sluggish reactions.

Bjorn took a deep breath. The club arched at his right side. Bjorn seized the arm. He'd meant to catch devil's wrist but wrapped his fingers around the forearm instead. Good thing Bjorn had large hands. His right hand lashed out and clamped around devil's throat. The goon gurgled behind the mask as Bjorn lifted him at arm's length. The baton clattered to the sidewalk. Devil clawed at Bjorn's hand and feebly kicked in the air.

"I am sick of your crap!" Bjorn snarled. Devil's eyes bugged out, visible despite the mask. "You tell Brackin! You got it?"

Devil nodded weakly. Bjorn drew him closer and hissed, "Consider yourself lucky." Bjorn flung devil away. The goon gasped for breath on the pavement.

Bjorn turned on the pair holding Tomas. They shoved Tomas at Bjorn and sprinted for the open van. Instinctively, Bjorn caught Tomas before he sprawled on the sidewalk. The van screeched away from the curb.

"We…we should get to my car." Why were words hard? The ground shifted below him, and it was Tomas' turn to catch him.

"We need to get you to a hospital," Tomas said.

"I just need…what…sit down." Bjorn staggered a handful of assisted steps. Was the sun going down? It shouldn't be so late.

Emergency medical assistance summoned.

* * *

Voices. There was an argument, but Bjorn couldn't make out the words. He recognized one of the voices. Bjorn squinted against dimmed lights.

"…but I'm his girlfriend!" *Grace?* Had he forgotten their second date, and he was her boyfriend? Bjorn grasped at the smoky fragments of recent memories.

"Miss, as I said, only family is admitted."

"Come on, Grace. Wait for his family to come back. Maybe they'll let you see him." *Tomas—right, Tomas was there when…something happened?*

Calibrating. Short-term memory disruption. Do you wish to view last video footage cached?

"Yes." Bjorn said. His mind was too fuzzy to fuss with mental typing.

The fight replayed in Bjorn's pinview. His recollection of the incident coalesced. They'd hit him over the head a couple of times with those batons. He was lucky they didn't cave in his head.

You have been treated for two skull fractures, a concussion, two fractured ribs, a bruised kidney, and multiple contusions.

"How long have I been out?"

Elapsed time since losing consciousness: 5 hours 37 minutes.

"I heard him! He's awake—let me in!" Grace demanded from the other side of the door.

"No. If you don't leave, I'm going to call security."

"What's going on?" The new voice was his father's. Great, how much trouble was he in now? What was the penalty for an all-out brawl in broad daylight?

"You must be Grace," Bjorn's mother said. "It's all right, nurse. Let her in."

The door flew open, and Grace rushed to the bedside. "*Dios Mio!*" She gingerly took Bjorn's right hand, careful of the IV line.

"I must be pretty gruesome." Bjorn grinned. Did he still have all his teeth? He didn't remember getting hit in the mouth. His lips were parched, but he didn't feel any dental gaps. "Trust me—the other guys look worse."

"From the police images, it looked like a massacre," Bjorn's father remarked with a grin.

"BJ, it isn't funny." Bjorn's mother turned to Grace. "Hello, dear, I'm Lynn Tovesson."

"Hello, Commander and Mrs. Tovesson. This isn't how I planned on meeting you," Grace said.

"Sorry. I meant to wait to get hospitalized until after our second date," Bjorn rasped. Was there any water? He was hungry and thirsty.

"Trip, don't try to get up," Bjorn's mother admonished. "What do you need?"

"Some water." Bjorn's head agreed with his mother—sitting up was a bad idea. "How bad is it this time?"

"You'll be out tomorrow, and back to school Thursday," his father replied. "Doc Cataldi came out from the base and treated you with trauma nanites. The staff here was pretty pissy about it. You'll be on light duty for a week to be safe. Good thing you have a thick skull."

"Good thing they didn't decide to shoot me and be done with it," Bjorn countered.

The commander switched to Icelandic. "What's this about? Is it a fight over a girl?"

"Don't be rude," Bjorn retorted in English. "No. It's because the same jerk I got into a scuffle with lost face. He figured a good beating would put me in my place."

His mother returned with a water bottle and handed it to Grace. Bjorn took a grateful sip from the straw, resisting the urge to slurp more water right away.

"Which is why I need to go back to school tomorrow," Bjorn said.

"Trip, the doctor said you should stay overnight." His mother glanced to the commander for support.

Grace added, "You shouldn't push yourself. Tomas said you fought off four on your own. You don't have anything to prove."

"I need to stare Mitch Brackin in the eye and show him I'm not scared," Bjorn stated. "I need to shut this down before he does something, like go after you."

"BJ, talk some sense into him," his mother pleaded.

"The boy's right." The commander met Bjorn's gaze. "If he wants to see this through, we should let him. Keeping him overnight was a precaution. He's still on light duty—no PT with Sergeant Silver and no hand-to-hand with Eddings. Stay off the base for a week and recuperate. In the meantime, handle this thing with the Brackin kid. If you don't do it your way, give me the video of the fight and I'll pay the Loki-cursed police to do their job."

Bjorn's mother's face was set in stone. How long would the commander be in the doghouse this time? "Fine. I'll go home and let Geneva know to warm some leftovers. I'm sure Trip is hungry after the nanites."

Grace watched Bjorn's mother leave before asking, "Are you sure you're up to this? Why don't you take another day to catch your breath?"

"Because I want to see if his buddies have any fresh bruises tomorrow," Bjorn replied. "He wasn't there, but I'm sure his cronies were among the crew, if not the entire group. I want him to see me walk in when I should be recuperating in the hospital. While he's still rattled, I want to tell him to back the hell off."

"I can see you're going to be a handful." Grace leaned over and kissed him.

"You're one to talk—I heard you out in the hall," Bjorn countered with a grin. "I'll see you tomorrow."

* * *

Bjorn awoke to an inventory of aches. The nanites had mended the worst of the injuries, but there were plenty of bruises.

"How are you feeling?" His mother asked from across the breakfast table. She pretended not to notice Bjorn's double helping of breakfast. He needed to replenish the tissues the nanites cannibalized to repair the damage to his body.

"I'm sore and I'm glad I don't have MST today." Bjorn dug into a pile of eggs. "I'll be wiped out after school, so it's as well I'm banned from Bear Town for a week."

"It means I get to cook a proper dinner," Geneva remarked with a hint of her German accent. Her workload had lessened since Bjorn ate many of his meals at the Berserkers' mess hall.

"Trip, you could invite Grace over for dinner," his mother suggested.

Bjorn repressed a quip about how he was supposed to take it easy. "I think she has debate team tonight. Why don't I find out her schedule for next week? We could plan something instead of putting Geneva on the spot."

"I enjoy a challenge," Geneva said.

"I guess you're right," his mother admitted. "I didn't know she was already your girlfriend."

Neither had he until he regained consciousness. "I think the excitement from yesterday jump-started things."

"Well, make sure you don't get too carried away in all the 'excitement,'" his mother remarked.

Bjorn blushed while Geneva chuckled.

* * *

A dull ache thrummed in his skull by the time Bjorn reached lunch. A handful of students whispered in huddles when they saw him, but no one was brave enough to mention the evidence of yesterday's fight on his features. One ear was still purple, red, and swollen. Another angry red mark amid a bruise on his forehead marked where nanites had closed a head wound.

Bjorn set his lunch on the usual table. Everyone watched him expectantly. "Tomas, thanks for having my back yesterday."

"I didn't do anything, man," Tomas protested.

"You kept two of them out of the fight, and you waited with me until the medics arrived," Bjorn said. "Seriously, thanks."

Bjorn's gaze swept across the cafeteria until he found Mitch and his coterie in their usual spot. Mitch pretended not to notice him from the moment Bjorn had stepped into the lunchroom. A few members of Mitch's entourage were missing.

"Are you sure you're ready for this?" Grace asked, a gentle hand on Bjorn's arm.

"If I wait, it loses the impact," Bjorn replied. "I'll be fine. It's not as though they'll jump me here in the middle of the cafeteria."

"I mean, are you sure you can keep your anger in check?" Grace inquired. "I don't want you to get expelled."

"I'll be fine," Bjorn promised. Hopefully he could keep his word. He marched across the cafeteria, mindful to not limp from the dull ache in his knee. A wave of silence followed him as students fell hushed at his passage.

Brackin watched him approach. Only a few droplets of sweat on his brow betrayed his nonchalant demeanor. "What do you want, Soggy? Still crying about falling in the water?"

"You know why I'm here." Bjorn spotted one of Mitch's buddies trying to conceal the bruises around his throat. Bjorn pointed at him. "You're the one with the devil mask."

"You can't prove crap," Mitch sneered.

Bjorn tapped his pinport. "I have pinplants. It means I can record video and audio and save it in my head, then download it to a slate or the Aethernet. Not only do I have video and audio, the police also have DNA evidence from the batons and mask fragments left at the scene, as well as all the blood. I also captured the VIN of the van when they had the door open."

Several members of the group shifted uneasily, peering at Mitch.

"My family has enough money to afford a police investigation," Bjorn continued. "Everyone who left a speck of DNA at the crime scene could go to a Re-education Camp. I suspect one or more of them would roll on who put them up to it in a plea deal."

Mitch's face paled. Society tolerated the behavior of misfortunates to an extent, but once you crossed the line you were sent away to be "educated" in how to think and behave properly.

"What do you want?" Mitch hissed through clenched teeth. Anger and fear warred across his face.

Aches and pains reminded Bjorn not to grin smugly. He kept his voice low, but loud enough for Mitch's compatriots to hear. "Simple. You leave me and my friends alone. If someone hassles us, I'll assume you're responsible. I'll have a choice between releasing all of this data and pressing charges or sending a squad of the family business to take you and your family somewhere to dump you into a pit with some hungry aliens."

"Mercenary activity is illegal off bases and startowns," Mitch retorted.

"Who's going to pay for an investigation?" Bjorn demanded. "You? Your family? These guys?"

All of Mitch's buddies found somewhere else to focus their attention.

"We have eight months until graduation. You have eight months to leave me the hell alone. Got it?" Bjorn punctuated the question with a cybernetic finger to Mitch's sternum.

"Fine," Mitch spat. "You're not worth the trouble."

"We agree on something," Bjorn said. Bjorn turned his back on Mitch and spotted Principal Figueroa staring from across the cafeteria. The security guard next to the principal had his radio out. Mitch muttered something, probably an attempt to salvage his pride in the eyes of his coterie, but Bjorn let is pass. If he got through the school year without any more fights, he'd be happy.

"Everything good?" Tomas asked as Bjorn sat.

"I thought the principal was going to call in the cavalry," Larcell added.

Amy shook her head. "He was waiting to see how it would play out. He waved off the guard calling it in."

"I think we have an understanding," Bjorn replied. "I may have put it on thick, but Brackin knows, and, more importantly, his buddies know, I have enough evidence to pin someone to the wall."

"So you're going to let them get away with putting you in the hospital?" Aisha challenged.

Grace had been holding her tongue, but her eyes spoke volumes. She wanted Bjorn to twist Brackin's head until his pasty face pointed the wrong way.

"I could throw down and bust some heads, or I could try to get them a visit from the police and a prosecutor-for-hire. It risks an ongoing escalation of revenge, and it would go beyond me. How long until they go after my girlfriend or my friends?"

"Girlfriend?" Aisha asked. "I thought you guys only had the one date?"

"Must have been a heck of a date. Way to go, big guy!" Larcell offered a high five but lowered his hand when Tomas glared at him.

"We've only had the one date," Grace said.

"I heard what you told the nurse last night." Bjorn grinned. "No take-backs."

*****

Chapter Twenty-Eight

Bear Town, New Mexico

"You certainly have a storied application, Mr. Tovesson." The hologram of the admission's counselor for the university folded her hands. "Coming back from such a catastrophic injury must be daunting. I commend you for your courage."

"Thank you." Bjorn didn't mention he knew there was a 'but' coming. He could tell from her tone.

"But your grades are not impressive. There are many students with higher marks who are more deserving of admission to college based on academic and socio-economic criteria." Her smile reminded Bjorn of Vurrg when they first took him to a Brazilian steakhouse. "However, given your family's economic situation, we would be happy to offer one of our guaranteed admission spots for $500,000. That doesn't include tuition or any other fees, of course."

"Of course," Bjorn replied. It was the same thing the other schools had told him. They were only interested if his family shelled out a huge sum of money, generally the equivalent of 10 years of tuition. Most students never had to worry about the tuition thanks to FedEd. "Unfortunately, my father has declined to fund my scholastic endeavors. I was hoping with my disability, having lost an arm, I would qualify for enough assistance to use my own savings to fund my education."

"Those conditions do not apply to mercenary family members. Perhaps if you did a few years as a mercenary you could afford a guaranteed spot on your own?"

"I see. Thank you for your time." Bjorn leaned back in the chair once the call disconnected and the Tri-V image faded. If your family won't pay, become a merc and pay your own way. Different school, but the song was the same.

It rankled him to admit she might be right. After all this time declaring he wouldn't become a mercenary, he might have to give in and pick up a MAC. He could do a three-year enlistment and muster out with enough to pay for school and living expenses until he graduated.

His classmates going on to college already knew what they wanted to do. Grace had received her acceptance message yesterday. Bjorn was still trying to cobble together his future at the last minute. He stretched before leaving his office. He'd been in there all morning doing the Tri-V interviews. He thought the spartan office would make a better impression than his bedroom.

"Not good?" Stefan watched him come down the hall to the reception lobby. "I'm sorry."

"It's my own fault," Bjorn muttered. "If I hadn't freaked out and gotten kicked out of Mesilla Prep, I might have had a chance. There were teachers there proud of the fact I wanted to buck the family tradition of becoming a mercenary. They were all lined up to give me glowing letters of recommendation. It's funny…they condemn us even as they hold their hands out for our credits."

"Us?" Stefan's tone was quizzical.

"You know—mercenaries." Bjorn sighed. "I'm going to pop by the mess hall to grab a bite and sulk."

"Don't you have a date?" Stefan inquired.

"Not until 1900 hours. I've been on base all day, but I skipped lunch for my interviews." Today had been his first day back with Eddings training group since the masked assailants. He would have gone back a week ago if his parents had let him, but he had pushed himself too soon in MST class. "I don't want to be cranky—crankier—than I am now."

"Have fun, young man."

Bjorn scanned the mess hall. He didn't see the commander, which was as well. He found an empty table to tuck into his tacos while catching up on reading from school. Bjorn propped his slate on the table even though he didn't need it. He could process the text much faster through his pinplants, but it weirded people out when he stared off into space with his eyes flicking back and forth. Why did he bother doing the class work? He could coast by and do as little as possible to graduate. Was it pride, or was he just plain stubborn? Either way, Bjorn was going to finish school as though he was going to college.

Bjorn was on his third taco and second chapter when his father plopped down across from him. After several seconds of watching Bjorn read the air, his father said, "I heard about the interviews. I'm sorry, son."

Bjorn marked his place in the text and shrank it out of view. "Why? It's what you want."

"I'm sorry because I know going to school is what *you* want," the commander replied. He leaned forward. "I spoke to your mother. If you still want to go to school, we'll foot the bill."

"It doesn't matter if I can't get in," Bjorn remarked around the remains of the last taco. He resisted the siren song to get another three. He was taking Grace to her favorite restaurant in four hours.

"I mean will pay for everything, including the guaranteed admission fee," his father said. "We have two conditions. Hear me out. One is you get at least a B average this year. The second is that the college is in Arizona, New Mexico, Texas, or Alaska. It will keep you closer to family, and I'll be damned if I'm going to give my money to some moonbat institution on one of the coasts."

"It's a lot of money." What was the catch? His father had been adamantly opposed to paying for Bjorn's education. There had to be some sort of strings attached for him to suddenly cough up somewhere between 12,000 and 25,000 credits.

"It's an investment. Hopefully it will keep you from running the company into the ground after I'm gone, or you'll get a good deal for it if you decide to sell."

Bjorn pushed back his tray. "After all this time, you're going to pony up the money?"

"I thought you might work it out on your own," his father said. "I think you could do as well working inside the business and taking net-classes. Your mother and I discussed it, and I was outvoted."

"So, since I'm a failure, now you're willing to help me." The tacos formed a lump in his stomach.

The commander gave him a cautioning look. "Don't spit in the wind, son. I'm saying I will help you out. Don't twist it up or over think it. My offer is on the table. Chew on it, but we have to let a school know before all of those spots fill up."

"All right, I'll consider it." Why wasn't he jumping for joy? His father was giving Bjorn exactly what he wanted, so why did he want to refuse it out of spite? Was it because his father's largess signified Bjorn had failed?

"I've got something else to show you," his father said. "Dump your tray and meet me outside."

Bjorn's curiosity was piqued by the time he reached the huge doors of Bjarnarsal. Even though it was almost autumn, the afternoon sun baked the parking lot. His father stood next to a vehicle best described as a fusion between a typical mercenary light personnel transport and an automobile from the mid-20th century. Where the LPTs used by the Berserkers were blocky, this vehicle's chassis was covered in curves.

"What's this?" Bjorn asked, intrigued. The surface was covered in a deep blue, almost black, glaze, but tiny motes glinted as light played across the vehicle.

"According to Vurrg, this was all the rage in Zuul LPTs about twenty years ago. His company had it here as a demo, but us Human mercs don't like our rides all curvy." Bjorn's father patted a fender. "I told him it reminded me of an old-school hot rod. That led to two hours of showing him pictures of cars from the 1940s and 1950s. Now his company is going to emulate those designs for Zuul civilian use. Their mercs won't go for all the chrome, but the civilians will go nuts over it.

"Vurrg asked if we wanted this old demo since his company didn't want to haul it home and it was doing him no good as a display model." The commander jerked his thumb toward the motor pool. "I asked Sergeant Silver to have his team go over it and ensure it was road legal. I was going to give it to you last weekend, but they had to redo the autonomous driving software so the local bureaucrats wouldn't get their boxers in a bunch."

Bjorn peered through the windows. The configuration of the interior was familiar—two seats in the front and the bench seat in the rear could fold down to expand the aft cargo space. The details caught his eye. As the Zuul designers were enamored with curves, there were few straight lines. "Wait, this is for me?"

"Yeah. I guess Vurrg thinks giving my kid a leftover relic will dispose me to giving his company a contract for those multi-role rumblers." His father held up a key fob. "If you drive it on manual, watch the throttle. Zuul love to go fast, and even after the motor pool techs reconfigured the pedals, the acceleration is still peppy."

Bjorn accepted the fob. "First you offer to pay for my school, and now you're giving me a car. Are you dying of some sort of alien disease or something?"

"Odin's Eye! Why can't you accept it when something good happens?" Bjorn's father shook his head. "You're too young to be such a damned pessimist."

Bjorn circled the transport. It had regulation license plates on the hatch above the rear bumper, along with a full-sized spare tire covered by a convex plate with the same blue-black glaze. "What's the deal with the paint job?"

"It's supposed to be laser-refractive, and the deep blue is the Zuul equivalent of our olive drab. It runs on electricity, same as our other vehicles. There are solar cells embedded in the roof. They won't keep the vehicle charged, but in a pinch, they'll get you a few kilometers. The back-up fuel-cell will give you one full charge. You'll need to refill it at a hydrogen terminal, so don't use it unless you're out of options."

"Thanks."

"Don't thank me," his father protested. "Thank Vurrg and thank the techs. They worked on this in their off hours. At least it was a better investment of time than the stupid CASPer axe."

"I will. In fact, I think I'll go and thank them now." Bjorn climbed into the driver's seat. Typical for a LPT, there was a half meter of ground clearance. He powered up the transport, and the instrument panels illuminated. He took a moment to scan the displays. The arrangement was different, but at least everything was in English.

The Zuul LPT leapt in reverse and screeched to a halt on the pavement. Bjorn's father crossed his arms and shook his head. Bjorn dug into the settings and decreased the sensitivity of the accelerator pedal. He eased out of the parking lot of Bjarnarsal and followed the road uphill to the motor pool.

"I see you got your new toy," Axe called as Bjorn clambered out of the transport. "Better be careful of the accelerator—it's a bit touchy."

"I found out. I hear I have you and your crew to thank," Bjorn said. "My dad said the crew worked on it after shift."

"It wasn't a big deal. In truth, I was trying to figure out how we were going to keep it secret until we heard you wouldn't be back until today." Axe appraised him. "You seem all right. I heard you took quite a beating. They flew Doc Cataldi to the hospital."

"It was four on one."

"I heard that as well. Eddings is itching to see the footage of the fight," Axe remarked.

Would Eddings scold him, praise him, or more likely both? "I'll send it to her. I'm sure she'll have some critique, but I owe it to her tutelage that I came through it able to form whole sentences. That, and your help with my southpaw."

"Do you know who was behind it?" Axel led him back to the garage, out of the sun.

Bjorn nodded. "I think I've dealt with it. He and his cronies are steering clear because if they don't I have enough evidence to get at least some of them sent away for re-education."

"How's the ride?" Wathen called. "I thought someone tried to mix a 1943 Deluxe and a 1951 Hornet on a LPT frame."

"I haven't had much time to shake it down," Bjorn replied.

"If you're taking it on a hot date, be sure to try the polarizing windows," Wathen suggested. "The controls are by the air conditioning. The windows have crystals you can adjust to make them one-way mirrors. You can see out, but no one can see in. The cops might pull you over if you drive around with the windows polarized, but it's great if you park somewhere and need some…privacy."

"Mammals," Egg clicked. The translator punctuated the word with a huff.

"Don't mind him," Wathen said. "He's annoyed because we got your axe fabricated, but logistics sent it to the warehouse in Houston since your CASPer is there."

"Shift isn't over," Sergeant Silver chided. "We still have three jobs to finish before 1700."

"Seriously, thanks to you and your people," Bjorn said.

"Don't sweat it, kid. I had some free time since you were recovering." Axe nodded toward the parking lot. "Do me a favor, and don't wrap it around a light pole. It's got a lot of get up and go."

"Don't worry, I'm not going to do any drag racing," Bjorn remarked. "In fact, I'm going to drive it around for a bit to get used to the controls. The commander said it was good to go on autodrive."

"It is, now that we've figured out how to convert Zuul measurements to metric and tweaked the programming. They go faster than us, and the Zuul don't worry as much about safe following distance. You're good to go if you want to put it on auto."

"Thanks again."

*****

Chapter Twenty-Nine

Las Cruces, New Mexico

"What kind of car is this?" Grace asked as Bjorn helped her up into the passenger seat. The small crowd eyeing the vehicle was wondering the same thing.

"It's a Zuul vehicle. My father has a friend who works for a Zuul company trying to sell transports, trucks, and rumblers to Human mercenary companies," Bjorn replied. Had Grace ever met a Zuul? The topic of aliens hadn't come up yet. "It's years out of date, so Vurrg gave it to my dad."

Bjorn closed Grace's door and circled the transport. "My dad had our technicians make it street legal on Earth," Bjorn continued once he climbed in. "I guess he got tired of me borrowing the family LUV."

Bjorn input their destination, Grace's favorite restaurant, and engaged the autodrive. The system responded in English and smoothly joined the flow of traffic outside the apartment complex. Bjorn had called ahead to make reservations; once they arrived at Crispino's Ristorante they didn't have to wait.

"I've never been here before," Bjorn remarked when they were seated. The bustling restaurant lacked the cookie-cutter vibe of franchise eateries. It was up-scale without elevating itself to snobby. "Are you a fan of Italian food in general, or this place in particular?"

"I have some fond memories here," Grace replied. "It's pricey, so my family only comes for special occasions. The last one was my *quinceañera* two years ago. My parents have to be frugal since Tomas and I are both in high school, and my cousin Corina starts next year."

"You never came here on a date?" Bjorn had tip-toed around the subject of previous boyfriends. He'd gleaned a bit of information from Tomas but hadn't probed for more.

"No. Adam's routine included three places, one of which was a taco truck. Cristian and I were only fifteen, so we were chaperoned to the pizza place, the roller rink, or the cinema." Grace picked up her menu. "How about Herman's? I'm guessing I'm not the first girl you've taken there."

Fair was fair. He'd open this can of worms. "I went there several times with my last girlfriend, sometimes on a date and sometimes with a larger group of friends."

The waiter appeared, and Bjorn prepared for the subtle implication he should present his UAAC up front so the restaurant could verify his funds. Instead, the waiter recited the specials of the day and took their drink orders.

"I think he realized we're not dine and dash kids," Grace remarked. "They're not usually dressed up, and they certainly don't roll up in a Zuul hot rod."

Bjorn skimmed the menu. Entries were both in English and Italian, so he ordered his pinplants to quit trying to overlay translations. The prices made Bjorn glad his father had covered the tab for Edding's hand-to-hand classes. A meal here would be a week of eating at a burger-and-fries joint.

The waiter returned to deliver drinks and take their meal orders. After repeating the entire order from memory, he hurried off.

"I half expected an Italian accent," Bjorn remarked.

"I think Luigi—Mr. Crispino—and one of the chefs are the only ones from Italy," Grace said. "The two assistant chefs are local, same as the rest of the staff. If someone faked an Italian accent Luigi would put his foot down because it wasn't 'authentic.'"

"You haven't said anything about your interviews," Grace said after they small-talked through the appetizers and salads.

Bjorn shrugged. "There isn't much to say. I don't qualify for scholarships or general admission. I didn't say anything because I didn't want to be a downer."

"If you don't want to talk about it, I understand," Grace said. "Don't hold back because of me, though. If you're going to be my boyfriend, I have to take the good and the bad."

"Are you sure you want that kind of baggage?" Bjorn asked with a half-hearted grin.

Grace reached across the table and took his right hand. "Yes."

Bjorn took a deep breath. He might as well get it out there, otherwise it would hang over their date like a rain cloud. "So, all three schools turned me down. Then my father threw me a curve ball and offered to pay to get me into college."

Grace's face lit up. "That's great! Wait, it's not great?"

"You're going to think I'm being stupid, but if I accept his offer, I'm a failure." Bjorn paused when she protested, then continued. "My whole plan hinged on succeeding based on my own talent and my own work. When football was my end game, it had nothing to do with my family being rich or being mercenaries. It was all about my skill and the effort I put into becoming the best football player I could.

"Even when I tried to get those scholarships and apply to those colleges based on my records, it wasn't because of where I came from or who I was related to. It was all on me, and they rejected me." Bjorn kept his voice even. Grace holding his hand helped ground him. "They told me I wasn't good enough, but my father's money was."

"Don't believe them." Grace squeezed his hand. "What are you going to do?"

"I haven't decided yet. I know the smart thing would be to take his offer." Bjorn shook his head. "I'm considering serving a tour as a mercenary to raise enough money for school."

"You could get killed. One out of ten mercenaries doesn't survive the first year." Grace's eyes were wide with worry.

"I don't know. I have some time to decide, so I'm not going to ruin the night by obsessing over it," Bjorn said.

"I won't say another word about it." Was she worried her new boyfriend was going to run off and get killed? Listening to the training cadre, a lot of relationships didn't survive enlistment in a mercenary firm.

"Good thing I didn't load up at the mess hall," Bjorn remarked once the main course arrived. "I like Italian as well as any other food, but this is amazing. I can see why it's your favorite."

"Is it better than Herman's?" Grace teased.

"Let's not get carried away," Bjorn countered with a grin. "I could eat at Herman's every day. This place is the best I've been for dining. There's a difference."

"I'll concede the point," Grace relented. "Where do you want to go after dessert?"

Bjorn had a spot picked out on Monte Vista, off a little used service road to the observatory. The Zuul PT—ZPT—would have no trouble navigating the terrain, but he wasn't about to suggest going parking this early. Not only would it be crass, it was still light enough someone might notice the blue-black vehicle weaving its way up the mountain road.

"Do you want to go to Club Jove?" Bjorn had scrolled back through Grace's social media. She'd been there several times last year.

"I picked the restaurant," Grace protested. "I want to do something you'll enjoy."

"I'll have a good time anywhere we go if it's with you."

Grace raised an eyebrow. "Did you practice that line? You're not the only one who can dig into a social feed. You went to Zagyg's forty-seven times last year. When we played putt-putt, we never stepped inside, and based on your score you didn't play miniature golf forty-seven times."

"Fine. We'll go to the arcade and I'll give you a tour of Bjorn's favorite games." Games he used to play with his friends. It had been months…was it long enough? "Maybe we can find a co-op game, but as soon as you're getting bored, let me know. The night is young, and I'm sure we can find something else to do."

***

Bjorn eased the ZPT into the congested parking lot. Vehicles crept through the lot among a swarm of pedestrians. He'd forgotten about the Saturday night cruisers. In the past, the autocar had dropped him off at the corner, and picked him up when called. He never paid attention to the older youths driving their cars around the block or threading them through the parking lot.

Old petrol cars mingled with sleek modern electrics. Sound systems competed for volume while vehicle-mounted lightshows flashed. Bjorn was driving manually but flipped the autodrive to stand-by in case someone or something darted in his path before he could notice.

The ZPT drew attention from the cruiser crowd. Spectators hooted and whistled as Bjorn drove by searching for a parking spot. He was about to admit defeat when a spot opened, and he snagged it before someone else could claim it.

"Who knew Zuul cars would be so popular?" Grace said. "Maybe they should market them to civilians on Earth?"

Civilians wouldn't have the money to make it lucrative unless the Zuul caught the attention of the wealthy. "The Zuul would probably charge too much."

"You'd be surprise what some of these guys spend on their cars," Grace remarked.

Several passing drivers called out to Bjorn as he rounded the vehicle to help Grace down. While she could climb down on her own, his grandparents had instilled in him at a young age to be a gentleman. Grace didn't bristle at his attempts at chivalry and smiled when he opened her door and held out his hand.

They weaved their way through the parking lot. Bjorn considered ordering his pinplants to quit flagging every vehicle and person—it was distracting. A few people recognized him as the driver of the ZPT and called out.

Match.

A red outline appeared around a parked car. It was Berto's. He hadn't considered if Berto would be here. Would Heather be with him? It would be too awkward to suddenly return to the car. Inside would be crowded; maybe they wouldn't run into each other?

Bjorn held open the door for Grace. His eyes dipped as she preceded him.

Image saved.

"Trip?" Ray caught Bjorn's attention as he led Grace through the crowded foyer. "I haven't seen you here in ages."

"I've been pretty busy," Bjorn said.

Ray's eyes flicked to Grace. "So things are going good, big guy? You should check out the CASPer sims. We've added a player-versus-player option to the usual scenarios." His attention returned to Grace. "Bjorn here is the top scorer on our sims."

Another customer demanded Ray's attention, so they slipped away into the crowd. "Top scorer on the CASPer game? Why am I not surprised?" Grace remarked. She had to lean close to make herself heard over the cacophony of games and people.

"The trick isn't being the best at shooting or jumping around, it's about anticipating the scenario and what the enemies are going to do." Bjorn stooped a bit so Grace could hear him. "It's not so different from being on the football field."

Multiple matches. His pinplants painted four figures in the crowd. He should have anticipated it. Heather, Berto, Mickey D, and Blair were ahead, near the CASPer sims.

Grace sensed his sudden tension but couldn't see over the crowd. "What is it?"

"It was bound to happen sooner or later," Bjorn replied. "My ex is here, with my ex-teammates."

Grace grabbed his hand and surged ahead into the crowd before Bjorn could protest. Blair was the first to spot him over the throng of people. Blair nudged Mickey D, who spent a second staring before she swatted Berto on the shoulder to pull his attention from Heather.

"What's up, *herm*—Bjorn?" Berto tried to sound casual.

Mickey D stepped closer. "There isn't going to be trouble, is there?"

"I'm not here to pick a fight," Bjorn countered. "My girlfriend wanted to see where I spent so much time last year."

Heather's eyes narrowed as she appraised Grace. Bjorn couldn't see Grace's expression, but he suspected it was similar. Grace clutched his hand tighter.

"We need a fourth to do a run—you interested?" Blair interjected. Both Mickey D and Berto turned on him. Blair shrugged. "Bjorn was always the best at this game, and we haven't beaten this new scenario yet."

"You're kidding, right?" Did they think playing a video game would make up for blowing him off after they picked sides?

"He doesn't want to play with us. Who could blame him?" Berto said.

"Rice bailed on us again," Mickey D remarked. "If the big guy is willing, we could give it a go. Who knows, maybe we could beat the Goka wave with him."

Goka were laser-resistant psycho cockroaches with knives. Even with his experience with aliens, Bjorn didn't want to meet a Goka.

"Maybe you should, *querido*," Grace suggested. She lowered her lashes. "We have some time before going somewhere more private."

Bjorn and Berto regarded each other several seconds. "Fine. I'm game," Bjorn relented. "If nothing else, I know Mickey D wants the experience for MST."

"Yeah, I'm on the advanced path as well," Berto admitted.

Bjorn knit his brows. "What happened to college?"

"Nick Cooper is our quarterback, and we're already 0 and 2. Two schools have changed their minds, and the other two are waiting to see how the season turns out." Berto cracked his knuckles, a nervous fidget. "Nick is more interested in his social media image than the game. Now scouts are saying I only did well because of you."

"Bullshit!" Bjorn retorted instinctively. "You were in the 99th percentile for high school running backs last year."

"That was last year. I've moved into the advanced MST track in case Cooper ruins everything," Berto stated.

"You can't become a mercenary," Heather protested. Bjorn remembered the objection well.

"Are we going to yammer all night or are we going to do this?" Mickey D demanded.

Bjorn turned to Grace. "You don't want to sit through half an hour of this, do you?"

Grace patted him on the arm. "I think it might be good for you." She raised on her tiptoes to kiss him and whispered, "Show them why you're the best."

"Fine, I'm in," Bjorn announced after another kiss. He swiped his Yack over the terminal to pay for the run. A scenario he didn't recognize was at the bottom of the menu—Chitin Valley. "Damn, it's a bug hunt."

"More like the bugs are hunting us," Mickey D remarked as she moved to her traditional spot in Pod Three. Blair was already squeezing into Pod Four. "The basics are our dropship is downed, and we need to get to the evac point."

Bjorn and Berto eyed each other as the stood between Pods One and Two. "Go on, man. You've always run Pod One."

"Things change." Bjorn spotted both Grace and Heather paying rapt attention. "If you've been leading them from One, it doesn't matter."

"The damn pods are the same!" Mickey D yelled. "Get your asses in them before we start burning time."

"Maybe she should be in charge." Bjorn stepped to his traditional pod and climbed in. It really didn't matter who was in what pod once the game began, but Bjorn had always been in the same one.

"Maybe. Mickey D, you want the sergeant button?" Berto called as he positioned himself in his simulation pod.

Mickey D reached for her pod's canopy. "Why? Bjorn will take charge as soon as it goes to hell." She hauled down the plastic shell.

Bjorn centered his feet on the footpads and slipped the haptic bands over his hands. He closed the clamshell canopy and the Tri-V lit up. In the center, a message blazed in orange: Error—haptic failure left hand.

Loki take it! The stupid machine wasn't reading the feedback from his cybernetic hand. What was he supposed to do now?

Scanning interface. Handshaking. Establishing link. Patching device OS to accept feedback.

"What's going on?" Mickey D called over the comm channel. "It doesn't show Bjorn loaded in."

"Give me a minute. The system is being twitchy about my prosthetic," Bjorn replied.

The orange text disappeared, replaced by the familiar graphics of the scenario launch screen. A quick cinematic scene played through the crash of their dropship. Bjorn took the opportunity to look over the loadouts of their CASPers. Everyone had a laser. Unfortunately, most of the insectoid mercenary races were laser-resistant to some degree. Two of the mecha mounted heavy MAC cannons and the other two had rocket launchers.

A voiceover rattled off mission objectives—namely make it to the evacuation point. Secondary objectives included taking a MinSha communication post to call their ride sooner and destroying a Jeha equipment depot. Jeha were giant millipedes, but they weren't mercenaries. They were consummate engineers and technicians.

The quartet fell into their traditional diamond pattern, with Bjorn at the point, Berto and Mickey flanking a few paces behind, and Blair bringing up the rear. Bjorn checked their ammo inventory. Plenty of laser juice, but limited MAC rounds and rockets. They were marching through a landscape of old ruins. There were plenty of places for enemies to hide. Bjorn ordered his pinplants to flag potential cover positions against enemy fire.

Sensors pinged movement and an energy source ahead. The dance was about to begin. "Save the MACs and rockets if at all possible," Bjorn stated. "I know MinSha take more laser hits than kinetics to kill, but we need the heavy hitters for the Goka. What's the story with the Jeha depot?"

"It's not hard to take out, but after the first couple of runs, we skipped it to save time and ammo," Berto replied.

"What good are the objective points if we don't get off the world?" Mickey D added.

"Have you tried looting it?" Bjorn slowed his pace. "Bugs on the left!" He deployed his laser shield in the nick of time. One pulse still skimmed his shoulder armor but registered as minimal damage.

Berto and Mickey D both returned fire with their laser carbines. The MinSha had cover, but one caught a laser pulse in its faceted ruby eye. Bjorn hunkered down and scuttled forward to a fallen stone column.

"I'd bet money there is a crew-served weapon behind the rubble pile to the right," Bjorn said.

Berto moved next to Bjorn when the MinSha changed targets. Mickey D and Blair had swung wide behind a partial wall to the right. "I saw the energy reading. We don't normally run into this heavy of opposition so quickly."

"It increases the difficulty rating each time we run it," Blair remarked. "Plus it randomizes elements so we can't learn it and fight our way through by rote."

"Very impressive, sweetie, but how does it help us?" Mickey D asked.

"Sweetie?" Bjorn stifled a chuckle.

"Shut up, Bjorn," Mickey D snapped. "If you can get those bugs' attention, we can go over the rubble and take out the crew-served weapon."

"Let's do this. I'll go lateral and you pop them before they can smoke me," Bjorn told Berto.

"On your count," Berto replied.

Bjorn counted as though they were on the line of scrimmage. At "Hike!" he broke cover behind his laser shield. The readout for the integrity of the ablative protection decreased precipitously. Fire tapered off as the MinSha broke cover to track Bjorn's path, and Berto picked two of them off. The mantis-like aliens swung their weapons toward Berto.

Bjorn fired his jump jets. The pod shook, but there was no faux acceleration like in the simulator rig in Bear Town. If the lovebirds didn't have the attention of the crew manning the heavy weapon, Bjorn would be the target in a skeet shoot.

Bjorn landed among the MinSha, crushing one to cushion his landing. Bjorn speared another with his CASPer's arm-blade. Two more fell by the time Berto joined the brawl. Looting the MinSha gave them the location of the communication center.

"How heavily guarded has the communication center been?" Bjorn asked.

"Better than the depot, but still not heavy," Berto replied. "There's usually two more groups of MinSha on the way to the extraction point, plus the Goka wave after the second cluster of MinSha."

"Mickey D, can you and Berto take the comm center?" Bjorn asked.

"Probably. It depends on how much they've upped the difficulty," Mickey D replied. If Berto was offended Bjorn hadn't asked him, he held his tongue. "What are you thinking?"

"We break the golden rule and divide the team. You and Berto take the comm center while Blair and I hit the depot. If I'm right, we should ransack the depot before we blow it up," Bjorn replied.

"Why are you so certain there's something useful in the depot?" Berto broke his silence.

Bjorn highlighted a section of the map and shared it with the rest of the team. "They made it easy to find and it's lightly guarded. You've been taking the easy points blowing it to kingdom come. I'm guessing if we're patient, there will be some useful munitions and gear needed to complete the scenario."

"It makes sense," Blair chimed in. "The designers tempt us into destroying the keys to victory."

"It isn't realistic," Mickey D grumbled. "I get what you're saying, but…"

"This is a game. If this was a sim-run at Bear Town, I'd expect the depot to be a trap," Bjorn replied. "The difference between a game and battle simulation is with the game you're a customer, so they put the means to win out there, but in a battle-sim the enemy isn't going to leave convenient ammo and supply packs lying around."

"The clock is running," Berto remarked.

"All right, Blair and Bjorn take the depot and rendezvous at the road junction north of the comm center," Mickey D ordered.

Bjorn resisted chiming in with anything else. If Mickey D was going into the mercenary business, being in charge would be more valuable to her, even if it was merely a game. He lumbered his CASPer forward, the pod shaking with each simulated step. In a minute, he and Blair were around the corner from the depot.

"I make three MinSha, spread evenly along a circular perimeter," Bjorn stated. His pinplants highlighted the locations in the shared map. There was a center structure, but each of the mantis-like aliens were far enough out they could see and cover their comrades. The rubble walls appeared too unstable to support a CASPer landing on them.

Blair opened a private channel. "You know, Berto and Heather feel bad about hurting you."

"They should," Bjorn retorted. "The two closest people in my lives screwed me over."

"They miss you."

"Shut up—we have bugs to kill!" Bjorn snapped and regretted it. Blair didn't deserve his ire.

"Sorry. Which one do you want me to go after?"

"I'm sorry, Blair. It's not your fault everything went to hell. I don't even know why I agreed to this." Bjorn highlighted one of the MinSha. "Let's finish this scenario, and I'll go back to my new life. When you fire on your target, get the structure between you and the one 120 degrees clockwise."

"Right. On your count."

"Two, one, hike!" Bjorn surged around the corner, cutting it as tight as the simulation would allow. The closest MinSha spun to face him, only to be skewered on Bjorn's arm-blade. The MinSha thrashed and scored the plating on his CASPer's arm before it went limp. Bjorn continued his charge ahead and to the right.

The dead alien occluded some of his cameras, but Bjorn was able to make out the mantis switching its aim from Blair to Bjorn. The MinSha's laser pulsed, the energy lost trying to burn through the dead bug's laser-resistant carapace. A second later another pulse flashed past Bjorn's suit's shoulder as the MinSha tried to aim around his deceased comrade. A third pulse skimmed his CASPer's shin armor. Bjorn launched his impromptu shield at his opponent and followed the corpse. By the time the MinSha disentangled himself and his weapon, Bjorn lopped his head off with a sweep of his arm-blade.

"Blair—sitrep?" Bjorn called.

"Mine is down, but I used a MAC round."

"Only one? Good shot." Even though Bjorn wanted to save the kinetic weapons for the Goka wave, one projectile shouldn't make a difference.

"You guys have been quiet," Mickey D called over the team channel. "We've taken the communication center and sent the message. What's your situation?"

"We've cleared the guards at the depot." Bjorn checked the virtual inventory. "Bingo! We scored a dozen K-bombs."

"Grab the goods and rendezvous," Mickey D commanded. A waypoint highlighted on the shared map.

Once they met up, a vindictive impulse urged Bjorn to blast Berto. It was a game, after all. His pinplants outlined Berto's CASPer, but Bjorn pushed aside the itch for petty revenge. It might give him a flicker of gratification, but it would ruin the run for everyone else.

"You lolly-gagging, big guy?" Berto called as the others set out.

Bjorn fell in behind them. "Checking my targeting system."

After two minutes following the road they found the next cluster of MinSha. Another crew-served weapon ensconced in the shell of a building made proceeding a deadly risk.

"Should one of us jump in?" Blair asked.

"I bet the MinSha infantry farther up would pick us off," Bjorn countered. Bjorn placed one of the K-bombs in his CASPer's left hand.

"It's a seventy-five-meter toss. You think you can make it?" Mickey D asked.

"One way to find out," Bjorn replied. The distance wasn't an issue if the software correctly translated Bjorn's strength. It was accuracy. The bomb wasn't a football, and the simulated CASPer hand didn't have the same grip. "When it goes boom, break left and engage the MinSha hunkered down in the rubble. Get among them as fast as possible and crack them like crab legs."

Bjorn armed the remote trigger on the K-bomb and heaved it. The trajectory was too flat to arc into the building from above. The K-bomb struck the wall halfway up and Bjorn detonated it. "Go!"

In the periphery of his Tri-V, Bjorn watched the walls of the building collapse, burying any opponents and weapons inside. Not the dramatic result he was hoping for but effective enough. Two laser pulses left smoking circles on his shield and another damaged a shoulder actuator, then they were among the MinSha.

"Attention, Squad Alpha, this is Dropship 1337 on approach to LZ. ETA is five minutes."

"We need to hurry before the Goka spawn!" Mickey D shouted.

"Too late!" Blair called. A black scuttling mass surged over the ruins along the road behind them.

"Move! Once we're halfway to the LZ, everyone arm a K-bomb!" Bjorn yelled. His rear camera showed the closing carpet of murderous insects. "Drop!"

Bjorn armed the K-bombs as they lumbered toward the landing zone. A timer displayed 3 minutes and 45 seconds remaining until the dropship arrived. The Goka swarm reached the K-bombs. Four thunderous explosions sent bug parts flying.

"Rockets into the mass!" Bjorn yelled. "No point in saving them!" He fired both of his munitions into the oncoming wave of insects, spreading his shots to cover as much area as possible. "Fire your MACs at any bugs who get through."

Bjorn watched the ragged Goka frontline sweep over the piles of carapaces and chitinous limbs. "K-bombs!" Bjorn bowled his explosive deep into the swarm and detonated it. It was his last. Three more explosions disrupted the swarm. "Throw what you have left!"

Two of the bombs landed within a meter of each other, reducing the field of effect. Despite the rain of destruction, several Goka persevered. MAC rounds shattered many of the survivors, but some scrambled through and drew sharp knives.

Two leaped at Bjorn. He snagged one out of the air with his left hand and crushed its head. Bjorn's arm-blade deflected the other, but it skittered back at him. The display showed two minutes.

Bjorn stomped on the Goka in time for another to penetrate the melee. It vaulted for his main canopy, but Bjorn blocked its path with his right arm. The insect sank a razor-sharp blade into the elbow joint. The arm flashed yellow in his CASPer status, and Bjorn's health bar decreased.

Bjorn flung the murder-roach into its dead fellows. He scraped another Goka off Blair's back—its knives were embedded in the CASPer's back. Blair's status showed several yellow lines and half of his health was depleted.

A loud bang reverberated through the pod as a magnetic accelerator round took off his empty rocket launcher and compromised the pauldron armor. "Watch it!" Bjorn snapped. Over a minute remained.

"Quit flailing around in the line of fire," Berto yelled back.

Bjorn snagged a leaping Goka, one of the last of the swarm, and hurled it at Berto's CASPer. The armored suit rocked as the alien slammed into the canopy armor. "Check your aim, clown!"

"Did you throw a roach at me?" Berto stomped on the meter-long insect.

"You shot me!"

"Hey, guys," Mickey D interjected.

"It was an accident!" Berto protested. His shoulder-mounted MAC swiveled as he drew a bead on Bjorn.

"Guys!"

"Like you accidently stole my girlfriend?" Bjorn snarled.

"If you hadn't turned into a nutcase maybe she wouldn't have left you!" Berto snapped.

Bjorn charged. "You sonuvabitch!" he roared. Bjorn reared back his left fist and hammered it into Berto's canopy. The pod shook from the simulated collision as he watched Berto's CASPer topple backward. Yellow flashes turned red to indicate damage to the arm of his own mech.

"You assholes!" Mickey D shouted.

As Berto's CASPer sprawled on the pavement, Bjorn could see over him, revealing the Tortantula. Instead of a Flatar saddle, a huge accelerator cannon was mounted on its back. Bjorn stared down the barrel of the weapon as its muzzle flashed. The pod rattled and went dark except for the red letters on the main display.

Game Over.

Bjorn tore off the haptic bands and yanked on the handle to raise the canopy. Luckily it was on his right side—he might have ripped the handle loose with his cybernetic arm. He clambered out of the pod. The other canopies opened.

Heather stood wide-eyed with her hands to her mouth, her eyes flicking from Bjorn to Berto's pod. She was probably wondering if Bjorn and Berto were going to continue their fight in the real world. Bjorn's blood hammered in his ears.

Berto hauled himself out of his pod and stalked toward Bjorn, spitting a stream of Spanish curses too fast for Bjorn to follow.

Unknown pejorative. Slur against your parentage. Suggestion of an anatomically impossible act. Go to hell. Unknown pejorative.

Grace watched Bjorn. Where Heather appeared torn whether to physically intervene, Grace coolly waited.

"You macho idiots!" Mickey D yelled. She slammed her hand on one of the pods as she stormed toward Bjorn and Berto. "You couldn't keep it together for another 45 seconds before your egos took over? You couldn't have your pissing match on your own goddamn time?"

Bjorn's righteous indignation and stoked fury deflated like a balloon. He still seethed, but she was right. "I'm sorry, Alison." Using her given name added some gravitas to his apology. She had taken the run seriously, even if it wasn't a military-grade simulator, and he'd ruined it.

Bjorn turned to Berto. "You, I'm not sorry. I hope we don't cross paths again—next time you piss me off might not be in a game."

Grace fell into step beside him as they headed for the door. "I'm sorry. I thought it might be cathartic."

"It's not your fault. I wouldn't blame you if you didn't want to date me after that display," Bjorn said.

She took his right hand and squeezed it. "We all have a past. What's important is how we move forward."

"I guess you're right. For a few minutes, it felt like old times, but it's the past, and I need to move on." The electronic cacophony of the arcade was replaced by the street noise of cruisers and the cheers of the crowd in the parking lot. "So where to from here?"

"By the time we get out of this parking lot and up to Monte Vista, it will be night." Grace lowered her lashes. "I can't make you forget the past, but I bet I can take your mind off it."

*****

Chapter Thirty

Las Cruces, New Mexico

Bjorn paused at the entrance to the kitchen. Both his parents sat at the breakfast table. His mother sipped coffee as she skimmed a slate while his father devoured a hearty stack of pancakes. The aroma of the bacon piled high on a plate had drawn Bjorn downstairs from his room despite still being tired. Sunday was his only day to sleep in, but his stomach won out over laziness.

"Good morning," his mother said cheerily. "How was the date?"

"Did you break the car in?" his father asked with a smirk.

"It was fine." Why did this feel like an interrogation or an intervention?

"Fine? You didn't get home until nearly 0200 hours," the commander said before renewing his attack on the pancakes.

"Do you want a play-by-play?" Bjorn asked. He surveyed the food in the warmers. More pancakes, hash browns, and eggs in addition to the bacon. He'd go easy on the pancakes and potatoes and load up on the protein-laden food.

"No!" His mother covered her embarrassment by focusing on her slate.

"What are you being dodgy about? Besides the obvious—which we don't need to hear about." His father wiped syrup-sticky crumbs from his beard and moustache—an argument against Bjorn growing out his own facial hair.

"I ran into Berto, Heather, and the others at the arcade," Bjorn replied.

The commander slurped his coffee before asking, "Do I owe for any damages?"

"No, I didn't break anything or anyone." Bjorn loaded his plate and poured a glass of orange juice. "Things got heated, but the only punches thrown were in a game."

"I'm guessing you and Berto didn't shake hands and make up afterwards," his father stated.

No kidding—did he really expect Bjorn to bury the hatchet with the friend who betrayed him? "You're right. If anything, it was a reminder of how much I lost."

"Heather was there?" Bjorn's mother set down her slate.

Bjorn nodded while he chewed a mouthful of bacon. "Nothing like being out with your new girlfriend and running into your ex-girlfriend." Grace had been coy about her conversation with Heather during the simulation run. "They got to hang out while my attempt to relive the glory days went up in flames."

The commander chuckled. "To be a fly on the wall, or better yet have a micro-drone so you could hear what they talked about."

"New girlfriend? So it's official?" Bjorn's mother swiped at her slate screen. "You updated your relationship status online and everything."

"So how long will you hide us from her family?" Bjorn's father asked over his coffee cup.

Bjorn's mother glanced sidelong at the commander. "Bjorn has nothing to be embarrassed about, BJ. There's no hurry; we've barely met Grace."

"He's worried I'm going say she's only into him because we're rich, and that I'll disapprove of her family because they're not wealthy," Bjorn's father stated. "I don't blame you, son. Those thoughts crossed my mind, same as when you and Heather got together."

Bjorn remained silent, working his way through the pancakes and hash browns.

"I like Grace," Bjorn's mother protested.

"For the record, so do I," the commander retorted. "She's a spitfire, and she'll keep Trip on his toes. The girl was in the room all of two minutes, and I could tell she wasn't angling to be a trophy wife. Don't pick out wedding arrangements, though. You're still too young. Don't even think about getting serious until after college."

"Assuming I go to college," Bjorn muttered.

"My offer stands. Hudson's Harriers went under because the CEO never met a bad investment he didn't jump on. There are worse things than learning how to handle the finances." The commander paused for another slurp of coffee. "I had to learn from my father, and I'm not as good at it as he was."

"Why not go to college?" Bjorn's mother asked.

"Maybe I want to see how I do on my VOWS next month?" Bjorn's eyes fell to his plate despite how badly he wanted to see their expressions.

"Now you're just being contrary," his father accused.

Bjorn's mother clucked her tongue. "You don't want to be a mercenary."

"What I want is to accomplish something on my own." Bjorn speared a sausage link.

"You don't have to decide now," his mother said. "So, when are we going to have Grace over for dinner?"

"Not next weekend. She'll be out of town for a debate meet," Bjorn replied. "She's free the following weekend."

"She's on a debate team? Son, are you sure you want to date her? You'll never win an argument." The commander grinned.

"BJ." Bjorn's mother shook her head. "Do you want to invite her over, or the whole family?"

"Let's see if Dad scares her off first," Bjorn replied. "If not, we can have Grace's family over the next month."

"What are you doing today, wise guy?" Bjorn's father asked.

"What? Homework—I don't have any plans." Bjorn double-checked his calendar in his pinview. He had about three hours of homework thanks to his pinplant making reading assignments a breeze.

The commander grinned. "Want to go to orbit?"

Bjorn raised an eyebrow. He could tell his mother was holding her tongue. He'd been to space twice, once with his father and again with a school group. "What's in orbit?"

"The EMS *Onikuma*—the latest addition to Bjorn's Berserkers. It's a mercenary cruiser—a Besquith design." The commander's grin widened. "It was spoils of war, but it needed repairs and some refitting."

"How the heck did you take a Besquith mercenary cruiser?" The Besquith were top-notch engineers, a fact often overshadowed by their reputation for blood-thirsty carnage on the battlefield.

"Khabar pirates mistook our hired transport for a civilian freighter. The dumb goats didn't expect to open the hatch and find a mercenary company." The commander laughed. "They were so pissed—at least the ones who survived."

"Were they related to the Khabar we ran into in Houston?" It seemed an unlikely coincidence, but Bjorn was suspicious of the goat-people.

The commander waved his hand dismissively. "I doubt the same goat-faced sonuvabitch you punched out in Houston managed to track me down to a random transport. If he did, the Gruff messed up."

"Wait, what's this about Trip punching a goat?" Bjorn's mother interjected.

"It wasn't a goat, it was an alien who was trying to rob us," Bjorn replied.

"He clocked the Gruff good," the commander remarked. Bjorn's mother scowled. "Don't worry, Lynn. My people were there. Trip wasn't in any danger."

"Did you get the smell out?" Bjorn asked, hoping to change the subject.

The commander nodded. "I don't think the Gruffs had it long. I suspect they stole it from some Pushtal pirates."

"What did you do with the survivors?" Bjorn asked.

"Since they weren't mercenaries, there was no ransom for their safe return. I dumped them off at Karma. Their leader, Brillo, was pissed. I thought he was going to spit nails." Bjorn's father guffawed. "Anyway, they signaled last night the cruiser was ready for inspection. I've got a dropship waiting at Bear Town. If you want to tag along and promise not to throw up all those eggs and bacon, you can join me."

A screaming VTOL passed over the house to kick up dust in the backyard. Bjorn checked the time—two minutes after the end of the neighborhood quiet time. The neighbors would be ticked, but they couldn't do more than complain.

"Let me grab my slate, and I'll meet you out back," Bjorn said. If he had known he was going to orbit, he wouldn't have wolfed down so many eggs. Bjorn raced up the steps to his room two at a time. Having their own cruiser untied a logistical knot in the Berserkers' operations. Getting a Besquith ship without having to fight the werewolves was a bonus. Not only were Besquith highly regarded shipwrights, their vessels had a reputation for spaciousness other races lacked.

The commander sat in the VTOL, watching impatiently as Bjorn jogged to the waiting aircraft. As soon as Bjorn strapped himself in, the flyer leapt into the air, accompanied by the shriek of duct-fan turbines. The VTOL lurched and bobbed as it swung west and howled toward Bear Peak in the San Andres range. In five minutes, they were circling over a landing pad in Bear Town.

"You okay, son?" the commander asked. "If you need to heave, do it now before we go to orbit."

"Did you invite me along solely in the hopes I'd vomit so you could give me grief about it?" Bjorn quelled his roiling stomach.

"Solely? No. I consider it a side benefit as long as you don't puke on me."

The dropship could carry a platoon of CASPers into battle, so it felt cavernous when Bjorn and his father joined Vurrg in the fold-out passenger seats.

"What do you think of the transport vehicle?" the Zuul asked, his muzzle parted in a toothy smile.

"It's really cool. It stands out in the crowd," Bjorn replied.

Vurrg tilted his head quizzically. "Is distinctiveness important?"

"For teenagers it is," the commander said. "Plus I'm sure he appreciates the spacious cargo accommodations."

"Splendid! I did not realize your son would be interested in hauling cargo," Vurrg remarked. The Zuul lowered his voice. "It also provides sufficient space for—"

"Yes, I know," Bjorn interrupted as his cheeks turned red. "It was quite sufficient."

"Excellent. Your father said you had a new mate," Vurrg said.

The lift alarm cut off Bjorn's stumbling attempt at a reply. The dropship thundered skyward, slamming Bjorn into his seat. Air-breathing scramjets soon surrendered to alien tech rockets as the atmosphere thinned. Fifteen minutes later, the G-forces abated as the dropship reached orbit.

"What brings you along, Vurrg?" Bjorn asked, hoping to deflect any questions regarding mating.

"Your father invited me. He is fortunate—as I understand it, the ship is only two hundred years old," Vurrg replied.

"It's two hundred years old?" Bjorn turned to his father. "You didn't say it was a relic!"

"Son, you have to understand, Galactic technology is built to last," Bjorn's father retorted. "It isn't how industry was on Earth, where everything has a planned obsolescence to drive the consumer purchase cycle. In the Union, assets such as starships are built to last. The flagship of the Winged Hussars is far older."

"I bet upgrading it to modern technology was expensive," Bjorn remarked. His guts flip-flopped as the dropship coasted through the satellite belt and micro-gravity replaced the faux push of thrust. The eggs roiled in his stomach.

"Technology in the Union advances at a glacial pace." His father watched him, gauging whether Bjorn was going to lose his breakfast. "Most of the work was refurbishing the ship after months of slipshod maintenance and switching systems to Human standard."

"That's crazy. A ton has changed in the past century. I can tell the differences in slates from the time I was born versus the ones the Berserkers use as tactical slates." Bjorn focused on the argument rather than his queasiness. "Heck, Binnig has had eight iterations of the CASPer since the Alpha Contracts."

"I can attest that Galactic technology changes very little," Vurrg interjected. "After the nanite revolution, there have been few advancements, and those have been incremental. The Galactic Union and the Science Guild have been around for millennia, and technology is hitting the barriers of what is physically possible. Devices can only be so small before you can't shrink them anymore. Materials have a finite limit of how much energy they can conduct. If there was a way to make a better slate, or a more efficient hyperspace drive, the Science Guild would have discovered it by now."

"Son, Earth is still catching up to the Galactic Union. Slates didn't get better—we figured out they were selling us crappy ones. The improvement in CASPers isn't because the Union is getting more advanced, it's because Binnig has gotten better at incorporating Galactic technology into their suits."

"Commander, we're preparing for final approach," the co-pilot called.

"Give me a scenic pass," Bjorn's father replied.

"Roger. EMS *Onikuma*, this is Dropship Bruin Actual. Requesting permission to land after a victory lap."

Bjorn could hear the reply. "Acknowledged, Bruin Actual. Port hangar is standing by."

The dropship spun on maneuvering thrusters and controlled bursts from the engines brought it alongside the *Onikuma*. The ovoid vessel stretched 120 meters in length. A pair of hangars pierced the waist of the ship, offset by a pair of extendable gravity decks. Defensive weaponry and shield nodes bristled on the hull, arranged to let the cruiser close in, release its dropships, and get out in one piece.

"I hate to admit it, but the Besquith are fine engineers," Vurrg remarked as he gazed out the window. "It's a shame such a splendid vessel fell into the paws of the Pushtal, then the hooves of the Khabar."

Bjorn stared at the metal ovoid hanging in the blackness of space. A freshly painted Bjorn's Berserkers logo adorned the hull. For all the talk of Besquith engineering, what made this ship any better than any of the other egg, sphere, and cigar shaped vessels orbiting Earth?

"Odin only knows how the Gruffs got it away from the Pushtal, but I'd guess in the same manner we acquired it. The greedy tigers thought they had a fat civilian transport, but instead it was full of

Khabar." The commander appraised the ship as the dropship circled it.

"I wouldn't think the Khabar could match the Pushtal," Bjorn remarked. After all, he punched one out.

"Never underestimate the value of surprise." Bjorn's father grinned. "It's how we took it, and I'd be willing to bet it's how the Pushtal stole it from the original owners. Somewhere there's some ticked off Besquith."

"Aren't you worried they'll come to reclaim the ship?" Bjorn didn't want to be the object of a Besquith's ire.

"The laws regarding prizes of war and salvage are pretty clear in the Galactic Union. We legally seized the vessel in a defensive operation, and more importantly, we paid the credits to duly register it with the Mercenary Guild and the Cartography Guild." His father rubbed his thumb and forefinger. "Most laws in the Union revolve around the appropriate guild getting their credits."

Bjorn lost sight of the *Onikuma* as the pilot spun the dropship and oriented toward an open hangar bay. As they slipped into the bay, the wall loomed a mere three meters from the window Bjorn peered through.

"No, there isn't much room to spare," his father commented, following Bjorn's gaze. "She carries up to six dropships and two shuttles. We can transport an oversized company into battle. The limiting factor is interface craft to deliver the troops to the surface."

"You could attach smaller transports to the docking points," Vurrg suggested. "A landing transport could carry one of your CASPer companies. I have an associate who would make a reasonable deal on one."

The dropship shuddered and magnetic clamps seized it and adjusted its parking position. Warning lights indicated the bay was still in vacuum.

"There's a Human phrase about putting your eggs in one basket," the commander remarked. "If the landing transport gets shot down, you lose the entire company, plus the transport and crew. It would break the back of a merc outfit our size."

The warning lights flashed, then changed color. "We've got atmosphere, Commander Tovesson. You're good to disembark," the co-pilot called.

Bjorn's father released his restraints and nudged himself so he could grab an overhead handle. Vurrg followed suit with the ease of a veteran space traveler. Bjorn unbuckled his harness but held onto his seat's armrest.

"Maybe we should have gotten you some magnetic boots?" The commander waited for the hatch to open.

"The trick is to stay within reach of something you can hang onto," Vurrg commented. "There is no worse feeling than flailing about in empty space."

Bjorn eyed the handle behind Vurrg and pushed off his seat. His pinplants highlighted his target.

Activate magnetic grip?

"Yes."

Bjorn began to spin as he swiped at the handle and missed by two centimeters. He raised his left hand to cushion the impact with the ceiling. His hand stuck to the metal even as he bounced away, giving him enough leverage to swing himself within reach of the intended handle. He flexed the fingers in his cybernetic hand to pop his magnetized palm away from the metal.

"At least you didn't brain yourself," his father said. "You've already met your concussion quota for the year."

The hatch sliding open interrupted any rejoinder Bjorn had. Cool air tinged with the odor of burning metal and solvents wafted into the compartment. It reminded Bjorn of the motor pool garage with the air conditioner set on full blast.

"Welcome aboard, Commander Tovesson." The woman greeting them wore a Berserkers dark gray uniform with a captain's insignia. Her ballcap bore a patch with a stylized bear riding a rocket and EMS Onikuma embroidered under it.

"Thank you, Captain Alderfer." The commander nodded and turned so Captain Alderfer could see past his bulk. "This is Vurrg, a civilian supplier, and my son Bjorn III. We call him Trip to prevent confusion."

"Welcome to the EMS *Onikuma*, gentlemen."

"Captain Alderfer is in command of all of our space and interface assets." The commander launched himself to the railing running along the wall of the hangar. "I know you have a lot on your plate, Norene. You can have someone give us the nickel tour, and we'll get out of your hair."

Vurrg followed Bjorn's father with practiced sureness. The captain was already pulling herself along the railing toward a hatch. Bjorn shoved off the dropship. As soon as he was within arm's length of the wall, he used his cybernetic limb to catch hold.

"You okay, son?" Bjorn's father called from the hatch.

Bjorn could feel the eyes of everyone in the bay on him. He tried to hand-over-hand along the rail but found it harder to break the magnetic grip than on a flat surface. He quickly improvised a routine in his pinplants to quickly enable or disable the electromagnets.

"I'll be right there." It was easier to not use the magnetic feature of his hand when pulling along the rail. "This is only my third time in orbit."

"You owe me lunch," Vurrg said to Bjorn's father.

"I guess I do. The boy didn't upchuck," the commander responded. "Let me guess—the Mongolian place in Houston?"

"You bet I would puke?" Bjorn hung onto the railing and fought the momentum of his body.

"For the record, I had confidence in you, young Bjorn," Vurrg said with a toothy grin. "Thank you for lunch."

Captain Alderfer led them into a curved corridor. Based on the bend, they must be close to the center of the ship. A vertical shaft opened in the floor and ceiling. Ladder rungs lined the wall of the shaft and a glowing arrow pointed up.

BTI: Welcome aboard, Bjorn.

Bjorn ensured he had a solid grip on a rung and followed everyone else up the shaft before answering. "*You're installed on the ship?*"

BTI: A node of this program has been installed on this ship to facilitate mission operations.

"Can you fly the ship?"

BTI: A certain degree of automation is available, but the vessel is too complex for this program to operate for extended periods or in operations approaching combat complexity.

An updating icon appeared in the corner of Bjorn's pinview. After a few seconds it vanished, in time for Bjorn to barely catch himself before colliding with Vurrg's feet.

"Son, are you getting dizzy or something?" his father called.

"Sorry, it's a pinplant thing." By now, his father accepted the excuse whenever Bjorn spaced out. Usually it was because he was distracted by something in his pinview. Usually.

BTI: I have updated your Bjorn's Berserkers facilities files and included the deck plans for the *Onikuma*. A wire frame of the ship appeared, with a blinking amber dot to indicate his current location.

"This is the bridge," Captain Alderfer announced at a heavily armored hatch. Several parallel gouges marred the surface of the hatch. Besquith claw marks? Were they from when the original owners lost the ship? "Besquith vessels have unified bridges and command information centers."

The room beyond was not as cramped as Bjorn had expected. The map in his pinview showed them midway up the ship right off the central spine. Tri-V consoles lined the chamber. All the stations and couches were on articulated arms.

"One advantage of Besquith ship architecture is you have plenty of room," Vurrg remarked.

Bjorn clung to the handrail. The high ceiling left plenty of space for him to drift embarrassed until someone fished him down. "I know Besquith are large, but isn't all the headroom wasted space?"

"All of the workstations are designed to rotate ninety degrees to face the bow of the ship," Captain Alderfer explained. "Operations, forward external view on the main display."

"Aye, Captain," a young man with a single private chevron replied. He tapped his console, and the ceiling disappeared behind a starfield. Earth arched across a section of the view, and an orbital station hovered in the distance with traffic buzzing around it. The man's station swiveled so he faced toward the huge Tri-V.

"Besquith design. Some ships rotate their entire CIC and bridge, but this is much simpler and easier to maintain," Vurrg said.

The next stop on their tour was the deck above, which included the commander's cabin. Bjorn wrinkled his nose when the hatch opened. While the faint scent of goat permeated much of the ship, he could brush it off as an artifact of his imagination. In this room the odor of goat, dried meat, and leather hung in the air.

"What in Odin's name is that?" Bjorn's father demanded. Bjorn peered over his shoulder. A tiger pelt rug stretched across the center of the cabin.

"Is that a Pushtal rug?" Bjorn asked. It would explain the smell, especially if it was fresh. It reminded him of the bear rug at his grandfather's house.

"Sorry, Commander. I thought they already removed it." The captain tapped a note on her tactical slate. "I'll have them get it out and dumped by end of shift."

"See that you do," Bjorn's father stated. "As much as everyone hates the Pushtal, I don't want word getting around that I keep the hide of a sentient as a decoration. Plus, it stinks up the place."

Bjorn's hand drifted to where his own grisly trophies were tucked under his shirt.

"Good thing I hadn't planned on staying up here," the commander added.

Bjorn followed his father into the cabin. For a shipboard cabin, it was spacious, but smaller than Bjorn's bedroom. As he looked around the cabin, his pinplants highlighted corners and contours. Bjorn spotted a small tubular object twenty centimeters long floating above a duraplex cabinet. Clear panels boxed in a stack of metal shelves. Was it some sort of trophy case? Bjorn magnetized his hand and pulled himself along the ceiling to the cabinet. He tried to fish the cylinder out of the space, but it was too tight to shove his hand in.

"Trip, what are you doing?" his father asked.

"There's something here." Bjorn held his left palm toward the object. It slowly drifted toward him until it bumped against his palm.

"Good thing it wasn't a bomb or some other booby-trap," the commander remarked.

"A bomb?" Vurrg's eyes went wide.

The metal cylinder had three bands marked with symbols. His pinplants highlighted the glyphs as Bjorn turned the item in his hand. "Do you want this, Captain?"

"Finders keepers. It's nothing the technical teams have noticed, even when they swept the ship for stray electronics," the captain said.

"It's probably full of Besquith erotica," the commander remarked with a chuckle.

"You think so?" Vurrg cocked his head.

"I was kidding," Bjorn's father replied. "I don't even know if the werewolves have smut. Why are you so interested?"

"Curious, maybe," Vurrg countered. "I doubt I would survive a Besquith alpha. The females are quite…aggressive."

"Keep it up and you might lose your free lunch." Bjorn stashed the cylinder to examine later.

The commander laughed. "It would be like a chihuahua trying to mount a German Shepherd."

"Now I might lose my lunch," Captain Alderfer muttered. "The next stop on our tour will be the mess hall. Commander, it will be a good opportunity to meet some of the crew."

"A chihuahua? There's no need to be insulting," Vurrg grumbled.

"Captain, are we still on schedule for departure in ten days?" the commander asked as they rose toward the mess and galley deck.

"Yes, Commander."

"What's in ten days?" Bjorn asked. "Do you have another contract?"

"Yup. An Eosogi corporation has hired us to root out some claim jumpers backed by a HecSha garrison," Bjorn's father replied.

"Will you be back in time for the VOWS?" Bjorn asked. The assessment would take place two weeks before Thanksgiving, two months from now.

"If everything goes according to plan. The target is two jumps away, so we'll be four weeks in hyperspace round trip. If we're two weeks on-world as planned, then I'll be back." Bjorn's father arched an eyebrow. "What does it matter? It's not as though my presence is going to make a difference on your scores."

"Because I'm going to knock it out of the park when I take my VOWS, and I want you to be proud of me," Bjorn replied quietly.

"Son, no matter what, I'll be proud of you," the commander replied. "A bear shredded your arm less than a year ago. You lost everything you'd been building toward, yet here you are, ready to kick Loki in the pills. You'd make a helluva merc, but you'll succeed whatever you decide to do."

"Damn, I might tear up," Captain Alderfer remarked.

"You get used to it," Vurrg whispered.

* * * * *

Chapter Thirty-One

Las Cruces, New Mexico

Bjorn turned the cylinder over in his hands. The markings weren't Besquith or Pushtal. GalNet entries had identified a few as Khabask, the Khabar language. It was a puzzle Bjorn didn't have much spare time to mull over, but he kept finding himself drawn back to it.

An alert pinged in his pinview. He needed to go pick up Grace for the dreaded family dinner. His parents acted as though they liked Grace, but Bjorn kept expecting the other shoe to drop, especially from the commander. Was he being paranoid?

Bjorn energized the ZPT. The Zuul-built vehicle was a hit at school as well as at Bear Town. As much as Vurrg raved about Besquith ship architecture, Zuul vehicle design was admired by Bjorn's peers. He decided to drive on manual despite the traffic. He found he relished being in control of the vehicle as opposed to letting the computers decide for him.

"*Oye!* Nice ride, Oso!"

Many of the locals recognize Bjorn, or at least his car. He waved in the general direction of the greeting as he followed traffic to Grace's building. This would be Bjorn's third trip to the family apartment.

A short, middle-aged man with a sun-weathered face opened the door. "You must be Bjorn."

"Yes, sir. I take it you're Grace's father. It's a pleasure to meet you, Mr. Garcia."

The man regarded him, unfazed by the fact Bjorn towered over him. "A pleasure to meet me? At least you have manners, *gringo*."

"I heard about your machete collection," Bjorn said as the man admitted him.

Mr. Garcia chuckled. "Good. With a machete, even the biggest man can be cut down to size."

"Mama! You promised Papa wouldn't threaten my boyfriend!" Grace called.

"I can't cook dinner and keep him away from the door, *menina*."

"I am not threatening your boyfriend," Grace's father protested. "I am sizing him up."

The kids watching the Tri-V in the living room didn't even glance away from their program.

"Well, you've had your chance to meet him," Grace said, taking Bjorn's arm.

"I am only getting started, *hija*." Mr. Garcia grinned wickedly. "However, I can see you are eager to drag your boyfriend to safety. I'll save my questions for later. Perhaps sometime soon Bjorn and I can sit down and talk man-to-man?"

"Papa!" Grace led Bjorn to the door.

"Is it wrong for me to want to get to know the boy my daughter spends so much time with?"

"I spend more time on the debate team, but you don't threaten Mr. Poore," Grace retorted. "Good night. Don't wait up for me."

"Sharpening my machetes keeps me awake," Grace's father retorted.

Grace sighed as she closed the door. "For the record, he can barely stay awake after ten and has never actually harmed any boy I dated. Once I have you over for dinner, he'll calm down."

A family riding the elevator down drowned out any chance for a conversation and limited Bjorn and Grace to holding hands. Out front a dozen locals were gathered around Bjorn's car, admiring the vehicle and debating its origin.

Bjorn unlocked the transport via his pinplants, which also flashed the lights. The crowd stepped back in case the vehicle went into autodrive mode. A boy a couple of years younger than Bjorn spotted him and Grace approaching.

"Is this your car?" the boy asked.

Bjorn nodded. "It's a Zuul personal transport. They love curves in their vehicles, or at least they did when this was made."

"See, I told you it wasn't Chinese," someone in the crowd muttered.

Bjorn opened the passenger door and helped Grace up.

"When I grow up, I'm going to a get a Zuul car," the boy declared.

"How're you going to afford an alien-built car on your government stipend?" someone teased.

The boy crossed his arms, staring at the ZPT. "Easy. I'll become a mercenary. Then I'll be able to afford an alien car. Maybe I'll get a flying car."

"I don't know if getting a car is worth becoming a mercenary," Bjorn remarked as he circled the vehicle.

"It's the only way a kid from the projects is going to get rich," the boy called after Bjorn. "Otherwise I'll be stuck here with these losers."

Bjorn closed the door, cutting off the crowd's response. He made sure everyone was clear before pulling out and joining traffic.

"Unfortunately, he's right," Grace said, watching the tower complex. "Unless you're smart, talented, or lucky, kids like him are stuck living in government housing and living off the government guaranteed income. He might be able to get a menial job to supplement the stipend, but then the government pares back the GGI by half of what you make. Meanwhile, the media shows mercenaries living the high life."

"While omitting the part about how many of them die," Bjorn added. The casualty rates for rookie mercenaries, especially in smaller, less established outfits, was high. Even in a big outfit, such as the Berserkers or one of the Horsemen, you could still get killed before you even reached the planet.

"I'm glad you're not becoming a mercenary." Grace patted his shoulder. "I'd be worried sick every time you left on contract. It would make concentrating on my studies hard."

"Yeah." Bjorn still hadn't taken the commander up on his offer.

"Mama wants you to come over for dinner next weekend," Grace said. Bjorn welcomed the change of subject. "You might not be facing aliens, but are you ready to brave my family for more than five minutes?"

"I can manage it," Bjorn replied. "Especially since every time I've been to your apartment whatever your mother has been cooking smelled delicious."

"Should I tell her to take it easy on the heat?"

Bjorn shook his head. "I love authentic Tejano food. I don't want it artificially hot the way some gimmicky restaurants get, but as long as I have a glass of water, I'll be good."

"I'll make sure you have plenty of water," Grace said.

* * *

"Does this whole swath of land belong to your family?" Grace asked as they rolled through the security arch.

Bjorn shook his head. "The Tovessons hold the southwest quarter, which is a bit over a hectare. We share the outer perimeter with three other families and split the security cost. The Stantons, our neighbors to the east, are always fussing with my father. If he could, the commander would buy out their property so he wouldn't have to listen to them anymore."

"What are they feuding over?"

"Mr. Stanton complains about the VTOLs coming and going. To be fair, they are a lot louder than the Stanton's or the Cheng's aircars." Bjorn swung onto the circular court at the heart of the neighborhood. An Egyptian-style obelisk dominated the center of the court, providing hiding places for more security cameras. Four driveways radiated away from the circle, each to a private gate.

"Wow, you guys have a ton of security," Grace remarked as the gate to the Tovesson estate swung open. "Do you have a lot of trouble?"

"No. People know if they try to break in, we'll have enough biometric and imaging evidence to nail them to the wall, assuming they even get out before the private security response team arrives." More tell-tales of the lopsided justice system. Bjorn parked the ZPT in front of the garage. "Criminals know wealthy families in neighborhoods such as this will pay to have them prosecuted, so they go after softer targets."

"In a way, that's messed up." Grace took Bjorn's hand and let him help her down.

Bjorn shrugged. "Public law enforcement is a limited resource, and the prison system has been overloaded for more than a century. It's why the cops wouldn't have had the time of day for a couple of school kids duking it out. Heck, the areas in and around startowns are worse. There's only private security and the risk of running afoul of armed mercenaries keeping the criminal element in check. While Galactic Union law applies in the starport, it takes a major crime to draw a Peacemaker."

Grace held his hand as they walked to the door. "I've never been to a startown."

"It's not as impressive as it sounds. They're mostly warehouses with a smattering of bars, restaurants, and hotels catering to the mercenary industry. Toss in a few tourist traps and businesses too seedy to run under Earth laws and you've got a startown." Bjorn held the front door open for Grace. He called down the hall, "We're here."

Grace's gaze swept across the foyer. The left opened into the living room half the size of her family's entire apartment.

"Your father is in the back yard with Vurrg," his mother responded. "Let me get him. Have a seat, and Geneva will bring you some refreshments."

"Who's Genev—" Grace clutched Bjorn's arm. "You didn't say you had a pet mountain lion."

What? Bjorn followed her frozen gaze. A large, tawny feline regarded them from one of the couches. His pinplants outlined the creature. Race: H'rang—Identity: Doctor Shur'im

"Dr. Shur'im? What are you doing here?" It was going to be enough of a distraction having one alien here, but at least most Humans knew about Zuul. The cougar-like H'rang were another story.

"Hello, you are surprised to see me, yes?" Dr. Shur'im rose from the couch. "Your mate is certainly surprised."

"She's never met a H'rang before. Grace, this is Doctor Shur'im. She installed my pinplants." Bjorn gave Grace's hand a reassuring squeeze.

"This is correct." The doctor bobbed her head. "My associate and I wanted to follow up with our star patient. It has been ten *mr'ufft* since your procedure—a *mr'ufft* is three to the third power days."

"Associate?" Bjorn would have missed the beige lump in an armchair if not for his pinplants outlining and highlighting the ElSha. "Frek?"

The form stirred and returned to a mottled green and beige skin pattern. "Did I doze off?"

Grace reacted with curiosity instead of trepidation as the lizard-like alien sat up. Perhaps his smaller stature made him less threatening.

"Frek designed and built my prosthesis," Bjorn explained.

"I'm working on the next iteration," Frek remarked as he stretched and yawned. "In another nine to twelve Earth month's you will have grown enough to merit a new arm. Depending on how much bigger you get, there may be one more upgrade. It wouldn't do to have your arms noticeably different lengths."

Geneva stood in the entrance holding a tray. "Iced tea? It's unsweetened, so I brought sugar and sweetener."

"Grace, this is Geneva." Bjorn accepted a glass with his left hand.

"Are you Bjorn's aunt?" Grace asked.

"Goodness no. I'm the Tovesson's housekeeper. I had to change your boyfriend's diapers." The stocky woman gave a hearty laugh.

"Really?" Of anyone, Geneva was best armed with embarrassing stories from Bjorn's childhood.

"Housekeeper?" Grace's tone grew cool. "Are you indentured?" Indentured servitude had been legalized decades ago to deal with rampant debt from earlier generations. The practice had fallen back out of favor but was still technically legal. After a generation of people working off their ancestors' debts through servitude, almost no one took out new loans where indentured service was a provision.

"No. My family came to the USA nation-state from Austria when my brother enlisted with Bjorn's Berserkers. My brother died on his second contract and our parents squandered his death benefits.

Commander Tovesson hired me on to help his wife. They pay me too much to qualify for GGI, and in turn I clean up after their caveman of a son." Geneva set the tray on a table. "Doctor, don't you want your milk?"

"H'rang are lactose intolerant," Dr. Shur'im replied with practiced patience. "Some water would be splendid."

"What is this milk?" Frek wandered over.

"Earth mammals secrete this fluid to feed their young," the H'rang explained, holding the glass out. "It contains a disaccharide H'rang cannot properly metabolize. However, since Earth mammals resembling us savor this secretion, Humans offer it to races they refer to as felinoid."

Frek flicked his long tongue into the glass. "Oh, that's tasty. It reminds me of *untranslatable* juice."

"Please, take it." Dr. Shur'im handed Frek the glass.

"Dinner will be ready in half an hour in the formal dining room," Geneva said before departing.

"Formal dining room? How many do you have?" Grace asked, averting her eyes from Frek lapping at the milk.

"Only the one, but we usually eat at the breakfast table in the kitchen," Bjorn replied. Hopefully Frek hadn't brought his own meal consisting of grubs or other creepy crawlies. "You get the fancy treatment."

"There she is!" Bjorn's father exclaimed. "We haven't scared you off yet?"

"No. Nice to see you again, Commander and Mrs. Tovesson," Grace said.

"I hope our guests didn't startle you, Grace." Bjorn's mother cast a sidelong glance at the commander. "They were a last-minute addition."

"Speaking of which, this is Vurrg." The commander gestured to the Zuul next to him. "We're business associates."

"Let me guess, you provided Bjorn's car." Grace's self-assurance returned.

"You are correct. I hope there was sufficient space for your—"

"The car is great," Bjorn interrupted. "What brings you by?"

"Your father mentioned you were having a dinner to welcome your new mate," Vurrg replied. "Having met your previous mate, I was curious as to the difference and eager to observe Human family rituals."

Bjorn winced. What was next? Were Khabar going to knock on the door?

"It's not how I described it, son," the commander protested.

"I read between the pages," Vurrg countered, grinning.

"Young Humans are prone to embarrassment and emotional outbursts," Dr. Shur'im remarked. She held up her slate. "Biometric telemetry reinforces this supposition. Perhaps we should cease discussing mates, yes?"

Frek stopped lapping milk long enough to comment, "Mammals."

"Yes, please, let's change the subject," Bjorn said.

Grace leaned close and whispered in his ear. "You're turning red. It's cute to see you flustered but don't burst a blood vessel."

Geneva returned. "If everyone would be seated in the dining room, I'll serve the first course."

"Thank Thor," Bjorn muttered.

Once everyone was seated, Bjorn's mother steered the conversation to more conventional topics. "Grace, what are your plans after high school?"

"I've been accepted to the University of New Mexico. I'm going to major in finance with the intent of going on to law school," Grace replied.

"A lawyer?" Bjorn's father raised an eyebrow. "It's a lot of school. It takes what, about six years?"

"It is a long time, Commander Tovesson, and since I'm going beyond a four-year degree, it won't be cheap." Grace paused as Geneva set the main course in the middle of the table, a steaming brisket. "The federal education grant only covers bachelor's degrees. Between savings, a matching scholarship, the Tauber Memorial Grant, and working a part-time job, I'll have it covered."

"You have been planning your course of action for long, yes?" The H'rang's tongue licked her muzzle as she eyed the brisket. "I have only been on Earth for two years, but your social support programs are complex. They vary by the districts you call nation-states and can hinge on cosmetic variations. I find some laudable and others laughable."

Bjorn noticed the slight lag indicative of reading a pinview. The doctor was using her pinplants to improve her English vocabulary.

"So you were here over a year before working on your first Human patient?" Bjorn asked, fighting a note of alarm creeping into his voice.

"You were not my first Human patient," Dr. Shur'im replied. "There is a growing Human population on one of our colony worlds. You are my first Human pinplant implantation."

"You're my first Human client," Frek added. "I know, adding an arm isn't as creepy as having her fish around in your skull with nanites and monofilaments. I'm glad to see you haven't torn it off yet."

"My vehicle seems to be the least disturbing contribution," Vurrg remarked with a laugh, watching as Geneva served the first round of brisket.

"I'll try some of your dead mammal flesh," Frek remarked when Geneva reached him. "If nothing else, I realize my dietary preferences distress Humans, especially when they are also eating."

Grace glanced to Bjorn quizzically. "He prefers bugs and grubs—preferably alive," Bjorn said, suppressing the urge to grin at her discomfort.

"I long ago learned to appreciate the ways Humans prepare meat," Dr. Shur'im stated, picking up her fork. "There is a significant Brazilian population on Vishall, and their *churrascarias* are…how do you say a religious experience…divine."

"The one in the Houston Startown is spectacular!" Vurrg exclaimed.

"You ate so much I thought they were going to kick us out," the commander remarked.

"The sign said all you can eat!" Vurrg protested.

Bjorn stole a glance at Grace. She appeared to have recovered from any initial apprehension and was watching the aliens' banter in fascination. *Good, they're not going to scare her off.* Bjorn had been concerned it was some sort of test on the commander's part, despite his claims of liking Grace.

Conversation faded until dessert. If Frek didn't find the cuisine to his taste, he kept it to himself. For Vurrg and Dr. Shur'im, there was no doubt they enjoyed the meal. While both races descended from carnivores, they had become more omnivorous with civilization.

"There is another reason we wished to speak to you, Bjorn," Dr. Shur'im said as she pushed back half a slice of Linzer torte.

"Are you not going to finish your dessert?" Vurrg asked.

The H'rang slid the plate over. "Be my guest. As I was saying, there is a reason Frek and I wished to speak to you with your family and mate."

Bjorn resisted the urge to reach for his pinlink port behind his ear. "Is there something wrong?"

Running diagnostics. All hardware and software functions nominal. User displays increased heart rate and elevated blood pressure.

"I told you Humans were pessimists. You owe me one credit," Frek remarked.

"You were correct." The feline turned her attention to Bjorn. "Nothing is wrong. We wish to discuss your education and future employment."

Bjorn furrowed his brow. "You want to give me a job? Doing what?"

"There is a growing market for our respective services." Dr. Shur'im gestured to herself and Frek. "Mercenaries find themselves in need of prosthetics, and many of them are seeking out pinplants. The most sought after pinplants are from a Wrogul, but he does not have the capacity to meet demand."

"Wrogul?" Bjorn's pinplants remained silent. "Another alien race?"

"Correct. I'll admit, his talents exceed my own. However, I have the advantage of being on Earth, and I charge significantly less than the Wrogul." Dr. Shur'im tipped her head toward the ElSha. "After Frek and I worked on your case, we realized a partnership would be beneficial."

"I don't see where I come into the equation," Bjorn said. "Even with college, I'm not smart enough to be an engineer or brain surgeon."

Frek gave a clicking laugh. "We want you to be a model."

"What?" Bjorn's tone bordered on incredulous.

Grace giggled next to him. "You could be shirtless and flex your cybernetic arm."

"A model is a living mannequin for garments, yes?" The felinoid tipped her head side to side in the equivalent of a Human shake. "No, we do not wish for you to be a visual aid. I believe the term is spokesperson, yes?"

"Do I need to have a logo on my arm or something?" Bjorn asked.

"We believe having the scion of a respected mercenary family speak on our behalf will carry weight, especially since he is a testament to our services," the H'rang stated. "In exchange, we will pay you. We can negotiate the amount, though we favor a model leaning heavily on a percentage of profits."

"It would be money to fund your education, son," the commander added. "I know you're reluctant to take what you consider a handout from me."

"You should ask for a percentage of revenue," Grace whispered. "Profit is too easy to tamper with. I'm still a fan of the shirtless idea."

"It would also give you an opportunity to get in on the ground floor of their business," Vurrg remarked, licking crumbs off his muzzle. "I am considering investing in their company."

"It sounds like a great opportunity," Bjorn said, poking at what was left of his torte.

"Here we go," the commander muttered.

"BJ."

"I need to think about it." Bjorn kept his tone level. Something was rubbing him the wrong way. This wasn't because of anything he had brought to the table; it was because he happened to get mauled by a bear. Did the commander have something to do with the offer? Pinplants were becoming more popular among mercenaries. Perhaps

Bjorn's father had suggested a flow of customers in exchange for a bit of employment charity?

"Your father said you are considering studying business to better run Bjorn's Berserkers once he retires. Perhaps you could practice on a smaller business, yes?" Dr. Shur'im suggested. "It would be useful to have a financial manager familiar with Earth regulations as our business grows."

"It's a generous offer, and it's a lot to process." Bjorn was keenly aware of his father's scrutiny. "To be honest, tonight was supposed to be about introducing my girlfriend to my family."

"Of course." The H'rang bobbed her head. "We can discuss this another time, yes? Yes."

"He's in a hurry to get this family dinner over with so he can take Grace upstairs," Bjorn's father said. The commander gestured upward with his fork. "The boy spent hours cleaning his room."

Vurrg grinned, Dr. Shur'im cocked her head, and Frek muttered, "Mammals."

"Perhaps he should have visitors more often," Geneva muttered as she collected dishes. Louder, she asked, "Does anyone want coffee or perhaps something stronger?"

The commander and Vurrg opted for stronger while everyone else but Frek opted for coffee, which he claimed made him jittery.

"Grace, are you originally from Las Cruces?" Bjorn's mother asked.

Grace nodded while trying to cool her coffee. "According to my *abuela*, our ancestors lived here since before First Contact. Bjorn said your family is from Alaska. Did you get tired of the cold?"

"My father bought a chunk of the decommissioned White Sands Missile Range from the feds fifty years ago," the commander replied. "Property around Houston went for a steep premium. Once the base at Bear Town was founded, it made sense to set up house nearby."

"*Afi* and *Amma*, my grandparents, still have a house in Alaska," Bjorn added. He didn't mention the bear attack. Grace had already heard the story.

After another half hour of Bjorn's mother interrogating Grace and an embarrassing story from when Bjorn was twelve, the aliens all made excuses to leave.

"Monday, after school, Frek and I wish to conduct diagnostics and measurements," Dr. Shur'im said. "Will this work for you? Yes?"

"Yes, it's fine." As much as Bjorn disliked getting poked and prodded, if he was going to need at least one refit for his arm, he didn't want to blow them off. Would there be another pitch of their business offer?

Vurrg patted Bjorn on the shoulder and gave a chuffing laugh, but the Zuul kept his remarks to himself.

"I bet you didn't expect a zoo," Bjorn murmured to Grace.

Grace shook her head. "Is it always so…interesting here?"

"No. My dad and Vurrg hang out some, but the other two were a surprise," Bjorn replied. "I think the commander pals around with Vurrg because he's not in the Berserkers, so Dad isn't his boss."

"I thought mercenaries were big on camaraderie?" Grace slipped her hand into Bjorn's.

"In general, but it's different when you're the commander. Would you want to order your friends into battle knowing some of them may not make it back?"

"Sounds lonely," Grace remarked. "Another good reason not to become a mercenary."

"We're going to go watch television in the sitting room and leave you kids in peace," Bjorn's mother said. "Grace, I can't wait to have your family over."

"Me too, Mrs. Tovesson."

"Son, be sure to get Grace home on time," the commander stated. "Good night."

After his parents disappeared, Bjorn gave Grace's hand a squeeze. "So, do you want to see my room?"

"I thought you'd never ask."

*****

Chapter Thirty-Two

Bear Town, New Mexico

"Quit swinging it as though you're chopping wood," Sergeant Axel Silver grumbled.

Bjorn hefted his battle-axe in a two-handed grip. "Why not? It tends to go poorly for the lumber."

"Because a log won't swing back while you're overcommitted." The sergeant stomped forward and adjusted Bjorn's grip. "I know it feels more powerful the other way, but you can't recover from a miss or maneuver the axe to block."

"I don't see why you're wasting time swinging that clumsy weapon around," Eddings remarked. She was perched on a steel drum in the shade of the motor pool garage. "You're one of my better students. By the time you'll be old enough to drink off base, you'll be terror in bar fights. Also, your stance is wrong—you're struggling to keep your balance on misses. It would tire you out faster in a real fight."

"He needs to be able to turn quickly," Axe protested. "He can't do that if his feet are all spread out."

Eddings sighed and hopped off the drum. "Step back, old-timer."

"Old-timer? Watch it, or I might put you over my knee." Despite the taunt, Sergeant Silver stepped back.

"It would be hard to do with two broken arms." Eddings turned to Bjorn. "Extend the weapon out, full swing. Feel how you're compensating with your legs, so your momentum doesn't topple you forward?" She tapped his left hand until he moved it higher on the haft. "He was right about your grip. You have a bionic arm; you can afford a little more choke on the haft." Next she kicked at his boots until Bjorn adjusted his feet to her satisfaction.

"You guys have been at this for how many weeks and you still haven't figured out proper stances?" Eddings stepped back out of reach. "Try the swing again. Better? Can you feel the difference in your legs?"

"Yeah." Bjorn swung the axe experimentally a couple more times.

"For the record, we're breaking new ground here," Axe protested. "Between the weapon and the student, I'm making some of this up as we go."

"It's why I suggested to Sergeant Silver we invite you for your opinion." Bjorn swept the axe in an arc. "Would the same principle apply to a CASPer?" Bjorn asked.

Axe scoffed. "For all the protest, you show a keen interest in CASPer operation. He's made three sim runs now, plus fourteen hours logged in live CASPers."

"Most of those hours are driving suits around the motor pool for the maintenance teams," Bjorn countered. Sure, there had been the one obstacle course run when one of the cadre troopers was so hungover he couldn't walk.

"Wow, and here I thought five hours behind rumbler controls was something," Eddings remarked.

Axe raised an eyebrow. "What were you two doing in a rumbler for five hours?"

"I have a girlfriend!" Bjorn proclaimed. He quickly turned to Eddings. "No offense."

"None taken. You're too young anyways," Eddings said. "I needed a driver so I could log time in the vehicle commander's seat, and my new driver is a lazy bum. Beta Bear could make a decent Casanova driver."

"Rumblers are a bit cramped," Bjorn remarked. "I thought we were here so Eddings could give her insight into my battle-axe training?"

Axel pointed at the double-bladed weapon. "You know he wants to use one of these with his CASPer?"

"In the hands of a battle suit, it would be a hatchet." Eddings shook her head. "I don't think the arm-blades are optimal but swinging a little tomahawk at an Oogar seems pointless."

"One, the CASPer battle-axe is scaled to match the suit," Bjorn retorted. "Two, it's more of a thought experiment. It's not as though I'm going to field a CASPer in battle."

"Could you put it in the simulator software?" Eddings mused. "I'm curious to see how it would work."

"He's already talked the battlefield tactical intelligence into mocking it up in the sim," Axe said.

"I didn't so much ask as my pinplants relayed the query and next thing I knew I had a virtual battle-axe." Bjorn tapped the side of his head. "Sometimes it's spooky the way the software anticipates me."

"The pinplants or the BTI?" Eddings asked.

"Both."

"Have the techs crunched the numbers to evaluate your damage output with the axe to someone else using a traditional arm-blade? I wonder how they compare," Eddings suggested.

"I'm sure those code monkeys have better things to do," Axe said. "All right, let's stow your toys so you can get to Eddings' class."

"Don't take too long, or I'll leave without you," Eddings chided. "I can't be late for my own class."

"Good thing you have a girlfriend," Sergeant Silver muttered as they collected the debris and unused targets from the day's "therapy."

"Very funny. Not only do I have a girlfriend, Eddings has a boyfriend," Bjorn countered. "Not to mention the fact I'm still a kid in her eyes."

"If you say so," Axe said, dumping an armload of logs into a bin. "From what I hear, Wick is a shifty piece of work. You're the heir-apparent of the firm and, from what the ladies say, a slab of beef."

"What?" Bjorn peered about in case the outburst drew attention. The only person in sight, Eddings, was engrossed in her slate.

"I'm calling it as I hear it, kid." Axe scanned the yard in case they missed anything. "Rumor has it even the commander is a fan of your new girlfriend. If she's all you've made her out to be, don't screw it up for some easy action."

"I didn't plan on it." Bjorn caught himself before he admitted he loved Grace. Heather had burned him. It made Bjorn reluctant to confess his feelings for Grace. *Love—am I jumping the gun? We've been dating for a couple months now. Is it too soon for the L word?*

"Good. Go ahead and get to your class," Axe said.

Bjorn snapped out of his thoughts and joined Eddings. They walked toward the half-empty warehouse she used for classes.

"Rumor has it your new girlfriend meets the commander's approval," Eddings remarked.

"Yeah. She came over for family interrogation last week, and I'll endure the same tomorrow," Bjorn replied. Why was his love life the subject of base gossip? "How did you hear?"

"What? Compromise my intelligence assets?" Eddings laughed. "Your father isn't exactly the quiet type and Stefan even less so."

Bjorn could imagine his father going on about Grace in the mess hall or before a meeting in a roomful of people. "I guess you're right. The commander says she'll keep me on my toes, and he's right. She's on the debate team and going into pre-law."

"Ouch." Eddings winced. "If you thought you had a chance of winning an argument, forget it."

"We haven't had our first one, but it'll happen sooner or later." Bjorn snorted. They were still in the honeymoon phase. "I'd rather box an Oogar."

"At least the commander approves of her. It has to make things easier on the home front," Eddings said. "I heard the cheerleader was a bit of a ditz."

Bjorn instinctively rankled at someone speaking ill of Heather, even after she broke his heart. "I guess. I don't know why you'd care."

Eddings scoffed. "Other than vicarious drama, I don't. It makes for small talk." She yanked open the door. "Time to learn something useful instead of waving around your Viking relic, Beta Bear."

* * *

"What happened to your experiment on running two guest restaurants on the weekend?" the commander asked as Bjorn plopped down with a plate of spicy Thai food. "I was hungry for Italian."

"It turns out a number of troops go to Las Cruces or down to El Paso-Juarez on Saturdays. Two vendors mean lukewarm sales for them both, and they might not break even on the day," Bjorn replied. "I talked to the restaurant operators and they agreed to rotate Saturdays. It turns out it was tougher on them to have resources dedicated here every other Saturday. Once a month is more manageable."

"So have you decided on Frek and Shur'im's offer?" The commander chewed on a generic chicken tender from the regular mess hall menu.

"I'd be a talking mannequin," Bjorn grumbled and dug into his pad thai. "I know, I know—it's a great deal."

"Son, can't you accept when something good lands in your lap?" Bjorn's father gnawed on another tender after dunking it in barbeque sauce. "Plenty of companies, including medical ones, have spokespeople and paid testimonials."

"What if I put the money toward the cost of my cybernetics and pinplants?" Bjorn suggested. "I'm going to need at least one new arm, so I might as well make it a Cadillac of bionic arms. Dr. Shur'im said she could add another memory bank and processor to my pinplants."

"What about your education?" his father asked, brushing flecks of breading from his beard with the back of his hand. "Son, you obviously have a head for business. Why not capitalize on it? Let me worry about the medical expenses. It's my thrice-damned fault the bear lived long enough to maul you."

"You forcing me to train relentlessly with the pistol *Afi* gave me is what saved my life," Bjorn countered. He shoveled a lump of spicy vegetables, chicken, and rice noodles into his mouth. Chewing slowly and savoring the heat bought him some time. "You lift off tomorrow for the contract. I can tell them I'll do it, and we can hash out what I'll use the money for when you get back."

The commander regarded Bjorn from under bushy brows. "Fine. Try not to get in too much trouble while I'm gone."

"Assuming I survive dinner with Grace's family tomorrow, I think I'll be all right," Bjorn said.

"I hear you've been using the base as your own personal playground," his father stated. "I haven't put my foot down because some of it has been helping the motor pool team, but don't forget these aren't toys. I'm tempted to tear Sergeant Orr a new one for letting you run a CASPer through the confidence course."

"The cadre was trying to scrape up an additional person so they would have two full squads," Bjorn protested. They could have run the exercise a trooper short, but it gave him an excuse. The commander knew it was an excuse. Was he going to drop the hammer and cut off Bjorn's access?

"Sounds pretty flimsy. Your mother will have my head if you get hurt horsing around in a CASPer or joyriding in a Casanova. Yeah, I know about you cruising around with Eddings." Bjorn's father leaned forward and lowered his voice. "You already have one girlfriend. Don't mess it up."

"Why do people think there's something going on?" Bjorn protested. "I hang out as much with Sergeant Silver."

"I don't want to see you make a dumb mistake, Trip."

"Because I have a history of messing up, right? I got kicked out of school, I lost my girlfriend, I alienated all of my friends, so now you think I'm going to cheat on my new girlfriend?" Bjorn spotted a few glances from nearby tables and reined in his temper. "You know what I do while I'm playing chauffeur for Eddings? I read homework assignments. If all I'm doing is driving from Point A to Point B in the desert, I have enough brainpower to spare for reading. Trish sits back in the commander station and uses every function possible because she wants her time logged."

"All right—calm down. It was a caution, not an accusation. I don't want to leave on an assault drop with you all pissy at me." The commander dropped half a chicken tender onto his tray. "I've a long list to check off before we lift tomorrow. Good luck with Grace's family, and good luck on your VOWS. If this contract runs into any hiccups, I won't be back in time for your assessment."

"Thanks. Try not to get shot down, blown up, or eaten," Bjorn said. "I'm not ready to run the family business, even if I'd only be a bean counter."

* * * * *

Chapter Thirty-Three

Las Cruces, New Mexico

"How'd it go?" Aisha asked before Bjorn and Grace even sat down.

"She means did your family scare off Bjorn?" Amy added.

Grace set down her tray. "Why would they scare him off? There were aliens at his family dinner."

"Because he's an only child, whereas you have a large, gregarious family," Amy said. "It can be overwhelming for someone not used to so much…togetherness."

"Mama adores Bjorn," Grace said, leaning into Bjorn. "He was so polite and respectful."

"Plus he asked for seconds," Tomas added. "If you want to get on *Tia* Gabi's good side, let her feed you."

"What about your father, the Machete King?" Larcell asked.

"He only mentioned his machete collection three times," Bjorn replied. He wanted to slip an arm around Grace, but it would have made eating lunch challenging.

"I think *Tio* Hector approves of Bjorn," Tomas said. "As long as Grace doesn't ditch her goals to become a merc wife."

"I'm not putting aside my aspirations for anyone," Grace remarked, patting Bjorn's hand.

"See, no problem there," Bjorn said.

"You forgot to proclaim you aren't going to become a mercenary," Amy remarked.

"It goes without saying." Bjorn eyed his lunch—mystery loaf in enigmatic gravy. "Your statement backs it up."

"It goes without saying," Larcell echoed. "The big man reminds us at least once a week."

"I think Tomas is right," Grace said. "Papa is warming to you. Mama may be picking out my wedding dress, but you've got six years to win my father over."

"For the record, you've already earned the commander's stamp of approval," Bjorn remarked. "He's already warned me not to mess up."

"A wise man." Grace wrinkled her nose.

"Please quit being the adorable couple," Larcell pleaded. "It makes us poor, lonely, single folk feel even…singler."

"You don't complain about Amy and me," Aisha remarked.

"Because you two are quiet and a little bit spooky." Larcell gestured with his spork. "I wouldn't be surprised to find out Amy has voodoo dolls of everyone."

"Do you want to see yours?" Amy offered.

"No!" Larcell cried, drawing attention from the surrounding tables. "The only thing keeping these two from being Homecoming royalty is he's not the football captain, and she's not a cheer…aw, shit. I'm sorry, man. I didn't mean—"

"Larcell, it's fine," Bjorn interjected. Even though he was right. "I don't care about being Homecoming King, or Prom King, or any of that crap."

Larcell let out a breath. "I wasn't thinking."

"Don't sweat it," Bjorn said. "It's in the past. If Grace wants, I'll buy her a sash and a tiara."

"I've never worn a tiara," Grace said, adjusting an imaginary crown. "It might go to my head."

* * *

"Listen up, maggots!" Sergeant Kimble shouted.

The advanced MST class settled into formation. "Seats are limited for the field trip to Houston next week. Only ten of you punks get to go, and I have to decide who gets a seat on the VTOL."

Bjorn raised his hand. Kimble's head swiveled as he zeroed in on Bjorn and stalked down the line of students. "Tovesson! Why are you interrupting my speech?"

"Sergeant, I might be able to prevail on my father's outfit to provide additional transportation," Bjorn suggested.

"Did someone name you logistics sergeant?" Kimble yelled. "No! Want to know why? Because there's more to think about than how many VTOLs we can scrape up. There will be MST students from other Las Cruces schools, so even if your daddy loaned us enough birds to fly everyone to Houston, there wouldn't be space on site to handle everyone. If we could bring more of you pukes, don't you think I could have scrounged up an additional bird?"

He'd really blundered into it. As much as it galled Bjorn, the best route was to eat some crow. "Sorry, Sergeant."

Sergeant Kimble glared at Bjorn. Bjorn focused on the sergeant's forehead. After several seconds, Kimble resumed pacing in front of the students. "As I was saying, I need a fair way to choose the lucky participants. The ten best times on the confidence course today get a ticket." Groans and mutters rippled through the formation. "What's that? Speak up, maggots!"

The students fell silent. "Since this is every man for himself, the last set of logs are locked," Kimble stated. He paused in front of Bjorn. "Corporal Baylor, give Mr. Helpful here a five second penalty for interrupting me." The training assistant tapped on her slate.

Bjorn bit back a protest. It would only lead to a steeper penalty if he opened his mouth. Kimble glowered at him, daring him to say something. Five seconds was still doable, but not guaranteed.

"Line up people, alphabetical by surname!" Sergeant Kimble ordered. "Go when Baylor says. Jump the gun and you're disqualified!"

Another attempt to handicap him? Bjorn would start near the rear of the pack, meaning slower trainees would be obstacles. Going to Houston wasn't a big deal for him, but now it was a matter of pride.

"Three…two…one…" Baylor paused, but years of scrimmage discipline kept Bjorn from biting at the false start. "Go!"

Bjorn wasn't the fastest over open ground, but he retained his football speed. If this had been an open sprint, he would have placed midway in the top ten. In two of the obstacles, Bjorn's size would work against him. Any climbing challenge would be a cakewalk.

By the second obstacle, Bjorn had passed two students. "Move it, Kraslow!" he shouted at the trainee ahead of him on the hand-over-hand challenge. While Kraslow descended the ladder at the end, Bjorn swung off the last horizontal rung and hit the ground running.

The elapsed time, including the five second handicap, ticked off in the corner of Bjorn's pinview, with his best three times below. He sprinted to beat Alvarez to the only unoccupied climbing rope. Traffic was his enemy, especially where his cybernetic arm would help him clear a challenge in half the time.

One of the other rope climbers stopped to gawk as Bjorn hauled his way to the top. He locked his left hand loosely around the angled rope. He would need to break out the dermal repair kit when he got home. By the time he arrested his slide at the bottom, Bjorn could smell burning plastic as the friction heated the high-tech polymer skin on his prosthesis.

Bjorn blasted past three more runners in the sandbox. The last obstacle lay ahead—the logs over water. His current time was running ahead of his third best now. Bjorn turned the last corner before the log pool. Trainees inched across the outer two logs, but the center one was clear. Bjorn surged forward.

It was too easy. Bjorn focused his view on the end of the log. The locking pin was missing. If the pin on the other end was gone, the log would spin freely. Of course it was gone. Any deviation off center and the log would spin, dumping him in the chest-deep pool.

A blue line illuminated the center of the log in his pinview. Easier said than done. Bjorn felt the log shift by his second step. On the third step, he threw himself into a shallow dive. Momentum carried him to the end of the pool. Bjorn hauled his drenched bulk out of the water and stumbled upright. The time had fallen below the third best.

Dig deep and wipe those smug grins off their faces. With the finish line in sight, there was no reason to hold anything back. His water-logged clothes and boots added extra kilos. Each step sprayed water and his leaden boots squished. *Fourth and long for the game.*

Bjorn could almost feel a football under his arm as he lowered his head and charged. Twenty yards to the finish line—one holdout from the global metric conversion. Fifteen yards and the third time blinked as his current time matched it. Ten yards, and his third best time had been supplanted. Five yards and Kimble's eyes went to his assistant's slate in disbelief.

Bjorn hurtled across the finish line. It took another ten yards to slow to a halt. Bjorn gasped for air and tried to ignore the stitch in his side. Lunch threatened to make an encore appearance. Why did this have to be at the end of the day?

Kimble shook his head. Bjorn checked the time in his pinview. No way ten other students beat him—unless they were as motivated. Kimble strode over to Bjorn.

"Tovesson, are you going to puke all over my pristine yard?" Kimble barked.

"Maybe, Sergeant," Bjorn wheezed.

"I knew you were bull-headed, but you're too stupid to know when you should lose," Sergeant Kimble said. "Congratulations—you're number six. Unless some of these stragglers are smuggling jump jets, you get to go to Houston, courtesy of the Dust Devils. Meanwhile, try not to die from a heart attack."

Bjorn nodded, still hunched over. It helped hide his grin.

*****

Chapter Thirty-Four

Houston, Texas

"You kids excited to visit startown?" Colonel Sebastian Walther addressed the high school seniors as though they were 10-year-olds visiting a theme park.

Bjorn wasn't sure which was worse—the patronizing commanding officer of the Dust Devils, or the rickety VTOL flyer reeking of over-heated metal and lubricant. The cadre from Mesilla Prep was on one of the Berserkers' VTOLs.

"You maggots stick with the group," Sergeant Kimble ordered. "No wandering off to get morphogenic tattoos or other bullshit."

Bjorn had a morphogenic design tucked away in his pinplant memory. The tattoos were animated, triggered by stimulus or command. Amy had illustrated the artwork, combining tribal tattoos with animated bear iconography. Bjorn vacillated on whether to get the ink. The commander would flip his lid, and if Bjorn entertained any notion of entering a white-collar profession, the tattoo would be a strike against him.

The VTOL lurched into a turn. Bjorn listened for signs of a turbine failure, but all four engine pods continued to scream. The rattle from the aft-left pod was barely noticeable, even as the craft shuddered.

"Relax. Hessie is an older bird, but she hasn't crashed yet!" Colonel Walther declared with a grin.

The pilot navigated the VTOL through the outer traffic belt of the startown, a buzzing ring of VTOLs, aircars, and older small aircraft. Bjorn spotted the control tower of the old Hobby Airport, now part of the Four Horsemen Museum.

The VTOL slewed and spun. Once again Bjorn thanked Odin for the wisdom to eat a light breakfast. The flyer slowed to a hover, then descended to land amid several other parked aircraft. The turbines went from an ear-piercing shriek to a dull whir. A cough and rattle sounded from the left rear turbine pod.

"Welcome to the Houston Startown!" Colonel Walther announced. "Sergeant Kimble, see these fine young people to the marshalling area."

"You heard the colonel, maggots!" Kimble shouted. "Disembark and fall in, two by two!"

A familiar black and gold logo caught Bjorn's eye from across the airfield. The VTOL sported the Berserkers' public emblem, as opposed to the black and gray tactical version used on vehicles and uniforms intended for combat. Bjorn didn't see the pilot nor any sign of the passengers.

"Tovesson, quit gawking!" Kimble yelled. "Squad, move out!"

At least the mid-October heat was tolerable—almost 30 degrees. Even with the extra warmth from the tarmac, it wasn't sweltering. Bjorn marched in the last row of the double column, triangulating the position of the Berserkers' warehouse based on visible landmarks.

Bjorn's Berserkers Houston Logistics Facility. A map appeared in his pinview.

"Sure, take all of the fun out it," Bjorn replied mentally.

No entertainment software is running. Shall we play a game?

"*No thanks,*" Bjorn replied. Sometimes the computer in his pin-plants creeped him out. Was the behavior a side effect of alien programming?

"Two hundred schools are represented here today," Sergeant Kimble called as they reached the conference center. "Don't embarrass me in front of the other one hundred ninety-nine! Goes double for you, Tovesson!"

The students joined the queue to enter the huge hangar turned conference hall. The last time Bjorn was here, the space was stuffed with displays emitting a cacophony of light and noise. Now rows of folding chairs were arranged in blocks. Propaganda posters touting service to society and the mercenary industry lined the walls.

"Funny how our teachers and the media bag on mercenaries, but schools bend over backward to help merc outfits recruit us," Teresa Gallardo remarked. She was one of two girls who qualified for the trip.

"It's because we supply eighty-two percent of the government's revenue," Bjorn said as they filed into their seats. "Without us, there's no Global Guaranteed Income, there's no FedMart subsidies, there's no FedMed Care, and there's no FedEd college grants. Just because they want to spit on us doesn't mean they won't hold their hands out for half our income."

"It's the first intelligent thing I've heard you say, Tovesson." Sergeant Kimble sat in the outermost seat of their row, next to Bjorn. "Now shut up."

Bjorn grunted but held his tongue. There would be two hours of speeches and presentations, lunch, then four hour-long group sessions. The students were allotted three hours for dinner and sightseeing before boarding the Dust Devil's VTOL for the return trip. In theory, the colonel, the MST sergeant, and the training corporal were supposed to ride herd over their charges while in startown. Bjorn would be surprised if they saw Colonel Walther again before 2000 hours.

Bjorn paid enough attention to clap politely with the rest of the crowd during the first wave of speeches and a video espousing the noble merits of the Off-World Levy. It was their duty to bravely go out into the galaxy so the masses back on Earth would have food on the table, a roof over their head, and a Tri-V set on the wall. No mention was made of the latest ill-fated attempt to raise the OWL to 66% from 50%. He devoted the rest of his attention to chewing through as much homework as possible.

"I actually envy you, Tovesson," Brackin muttered as they waited in line for their vat-meat sandwiches and chips.

"Why?" Mitch had steered clear of Bjorn since their last confrontation.

Brackin scanned the crowd. "You were checked out for the rah-rah snooze fest. I bet you were watching videos on the computer in your skull."

"I was doing homework," Bjorn countered. "Might as well get something productive out of the time."

"It's all grown in the same lab, so it doesn't matter. Pick a sandwich and move it!" Kimble called from behind them.

The sergeant was right. The vat-grown meat was all the same. Bjorn grabbed the largest sandwich and followed his classmates to their assigned break-out room. Despite the cavernous space in the repurposed hangars, there wasn't space to set up a cafeteria for 2,400 people.

"Sergeant Kimble, where are we going for dinner?" Miguel "Mojo" Mojica asked. He set down a plate with three sandwiches. The guy was a bottomless pit. Bjorn didn't know how Mojo wasn't fat with the way he ate.

"Ask Tovesson." Sergeant Kimble unwrapped his sandwich. "He's the local expert."

The perfect way to keep Bjorn from slipping away on his own—saddle him with a bunch of classmates.

"I bet he knows bars where we can get served," Gerald Fitz suggested.

"The hard part isn't getting served. It's getting through the door," Bjorn said. "Any bar worth a damn has a bouncer to keep out tourists like us."

"What about the other bars?" Fitz asked. "I don't care if the beer is some artesian brew."

"Do you care if you walk out with both kidneys?" Bjorn took a huge bite of his sandwich. The meat was bland, and the veggies were soggy. Dinner was already sounding good. He took his time chewing to stall while composing his next statement.

"Most of the places here take Galactic Union credits, and the exchange rate sucks. There are no FedStops in startown," Bjorn said. The small convenience versions of FedMarts were ubiquitous elsewhere, but nothing in startown would accept stipend transfers. Business was done in hard currency or through a Universal Account Access Card. The latter used Galactic Union credits.

"There is the meal allowance," Corporal Baylor suggested. "The sponsoring mercenary companies provided ten credits per student as per diem."

If Sergeant Kimble's eyes were lasers, they would have flash-fried Baylor. "Those have to be processed through a Yack with a mercenary account."

"So where are you taking us?" Mojo asked.

Kimble fumed. Bjorn didn't envy Baylor once Kimble got her alone. She had cost him 100 easy credits.

Bjorn took a breath. "Sergeant, I have a suggestion."

Kimble's head resembled a tank turret as his glare swept to Bjorn. "It better be a good one, Tovesson."

"Do you know the Hunnu Mongolian Barbecue? I could feed this crew for five credits a head, and I have a mercenary certified UAAC." Bjorn held out his Yack. The Bjorn's Berserkers logo appeared on it. "If you have other engagements here in Houston, you could transfer fifty credits to me, and I'll take the squad to Hunnu." It would also leave Sergeant Kimble with 50 credits, the equivalent of $2,500 if converted to Earth dollars.

Kimble's eyes narrowed as he studied Bjorn. "Tovesson, you're batting a hundred. That is the second smartest thing I've heard you say." Kimble pulled out his slate and his Yack, a thumb-sized slab of plastic. A few typed commands later, Kimble tapped his Yack to Bjorn's. "All right, maggots. You're Tovesson's problem for dinner, but if you lose track of him you fend for yourself—no allowance. Any questions? Good. Now let me finish this tragedy of a sandwich in peace."

The sessions were 50 minutes long to give presenters time to rotate rooms. The CASPer trooper presentation was full of glory and riches. They were the most lucrative mercenary roles and almost guaranteed to bring you face-to-face with a variety of terrifying aliens who wanted to eat you.

Flight and shipboard positions required additional training and were ideal for those who scored better on the mental portion of their VOWS. Since this bunch was selected for their physical prowess there was little interest from the Rio Grande High School squad, save for Kemmi Anderson. She wanted to helm a starship and aspired to join the famous Winged Hussars.

Logistics was another specialization better suited to the more intellectual. It was the least glamorous of mercenary duties and the lower levels were often filled by contractors, but it was so hard to draw in recruits the Mercenary Occupational Specialty warranted its own presentation. You might not get rich in logistics, but you were less likely to be murdered by a giant spider.

Infantry and armor were rolled together in the fourth presentation. Whereas CASPers were sometimes referred to as augmented infantry, or auggies, non-powered infantry was labeled standard infantry. They were often used in defensive duties, but fewer companies used them due to high attrition and low demand. Armor was the red-headed stepchild of the mercenary business. Armored vehicles packed more punch and carried more armor than CASPers, but they were less agile and therefore vulnerable to close-in enemies.

"How much homework did you do?" Brackin asked after the polite applause faded for the last presenter.

"A little." Bjorn was about to admit he'd been in a virtual chat with Grace during the space and flight crew presentation. He'd paid rapt attention during the logistics session—even in the civilian world, logistics was a crucial component. The armor presentation made him worry about Eddings.

"Don't forget where we parked, maggots," Kimble declared after the presenters left the room. "Pad 17. If you're late, you'll get left behind, and you can hitchhike home. You have three hours to get dinner, try to find Sirra'Kan anime, and get kicked out by a tattoo parlor."

Bjorn flagged the landing pad on the map in his pinplants with a timer set for him to arrive five minutes early. When he returned his focus to his surrounding, Kimble was gone, and Baylor fidgeted in her seat.

"Can we get dinner now?" Mojo asked.

Bjorn had made reservations after lunch and paid the five-credit reservation fee. Half the money would go to the server, so Bjorn didn't begrudge it. "Our table is scheduled in thirty minutes. Let's go."

"Does this place have real meat or vat-meat?" Fitz asked.

"It's real, not lab-grown." Bjorn replied.

* * *

Patrons packed the waiting area, and Bjorn wove through the crowd. The hostess glanced up, craning her neck to meet Bjorn's eyes.

"If you want a table, it's at least an hour wait," she said apologetically.

"I have a reservation under Bjorn Tovesson." Planning trumped luck.

The hostess peered at her slate. "Would it be Bjorn's Berserkers?"

"No." He hadn't mentioned the Berserkers when he made the reservation, so why would she ask…? Bjorn scanned the lobby and spotted Mickey D standing next to Sergeant Sorenson. Sorenson had retired from active duty with the Berserkers to assume the role of MST Sergeant at Mesilla Prep. Bjorn's father could have raved about Hunnu to Sorenson, assuming the sergeant hadn't already known about it.

Sorenson spotted Bjorn and gave a subtle nod. The sergeant thought it was a waste Bjorn wasn't going to be a mercenary. Bjorn turned away before Mickey D could notice him.

"Here we go—Tovesson, table for ten." The hostess flagged down a server. "Sarnai will show you to your table."

Bjorn waved the rest of his group forward. Mickey D caught sight of him and whispered to someone obscured by the crowd—it had to be Berto. Great. Maybe they'd be stuck waiting for an hour, but no, they had a reservation.

Once they were seated, the server explained how the bowls and grill worked, along with their drink options. Surprisingly, only one student of their cohort ordered beer. Good, Bjorn didn't want to babysit drunks.

While he waited for his meat at the grill, Bjorn watched the Mesilla Prep students go to their table. Fortunately, it was on the other side of the dining room from Bjorn's group. They could avoid each other and there'd be no drama.

Bjorn wrinkled his nose. Under the grilling meat, he caught a whiff of something pungent and earthy. It only took a moment for Bjorn to spot the Khabar, standing two paces back and to the left. Bjorn's pinplants flagged the goat-man as the Gruff surveyed the meat offerings. Bjorn turned away before its gaze reached him.

Bjorn watched the Khabar's reflection in a polished steel cleaver hanging above the grill. After a moment, the alien turned away. Bjorn collected his cooked meat and followed the Khabar with his eyes.

The creature slowed as it passed the Mesilla Prep students. It was casing them. The Gruff skulked back to the lobby and joined another of its kind.

Bjorn couldn't make out their speech over the crowd noise, but they appeared to hold a hushed conversation. One disappeared through the crowd in the lobby while the other waited, clutching a table-beacon.

The Khabar weren't the only aliens, Bjorn noted as he returned to his table. A pair of Zuul sat across from a Jivool at a table cluttered with empty bowls. Four jittery, weasel-like Zuparti shared another table. The only one paying the aliens any attention were younger diners. To the mercenary personnel who composed a large portion of the customers, the presence of the aliens was another Saturday.

"What's wrong, Tovesson? Afraid you'll have another scuffle with your old playmates?" Brackin grinned with a mouthful of rice.

"No, it's the Khabar I'm concerned about," Bjorn replied. How did Brackin know about his dust-up with Berto? Was the video so widespread or had Brackin sought it out?

"The what now?" Brackin chewed noisily.

Bjorn resisted the urge to point. "The goat-dudes. A few months ago, some of them tried to mug my father and me."

"Now you assume all goat-people are criminals?" Brackin laughed. "You're the judgmental one, but people call me a racist."

"Because you are one," Kemmi hissed from the other end of the table. "You and the rest of your—"

"How about we don't have a political fistfight in a restaurant?" Bjorn interrupted. He agreed with Kemmi but didn't want any distractions if the Khabar were up to no good. Did it make him a xenophobe?

The Khabar kept glancing in the direction of the Mesilla Prep students. After fifteen minutes, the table alert in the Gruff's hand flashed. The goat and his partner followed a waitress to a table, collected their bowls, and joined the crowd around a grill.

"What are your sinister goats doing now?" Brackin asked as he sat down with his second bowl. "Think they'll take another crack at robbing you?"

"Up yours," Bjorn muttered.

"What happened to the ones who tried to mug you?" Mojo asked.

Bjorn caught Brackin's eye. "I punched one out in the street. My father and another Berserker shot two more." Brackin became interested in the contents of his bowl.

"You think they're out for revenge?" Teresa asked.

"I'm not even sure if these are the same billy goats," Bjorn remarked. "They seem interested in the Mesilla Prep kids, not me."

"I'd say count yourself lucky," Kemmi commented. "It's not your problem. You sure as hell don't owe those Mesilla snobs anything, not after the way they did you wrong."

Evidently everyone in school had seen the video.

"Mojo is never going to finish," Brackin groused 45 minutes later. Mojo shrugged over his fourth bowl.

"I closed our tab. This is his last bowl." Bjorn watched the Mesilla Prep students file out through the crowd. One of the Gruffs pulled out a slate and tapped on it. Bjorn tossed his napkin on the table and stood. "You all can do what you want but don't miss the ride home."

"Where are you going?" Brackin asked.

"If I'm right, something is about to go down. If I'm wrong, I'm going to go check on my CASPer." Bjorn headed for the door, weaving among patrons and servers.

Outside, a crowd milled in commotion. Bjorn spotted Mickey D staring down the road. "Move it!" Bjorn bellowed at the throng in front of him and plowed between whoever didn't get out of his way.

Berto was the first to notice Bjorn emerge from the mass of onlookers. He faltered for a moment before blurting out, "A bunch of goats kidnapped our sergeant!"

"Shit, you called it, Tovesson," Brackin said from behind Bjorn.

"What happened?" Bjorn followed Mickey D's gaze, but there was nothing but scattered traffic. An autocab swung from straddling the curb back onto the roadway.

"There were six goat-people. Four held us at gunpoint while two more smacked the sergeant with stun batons. They hauled him into the back of a truck and took off," Berto said.

Bjorn brought up a map displaying the web of streets and accessways through the startown. Nabbing the sergeant didn't make much sense. The kids would be worth ransom. All the sergeant would be good for…

"Loki's Get!" Bjorn swore and highlighted the Berserkers' depot at the starport. *"Ping and display all Berserker assets within 5 kilometers."*

BTI: Hello, Bjorn. This is the local node. How may I be of assistance?

How many nodes were there? "Aliens have kidnapped Sergeant Sorenson. I think they are going to attempt to use him to break into the logistics depot. Lock out his access."

BTI: I'm sorry, but you don't have clearance to lock out an account.

Bjorn spotted a blinking dot a block away. He zoomed in on it. *Rumbler LT-109.*

"Where are you going?" Mickey D called as Bjorn dashed up the road.

"The rumbler!" he yelled over his shoulder. "Highlight shortest civilian traffic route from here to the logistic depot."

An amber line flashed on the map. The starport and surrounding startown were laid out like spokes on a wheel. Civilian traffic would have to go to the outer rim and circle around. Certified vehicles could drive to the inner loop bordering the starport proper.

Bjorn spotted the parked rumbler. He cast the virtual key and start-up order from his pinplants. *"Highlight shortest mercenary traffic route from here to the depot."* A green line manifested with a blinking blue box highlighting the security gate. If there was traffic, he'd be stuck.

The rear ramp dropped as Bjorn approached. A dull hum sounded from the fuel-cell powerplant waiting to send juice to the electric motors. The rumbler was a logistics transport model, not intended to see combat. It was unarmed.

"Tovesson? What are you doing?" Brackin shouted.

"Who the hell are you?" Berto demanded. A block-long sprint, and he showed no sign of being winded.

"I'm in his MST group? What's your—shit! You're the best friend who screwed him over!" Brackin laughed while catching his breath.

"Bjorn, what are you thinking?" Mickey D asked. No one else had followed them. Hopefully someone was calling the authorities, for all the good it would do.

"They're going for the warehouse—the logistics depot here at the starport," Bjorn replied. "They need access to get through the yard gate and into the warehouse building. It's why the Gruffs nabbed Sorenson."

Bjorn clambered forward to the driver's compartment, squeezed into the seat, and secured his safety harness. "Last one in raise the ramp!"

"We'll never catch them," Brackin remarked.

"Bettie, have the Officer-In-Charge and all local personnel been notified?"

BTI: Alerts have been sent. Responses are pending.

"Better strap in!" Bjorn yelled as he threw the throttle forward. The armored vehicle lurched and spun about to head toward the starport. Bjorn checked the map. There had to be a way around the checkpoint.

BTI: Negative. There are no unobstructed paths.

"What about obstacles vulnerable to 25 tons of rolling metal?"

The end of a dead-end alley flashed orange. A low concrete berm secured a double layer of steel fencing.

BTI: Breaching the perimeter fence will alert security.

"Even better."

"Big guy, did you miss the part where they have guns?" Berto hunched in the opening to the driver's compartment, bracing himself as Bjorn swerved around an autocab.

"They're going to try to rip off the Berserkers' supply depot. It's full of weapons and ammo. I bet if we beat them there, we can scrape up enough guns to hold them off until the security forces arrive." Armored wheels screeched on fused pavement as the rumbler skidded around a corner and caromed off a wall.

"Who taught you to drive?" Brackin yelled. A dull boom reverberated through the hull of the vehicle. "Shit! Are they shelling us?"

"Bettie, what was the detonation?"

BTI: Working.

His pinplants flashed external views across the top of his pinview. In the distance, a gout of flame and smoke rose into the evening sky. A blue circle on the other side of the starport flashed on the map amid rented storage warehouses.

BTI: Emergency alerts indicate an explosion. Security forces are responding.

"It's a draw play," Bjorn said aloud.

"What?" Berto grunted as another turn flung him against the wall.

"I bet a credit to a burrito the Gruffs set off the explosion as a diversion," Bjorn said. It meant there were more of them than the handful who grabbed Sergeant Sorenson.

Bjorn pulled up a personnel roster and found Sergeant Sorenson's entry.

"Requesting remote log-in—ID: E.Sorenson."

BTI: You are not Sergeant Erik Sorenson.

"Requesting remote log-in—ID: E.Sorenson."

BTI: Verification required. Passcode, UAAC, or Biometric?

"Passcode 123456."

BTI: Incorrect passcode

"Passcode admin."

BTI: Incorrect passcode

"Passcode qwerty."

BTI: Incorrect passcode. Credentials for E.Sorenson locked until cleared by a superior officer or technical support.

Warning—Collision Alert! The blue text flashed in his pinview and on the rumbler's Tri-V.

The fence loomed ahead. Forward-looking LIDAR—light detection and ranging—showed the concrete berm was 30 centimeters high—enough to anchor the fence but not enough to halt a hurtling armored vehicle.

"Mierda!" Berto hissed when he realized what Bjorn intended and scrambled aft.

"Hang on!" Bjorn slammed the throttle forward to the stop. The area across the roadway would be tarmac with plenty of space to turn around. Bjorn muttered a quick prayer to the Norns that no vehicles were passing by on the other side of the fence.

Warning—Collision Alert!

The blocky nose of the rumbler punched through the fence before the first set of wheels hit the berm with a bone-jarring crunch. Bjorn clutched the bottom of his seat with his left hand and the harness bit into his shoulders. Shouts echoed from the rear of the transport only to be cut off as the second pair of wheels bounced over 15 centimeters of shattered concrete. The rear wheels hitting five centimeters of concrete gravel was little more than a speed bump.

The rumbler bounced across six lanes of road and onto the tarmac, where a dozen ant-like Altar scurried for cover.

Warning—Collision Alert!

Bjorn stomped on the brakes and yanked the controls into a left turn. The external cameras showed a spray of sparks as the rumbler slid sideways toward a freighter and pallets of cargo. As soon as the rumbler was 90 degrees to the ship, Bjorn released the brake and threw the throttle forward again. Metal screamed on pavement until the wheels found enough traction to throw the vehicle forward. They missed a landing strut by less than two meters.

Incoming alert from starport security—halt your vehicle and await apprehension.

BTI: All security forces are responding to the explosion.

"I don't need the voices in my head to start arguing," Bjorn muttered. The logistics depot entrance was off the spoke road ahead and on the left. Bjorn slowed enough to not skid through the turn. The checkpoint on the spoke road was designed to limit access into the starport proper; outbound traffic was unhindered. There were customs checkpoints at the egresses from the startown to deal with outgoing vehicles and goods.

There were no signs of vehicles lying in wait near the gate into the Berserkers' facility. Bjorn queried the system for access.

BTI: Your access is not on the facility roster.

'Sonuvabitch!" Bjorn blurted. They couldn't have much time.

"Verify facility inventory. There is a CASPer assigned to me in the facility."

BTI: Inventory confirmed.

"I wish to access my equipment."

BTI: Facility access granted.

The gate whirred open. The walls around the depot were rebar concrete, but the gate was sheet metal, the same as the fence Bjorn had plowed through. Once in the yard, Bjorn swung the rumbler around and parked it flush and parallel to the gate. If someone rammed the gate, they would be in for a nasty surprise.

"All out!" Bjorn called and unstrapped from the driver station.

He crawled into the aft compartment where Mickey D and Brackin were tending to Berto with a first aid kit. A nasty cut on his head bled through an impromptu bandage.

"Dumbass didn't belt in before you played wrecking ball," Brackin remarked.

In a non-combat vehicle, there'd be no trauma nanites. The kit was little better than its counterpart from a century ago.

"We need to get inside. Hopefully we can find a nanite applicator while we gear up for the Gruffs." Bjorn said.

Berto smiled, then winced. "It's all good, *hermano.*"

"Carry him." Bjorn dropped the ramp and let Brackin and Mickey D precede him. After Bjorn secured the ramp, he ordered the rumbler to lock-up and kill power to the wheel motors. He left the fuel cells running in case they needed to get moving again in a hurry.

Bjorn held his breath as he pressed his right hand against the lock panel. A green light winked on and a click sounded. Bjorn let his breath out as he held the door open so they could carry Berto inside. A small truck and two larger ones rolled to a stop outside the gate.

"They're here," Bjorn announced as he closed the door.

* * * * *

Chapter Thirty-Five

Houston Texas

Incoming message—Captain Davis.

"Kid, what the in the name of Hel is going on?" The captain wore a colorful Hawaiian shirt and a baseball cap.

"The BTI alert should have the basics. I'm holed up in the depot with a few other MST students. I figure we can arm ourselves from stores and hold off the brigands until relief arrives," Bjorn said. "Although, it might take a while, since the Gruffs also set off an explosion to pull security forces to the other side of the starport."

"Are you mental?" Davis ran a hand down his face. "Most of the gear was emptied out for the current contract. You're defending some cleaning supplies and leftovers. Get out of there."

"We're pinned in," Bjorn countered. "Plus, the hostiles still have Sergeant Sorenson."

"Try to get to the back wall and slip over," Captain Davis ordered. "I can have a squad in the air and there in an hour, plus a fire team of infantry cobbled together locally in thirty minutes."

"We'll hold them off until then," Bjorn said.

Captain Davis snorted. "You're a kid."

"I'm a Berserker." Bjorn closed the comm channel. "Closest relief is thirty minutes, real firepower is an hour away," Bjorn announced.

"Is this place supposed to be empty?" Mickey D asked.

Bjorn scanned the floor, most of it bare. *"Bettie, I need an inventory."*

The list was woefully short but included an infantry squad kit. Bjorn led the others to a stray crate along a wall. There were ten sets of body armor, ten battle rifles, 30 loaded magazines, and ten personal first aid kits. Bjorn opened a first aid kit and handed the trauma applicator to Mickey D.

Berto hissed in pain as she sprayed a dose over the wound in his forehead.

"Oh yeah! Want me to get on the roof and plink aliens?" Brackin grabbed a rifle and slapped the magazine in place.

"If you don't want the full armor, at least take a helmet," Bjorn said. "The Gruffs might shoot back."

"Whatever." Still, Brackin accepted the helmet before he trotted toward the stairs winding to the ceiling.

"Bettie, give me the external camera feeds."

A row of images appeared across the top of his pinview. Bjorn focused on the front gate, where several Khabar milled about, arguing. They appeared to reach a consensus and cleared away from the gate to make room for the smaller truck.

"They're going to ram the gate," Bjorn stated.

Mickey D scoffed as she slipped a set of body armor over her head. "Unless they have another rumbler or a heavy truck, good luck."

"Hey, can anyone hear me?" Brackin called over a comm channel. The helmets had built-in communication gear. "I don't think these idiots know there's an armored vehicle in their path."

"I read you," Bjorn replied. "Don't shoot until they try to come over the wall."

"Are we going to defend an empty warehouse?" Berto asked. "All I see are a dozen big metal crates."

"Those are CASPer vaults," Bjorn countered. "They're used to make transporting CASPers easier."

"CASPers? Let's suit up!" Berto cried.

Mickey D paused from tightening the straps on her body armor. "We have a dozen CASPers? Let's stomp some goats!"

BTI: CASPer inventory: 1. Designation CASPer BBXX3.

"Loki's Get!" Bjorn smacked an empty CASPer vault. "The only CASPer here is mine."

"Of course it is," Berto muttered. He struggled to his feet.

"Fine, one CASPer versus a dozen aliens with small arms—I'll take those odds," Mickey D stated. "They'll probably wet themselves and run."

Bjorn walked to the vault holding his CASPer. "You're right. They wouldn't know it's a stripped-down model."

"Wait, what?" Mickey followed Bjorn. "Doesn't it have weapons?"

"An integral laser and an arm-blade," Bjorn replied. He seized the handle, braced his arm, and hauled the door open.

"Okay. Laze a few goats, and I bet the rest will beat hooves," Mickey D said. "I'm going topside to try to keep them from coming over the wall." She jogged toward the stairs, body armor rattling.

"Even without football, you get to be a big damned hero," Berto remarked.

"Stomping a couple of these goat bastards doesn't make me a hero," Bjorn countered. He found the manual release for the canopy. He noticed a huge battle-axe resting in place of an external carbine.

"How are you going to drive a CASPer without a haptic suit?" Berto asked.

Bjorn tapped the side of his head. "Pinlink. I can plug in directly." He scaled the suit and twisted to lower himself into it. "You should grab a gun and body armor but stay low. You took a nasty head wound. The nanites may have stopped the bleeding, but I wouldn't be surprised if you still have a concussion."

"Afraid I'll steal your glory?" Berto asked.

"I don't want Heather to lose another boyfriend." Bjorn plugged in his pinlink and pulled the canopy closed. Seconds ticked by while his pinplants shook hands with the CASPer operating system.

CASPer BBXX3 online.

"Expedite start-up sequence."

The interior of the suit lit up from Tri-V displays, but the view switched as the HUD fed directly into his pinview. Several overlays appeared, along with status displays. *Ten shots for the laser!* Hopefully the goats would back off after the first couple. They didn't know the CASPer wasn't at full strength and might miss the vacant shoulder mounts.

A quick scan of the inventory list revealed a crate identified as CASPer leftovers. There could be some laser magazines. A full magazine would give him 50 shots.

"Berto, find a crate marked 'CA MISC 01.'" Bjorn checked the location in the inventory—it was blank. "Try the three pallets by the stairs where we found the infantry kit. It seems to be the junk pile. I need more laser ammo."

"Right." Berto seemed steadier as he disappeared to the rear of the building.

"Oh, that had to hurt," Brackin remarked over the comms. Bjorn checked the cameras. The truck had slammed through the gate into the side of the rumbler. The armored vehicle slid a few centimeters, whereas the entire front of the truck was crumpled. Smoke rose from the ruined vehicle.

Over the audio pick-ups, Bjorn heard the distinctive *pop* of battle rifles firing from the roof as Khabar climbed the ruined truck to peer over the gate. Two goats fell backward, and the rest ducked.

Brackin laughed. "We've totally got this. The aliens can't get to the rumbler without us picking them off."

"You had to open your big mouth!" Mickey let loose a string of expletives. "We have a complication."

Bjorn flipped through the camera feeds. One showed the rear-most large truck. A Besquith stood on its lowered ramp. Behind the werewolf, a Tortantula emerged.

Bjorn grasped the hammer among the bear claws. "Thor lend me strength. Bettie, relay to Captain Davis and any approaching units—the hostiles include at least one Besquith and one Tortantula."

"Big Guy, this changes the equation," Mickey D called over comms. "The wolf and spider will shred us."

"New plan. I'll draw their aggro, and you three slip out and go over the back wall." Bjorn cursed the architect who put all the doors facing the front of the building.

"This isn't a sim-game, Bjorn." Gunshots punctuated Mickey D's statement. "You can't take both baddies in an underarmed CASPer."

"I only need for them to follow the ball. Once you're clear, I'll use my jump jets to get away," Bjorn said.

Jump juice—0%.

Awesome. The previous owners must have considered a tank full of the highly volatile fuel too dangerous for trade shows.

"Whatever you're going to do, Tovesson, you better hurry," Brackin shouted into his microphone. "The goats got wise and are sending the big boys!"

The Besquith leaped from the wrecked truck to the top of the rumbler, and glared at the rooftop before diving in front of the armored vehicle. The Tortantula clambered up the wreckage and over the gate.

Bjorn lumbered toward the loading dock. The metal door clattered upward at his command, drawing the attention of the aliens. He checked the cameras—the Tortantula was ignoring the small arms fire glancing off its armored carapace while the Besquith was hunkered behind cover. It had taken three rifle rounds with little more annoyance than wasp stings, but it wasn't eager to give the enemy free shots.

Bjorn hopped off the loading dock and toppled face first to the concrete with a resounding *crash*. The stupid CASPer only had one gyro set! The Tortantula scrambled across the top of the rumbler, sensing a vulnerable target.

"Rumbler LT-109—activate theft alert."

The lights on the armored vehicle flashed and klaxons screeched. The Besquith dashed away from the vehicle, chased by gunfire, and the Tortantula spun to face the new threat. Bjorn shoved himself upright and regained his feet.

"Targeting systems," Bjorn commanded the CASPer. A single blue dot appeared to track his laser's aim. *"Are you kidding me?"*

The CASPer only has the most basic functions. A wireframe overlay swept across his pinview as his pinplants highlighted threats and the last known locations of projected enemies.

The Besquith was gone. It was blitzing into the secondary. "Shit! Get off the roof! The werewolf is scaling the walls!"

Bjorn moved away from the building. He needed to draw the hostiles' attention away long enough for the others to exit the open loading dock and get around the corner furthest from the aliens. A blue outline flashed as one of the Khabar risked a peek over the wall. Bjorn's shot was low, so he didn't know if the laser had enough energy to burn through the wall and still nail the Khabar, but the Gruff disappeared.

Nine shots left.

Another volley of gunfire echoed from the roof, but there were no *spangs* of bullets hitting concrete or spider armor. A roof camera showed the Besquith ducking. It must have its claws sunk into the wall of the building. The roof hatch wouldn't delay it long.

One of the differences between Tortantulas and Earth spiders was the alien had a ring of ten eyes around its head. Even hunched down, it had tremendous peripheral vision. Two of those eyes locked on Bjorn. Bjorn fired two shots as fast as his laser would cycle. One pulse sizzled off the aliens' carapace, narrowly missing a pair of sockets, likely eyes lost in previous battles. The other flashed above the spider.

Seven.

"Bjorn!" Berto hurled the magazine for a CASPer integral laser the size and shape of a 500-milliliter soda bottle to Bjorn. He instinctively reached to catch it. The capsule bounced off the CASPer's armored hand and spun across the pavement.

The Tortantula snatched the magazine. If it didn't know exactly what it was, the alien knew Bjorn needed it. It tauntingly waved the magazine in its manipulator arm. Bjorn dimmed his cameras as he drew a bead on his target.

The laser pulse flashed through the rugged polymer exterior of the capsule. The magazine held enough volatile chemicals to power 50 laser shots. Four ignited immediately and additional cells cooked off in each direction away from the impact.

The Tortantula shrieked as its prize incandesced in its face and fused to its manipulator appendage until the limb burned off.

Six. Worth it.

Small arms fire *pinged* off the CASPer armor as the Khabar gathered their nerve. It lasted the two seconds required for Bjorn's laser to cycle. This time the laser pulse skimmed the top of the wall, flash-frying the Khabar's head.

Five.

Motion highlighted in his pinview. The Besquith slid down the side of the building, its claws throwing sparks as they shredded the metal surface. Bjorn's hasty shot flashed against the wall above the Besquith.

Four.

The Besquith was intent on potential prey inside the warehouse. Berto couldn't be far from the door, and the others would be moving toward it.

"Hey, furball!" Bjorn yelled over the CASPer's speakers. At least the sound system was useful at trade shows. "Valhalla awaits!"

"Load music—LZ-IS-001. Full volume."

Guitar licks echoed off the concrete, followed by a high-pitched wail. "We come from the land of ice and snow…"

The Besquith whirled around and ducked aside. Smoke from Bjorn's laser trailed from its fur, eliciting a snarl.

Three.

A maw full of shark-like teeth split open on the Besquith's face. Bjorn watched the laser cycle timer count down as the werewolf dashed forward. Bjorn triggered the laser a fraction of a second after the Besquith lunged. Fur, hide, and muscle cauterized on the creature's shoulder, but it didn't stop the Besquith from slamming into Bjorn.

Countless sessions of Eddings' training paid off as Bjorn instinctively shifted his stance to keep from being bowled over. Sparks flew as the Besquith raked the armor on Bjorn's arms as he shoved the alien away.

The staccato fire of a battle rifle rose above the clamor of classical music and the snarling Besquith. Berto fired another burst into the werewolf from the corner of the warehouse. The Besquith howled and decided the unarmored nuisance appeared more appetizing.

"No!" The Besquith ignored the laser pulse that amputated its tail, leaving a cauterized stump.

Two.

The CASPer was too slow. In a second, the Besquith reached the corner of the building as Berto backpedaled out of sight. The cycle timer showed a second remaining. The Besquith howled triumphantly, eager for the kill.

Whoompf! Mickey D fired an incendiary flare from her battle rifle's grenade launcher into the Besquith's face. The alien howled. The signal flare incinerated one of its eyes as it bounced off its skull. A salvo of gunfire followed the flare, staggering the Besquith as Mickey D and Brackin emptied fresh magazines into the beast.

Bjorn tracked the Besquith with his laser as the alien toppled backward. "Way to go! Let's—"

The Tortantula slammed into Bjorn, sending him skidding across the pavement. He rolled on his side and fired. The laser struck the spider's thorax armor, leaving a scorch mark but little else.

One.

"Go!" Bjorn yelled over the comms. The spider charged as Bjorn fought to regain his footing. It batted aside his arm as his laser blinked ready. The pulse dissipated in the pavement.

Zero.

Bjorn snapped out his arm-blade. Talk about bringing a knife to a sword fight. The Tortantula raised its bladed fighting limbs in response. Bjorn knew how to kill it—he'd done it before in the sims. He stepped forward and drove his arm-blade for the spider's head.

The Tortantula caught his blade between its fighting limbs in a cross-block. It wrenched its bladed arms and the CASPer blade snapped off. The Tortantula smacked Bjorn with a backswing, sending him stumbling back as he fought momentum.

Bjorn scanned his weapon inventory. The arm-blade was toast, the laser was empty, and where he should have a MAC, there was only the axe. Bjorn wrapped his hand around the haft and released the magnetic couplers holding the axe in place.

The Tortantula tilted its head. The two front-facing eyes were blackened. The ones on either side of the burned eyes watched the axe warily. Bjorn choked up on the handle; he would need to fend off the spider's fighting limbs.

The Tortantula pounced, its bladed limbs flashing down. Bjorn sidestepped one and batted the other aside with his axe. Reversing his swing, he drove the huge double-bladed weapon into the joint of the closest fighting limb, shearing the arm off.

The Tortantula hissed and raised its remaining fighting arm. Bjorn slammed the end of the axe into the spider's head, rupturing the two burned eyes and gouging another with the curved axe blade. The spider lashed out with its bladed limb. The serrated edge carved a gash into the side of the CASPer's armor, and Bjorn felt a burning pain across his lowest rib.

The Tortantula's fangs scraped at the armored canopy, eager to get at the juicy prey inside. Bjorn brought the axe down, throwing all his strength into the swing. Yellow alerts flashed as his left arm's actuators struggled to keep up with his cybernetic arm. Twenty kilograms of hardened titanium-molybdenum cleaved into the Tortantula where the fighting limb joined the thorax. The bladed appendage fell limp to the tarmac.

Bjorn jabbed his CASPer's right fist at the Tortantula's good eyes while he ripped his axe free in a spray of blue ichor. Bjorn brought the axe down again, ignoring servo warnings in his left arm, and buried the blade into the Tortantula's head. The alien spider slumped to the pavement.

Warm wetness trickled down Bjorn's side. How bad was he bleeding? Why hadn't the automated trauma system responded?

Trauma nanite stores—0%

Gunfire erupted on the road on the other side of the fence. Several angry bleats were cut off. One of the large trucks lurched in reverse, only to crash into the other cargo truck.

BTI: Relief forces on perimeter.

"Kid, are you there? This is Sergeant Jackson."

"Welcome to the party, Sergeant," Bjorn replied. Spots swam before his eyes and his pinplants warned of low blood pressure. "It sounds like you took care of our gate crashers. Be advised there are three friendlies in the facilities in addition to myself. They're all Human."

"Let them know not to pop us as we come over the wall," Sergeant Jackson said. "The gate is blocked."

"Sorry. I'd move the rumbler, but I'm busy bleeding all over the inside of my CASPer." There were nanites in the medkits with the infantry gear. Bjorn shuffled his CASPer toward the loading dock.

"*Hermano*, let us hook you up," Berto called over the comms. "I wouldn't want Grace to hear I let her boyfriend bleed out."

* * * * *

Chapter Thirty-Six

Houston Starport, Texas

"I want to see my son!" Bjorn's mother rarely raised her voice, but Bjorn recognized the tone. His father referred to it as "defy me at your own peril." The guard must have recognized it as well—he quickly stepped aside.

His mother rushed in, followed by the bear-like Jivool Peacemaker. Bjorn resisted the urge to reach for the claws dangling on his chest.

"Why isn't he in a proper hospital?" she demanded, halting the Jivool in her tracks.

"The infirmary was closer and had sufficient facilities to tend to the wounded cubs," the Peacemaker replied. "No organs were seriously harmed. Trauma nanites have mended the worst hurts, and your cub is receiving replacement blood."

Bjorn bristled at the cub remark but knew better than to get smart with a Peacemaker. If the Galactic Union was the Wild West, Peacemakers were the marshals of old and then some. They were the law enforcement arm of the Union, and they had broad discretion with the power to back it up.

"Trip, how do you feel?" His mother checked the slate at the end of the bed.

"A bit woozy, and I feel as though I was trampled by all eight of Sleipnir's hooves," Bjorn replied. His side still burned as the nanites finished their work. "How's Berto? They won't tell me anything."

"The other cub sustained a head trauma. He has received trauma nanites, same as your cub," the Jivool stated.

"Where are his parents?" Bjorn's mother asked.

The Jivool shrugged. "They have been informed of their cub's injuries and detainment. They are unable to obtain expedited transportation."

"Trip, I need to make a few phone calls. Rest while we get this sorted out." Lynn Tovesson turned to the Peacemaker and narrowed her eyes. "I already have a lawyer on the way. She'll want a list of charges upon arrival."

"I thought your father commanded Bjorn's Berserkers," the Jivool remarked after the door closed.

"He does, but it doesn't mean he's the boss at home," Bjorn replied.

Bjorn awoke three hours later. He must have drifted off shortly after his mother left. There wasn't much to do since they had taken his slate. Either the device was powered down, out of range, or jammed, as his pinplants couldn't handshake with the device.

His pinplants found an open Aethernet access node. It was better than nothing. Message indicators scrolled down his pinview, most of them from Grace. The last one was time-stamped fifteen minutes ago.

"I'm here—at the starport with your mother. She had the panther doctor who implanted the hardware in your skull flown to Houston to check on your BFF and invited me to tag along. Let me know when you get this."

Four minutes later, Grace was at the door arguing with the guard. Two minutes later, the door opened.

"Is this going to be a thing?" Grace surveyed him. How bad was he banged up? Bjorn hadn't seen a mirror. "This is the second time you've been hospitalized in three months."

"Last year I was only put in the hospital once—although it was for a few weeks," Bjorn mustered a grin. "I'm not in as bad shape as I look."

"Brackin is crowing on social media he took down a Besquith." Grace took Bjorn's right hand, careful of the IV line. The blood had been replaced with saline.

"I'm sure Loki would make it an edda, but Brackin had a lot of help," Bjorn remarked. Of course the jerk was claiming credit. Was he free, or had Brackin boasted online before the security forces swooped in?

"He also claimed you killed a Tortantula with a battle-axe," Grace added.

"To be fair, I was in a CASPer, and I suspect the spider wasn't in her prime." It would explain why a Besquith and a Tortantula were playing heavies for a Khabar gang—they couldn't cut it as mercs among their own races. "I wouldn't be surprised if the same was true of the werewolf."

Grace leaned over and kissed him. "I'm going to check with your mother. She's arranged a room for us."

"Us?" Bjorn raised an eyebrow.

Grace patted his hand. "No, not you and me. You're stuck here overnight. Mrs. T flew out Heather and Berto's parents. Heather and I get to be roomies tonight. Doesn't that sound fun?"

"Um…" Would they talk about him? If he was lucky, they'd ignore each other. They were going to talk about him. "Remember, I was younger when I dated her."

"Good. She does have some dirt on you." Grace winked. Bjorn watched her walk to the door.

Video file saved.

Grace paused, then stepped aside to let Heather enter the room.

"Hey." Heather stopped halfway to Bjorn's bed.

"I thought you'd be checking on your boyfriend." Bjorn kept his tone neutral despite the roiling emotions.

"He's sleeping. The doctor your mom brought gave him some specialized nanites for brain injuries, so he'll be out until morning. I wanted to say…I'm sorry." She closed the remaining distance. Tears threatened to well out of her blue eyes and smudge her make-up. "Not for breaking up with you, but for the way I did it. You deserved better, but I was afraid. Also, thank you. You could have let Berto die."

"No, I couldn't. Besides, he saved my bacon. Valhalla has no room for cowards and back-stabbers," Bjorn remarked.

Heather flinched.

"I didn't mean—"

"I know." Heather wiped at her eye, leaving a trail of eyeliner. "Can you forgive us?"

Bjorn's tongue was thick in his throat. "Maybe. Some hurts take a while to heal."

"Are you going to be a mercenary?" Heather tried to wipe off the smear but only spread it.

Bjorn took a deep breath. "I don't know."

"A year ago your answer would have been 'hell no.'" She smiled weakly. "When you decide, tell her. She deserves to know."

Bjorn nodded mutely.

Heather kissed him on the cheek. "Take care of yourself."

* * *

"I've concluded my investigation, at least as far as your involvement goes," the Jivool stated, its beady eyes focused on Bjorn. "The charge of unlawful mercenary action within a Galactic Union starport is dismissed as the conflict occurred within the confines of the leasehold, and you were acting to defend persons and property within said leasehold. I believe you may refer to it as the 'Castle Doctrine.'

"The starport operating authority, under auspices of the Merchant Guild, has seized the suspects' transport, so you cannot claim it as recompense. In addition, there are a few fines levied against Bjorn's Berserkers for the actions of their operators before reaching the leasehold. It is a matter between the Berserkers and the starport, and not part of this investigation." The Jivool turned to Bjorn's attorney. "I would recommend paying the fines and moving on, off the record of course."

"What about the Khabar?" Bjorn asked. He didn't want to have to watch over his shoulder for ticked off carnivorous goat-people.

"Most of the survivors were apprehended, however the leader, a Khabar named Brillo, eluded capture and is believed to have fled off-world," the Peacemaker replied. "According to his talkative minions, Brillo was vexed at losing a pirate vessel to your father. For some reason, Brillo believed a platoon worth of CASPers were in the depot in easy-to-transport containers."

"So my client is free to go?" the attorney asked.

"As far as I'm concerned. There is one last thing I would discuss." The Jivool slid a card across the table under one of its claws. "Earth has yet to have a successful Peacemaker candidate. Mr. Tovesson, I believe you should apply to the academy. From what

I've learned over the course of my investigation, I think you would make an excellent candidate."

Bjorn pocketed the card. "Thanks. I'll think about it, but odds are I'll want to stay closer to home."

* * *

Bear Town, New Mexico

Bjorn shifted restlessly as he tried to concentrate on his homework. The commander had sent a short message as soon as he touched down.

"Get your ass to Bear Town."

It had been four weeks since the incident in Houston. In the excitement of taking his VOWS, Bjorn had almost forgotten his father hadn't been there for the resolution. The Peacemaker had cleared Bjorn, but the starport still wanted their pound of flesh.

"I have a note to send you straight to Bjarnarsal," the guard at the gate said. "The commander wants to see you right away."

Bjorn wove the ZPT through traffic; the base was abuzz with post-mission activity. Bjorn checked the after-mission roster and was relieved to find Eddings had survived. The Berserkers lost two Casanova crews, five CASPer troopers, and eleven infantry troopers. Despite succeeding on the mission, it was the bloodiest butcher's bill they'd paid in a long time.

* * *

"Breaching Starport security—10,000 credits. Repairs to the logistics depot—2,000 credits. Unsafe vehicle operation tickets—347 credits." The commander set the slate down.

"Nothing to say about my 1133 on VOWS?" Bjorn retorted. He'd come close to maxing out his scores, but he lost a few points on speed challenges and mental exams. If a murderous spider the size of a car hadn't attacked Bjorn a few weeks earlier, he might have cracked 1140. Still, it was the best in his school, and almost certainly the state. Houston, Texas and Carmel, Indiana had a few prospects in professional merc finishing schools who could challenge his score, but it rated in the top percentile.

"Why did you charge in with a bunch of other kids in tow?" his father demanded.

"They followed me, and they acquitted themselves well. The goats had one of our men and were going after one of our facilities," Bjorn countered. "How could I let it stand?"

"It was almost empty!" The commander tossed the slate on the table.

Bjorn shifted uncomfortably. The Defense of the Empty Warehouse wouldn't make for a heroic edda. "By the time we found out, it was too late."

"You disobeyed Captain Davis' order."

"Only because it would have placed us in jeopardy. The Khabar were already there and could have picked us off," Bjorn retorted. "Tell me you would have done any different!"

His father grabbed the slate and watched the replay from the various security cameras again. "An 1133 isn't bad. I only had a 1079. Too bad you don't want to be a merc."

Bjorn leaned forward. "I don't know if it's always been in my blood, or only since the Kodiak tore away my plans with my arm. I've been determined to succeed on my own merits. Turns out fighting is my strong suite. I just didn't want to admit it."

"What about college?" the commander asked.

Bjorn shrugged. "I can take a business degree online and get plenty of practical experience here."

The commander ran his hand down his beard as he gazed at the slate. "Are you sure?"

"Yes."

"Your mother is going to kill me," the elder Tovesson grumbled. "You still need to finish high school. Be sure to do all the Homecoming, Prom, and whatever other crap kids do. I'm not going to be the one to deprive you of what's left of your…your school years."

Bjorn nodded. He didn't bother to tell his father Homecoming was two weeks ago.

"Have you told Grace?"

"Not yet," Bjorn replied. "I needed to talk to you first. You might have told me to go to Hel."

"Good luck with that conversation," the commander remarked.

"I'd be surprised if she doesn't already suspect," Bjorn said. "I figure, if nothing else, we have the rest of the school year, and however long until you have me report for duty afterward."

"I'm not cutting you any slack, and I don't care how many hours you've logged in what, you're going through training cadre." The commander tapped at his tablet. "If everything goes according to plan, we'll assemble a cadre at the end of July."

Bjorn nodded. "Valhalla awaits."

# # # # #

About the Author

At thirteen years old, Jon Osborne discovered a passion for two things—writing and telling stories. Instead of doing what a normal author-to-be would do and write stories, Jon wrote for his school newspaper and told stories through the medium of running role-playing games for his friends.

Journalism helped pay the way through college, and gaming garnered him lifelong friends. After college, journalism didn't pan out as a career, but Jon continued creating worlds and forging stories with his friends.

Fast forward almost 30 years; Jon was still a gamer who dabbled with writing. A long-time friend and fellow gamer who had found success as an author, Mark Wandrey, convinced Jon to submit a short story for an anthology. Jon's story was accepted, and it gave him the impetus to finish his first novel, "A Reluctant Druid."

Living in Indianapolis, Jon still games and continues to write. You can find out more about Jon at http://jonrosborne.com/. Fans who sign up for his mailing list will receive "Chapter 0" of "A Reluctant Druid" and be the first to get the news about Jon's newest books and stories.

* * * * *

Connect with Jon R. Osborne Online

Website: http://jonrosborne.com/

Amazon: https://www.amazon.com/Jon-R.-Osborne/e/B073PKR8GS

Facebook: https://www.facebook.com/jonrosborne/

Twitter: @druidoz

Did you like this book?
Please write a review!

* * * * *

The following is an

Excerpt from Book One of the Revelations Cycle:

Cartwright's Cavaliers

Mark Wandrey

Available from Seventh Seal Press

eBook, Paperback, and Audio Book

Excerpt from "Cartwright's Cavaliers:"

The last two operational tanks were trapped on their chosen path. Faced with destroyed vehicles front and back, they cut sideways to the edge of the dry river bed they'd been moving along and found several large boulders to maneuver around that allowed them to present a hull-down defensive position. Their troopers rallied on that position. It was starting to look like they'd dig in when *Phoenix 1* screamed over and strafed them with dual streams of railgun rounds. A split second later, *Phoenix 2* followed on a parallel path. Jim was just cheering the air attack when he saw it. The sixth damned tank, and it was a heavy.

"I got that last tank," Jim said over the command net.

"Observe and stand by," Murdock said.

"We'll have these in hand shortly," Buddha agreed, his transmission interspersed with the thudding of his CASPer firing its magnet accelerator. "We can be there in a few minutes."

Jim examined his battlespace. The tank was massive. It had to be one of the fusion-powered beasts he'd read about. Which meant shields and energy weapons. It was heading down the same gap the APC had taken; the tank was heading toward Second Squad, and fast.

"Shit," he said. He had to stop them.

"Jim," Hargrave said, "we're in position. What are you doing?"

"Leading the charge," Jim said as he jumped out from the rock wall.

*****

Find out more about Mark Wandrey and "Cartwright's Cavaliers" at: http://chriskennedypublishing.com/imprints-authors/mark-wandrey/.

*****

The following is an

Excerpt from Book One of the Salvage Title Trilogy:

Salvage Title

Kevin Steverson

Available Now from Theogony Books

eBook, Paperback, and Audio

Excerpt from "Salvage Title:"

A steady beeping brought Harmon back to the present. Clip's program had succeeded in unlocking the container. "Right on!" Clip exclaimed. He was always using expressions hundreds or more years out of style. "Let's see what we have; I hope this one isn't empty, too." Last month they'd come across a smaller vault, but it had been empty.

Harmon stepped up and wedged his hands into the small opening the door had made when it disengaged the locks. There wasn't enough power in the small cells Clip used to open it any further. He put his weight into it, and the door opened enough for them to get inside. Before they went in, Harmon placed a piece of pipe in the doorway so it couldn't close and lock on them, baking them alive before anyone realized they were missing.

Daylight shone in through the doorway, and they both froze in place; the weapons vault was full. In it were two racks of rifles, stacked on top of each other. One held twenty magnetic kinetic rifles, and the other held some type of laser rifle. There was a rack of pistols of various types. There were three cases of flechette grenades and one of thermite. There were cases of ammunition and power clips for the rifles and pistols, and all the weapons looked to be in good shape, even if they were of a strange design and clearly not made in this system. Harmon couldn't tell what system they had been made in, but he could tell what they were.

There were three upright containers on one side and three more against the back wall that looked like lockers. Five of the containers were not locked, so Clip opened them. The first three each held two sets of light battle armor that looked like it was designed for a humanoid race with four arms. The helmets looked like the ones Harmon had worn at the academy, but they were a little long in the face.

The next container held a heavy battle suit—one that could be sealed against vacuum. It was also designed for a being with four arms. All the armor showed signs of wear, with scuffed helmets. The fifth container held shelves with three sizes of power cells on them. The largest power cells—four of them—were big enough to run a mech.

Harmon tried to force the handle open on the last container, thinking it may have gotten stuck over time, but it was locked and all he did was hurt his hand. The vault seemed like it had been closed for years.

Clip laughed and said, "That won't work. It's not age or metal fatigue keeping the door closed. Look at this stuff. It may be old, but it has been sealed in for years. It's all in great shape."

"Well, work some of your tech magic then, 'Puter Boy," Harmon said, shaking out his hand.

Clip pulled out a small laser pen and went to work on the container. It took another ten minutes, but finally he was through to the locking mechanism. It didn't take long after that to get it open.

Inside, there were two items—an eight-inch cube on a shelf that looked like a hard drive or a computer and the large power cell it was connected to. Harmon reached for it, but Clip grabbed his arm.

"Don't! Let me check it before you move it. It's hooked up to that power cell for a reason. I want to know why."

Harmon shrugged. "Okay, but I don't see any lights; it has probably been dead for years."

Clip took a sensor reader out of his kit, one of the many tools he had improved. He checked the cell and the device. There was a faint amount of power running to it that barely registered on his screen. There were several ports on the back along with the slot where the power cell was hooked in. He checked to make sure the connections were tight, he then carried the two devices to the hovercraft.

Clip then called Rinto's personal comm from the communicator in the hovercraft. When Rinto answered, Clip looked at Harmon and winked. "Hey boss, we found some stuff worth a hovercraft full of credit…probably two. Can we have it?" he asked.

*****

Get "Salvage Title" now at:
https://www.amazon.com/dp/B07H8Q3HBV.

Find out more about Kevin Steverson and "Salvage Title" at:
https://chriskennedypublishing.com/imprints-authors/kevin-steverson/.

*****

Made in the USA
Monee, IL
24 January 2020

20811846R00223